ARIA

ARIA

Nazanine Hozar

VIKING
an imprint of
PENGUIN BOOKS

VIKING

UK | USA | Canada | Ireland | Australia
India | New Zealand | South Africa

Viking is part of the Penguin Random House group of companies
whose addresses can be found at global.penguinrandomhouse.com.

Penguin
Random House
UK

First published in Canada by Alfred A. Knopf Canada 2019
First published in Great Britain by Viking 2020
001

Copyright © Nazanine Hozar, 2019

Printed and bound in Great Britain by Clays Ltd, Elcograf S.p.A.

A CIP catalogue record for this book is available from the British Library

HARDBACK ISBN: 978–0–241–41790–4
TRADE PAPERBACK ISBN: 978–0–241–41791–1

www.greenpenguin.co.uk

Penguin Random House is committed to a
sustainable future for our business, our readers
and our planet. This book is made from Forest
Stewardship Council® certified paper.

For my mother, Toba

I saw many things on the face of the earth.
I saw a child who was smelling the moon.
I saw a door-less cage in which brilliance was fluttering its wings,
a ladder from which Love was ascending to the roof of Heaven.
I saw a woman pounding light in a mortar.

SOHRAB SEPEHRI (from "The Footsteps of Water")

prologue

1953

Mehri opened her eyes. She was lying on a mound of carpets. "Does he look like his father?" she asked.

The old man, Karimi, was holding the baby. "She doesn't know?" he whispered, turning to his wife.

"She feels it," Fariba said, glancing at Mehri. Fariba was much younger than her husband, and she was Mehri's one friend.

"I can tell she doesn't know," Karimi insisted.

"Keep quiet. Are you massaging the baby like I showed you?"

"Yes, yes." He rubbed the baby's chest and back.

"What have we got ourselves into?" Fariba said. "Keep rubbing." She grabbed a chunk of meat from the cooler and put it in a frying pan. "It's for the mother. Not for you," she said to her husband. She glanced back at Mehri. "She ruined her life the moment she laid eyes on that man. I told her to work for you, here at the bakery, instead. But she said she'd rather be his wife. Now look what's happened."

After a minute, Karimi asked, "Wife, why doesn't the baby make a sound?"

"Because her eyes are blue," Fariba said. "And she's cursed, like her mother."

—

MEHRI HAD STAYED motionless under a blanket for hours, her back against the wall. She was ashamed to look at her friend.

"I warned you about marrying him, didn't I?" Fariba said. "How many times did I say he'd beat you?" At last, Fariba wrapped the baby, pressed her against her own breast, and approached Mehri. "Don't you want to hold her?" she asked.

Mehri said nothing.

"You can't pretend she doesn't exist. Yes, she's a girl. But it's not so bad."

"He's going to kill me," Mehri said.

Karimi was leaning against the wall, too, his face hidden behind his paper. But his hands trembled. They ached from helping Mehri give birth. And now he was embarrassed to look at her.

"You know, husband, if we had a radio, you wouldn't need to read the paper. You can barely hold it up," Fariba said to him. "They say there are so many things to hear on the radio. Little plays. Would be nice to hear one of those." She turned away from Mehri and lit a match to the coal in the stove.

Karimi pushed his reading glasses to the tip of his nose and folded the paper. "Nonsense," he said. "You worry about your little radio when most of those northerners are showing off their televisions. And all those years ago I taught myself to read—so why shouldn't I read the paper? Nobody else back then knew how to read. Not my mother, not my father. I was the only kid up and down these streets who could do it. Figured out the letters on my own, and you—"

"What's a television?" Mehri asked suddenly, looking up. She caught a glimpse of the baby's hair under the light. It was a reddish brown, like the father's.

"A movie screen, only smaller," Karimi said, without looking up. "It's small enough to fit in a room. They have them all over the North-City. Mossadegh was on one the other day."

"Why was our prime minister on television?"

"To show he was alive. Somebody tried to kill him. Probably the filthy British." Karimi turned back to his paper. "Damn them all. If it isn't the communists, it's the English, and if it isn't the English, it's those darned turban lovers thinking they're as good as God. If it isn't—"

Fariba slammed down the kettle. "This poor girl nearly died tonight, and you worry about your politicians?"

"None of your scolding in front of her," Karimi said. "And dammit, nobody loves this country anymore. Except *him*. Mossadegh is great. Great, I'm telling you!"

Mehri closed her eyes again and pretended to sleep.

"This is a woman's matter," Karimi added, more softly, nodding at Mehri. "You want the neighbours to talk? We can't keep her here."

"That's all right, Mr. Karimi," said Fariba, "you just sit right there and drink your tea and read your paper. Just think about what your great Mr. Mossadegh would think of you."

FOR THE NEXT two days, Mehri refused to hold the baby, even when the father, Amir, kicked at the door of Karimi's bakery downstairs. Fariba hollered at Amir from the second-floor balcony that his son was no son, but very much a girl.

Amir said, "Then bring her down so I can kill her."

"You need to name her," Fariba said, turning to Mehri. "Now."

But by the end of the day, the infant was still nameless. And Amir still sat at the door, waiting to kill the child.

"He barks at people when they walk into the bakery," Fariba said. She bounced the baby in her arms. "I had to feed her dry milk, you know. Not good for her." Fariba shifted her weight where she sat on the Persian rugs covering the floor. She gulped down the last of her gin from a tea glass. When she was finished, she slapped the glass on the rug. "There's always your brother."

"He won't help," Mehri said.

"You've always said that, but you don't know. And that boy Amir would rather kill his daughter than pay for her. Got anybody besides your brother?"

"No."

Karimi entered the room and sat beside his wife. "You still unwell, child?" he asked Mehri. His voice was kind but weary. He had known Mehri since she was thirteen, a younger friend of Fariba's, who was five years older. He could hardly bear to see her pain.

Mehri covered herself with her veil and cast down her eyes. She bit into a soft corner of the material. It hadn't been washed for weeks. Sometimes when she walked the streets she wondered if others could smell her.

Fariba unfolded her thick legs and stood up, the baby in her arms.

"Wife," Karimi said, rising as well. "Put the baby down and come here."

They whispered as they walked into the next room. Mehri could hear them—only pieces and bits, but enough.

"I can't do it," she heard Karimi say.

"Are you ready to pay their way?" Fariba said.

"This is my house. Don't you forget where your place is, woman!"

"She's my friend. I do what I want with my friends. And I know that girl. She's lying about her brother."

"The government won't do anything for a family like that," Karimi said.

"That's their people's burden, then," Fariba said. "I don't know what to tell you, husband. If it weren't for the laws—"

"Other than the laws, what do we do about *him*?"

"Him, we'll figure out later. I'll cut off his orange-haired head if I have to."

THE BAKER AND his wife were still talking when Mehri picked up the baby and stepped out through the back door. In the snow, she loosened her veil and pulled out her hard, blackened nipple. Her breast ached in the frozen air. She brought it to the baby's lips, but the milk dripped away. She was cold, but the baby's skin was even colder. Above, a cloud hid the moon. A veil of snow had begun to cover the city. She felt wet blood dripping down her legs. It made a trail behind her. Amir could find her if he followed it, like a lone wolf trailing its prey.

But Mehri knew how to outmanoeuvre him. As a beggar-child she had made her way in Tehran's northern streets, where the rich lived, and where some of them had given her something to eat. Most days she had received nothing, unlike her brother. But he was the boy.

When she reached Pahlavi Street, which connected the south to the north and divided worlds and existences, she found it changed from what she remembered: almost empty, almost silent, its ghosts were speaking and its rich were long asleep. By the light of the street lamps, she could see the snowy roads that rose to the tips of the Alborz Mountains, twenty kilometres away. As a child, she had dreamed of reaching those mountains. She would open her arms and fly to them, just like the phoenix in the old tales. She used to wonder if, from up there, one could see the city's secrets. Once past the city's valleys, did the mountain people breathe more freely? She would imagine the rich on their picnics along the mountain's slopes and beside its rivers.

After three hours of walking, she was somewhere in the city centre. Her legs shook. They ached and ached and ached to the beat of war drums, her muscles pounding against bone. Her entire body ached. Her sex ached most. She wondered what would happen if the baby fell from her arms. Would it freeze and become a message to the future world: beware of birth, beware of life, beware if you arrive and are unwanted? If the baby fell, would its skull explode? Would all its bones break? Or, just like it had done in birth, would the child overpower everything around her and force her body into the world?

As Mehri walked, the city revealed itself to her. Structures and freeways unfolded and laid bare the world of the privileged. Here, in the city centre, the buildings grew taller; seen this close, they were as vast as the mountains that framed them. On one side of the street stood the tallest building she had ever seen. There was a picture of an old man on it: the prime minister, Mossadegh. She recognized him. Everyone knew his face now. She looked at it for a while, then carried on, past the parked cars and the few vehicles driving gently through the night. Even the shapes of cars had changed since last she had been here, she thought. They were more streamlined now, and in colours she hadn't seen before.

Now the streets and sidewalks widened. Mehri's toes hurt from the cold. The baby was oddly silent, as if she knew what her mother was about to do. Mehri touched her sore thighs, shuffling her hand past and through the veil's three layers, one for piety, one for culture, and the third for warmth. She picked up a handful of snow, cupped it under her veil to where she had been torn open and tried to wash the stain off, but the cold only stung her more. Blood stained her fingers. She put her nipple into the baby's mouth again, but the baby still wouldn't drink.

She walked another hour before reaching the centre of a major intersection. At the edge of the street, strands of grass tried to push through the snow. Mehri looked around. Everything was new here, everything was modern.

From this cross street there were four directions in which to go. She could walk back south, go north, or stay here on the streets that led east and west. To the west, there it was again—the picture of the old man, this time on newspaper pages glued to brick walls. Eastward the street was narrower, flanked by small trees that had lost their leaves for winter. One was different. It was a mulberry tree, which she recognized from her childhood, having spent hours picking fruit from one with her brother. They would collect thousands of mulberries in tin cans and leave them to dry and turn sweet before selling them. By nightfall they would have enough money for food—perhaps some meat to keep their muscles working.

Mehri had never imagined herself becoming a mother. Life had never seemed as if it could last that long. But now life had sped toward her, crashed into her, developed in her organs, between her muscles and veins, month after month, and then exploded out of her in the form of the being she now held in her arms. She wanted badly to bring the baby closer, even to kiss her. Instead, she touched her hand to the bark of the mulberry tree and felt its grooves. The baby whimpered for the first time, as though in protest, as though begging for some mercy.

Mehri walked on. She saw another mulberry tree, and beside it, an open alleyway. From within the alley came a stench of waste. She covered her face with her veil and entered. Paper garbage bags had been left out on either side. Holding the baby in one arm, she walked between the rows, searching for the right place. She felt nothing and had no awareness of time. The baby hardly stirred as Mehri placed her on the ground. For several minutes, neither mother nor child moved. Moonlight shone on the infant's face, and for the first time Mehri looked clear into her eyes. She and her baby shared the same eye colour, as Fariba had said. She bent down and caressed the baby's cheeks, her chin and brow. In the moonlight she saw that blood from her fingers had stained the baby's face. But there was nothing she could do about that now.

At last, Mehri stood and turned around. She walked away—so far that not even the moonlight could help her see her daughter again.

TRUCKS RUMBLED ALONG the gravel road in the dead of the night, vibrating like a line of ants, thick tarpaulins shaking as engines whirred and wheels lifted dust, fogging the cold February air. Behrouz Bakhtiar closed his eyes. A film of dirt coated the skin covering the thin bones of his face. He watched by moonlight as four eight-wheelers filled with young men from the provinces rolled away.

He would not be driving the young men home as usual. This was the first night of his four days off. He would instead place a cigarette in his mouth, light it with the last match he had in his pocket, and walk home down the red mountain, where earth mingled with snow, then stride through the city from north to south. This was his Tehran, and he was its secret guardian, the angel perched on the mountaintop counting buildings, trees, lights, and people who walked about like insects, unaware of being watched.

Strange how people are, Behrouz thought, the cigarette between his thin lips. And he began his walk down and through the city just as he had planned, just as he had been anticipating all day.

He slid down the slopes effortlessly, taking a drag from his cigarette every once in a while. He whistled when the mood struck him. He had walked this path many times, since he had first learned to drive up the mountain. How old had he been, seventeen? He was thirty-three now, so that made it sixteen years. With time off multiplied by sixteen, that made about four thousand times he had walked up and down the slopes of Darakeh.

Sometimes, of course, the generals gave him permission to drive down and save himself the three-hour walk. And when Behrouz first got married, the general in command had not only encouraged him to drive, he'd let him off early to encourage husbandly duties—but not without reminding Behrouz how old his new wife was. "Think that wife of yours'll be able to handle fresh little you?" the general had said.

Behrouz had married Zahra when he was nineteen, upon his father's urging. "The Prophet was a boy, his wife was forty when he took her," his father had said. But Zahra was no prophet's wife. She was thirty-six, had never married, and had a son, Ahmad, who was the same age as Behrouz. Ahmad hadn't come to the wedding. That night, when Behrouz asked his new wife where her son was, Zahra replied, "Somewhere in the prison halls." Then she had forced herself on him.

When he'd first started driving trucks in the army, Behrouz had been more talkative. The soldiers liked him. They would reveal themselves, telling him about their lives on the farms or in small towns. If they were Tehrani boys, they talked about their schools and their girlfriends. The only one who had never opened up was a member of the royal family—a cousin of the king. But Behrouz supposed that was different. He had been ordered not to look the boy in the eyes.

Behrouz had begun learning to drive at sixteen because he wasn't strong enough to fight, or smart enough to read. His father had taught him the basics. He could have sold bread on the streets like his father, or worked the oil mines like his uncles. But the one time he had suggested this, his father slapped him so hard, Behrouz saw stars for days. And that was the end of that.

Now, as he walked, the red dirt beneath his boots remained frozen. Three nights ago there had been a storm. But now the snow had settled and was packed along the path. The walk wasn't as bad as he'd expected. He swiftly made it down Darakeh, to the northern tip of Pahlavi Street. Here there were cobblestone roads and the houses were old. He'd heard that the king's father once lived here.

He walked past the old car parked along the street, searching his pocket in vain for another smoke. A man was walking toward him.

"Could I trouble you for a cigarette?" Behrouz asked. He had learned how to speak politely, like the people did up here. The man pulled out a single smoke from his pack. Behrouz took it and placed it between his lips. The man held out a lighter, its flame flickering in the slight breeze.

"Thank you," Behrouz said, and began to walk away.

"No money?" the man said.

Behrouz waited.

"No money?" the man asked again.

"You want money for the light?" Behrouz said.

"What do you think?"

Behrouz searched both pockets awkwardly.

"Only kidding. Stupid man." The man laughed as he walked away.

Behrouz stepped up his pace and cut through alleyways. He knew he was somewhere in Youssef-Abad district, midway through the city. He normally walked the main street, but tonight he felt like a change. Streams of sewer water ran in the gutters, but blossoming mulberry trees flanked the roads. This district was one of his favourites. He liked the corner shops and the cinema and cafés, which were old but patronized by rich people.

He was staring at the letters on the front of the cinema when he heard the cry—like a cat in pain. He walked closer to where he thought the sound was coming from, but water gurgling in the gutter muffled its location. He crossed into another alley—nothing there. He continued to move from alley to alley, jumping over gutters. The more he found nothing, the more urgently he searched. His only help was the moon; there were no lights in the nearby homes; it seemed the rest of the world was asleep.

He finally reached the mulberry tree, which was flanked by rows of garbage. Staring up at him was a pack of wild dogs. He imagined them tearing the tiny creature who had made the sound limb from limb.

He grabbed a stick from the ground and charged. But none of the dogs moved. How long had they been there? As he neared, the dogs sat and watched quietly. At last, Behrouz bent down and lifted the baby into his arms. The dogs sniffed his feet, turned and left.

He sped toward the edge of town, past abandoned buildings in which the poor secretly lived, past stacks of cardboard where the even poorer slept. He wondered how long the child had gone without food. The stores were still closed, but his wife must have bought some milk, he thought frantically.

The baby didn't look more than three days old. His head hurt. The stars whirled in the sky. At last, not far in the distance, he saw the pale outline of his house.

FOR THREE HOURS, Behrouz sat in his living room, trying to feed the child. He had woken a sleeping neighbour, who had found some milk, though the baby threw up most of it. Now, once again, he dipped the cap of his fountain pen into the bowl of milk beside him on the floor. He held the tiny vessel to the baby's lips, careful not to tilt it too far. The milk flowed onto her lips, but only a few drops got in. He wiped her face clean with the back of his pinky finger. In a minute, he would try again.

Zahra was sleeping. Her son, Ahmad, out of jail only two days, had left his dirty boots on the kitchen table. He'd landed in prison for cutting someone's fingers off, and Behrouz knew he would already be back to stealing.

By morning, Behrouz was struggling to keep his eyes open. From the north-facing window, he watched the rising sun. The rays crept toward him, along the floor. In the bedroom, his wife still slept soundly. He got up, walked into her room, and stood at her bedside, the baby to his chest. Zahra lay tightly wrapped in her blankets. She was fair-skinned, with straight, fine hair that turned a shade of light brown in summer. She liked to curl it these days, using little plastic rolls.

He returned to the living room and laid the baby gently on the floor. Then he walked quietly back to the bedroom.

"We have to talk," Behrouz whispered.

Zahra covered her eyes to block the sun. "You're home. Figured you'd be killing yourself with opium all night."

"Come with me." He pulled her out of bed.

In the living room, the baby's arms and legs shook and she struggled like an overturned insect.

"I think she's hungry," Behrouz said. "I gave her some milk, but she hardly drank. She needs to suck it, I think."

Zahra backed away from the infant. "Where did you find it? Is this some mess of yours we have to fix?" Her voice was sharp.

Behrouz picked up the baby. "Nothing like that," he said. "Last night in the alley, there was waste all around her. I found her in Youssef-Abad."

"That's the North-City," Zahra said. "What were you doing with those people? Listen to me: You put that baby where you found it so the trash who are her people can take it back."

"There were dogs around her. I don't know what they wanted, but—"

"Get it out of my house. And I know you do your own nasty business. You never touch me—as if I were made of fire and would burn you. But men are men. You must be touching somebody." Zahra grabbed the baby's face. "Did you take a look at its eyes? They're blue. I swear on Imam Hossein you've brought a blue-eyed devil into my house."

"Her eyes are green," Behrouz said.

"No. There's blue in them. You've brought evil into this house, Mr. Bakhtiar."

Behrouz listened silently as Zahra walked away and into the bedroom, still shouting at him. Fourteen years with her and the rage had only worsened. He looked at the baby. Zahra was right. There was blue in those eyes. He couldn't think how to comfort her. It had been so easy when he'd been a little boy and would play pretend. He would rock his baby, feed his baby, just like the neighbourhood girls did. And he'd been careful to never let his father know. But now, here was a real baby. The only thing he could think to do was speak to it, human to human. Not human to doll or master to slave. Yes, he would do what humans had always done, from the first crack of life.

"Want me to tell you a story?" he whispered to the little girl. Her wrinkled eyelids were shut tight, as if she would never want to face the world. "Want me to tell you the story of the Tooba Tree?" Behrouz said again. And so he began, hoping to drown out Zahra's shouts. "Past the clouds and the sky, way up in heaven, there is a tree, the Tooba Tree, from whose roots spring milk, and honey, and wine."

"I curse the day I married a boy," Zahra yelled from the other room.

Behrouz kept on: "Milk to nourish you, honey to sweeten you, wine to take you to the land of dreams."

Zahra yelled louder. "Think you were my saviour, Mr. Bakhtiar? You only made hell last longer."

Behrouz lifted the baby closer to his lips and whispered in her ear. "The Tooba Tree belongs to the orphans of heaven, for there is nothing that matters more, my little one."

He stopped and listened for Zahra again, but she had finished her rant. The baby had opened her eyes but was falling back asleep. "You sang to me from that alley," he whispered to her, "and I heard your song. Yet if I hadn't, and if you had not been saved, the Tooba Tree would have been waiting for you and you would have been all right just the same." Behrouz paused. He wondered if saving the little girl had been the right thing to do after all. But, since he had saved her and forced her into this thing called life, there was one more thing he needed to do.

"I used to love music, you know, when I was a little boy," he said, putting his pinky finger in the baby's mouth so she could suckle. "I used to sing, in secret, so my father wouldn't know. I used to sing arias. Know what they are? Little tales, cries in the night. If you sing an aria, the world will know all about you. It will know your dreams and secrets. Your pains and your loves."

Behrouz heard Zahra throw a pillow against the bedroom wall, and paused. After a few moments, hearing nothing more, he kept on. "I'll name you Aria, after all the world's pains and all the world's loves," he said. "It will be as if you had never been abandoned. And when you open your mouth to speak, all the world will know you."

part one

ZAHRA

1958–59

1

The doll lay hidden under the dirt in the garden, part of its head exposed and facing her, as though it had been waiting for Aria to rescue it from the garden bed. Even from a distance, Aria could see that its eyes were the same colour as hers. She lay on her stomach and reached out an arm for it, but the doll was too far away. Aria was small for her age; any other five-year-old girl would have been able to reach the doll, she thought. She looked down at herself. The dress her father had given her last month had already turned grey. She was making it worse now, crawling through the dirt. She'd be in trouble.

One of the doll's eyelids was half closed, but it opened when Aria at last grasped and shook the wooden body. She winked back at it. Then she crawled back out of the dirt, holding the doll to her chest. She stood on her tiptoes and peeked in through the window that overlooked the garden. Zahra was inside somewhere, and if she found Aria like this, she would do mean things to her again.

Her father had been away for a week, working in the barracks and military camps. This meant Zahra would feed her only once a day, because a little girl like Aria deserved nothing more. Sometimes, Aria would swipe Zahra's food from the table when Zahra wasn't looking.

Aria skipped around the courtyard clutching the doll in her hand. She leapt over imaginary canyons that opened in the cracks of the cobblestones. When fire burst up to the rim of the canyons, she jumped high. Then she ran to the courtyard's fountain for a drink. The cement basin around the fountain was small, and she liked to play inside it on hot summer days. But the neighbours, who took turns washing their dishes in the basin, disapproved. And when Zahra had found out, she'd given Aria a few good beatings to set her straight. Today she had another mission: cleaning her new doll. She pretended her Bobo had got it for her. She didn't call him Baba the way other children did their fathers.

She knelt against the basin, removed the doll's dirty dress, and dipped it into the water. It soaked a good while as Aria ran her fingers through the doll's matted hair. When she was done, she wiped the doll clean with the front of her own dress, the least dirty part. Then she picked up the doll's dress. There were flower petals along the creases. She rubbed the fabric of the dress against itself like she'd seen Zahra do whenever she washed their clothes. Once the dress was clean, she clothed the doll and laid it carefully on the grass beneath the basin to dry. Then she lay down beside it and fell asleep. Under the sun, she dreamt of a woman who told her how lucky she'd been to find the doll, and that she should forget about hunger if she wanted to be a good warrior. She slept deeply and dreamed of other things, too, such as lions in the desert and nomads on the mountain.

When Zahra pulled her hair, Aria awoke, too shocked to cry. Zahra smacked Aria's face with the back of her hand, knowing that inflicted the most hurt. Blood dripped from a cut on Aria's cheek left by Zahra's wedding ring.

Across the courtyard, a neighbour, Mr. Jahanpour, watched from his balcony. He went inside, slamming the door behind him, then came back out with a megaphone. "Madam . . . madam, please, this isn't godly. I advise you not to—"

"Mind your own business, you shit of a man!" Zahra shouted.

Mr. Jahanpour tried again, the megaphone blasting his voice. "Madam, all this is really not the right way to go about things."

Zahra stopped her blows. "Listen, Mr. Saviour, she's my shit of a daughter. I do what I want with her."

"Madam, I told you last time to control your temper on the girl. She was only playing. I was watching."

"So you're as much a pervert as you are an idiot," Zahra said. "Put that thing away. Why have the whole neighbourhood hear you?"

Mr. Jahanpour stood silently as Zahra pulled Aria into the house, the little girl kicking at the air in protest. "Go to the balcony," said Zahra, and shoved Aria there. "No breakfast, no lunch, nothing for you."

"I don't want to eat anything, anyway!" Aria shouted.

Zahra clicked the lock to the balcony door.

From where she was now, Aria could see Mr. Jahanpour in the courtyard, kneeling beside the garden where she'd been playing only moments before. His arms were behind his back and he was peering at the bed of reeds. Then he looked up at Aria's apartment.

"We share this space, stupid woman," he said. "It doesn't belong only to you."

He bent down and pulled out a reed, and now Aria could see that Mr. Jahanpour's son stood behind him. The boy lingered around his father, then strolled over to the basin and the patch of grass where Aria had left her doll. He grabbed the doll and ran inside. His father followed.

"Tell him to give me my doll back," Aria yelled after Mr. Jahanpour. But he did not answer.

—

IT WAS ALMOST dark when Aria awoke to the sound of a bang.

"Wake up!" an urgent voice said.

Aria rubbed her eyes. She pressed her head between the rails of the balcony.

"Who is that?" she asked. "I can't see you."

"Down here."

A figure stepped under the moonlight. It was the neighbour's boy.

"I live across from you," he said. "That's my mama in the kitchen." He pointed to the apartment opposite Aria. Through the window, she could see a woman standing over a steaming pot.

"What do I care? Give me back my doll. I saw you take it."

"I knew it was yours. I took it so I could give it back to you. I saw your mother smacking you. Did you hit her back? My Baba says that if he ever hits me like that I'm allowed to hit him back."

"Give me my doll."

"Wait. I need you to help me with something. See the big tree in front of you?"

The boy pointed to a tall cherry tree near the centre of the courtyard. Its branches had grown so long that they brushed against her balcony.

"What do you want with the tree?" Aria said.

"Can you reach the branches from where you are? My ball is stuck in there," the boy said.

"No. First you give me my doll."

"I can't. I'd have to throw it up to you and I can't throw that far. But my Baba says I'll be real strong one day, just like him. Want to see my muscles?"

"I hate your muscles," Aria replied. "And my Bobo's strong, too."

"What's a Bobo?"

"Like what you have, idiot," said Aria. "My father."

"Then why do you call him Bobo?"

Aria leaned over the balcony. "Don't you have school tomor-row?"

"Just shake the branches a little," the boy said. "The ball will fall."

"I can't talk to you. You'll get me in trouble."

"Listen, if you help me bring that ball down, I'll bring you a present after school tomorrow, *and* give you your doll."

"I don't need presents," Aria said.

The boy sat cross-legged on the ground and sulked. "I hate you," he shouted. "You're a stupid little girl."

"I'm big," Aria said. "I'm very, very big." When he didn't reply, she added, "I'm five years old. When it snows I turn six."

"Listen, will you please shake those branches? My neck hurts looking up and talking to you."

Aria moved closer to the balcony railing. "What's your name?" she asked.

"What's yours?" the boy asked.

"I asked you first," she said.

"Kamran."

"I've never heard that name before."

"You're only five years old. Give yourself some time."

"I'm Aria."

"Aria?" he laughed. "That's a boy's name."

"I am *not* a boy."

"Fine, you're not a boy. Are you going to help me?"

"Maybe." Peering down through the railing, Aria noticed something strange about this boy, about his face, his lips. "Did your father hit you?" she asked.

"No," the boy said.

"Why are your lips smashed open. Did you fall?"

He seemed embarrassed. "That's just my . . . It's my . . . I was born with it. My mouth is kind of inside-out."

"Inside-out? Can I call you inside-out-boy?"

"No, you cannot," the boy said.

"Okay, I won't. If you keep your promise about the present," Aria said. She walked to where she could almost touch the branches, but they were still too far away to reach. "I can't," she shouted down.

"Stand on the base of the railing," Kamran replied.

She did what he told her, stretching out as far as she could. "I got one!" she said.

"Shake it as hard as you can."

She shook the branch and heard the sound of the ball bouncing on the ground. The boy grabbed it and ran off.

"Don't forget about my doll, Mr. Kamran! Boy with the inside-out mouth and smashed lips!" she shouted into the darkness.

KAMRAN HELD HIS ball tight. He slid the metal door to his family's apartment aside with his foot, ran up to his room, and hid the ball under his bed. On his way down, he stopped for a moment at the window where he had been watching the Bakhtiar girl for months now, ever since she had been allowed to play in the garden. He was upset she'd noticed his cleft lip. But then again, everyone eventually did. Thank goodness he'd had the idea of throwing the ball into the tree. It was the best way to meet her. And she wasn't as strange as he had thought. She was a little nice, even. What was strange was her boy's name. Aria. He knew what it meant. His father had told him once. The Iranian race. But only boys were ever named this.

In the kitchen, his mother was feeding his little sister, who was now two. He opened the icebox. There was nothing inside but bread.

"Don't touch," his mother said. "It's dinner."

Kamran sat at the table and watched his sister suckle at his mother's breast.

"What were you doing with that girl?" his mother asked.

"Playing," he said.

"She's a bastard girl. Stay away from her."

"She has a mother and a father," Kamran said.

"Not real ones. She's a throwaway girl. From the street. And her eyes are blue. That means the devil's in her. Stay away or the jinn will come to your bed at night. Khanoom Kokab down the street took a stray in once. Everyone in her family died, even her cat. Now this girl's got blue eyes. Even worse."

"Her eyes are green," said Kamran. "I think."

"How can you see in the dark, son? Devil children are from jinn, and what do jinn do?"

"They trick us," Kamran said.

"Good. So don't be fooled. Everything she'll ever tell you is a trick. Even the Prophet, peace be upon him, will swear to it."

"Were there jinn in your town when you were little?" Kamran asked.

"In Yazd, all we ever had was dust, jinns, and Jews. And the fire temples, where the Zoroastrians do their hocus-pocus. Jinn, hocus-pocus; Jews, hocus-pocus; Zoroastrians, hocus-pocus. I bet with those blue eyes that girl's a Jew or a jinn's daughter."

"Kids at school say jinn aren't real. They're made-up stories from the small towns."

"Yazd is no small town. It was the capital of the world once. And if you don't know that this land was made by jinn, then I don't know what you've learned."

His mother loosened her headscarf and Kamran eyed the rotten tooth in her mouth. The tooth beside it had already fallen out. When the rotten one falls, he thought, she'll look like the stupid women on the streets.

"Kids at school say if you drink milk your teeth get pretty," he said.

"Milk is for babies," she replied.

"Can Baba get milk for us tonight?" he asked.

"Read the time for me and tell me what it says." His mother held out the watch on her wrist.

"It's stopped," Kamran said. "You haven't winded it."

"I haven't wound it," she said.

He corrected himself. "Wound it. Anyway, you can't have a winding watch if you can't tell time."

His mother jangled the watch. It was loose on her. "It was a wedding gift from your father. Maybe you'll teach me to read time. That's what good boys do for their mothers, huh?"

Kamran heard footsteps at the door and turned around.

"Now go help Kazem," his mother said, turning back to his sister.

Kazem was Kamran's father. He used his mother's maiden name, Kazemi, but everyone in Yazd had called him Kazem since his childhood. When Kamran's mother had married him, the name stuck. But Kamran only called his father Kazem when he felt sorry for him.

Kazem was carrying two full bags. Kamran took them, put them on the floor, and began to empty the contents. In one bag were rags and two jars of milk. In the other, he found two loaves of bread and three rotten apples. "Is that all?" Kamran asked.

"For tonight." His father held up his hand to show Kamran's mother. A bloodied bandage was wrapped around it.

"Oh! What did you do, husband?"

Kazem sat on the sofa. Dust rose and made him cough. "Let's see what I did. Come here, son." He unwrapped the dressing, revealing a mangled finger, swollen and blue. He passed the wrapping to Kamran. "You see, son, what I did was stupid. The bricks are supposed to go on top of each other, but not exactly on top. Layered, see? One brick sticks at the centre of the two under it. Mortar in between, layer on, pop, stick the new brick on top, pop. Real fast: mortar, brick, mortar, brick. Go too fast, and here's your poor finger." He held it up and laughed at his son's terrified face. He ruffled Kamran's hair. When he laughed he wheezed because he smoked too much, and the dust from the bricks had entered his lungs. "It's all right," he said. "Everything heals."

"Can you work?" Kamran asked.

"Don't you worry," his father said. "And one of those jars right there is yours. You drink up. My pretty son's got to have pretty teeth."

He ruffled Kamran's hair again and walked to the kitchen. He kissed his daughter, who'd fallen asleep at her mother's breast. "The other jar's for you," he said to his wife. "No protests. Money will come. I'm going to bed."

"Your son was playing with that jinn girl tonight," Kamran's mother said.

"Stop it, Mama." Kamran turned to his father, pleading. "She gave me back my ball."

"We're sure she's a jinn, now?" Kazem said.

"She's a devil-bastard child that came off the street," his mother replied.

"Then I would be careful with that ball from now on, son. Who knows what spells she's put on it." Kazem laughed and winked, but Kamran couldn't tell if his father was joking, or if Aria was indeed a jinn's daughter.

2

The new fellow dipped his face into the bucket. Water sparkled against his dark skin and ran down his neck to hide beneath the thick cotton of his uniform. Behrouz thought he'd met all the new boys, but this one he had somehow missed. The boy dipped his head again and splashed water through his black hair. The regiment had just finished their afternoon run.

Behrouz stubbed out his cigarette and approached.

"Towel?" he asked. He threw one over without waiting for an answer.

"Thanks," the new fellow said. No one else had a towel. "Guess I'm the special one." He laughed.

"You've got a captain badge there." Behrouz lit another cigarette and offered it.

"Don't smoke. But thanks," the boy said.

"You're older than the rest of these guys. But still young for a captain." Behrouz took a drag of his cigarette. His heavy-lidded eyes narrowed as he breathed in. He scratched at the growing beard on his face and exhaled. "Name's Behrouz." He held out his hand.

"Rameen."

"Nice to meet you, Captain," said Behrouz.

Rameen laughed. "Don't call me that. Just Rameen. You the cook?"

Behrouz blew out more smoke. "Sometimes. Driver, mostly."

"Oh yes. I think you brought us up."

"I didn't see you in the back of the truck with the others."

"I came up with the generals," Rameen said. "By us, I meant my men. You don't look old enough to be a driver. Why don't we have you suiting up with the boys? Bet you could use a rifle just fine."

Behrouz shook his head. "Been driving a long time now. You up here for a while?"

"Long as they'll have me." Rameen wiped at his neck again. "Doing the mandatory time. I'll be out of here soon enough. I've got more important things to do."

Behrouz nodded.

"My tent's over there. Small one next to the big dorm." Rameen pointed to the top of a hillock where the dormitory tents were set up. "You ever get bored, come say hi." He smiled, revealing perfect teeth. He looked like a movie star.

"Got a fancy place already?" Behrouz said. "People will think you've done somebody a favour."

Rameen laughed again. "Not bad for twenty-two. And right out of college."

Behrouz said nothing. He put out his cigarette between his and Rameen's feet.

"Thanks for the towel," said Rameen, handing it back.

"Keep it. I'm off to make dinner." Behrouz patted his shoulder and walked away.

At dinner, he looked for Rameen but couldn't find him. When most of the men had returned to their bunks, he filled a plate with rice and eggplant stew. In the dark, he found Rameen's tent.

"Captain?" he said quietly. It was cold, and his hands shook and he spilled some of the stew. He heard the rustling of papers and the closing of a drawer.

"Be right there," Rameen called. A moment later he unzipped the tent's opening. His face was sweaty.

Behrouz pulled back the flap. "For you," he said.

"Come in," Rameen replied. "Bet it tastes better with your cigarette smoke all over it."

"Sorry." Behrouz flicked the butt outside.

"Only kidding. Really. This is too kind."

"Seemed like you didn't have time to make it to dinner, so I thought . . ."

"Much too kind," Rameen repeated. "Have a seat." He motioned to the tightly made bed at the head of the tent, but Behrouz chose a nearby chair. Rameen sat on the bed with the plate in his lap. Soon, however, he set it down, walked back to his desk drawer, opened and shut it again.

Behrouz smiled.

"It's nothing," said Rameen. "I just don't want things falling out. You made this?" He took a whiff of the stew.

Behrouz nodded.

"Excellent. Excellent," Rameen said. But he stared at his plate, and Behrouz wondered why he was so scared.

IN THE MORNING, Behrouz looked again for Rameen. But he didn't see him then or all day, and that night he skipped dinner. He returned to the tent he shared with five other men, lay on his bed, grabbed the book under his pillow, and held it to his chest.

Cyrus, one of his bunkmates, threw a hat at him. "Bakhtiar, you only know how to hug books?" The others, freshly returned from the canteen, laughed.

Behrouz put the hat on. "I've already read it," he said. "Just thinking about it now."

"He couldn't read a street sign if he saw one," said Cyrus. Again the others laughed.

Behrouz reached for his pack of cigarettes, shook one out, and lit it.

"We can smoke in tents now?" said Cyrus. "Didn't know the rules had changed."

"I can. You idiots can't hold a cigarette unless your mommies do it for you."

"Cyrus had a nanny. The rest of us had mommies," said another of the men.

The front of the tent opened and in walked Rameen. Behrouz killed his cigarette. The others stood at attendance.

Rameen laughed. "At ease, gentlemen. How about a cigarette, Mr. Behrouz?"

Behrouz held out the pack. Rameen put a stick into his mouth. He waited for Behrouz to light it.

"So is it true, Mr. Cyrus?" Rameen looked up, taking a drag. "You had a nanny?"

"No, sir," Cyrus replied. "My grandmother raised me, sir."

"Oh, so both a nanny and a mommy?" said Rameen. The other men laughed. But Behrouz remained still. Rameen eyed him, then noticed the book on his bed. "Like to read, do you?"

"He just pretends, sir," Cyrus said.

"Shut up, granny boy," Rameen replied. "Well?" he asked again. Behrouz nodded.

"Not just any book, I see." Rameen studied the cover. He winked at Behrouz.

"Here. Brought you dinner." Rameen handed Behrouz a paper bag. "Someone who smokes so much can use all the food he can get."

"Thanks," Behrouz said stiffly, taking the bag.

"Feel sick or something?" Rameen asked.

"Just lost my appetite tonight."

"Well, I'm returning your favour." Rameen nodded at the other soldiers and left the tent.

Behrouz placed the food on his bed and lit another cigarette. His hands shook slightly.

"Someone has a favourite. Are you bending over for him?" asked Cyrus.

"You're a piece of shit," said Behrouz.

Cyrus sat back on his bed, folding his arms under his head. "If you can read those big books, how come you never read them to us?"

"Like you'd understand them," said Pasha, a Turkish boy from Tabriz.

Behrouz put the food under his bed, lay back, and held the book to his chest again. He stared at its cover and tried to make out the words. He'd been trying for a year. He knew what the book was. He knew that Rameen could have arrested him for having it. He put a hand to his chest to feel his heartbeat.

THAT NIGHT, AFTER hours without sleep, Behrouz left his tent. Only Cyrus was awake.

"Where you going?" Cyrus asked.

"To see where little village boys like you get sent for spankings," Behrouz replied.

When he entered through the tent flap, he found Rameen at his desk. "This is an early visit," Rameen said. He didn't look up.

Behrouz fished in his pockets, and remembered he'd forgotten his cigarettes. "What are you writing?" he asked.

"A report on banned books," Rameen said. "Like the kind you have." He looked at Behrouz, then broke into laughter. "You like reading that book, do you? If anybody else had seen it, things would be different."

Behrouz nodded.

Rameen got up from the desk and walked over to his bed. He sat and leaned against his bedpost, his shoulders square against it. By the way his uniform rested on his frame, Behrouz could tell his body was strong, muscular. He watched as Rameen stretched his long legs.

"This place must be different from where you come from," said Behrouz.

"Not so different. There are as many idiots here."

"I mean the small beds, the mess-hall food, the cold."

"Your food is perfect." Rameen smiled.

"You're young yet. You may change your mind," Behrouz replied.

Rameen reached under his mattress and pulled out something. "You want to read it now?" he asked. It was the same book Behrouz had. "Let's look together." He patted the bed. "Will you read aloud for me?"

Behrouz reached for his cigarettes again, even though he knew he had none. Then he sat on the edge of the bed with his back to Rameen, who held the book over his shoulder.

Behrouz took it. He turned a page. He opened his mouth. Nothing came out.

He tried again, yet the words on the page were not forming on his lips the way he had always dreamed they would.

"I knew it," Rameen said, sitting up. "You can't read, can you?" He grabbed the book back. "Why do you carry it around if you can't read it?"

Behrouz scratched his neck, his fingers running over his Adam's apple. "I know what's in it," he finally said, not turning around. "My wife read some of it to me before she got tired."

"You're married? And your wife can read but you can't?" Behrouz felt Rameen shift on the bed. "That doesn't answer my question," he said.

Behrouz looked around the dimly lit tent, hoping that somehow its silence and shadows would give him an answer. But in the end, he could only hang his head. "She worked for some people. They paid for lessons. She reads a little."

"Want me to teach you?" Rameen asked.

Behrouz said nothing.

"You know what can happen to me if they catch us, though? Not too many captains teach their men how to read books that scare the Shah. The secret police would be outside this tent before you know it." He laughed, and Behrouz realized that Rameen was enjoying himself.

"I've only heard stories," Behrouz replied quietly. "But one should be careful about the stories one hears. People like to turn one lashing into a hundred."

"One lashing is enough, as is one execution," Rameen replied. His tone had changed. "If I were you, I'd learn to read every book on that list to show up those scum."

"No one believed the boy who cried wolf for a reason," Behrouz said.

"Let's drop it." Rameen turned Behrouz around to face him. "Want me to read to you? Yes, that's it. I should read to you."

But now Rameen did something surprising. He began to undo the buttons on his shirt. "Never washed this yesterday. Stinks to the heavens." The sun was beginning to rise. He let his shirt slip off his shoulders and collect behind his back. "Do you mind?"

He handed the shirt to Behrouz, who took it without looking him in the eyes. Rameen rose off the bed, opened a drawer, and took out a new shirt. As he unfolded it, the muscles on his back moved. Behrouz named them: lats, triceps, shoulders. "Do you exercise?" he asked.

"On a cold day in hell," Rameen replied. "I've never worked for anything, Mr. Behrouz. My life has been a song of unwork. But I'll work for you. I'll read to you. The way your wife does." He smiled.

"Teach me," said Behrouz.

"Teach you? I said I'd read to you. Better, isn't it?"

"No, teach me." Now Behrouz stood up, too.

"Fine. I will read to you, and I will teach you." Rameen dropped the shirt he'd been holding. "Maybe you will teach me, too."

He walked toward Behrouz, placed his fingers on his eyes, and closed the lids. "Only once," he said, and kissed Behrouz's lips.

3

Aria played with her doll on the balcony. Zahra had put her out there again, though Aria had already forgotten why. The air was cold, but not enough to hurt. She decided to pretend that the doll needed warmth anyway, so she held it tight and blew warm air against its porcelain face. "I'll warm you, I'll warm you," she said.

"Keep your voice down," Zahra shouted from inside. "I didn't put you out there so you could make a ruckus. The neighbours will complain."

"The neighbours love me," Aria shouted back, risking a beating. She held her breath, letting it out only when she was sure Zahra wouldn't come find her. "Kamran loves me," she whispered to her doll. "And his baba loves me. They live right there, see?" She pointed to a window on the other side of the garden. "They cook food and tell each other stories and Kamran goes to school." She stroked the doll's golden hair. "I'll go to school one day, and if you're good and quiet I'll take you in my pocket. Kamran will play with you. If you're good. And if you're bad I'll give you to Zahra and she'll punish you because you deserve it." She watched the lights flicker in Kamran's window. His family sometimes used candles at night. She wondered what he was doing now—perhaps

playing, drawing pictures, or reading school books about fantasti-
cal characters with powers beyond imagining.

She searched through the window for a glimpse of Zahra, hoping she would have a change of heart. But as the minutes passed,
Aria turned away with a sigh and settled in for a few more hours
on the balcony, until Zahra let her in.

KAMRAN WASN'T PLAYING or dreaming of superheroes. Instead,
he was watching his father suffer.

Kazem was trying to untie his shoelaces, but he couldn't move
two of his fingers.

"Your finger is green, Baba," Kamran said.

"Just the tip," Kazem said.

"The other one's red." Kamran pointed to the middle finger.

"So it is," said his father.

The next day, a Friday, was usually a day off so everybody could
go to mosque. Instead, in the morning Kamran got ready to go to
work. He was going to stand beside his father and watch him lay a
brick, mortar it, then lay another. His father did not have the day off
because he was making a building for an important businessman.

Kamran held his father's wounded hand as they walked up
Pahlavi Street toward the North-City. He couldn't hold his father's
other hand because that was his good one, the one Kazem used to
carry his trowel, hammer, and filler. His hands were so big they
could hold all the tools at once. Kamran tried not to touch the part
of his father's finger that was turning green.

At the work site, there were bricks and mud and tools of all
kinds. Dust was everywhere. In the centre of the site, four rows of
bricks made a large rectangle. The bricks came up to Kamran's chest.

"I brought you just in time to do a row," said his father, setting down his tools. "You have to be my other hand today." Kazem dipped his trowel into a bucket of wet mortar, slapped it on top of two bricks, and picked up a new brick with his good hand. He slammed it on the mortar, so that it fit on top of the other two, precisely in the middle. "You try." He handed Kamran the trowel.

Kamran looked up at his father for reassurance, but the sun was in his eyes.

"It's going to be a hot day," his father said. "That's good for us. The mortar will dry faster. But it also means you work faster."

And Kamran did work fast. Sometimes dust got in his throat, but he coughed it away. He didn't complain because his father didn't complain, not even as his finger became greener. By the afternoon, the green had taken over much of his fingernail.

After seven hours, the sun was burning Kamran. He and his father hadn't brought any water with them. He stuck his tongue out to cool it, but it quickly became covered with dust. "Are you trying to drink dust, son?" asked his father. "They're supposed to come round here with water jars."

"They never come around with nothing," yelled a mason working beside them. "They haven't fed us in two weeks, Jahanpour. Last time they paid us was when? Take your son and put him back in school."

"No, brother, take him up to Qom and make him a holy man," said another, younger one Kamran had noticed earlier that morning. He was bigger than the other men. "If there's anyone who isn't hungry, it's those holy ones," he said.

Kazem laughed. "You want to be a mollah, son? Want a turban for your head?" All the men laughed along with his father; Kamran wanted to scream, "Stop!" but he said nothing.

A moment later he collapsed.

Kamran woke to the sound of a man yelling at his father. This man wore a suit, tie, and gold watch with diamonds, hundreds of them. He was also wearing a pinky ring, and it too was encircled with diamonds. On his shoes were little gold buckles in the shape of a lion with a sun behind it. Kamran recognized the symbol as the same one he saw on flags.

He watched as the man grabbed his father's bad hand, the one with the green finger. The man shook it, then flung it away.

Kamran stood up, then fainted again. Somebody caught him. Somebody else poured water into his mouth. The man in the suit was still yelling. Kamran opened his eyes. The yelling man had brown hair and was wearing sunglasses.

"I'm sorry, Mr. Agassian. I thought he could help me," Kamran heard his father say.

The yelling man spit in Kazem's face. A few other men in suits pulled him back. The yelling man began walking in a circle. Then he stopped and came toward Kamran. He bent down.

"Are you okay, son?" he asked. He reached out and stroked Kamran's hair. "Come on. Don't stop. Keep giving him water," he said curtly to the others. The veins in his neck popped out.

The water was good. Cold.

"Why aren't you at school, son?" the man asked him.

"It's Friday," Kamran replied. He looked around at the staring faces. "My Baba needs a hand. Can you get him a new one?" he asked.

The man stroked his hair again. "I'll see what I can do," he said. He rose and walked back toward Kazem. "You pull something this stupid again, Jahanpour, and I'll have you out living on the streets. Understand?"

"I do, Mr. Agassian," said Kazem.

"And then I'll have your son taken away from you, you mule."

Mr. Agassian played impatiently with his belt. His diamond ring sparkled in the sun. Now another man was running toward them.

"Hurry up. Get it to him," Mr. Agassian shouted. The runner stopped in front of Kamran, took a sandwich out of a bag, and shoved it into Kamran's mouth. Kazem lowered his head.

With his mouth full of bread, Kamran said, "Mr. Agassian, if you can't find my father a hand, can you please find him a finger?"

"I'll find him a new finger as soon as you get home and get some sleep." Mr. Agassian smiled. A black car, so shiny it reflected the sunlight, drove up beside him. There was a symbol like a peace sign on it. A back door swung open and Mr. Agassian got inside. As he watched the car drive away, Kamran wondered where in this city Mr. Agassian was going to find a new finger for Kazem.

A MONTH LATER, Kazem lost his finger.

The neighbours had told him to see a doctor, but Kamran's mother said doctors did magic things and put curses on families. Kazem's mother used to say the same. In the end, a butcher chopped off the finger with a big knife. Weeks after that, the finger next to it, the middle one, went yellow and pus came out of its fingernail. The butcher chopped that one off, too.

The next day, Kazem went to work. That evening, he told Kamran the story of what had happened.

When Kazem had to climb the side of the building with rope for the laying, he did it just fine. His left hand was strong and he used his feet to push himself up. He had his tools in a bag, which he held with his teeth. Up top, on the scaffolding platform, he took out his trowel. The mortar had been readied. His hand ached. A thin bandage was wrapped around it. He'd told the butcher not to make the cloth too thick so he could hold his trowel, which he picked up now. He wrapped his thumb, pinky and ring fingers around the handle. His hand hurt even more badly, but he managed to put a few slabs of mortar on the top layer of bricks.

When the day was over, Mr. Agassian came to check the work. The men lined up.

"How many bricks?" the contractor asked the first man in line.

"Two-fifty," the mason answered.

"How many bricks?" he asked the next in line.

"Two-sixty."

And then the next: four hundred, three-twenty, four-fifty, five hundred.

When it was Kazem's turn, another mason shouted, "Thirty!" before Kazem could answer. "You can't have a cripple working here."

As he related this story, Kazem ruffled Kamran's hair. "So they gave me my last pay. I got you your milk." He removed eight jars from the bag, nearly dropping one. Then he took out six loaves of bread, two packs of cigarettes, and one piece of goat's liver. "We're eating well tonight, son," he said.

The next day, Kamran didn't go to school. Nor did he go ever again.

From his bedroom window that night, he watched Zahra hit Aria and force her onto the balcony. Hours later, deep into the night, Behrouz came home. Unable to sleep, Kamran watched him from the window, too. He looked on as Behrouz found Aria lying on the balcony floor, took her in his arms, and rocked her gently back to sleep.

KAMRAN SNUCK OUT of the apartment. He took his school bag and books so no one would suspect him. He knew how to play tricks. He walked through the quiet alleyways. Above him, the hanging lights that he often saw at New Year and Ashura guided him. It wasn't Ashura yet, but the lights were there, waiting.

Early morning was the quietest time in the Bazaar. Before the sun could break through the cracks in the domed ceilings and arched entrances to the shop-lined alleyways, a lull fell over the carpets and the confectionery and the jewels locked away in underground safes. He stood under a hanging rug and inhaled. The carpet was twenty feet long, secured by six hooks dug deep into bricks in the ceiling. He briefly wondered if his father had laid those bricks, but then he remembered how much older the Bazaar was. He touched the rug. In certain parts, mostly near the centre and the corners, he could feel the silk. There were more rugs beside this one, all hung in a neat row from hooks in the brick. If there was an earthquake this whole bazaar would crumble. He imagined the scene: thousands of bodies under rubble, babies, mothers, and poor merchants, dead, leaving their starving families behind. And he would be there, too, but alive. He would rush to give aid, flinging the bricks off the injured as if they were feathers. He would see a beautiful girl, grab her hand, and pull her out of danger. He would hear a baby's cry. Frantically, he'd search under brick and stone, under giant carpets as heavy as ships, until he found the baby and resuscitated him back to life. Sadly, the baby's mother would be dead, but Kamran knew she'd be eternally grateful to him for saving her son's life.

He sat on the clay step by the carpet shop and could see some light down the alley. The sun had broken through. But he was too tired to move from the step and fell asleep there.

He awoke to the sound of chains being unlocked; the shops were opening. There were shouts and orders to take inventory. Some merchants grumbled unhappily with their neighbours. "Tell your mule of a boss to pay me my share," he heard a man say. The man was walking back and forth beside him, in and out of his shop.

"Why the fuck you sleeping in front of my shop, boy?" the man said. "Hurry out of here."

Kamran eyed him. The man was big. Several rolled carpets stood like columns outside his shop. He hoisted two, one on each shoulder, and turned to carry them in.

"Do you need help?" Kamran asked.

The man laughed. "You, help me? With what? Wiping my ass?"

"Here, let me try." Kamran grabbed the end of one of the carpets on the man's shoulder.

"The hell you will." The man whipped around. The rolled carpet hit Kamran in the face. He fell down, but quickly stood up again and tried to lift one of the carpets lined up outside the entrance. "I can help you," he said again.

"Leave it alone, you shit," the man said. He pushed Kamran aside and lifted the carpet himself. "What do you want, money?"

"A job," said Kamran. "My father lost his job. We need a lot of milk for my sister."

"Well, you can't work here," said the man. "You can't even lift a rock yet." He grabbed Kamran's school bag and threw it into the alley. Then he went inside and shut the door.

Three shops down was a sweet store. It sold not only Persian sweets, but American ones, too. Kamran could tell this from the colourful boxes and the type of writing on them.

"But you're wrong," the sweet-seller said when Kamran pointed out the boxes. "This one's German, and this one's Dutch. This one's Swedish or Swiss, not sure which. You tell me how much money your mother gave you, and I'll tell you what you can buy."

"I don't have money," Kamran said. "My father lost his fingers, so I am working, but—"

The seller, who had opened a box of candy for him, quickly closed it and put it away. "Go on, son," he said, not unkindly. "I don't hire children. But, you know, when I was a kid I used to collect dried mulberries and sell them to anybody for half a rial. I did that for a while. Then I went down to the garbage dump and looked for watches. You'd be surprised what you can find. I'd give them to the jewellers who knew how to fix them and then I resold them. Folks never had a clue. If you don't want to do that, go talk to the bead-man over there, at the corner."

Kamran crossed into the alley as the sweet-seller had told him to, and slowly walked five stores north. He already knew the bead-seller. A few months earlier, the owner had hired him to sweep around the shop before and after school. On the corner, he passed a veil shop, and beside it, a place that sold big sheets of paper with pictures of men wearing hats, men with guns hanging off their belts. He stopped outside a tiny shop that was half the size of the others. On the curtain over its doorway were the words "MOHREH-FOROUSH, Bead-Seller," written in coloured beads of all different shapes and sizes. He went inside. On the stall walls were pictures of little girls wearing beaded bracelets and neck-laces. Other photos showed beads strung and shaped into animals and houses. Behind the counter was a burly man with a beard but no hair on his head. He was concentrating on making something and sweating profusely.

"You're late," the man said, without looking up. "One more time and that's that."

"I was busy," Kamran said. "My sister needs milk. I was getting milk."

"Get milk on your own time," the man replied. "Now, do you know what I'm doing here?"

"No," said Kamran. He allowed himself a flash of hope and excitement.

"Come have a look then."

Kamran went around the counter. He knew what this meant. After months of being paid in small coins, and after sweeping the shop for endless hours, the bead-seller was about to change Kamran's life. The man held the beads close so he could see. "There are about a hundred beads in that box. You take one, in the right order, first blue, then green, then white, then red, string them on here, tie it up. Easy. But do it fast. Understand?"

"Yes," said Kamran. But he already knew how. He had watched closely as the man made bracelets and necklaces. On some nights, when the bead-seller closed shop, Kamran had snuck back inside and practised making bracelet after bracelet in secret.

"Once you're done, loop them around, like this. You loop them four times, and it looks like there's a flower at the centre of the necklace. Got it?"

"Yes," Kamran said. His heart beat fast.

"See my hands?" The man spread out his right palm. "They're big. My fingers fat. You finish this kind of necklace in five minutes, you get an extra toman a day. Bracelets are faster to make, but cheaper than other things. More you do, more you get. Understand?"

Kamran nodded.

That night, he ran home with his extra money and stuffed it in his pillowcase. For now at least he no longer had to beg other Bazaaris for a job. He went into the living room. His father was asleep on the couch. Infection had run through Kazem's body and his skin had yellowed. Sometimes he didn't make sense when he talked. Kamran kissed his father's forehead and went to the kitchen. His mother was making halva for Ashura. She had set a row of twenty bowls on the table.

"Take these to the neighbours," she said. "Start with the poorest ones. Give two to the bastard's mother so maybe the bastard won't rot in hell."

"Her name is Aria," Kamran said.

"Bite your tongue. I told you to never say her name under my roof."

Kamran piled as many of the bowls as he could carry on top of each other and went outside. He could hear the sound of drums and the music starting. Already, men were practicing for Ashura. Already people were wearing black, and some had started to cry and wail. He delivered his gift to the neighbours, leaving Aria's family for last. But when he made his way back to the Bakhtiar home, he paused outside the door. Inside, he could hear that Zahra was shouting at Aria again. He set down the tray, took the two remaining bowls, and went to the cherry tree. With one hand, he struggled up its trunk. He found a thick branch and left the bowls there. He and Aria would eat the treat later, together, he thought, when no one was calling her a bastard, and when no big giant men were yelling at him.

He shimmied as far along as he could on a branch, reached into his pocket and took out one of the bracelets he had made that day. It was white. He had painted Aria's name on it. He threw it on the balcony, into the corner where Aria always slept. Then he hopped down, ran back to his room, and changed into black.

4

In Behrouz's absence, Zahra raged, and Aria did whatever Zahra told her to do. Most of her time was spent washing clothes.

She waited for Kamran every day. Lately, she'd noticed he was coming home dirty, his hands covered in mud.

"Don't they make you wash your hands at school?" she asked him.

Kamran hadn't told her he'd stopped going to school. He was hanging off the cherry tree, trying to think of an answer, when he heard Zahra call out. "Aria, get some bread. You've been worth nothing all day!"

"Does she think you're a dog or something?" Kamran asked as he tried to climb from one branch to another.

"I think she likes dogs," Aria said.

"She's out of her mind, that woman. Dogs are the filthiest things."

"Who says they are?"

"The Prophet does, peace be upon him." Kamran dangled off a thick branch.

"The Prophet's stupid."

"You shut your mouth," Kamran said. "Look, Godzilla's coming."

Zahra was marching toward them with a stick in her hand. Aria began sliding down the tree.

"Didn't I tell you to get some bread? You deaf now?"

"We were talking," Aria said.

"Children shouldn't be talking, they should be shutting up." Zahra tried to hit her again, but Aria was quick and had already made it to the door of her apartment. She turned and waved. "Bye!"

Kamran waved back, clinging to the branch with one arm. His hands still hurt from work that day.

Inside, Zahra threw bills at Aria. "Here, go buy the bread."

Aria walked quickly. Her sandals, torn and too big, fell off every three or four steps. She passed old brick and stone houses, the kind that were so old the tenants had put up cardboard in place of windows. Some had even piled cardboard to make roofs.

The street began to fill with people. "Move!" someone yelled. It was an old man walking behind her. He pushed her aside. Soon she could hardly take a step. From the scent of roasted pistachios and almonds, she knew the bazaar was near, which meant the bakery must be, too. The smell of smoked liver and burnt charcoal wafted from the meat vendors along the road. She could see rows of rugs hanging along the street wall. The cheaper ones were always outside. When she moved under the bazaar dome, everything would be fancier.

"Liver! Pistachios! Almonds!" called voices around her. "Get out of the way, child!" a veiled woman said. Aria ran away from her, toward the mouth of the bazaar. Rows of hanging Persian rugs blocked her view. She ran under one, then another, and on and on, pushing back each one as hard as she could. The fringe at the end of each rug brushed against her unwashed and tangled hair.

"Child, what are you doing?" shouted one of the merchants. He spoke in an unfamiliar accent and Aria guessed he was one of the Turk people who came down to the city from the provinces. Another merchant saw her, too, and the two men both started after her. But they were too tall to duck under the rugs, and Aria laughed as she ran away.

On the other side of the rugs, an endless corridor of shops and vendors stood before her. She looked as far down the hall as she could to see where it went, but it seemed endless. She could smell kabobs nearby and saw a man waving cardboard over them so they would cook faster. She turned in the direction of the bakery but was pushed again, and this time she fell down. The bills Zahra had given her fell out of her pocket. The man who'd pushed her helped her up, but when she stooped to collect the bills, they were gone. She searched the faces around her, darting her eyes from vendor to vendor. She scanned customers, looking at their hands to see if money was crumpled between their fingers. But it seemed that all of it, everything Zahra had given her, was gone.

She tried not to cry, but still the tears came. "What's the matter, child?" a woman asked. She wiped Aria's face with her veil, then quickly left.

What would Zahra do to her? Dazed and afraid, Aria walked through the bazaar until it was dark and most of the shops had closed. At last she headed back south. As she passed each vendor, she caught the smell of freshly baked bread. She walked past the cobblers and ironworkers, until, at the corner of the block, she saw the bakery.

Inside, a tall, lanky boy with a dark neck was kneading dough. Aria watched as he lifted it with one hand and slapped it into a firepit in the wall. "Closed," he said with a South-City accent.

"There's no sign that says closed," Aria replied.

"Deaf?" he asked.

"I told you, there's no sign." She looked at the bread stacked around her. "Can I take some bread and pay you later?" she asked.

The boy called out to the back of the shop. "Stealing child, stop stealing! Mr. Karimi! Thief, thief!"

Asghar Karimi rushed outside. "Son, you make a ruckus like donkeys make sex."

"That stupid girl took off with some bread," the boy said.

"Is that the stupid girl, standing there?" Karimi asked, pointing at Aria. The boy stared back at him.

"Can I take some and pay for it later?" Aria asked.

"Is that how it works?" Karimi said.

"I lost my money. Someone at the bazaar stole it."

"She's lying," the boy muttered.

"Shut up," Karimi said. "I should get my wife to come bite your tongue out."

"Well, even if you say no, I'm going to take it, anyway," Aria said. "But I'll bring your money back."

"I'll call the police then. They'll come get you." Karimi watched her closely now, curious.

Aria inched closer to a pile of Barbari bread.

Karimi had baked the bread himself that morning. "Those are for a client," he explained, his tone more gentle. "She's coming to get them tomorrow." He placed a hand in front of the boy, and when Aria reached out and grabbed the bread he pushed the boy back and held him still.

Aria ran out and away as fast as she could.

Karimi let her run, then sent the boy home. By the time he had turned off the lights, he was certain he knew who the girl with the red hair was.

—

BEHIND AN OLD brick wall, a mile from the bakery, Aria took several bites before remembering she had better keep some for Zahra. Maybe then the punishment wouldn't be as severe. As she was folding the bread like a paper boy folds newspapers, she heard footsteps. She saw a male figure approaching, appearing in and out of the shadows as he walked under the street lights along the road. For a moment Aria felt scared, but something about the gait of the man, the way he moved, was familiar to her. When he finally stepped directly under a light she caught her breath.

It was her father.

She wanted to shout, but a stronger instinct took hold and she ducked behind a car parked by the road. She watched as he took a deep drag from his cigarette, looked in both directions along the street then crossed it. His footsteps were heavy, grinding gravel under the thick heels of his freshly waxed shoes. She remembered her father saying that the army had taught him three things: how to iron, how to polish, and how to swallow pain whole.

Once he got to the other side of the street and was headed down the sidewalk, Aria followed him. She followed him the whole mile back to where she had started, near the bakery. Several times she wanted to call out to him so he could lift her and hold her and take her home, tell her a story, maybe the one about the lion and the lamb at Persepolis, or about the Tree of Orphans in heaven. And maybe they would share some bread and he would tell her she was a good girl for not listening to Zahra because Zahra was not good. And then maybe he would tell her that he was going to take her away, to a land where there was only good, where there were no Zahras, only boys with dark necks who would climb peach and cherry trees with her. Maybe he would promise that she wasn't in trouble and that he would take care of her for the rest of his life.

But she stayed away, because maybe he was doing something she wasn't supposed to know about, and if he found out she knew he would hate her, like her real parents must have.

She followed him down a sidewalk, through an alley, and across another road. There, he stopped at a door and knocked three times. Someone opened the door and he talked to them for a while. Then the door closed and Behrouz moved on. He didn't stop at the neighbouring home, but at one a couple of doors down.

There, the same thing happened. A door opened. There was just enough light from the street lamp to let Aria see it was a woman. The woman was old. She said something and it looked like she was pointing her finger down the road. Behrouz turned his head and looked in that direction, nodding a few times. The door closed.

Behrouz moved down several more doors. On the other side of the road, hidden behind parked cars, Aria followed him. He stopped at another door, knocked. No one opened. He knocked again. Then a light turned on but still no one opened the door. He moved on, knocking on door after door. Some opened, some did not. He turned to cross the street.

Aria slid under a car so he wouldn't spot her. She could only see his shoes as they shuffled along the pavement. He was wearing his nice ones, and there was a gleam of light along their dark leather. Now, thinking about it, Aria realized her father was wearing his finest clothes, even a tie, something she hadn't known he possessed. She'd seen him in his uniform and sometimes the black trousers and white shirt he liked to wear on days off, but never a tie.

She'd grown tired, and imagined falling asleep there under the car. And no sooner had she thought this than she almost did. She kept her eyes open long enough to peek out and see a final door open to Behrouz—the door of the bakery she had stolen from earlier. She watched as the baker asked, "Can I help you?" To which Behrouz replied, "Yes, I am looking for someone." And then she could no longer keep her eyes open.

When she woke up to the roar of an engine, day was about to break. Behrouz was long gone. She stumbled out from under the car, to the horror of the driver, who exclaimed the names of Saint Fatemeh Zahra, the Prophet's daughter, and Saint Imam Reza and Saint Imam Hossein. "You will be Satan's favourite child, you stupid girl!" he said as he drove off in anger.

Aria found she'd been clutching the bread all night. Hungry again, she tore off a piece with her teeth and chewed at it all the way home. When Zahra saw her, she slapped her across the face with the back of her hand. Then she grabbed a twig from the cherry tree that she always kept handy, and hit Aria's cheeks and neck. "You'd better hold tight to the rest of that bread because it's the only food you'll be getting for a week," she shouted.

Finally Zahra sent her to the balcony again so that the neighbours could see what a demon she was. Aria spent the rest of the day huddled there until she fell asleep. When she awoke the next morning, she found a beaded bracelet placed beside her head. All the beads, except four, were white. The other four had letters painted on them. Four alien images.

If she'd been able to, she would have read her own name.

5

After walking through the city, Behrouz did not go home. Instead, he returned to the camp on the mountain. He had to be there every Friday to drive the regiment on the mountain down to the city mosques for Friday prayers. There they would be joined by the regiment that had stayed in the city. The main barracks were downtown, beside Laleh Park, and the regiments took turns each season, the men running or marching up and down the mountainsides, breathing in the cold air in case they were ever fated to engage in mountain warfare.

Behrouz had not seen Rameen since their night together in the tent, but now here was the young captain sitting beside him in the truck. Behind them, tucked in the back, were twenty other soldiers, boys who occasionally caught Behrouz's glance in the rear-view mirror.

"You're quiet," said Rameen. He touched Behrouz's hand as it rested on the gearshift.

Behrouz flung his hand up and caught Rameen on the right cheek. He was aware that some of the soldiers might be able to observe them through the square opening between the back of the truck and the front seats.

"Be careful," Rameen said lightly. "They'll think we're lovers." For the rest of the drive, the two men didn't speak a word.

IN THE MOSQUE, the mollah talked about nature. He talked about some sparrows he'd seen on a trip to the Caspian, among them a fledgling baby that had flown into a car windshield and died.

"When death comes," the mollah said, "it is God's will. And if indeed the baby bird died, it was his own fault, for he was flying in the path he should not have, and so it is better that he died, for his wrong way of flying was leading the flock astray . . ."

Rameen shut out the mollah's voice and turned to Behrouz, who had tried to sit away from him, without success. Rameen had followed him and slipped in beside him.

"He's a puppet mollah," Rameen whispered. "I know exactly what he'll say next." He lowered his voice to a baritone. "Stray not off the proper path, my sons, because if you get a bullet in your head, it's not the Shah's fault, nor SAVAK's fault."

The mollah continued: "So stray not off God's chosen path, my sons, for if misfortune befall you, curse Him not for bestowing his punishment, for verily, He, the All-Knowing, All-Merciful, has given us His rules, and His rules we must follow."

"Well, that was much the same thing," Rameen said.

"Shut your mouth," Behrouz murmured, but he couldn't help smiling. There was no place so humorous as the most sincere one. He had always thought this. Even as a boy he would laugh in the mosques. His father, a great Bakhtiari man, full of the blood of the Persian gypsies, would smack the back of Behrouz's head again and again, his reddened face shamed by the gaiety of his son. It was on those Fridays, in those mosques, that his father began to doubt him, Behrouz thought, and the seeds of his marriage to Zahra were sown. "It's because your mother died before you could walk, isn't it?" his father would say, and hit him again on the head. "Are you trying to be the woman this house never had?" But his father's friends and brothers assured him that his son's humorous remarks and delicate movements were the fruits of a changing Tehran, with its flashy kings and Western cars. But that never stopped the beatings, aimed at rushing Behrouz's body into manhood. And the trips to the mosques became more frequent.

Now Rameen was scrunching up his forehead, feigning immersion in the mollah's words.

"Stop it," Behrouz said again, attempting to be stern.

"You're the one who wants to read those forbidden books. This guy's one of those pig mollahs who says what SAVAK tells him to say. They're all pigs, but this one's really a pig."

Behrouz avoided his eye.

"You're not a God-lover, are you?" whispered Rameen.

A few of the other men were looking at them now. Rameen tugged at Behrouz's shirt. "God-lover, God-lover," he said. But Behrouz ignored him and took a notepad from his pocket. He began scribbling, thinking that if there were any secret agents in the room, they would see that he was but a simple driver heeding the words of a wise mollah.

At the next several Friday prayers, this became Behrouz's routine, pretending to be the studious student in a band of uncertain boy soldiers.

Some weeks into this game, Rameen moved in close to Behrouz's ear and whispered, "If the SAVAK catch you one day, what do you think they're going to say when they see a notebook full of scribbles?"

"Well, captain," Behrouz said, "I'll tell them it's my own form of writing."

"Then they'll ask you to explain its logic. And because you won't be able to, they'll accuse you of being a communist spy with his own code, lieutenant."

"I'm not—"

"Doesn't matter what you are or what you aren't. They'll make you into what they want you to be, what works for them. Come to my tent tonight. It's time I taught you how to write."

That night, Behrouz hesitated. He hesitated for so long that Rameen finally gave in and went to fetch him. He found Behrouz behind his truck, smoking opium through a pipe.

"Don't let anyone catch you with that. They're outlawing it."

Behrouz closed his eyes. He tilted his head back.

"Come with me," said Rameen.

Behrouz followed him. The high from the opium blurred his vision, and though he knew where he was, the sounds of the soldiers laughing as they played rook, as they clanked their teacups together and filled the mountain air with fumes from their cigarettes, as these same soldiers drew the shape of women in the dirt and dreamed of the day they could return to their villages instead of playing toy militia for the Shah, made Behrouz feel that nothing was real, and that what he was hearing and seeing through opium lenses was a dream evaporating as quick as smoke. He felt as if he were going to cry.

He stopped in the path midway to Rameen's tent. "I have to tell you about my daughter," he said. "She came to me like magic. But I'm afraid sometimes. I'm afraid that she's not real. That she's a mirage, a reflection in a pond that I mistook for a child."

Rameen was standing on a damp patch of grass. He listened carefully. Then he held out his hand. "Come," he said. Behrouz took his fingers.

—

WHEN BEHROUZ HAD first learned to drive, no one had told him about the hazards of winter: how tires got stuck, or how roads were blocked by fallen boulders weighed down by snow. When more things are added to the world, he thought, you have to be sure the world can take it.

When he had added Zahra to his world, his life had almost crumbled under the weight. "We're all sinners," his father had told him. "So, she has a child. And is unmarried. It's all part of God's plan. But you . . . You be the man, son. Stand up. Save her. That's what men do." Zahra was a distant cousin, left violated and destitute by some family she'd worked for, who had made her way to him through the family gossip trails. The day his father had decided on the marriage, Behrouz punched his chest twenty times, then punched his own head, and then the wall. If only he had tried to be intimate with other girls. But he never could. He had never tried with anyone, woman or man. Shame had always shadowed him. But in the end, pity had brought him around. No other man would want a thirty-six-year-old sinner. He had saved Zahra. It was part of God's plan.

Tonight, in the snow, he felt like he'd been driving for days. It had been three weeks since he'd slept in his own bed, beside Zahra, feeling her hate. Instead, he'd been confined to the cracking surfaces of bunkers and bunk beds topped with thin layers of foam. Even when he kept company with Rameen, it never felt nice. He wasn't going to sleep there again tonight, either.

He shook the pain out of his hands. They'd been aching for a while, but he kept them tight on the wheel, determined to steady the truck. It wasn't easy driving a truck this heavy down the mountainside. Gone were the days of his long walks, of being awed by the city. Ever since the *coup d'état*, not only had those walks become a thing of the past, his view on everything had changed.

It was as if a flower had been rooted out of him. It had been five years, and no one talked about the "sudden arrest" of the prime minister anymore—no one except Rameen. "He had it coming you know. Mossadegh," Rameen had once told him. "If only he'd co-operated with the Russians. Stubborn man."

"Don't the Russians make everyone into a Soviet?" Behrouz replied hesitantly. What did he know about such things? Still, he carried on. "We'd all stop being Persians, and Kurds, and Turks. Gypsies. I thought—"

"You haven't read the books. What do you know?" Rameen cut him off, agitated. He was quick to shut down when questioned. After that, Behrouz had stopped talking to him about politicians.

He drove on. The last time he'd returned home, Behrouz found Aria on the balcony. Zahra had banished her there again. He'd taken her in his arms and rocked her to sleep, then fallen asleep himself. The next morning, he took her to Laleh Park. He saw, to his alarm, that she was so thin she could slide through the bars of the park gates.

This time, he had a plan. Rameen had made him promise to stick to it.

When he arrived home, well into the early hours, he found Aria asleep on the front steps. Zahra wasn't home. He nudged the girl awake, lifted her into his truck, and began the journey back to the barracks. She would live there from now on. Away from Zahra.

The ride was long, and Aria slept all the way. Behrouz glanced over at her, and the bruises on her arm made him feel helpless. He noted how tightly she held her doll, and glanced at the six bracelets around her wrists, wondering where she had got them. His mind raced, jumping hurdles and flying across vast fields.

When they reached the mountain's snow-covered bottom, Behrouz stopped and lifted Aria out of the truck. He didn't want to risk driving up the slopes of Darband at night in the winter. They would walk the rest of the way. He carried Aria as long as he could, then set her down and held her hand as she sleepily placed her feet on the small mounds of dirt and rock that made the path up the slopes.

If they were to keep going, he thought, they would reach Mount Damavand, far beyond the city. They would go and go until they crossed into Russia and got away from this hell. What would it be like, to just walk and never stop? Would anyone here miss him? How far could he take his little girl? To what worlds would he help her travel?

On Darband, there were many paths to take. One led to trails and small cafés lined alongside the mountain. The other went to the army camps, and still another to the Kremlin.

"Bobo? Do you walk this way all the time?" Aria mumbled. She was half asleep still.

"Yes, I do."

"Are we going to your work?"

"Yes," Behrouz said.

"What do you do?"

"I drive. I've told you before."

"Drive soldiers? Can you tell me from the beginning? Can you tell me the story?" She clung to him as they walked.

"Yes. I drive between stations, down to the city and back sometimes, and take the soldiers around, or get them things."

"And that's why you're away so long?"

"Yes."

"And that's why I have to stay alone with Zahra?"

"Yes."

She almost fell, but he pulled her up, squeezing her bruised arm. She didn't say a word. Beneath her, a mix of sediment and snow crumbled and slid toward the mountain's base. The angle wasn't steep, but she was small.

"Bobo, does Zahra hate me?"

"I don't know. Sometimes I think she hates herself." She had likely grown to hate herself more since marrying him, he thought, but did not say so.

They came to a hill. Here, the snow had melted and the grass was pushing through. It was nearly daylight. A narrow dirt road, now dry, meandered higher and higher. This was the path to the barracks.

A voice called to Behrouz from the top of the hill.

"Bakhtiar, that you?"

It was Rameen, waiting for them. He appeared from behind the shrub.

Aria hid behind her father's legs.

"This is my daughter, Aria." Behrouz exchanged a smile with Rameen.

Rameen squatted down to eye level with the girl. His wide grin revealed his dimples.

"Aria? That's a boy's name, isn't it? You gave your girl a boy's name, Behrouz? Nice to meet you, Aria." He shook her hand.

"Not a boy," Behrouz said. "After a song. Aria. That's a song."

"A song?"

"Any song," Behrouz replied.

"Is it Latin?" Rameen winked at Aria.

"I don't know about those things, Mr. Rameen," said Aria shyly.

Behrouz bent down to Aria's level, too. "I'm driving up to Mashhad tonight. Rameen's going to look after you."

He straightened. "I have to go," he said to Rameen, who nodded.

Behrouz hugged Aria. "I'll be back by morning," he said. "You'll be fine."

BY LATE MORNING, Behrouz still had not returned.

Aria had slept the night in Rameen's tent, but when she awoke, Rameen was not there and she was alone. The men must have climbed higher up the mountain without her. She could see smoke from their fires not too far away. She decided to follow them.

Their camp was at the edge of Darband now, near Tochal, the first mountain of the Alborz. From there, if the soldiers kept walking, they would get to Damavand. That's what Bobo had told her. She set out after them and very quickly lost a shoe. One foot followed the other as she climbed steadily, covering her face to fend off the sun. After a while, she lost track of how long she'd been walking. She stopped to lie down, but the dirt was too hot, so she squatted instead and closed her eyes. Then she opened them again quickly, worried she'd lose sight of the smoke from the men up ahead.

She got up and began again, noticing how the red earth had tainted her white dress. Her feet were cut and bloody. Bits of sand and rock had collected between her toes. She bent down to clear them, carefully scooping between each toe. The air was beginning to cool and she felt a thin breeze rising. She considered her situation. Behrouz had said he'd be back in the morning, but he hadn't come. And Rameen had promised he'd take care of her, but he'd left, too. Then, in the distance, she could see someone running toward her.

"Did she come up here all by herself?" Rameen shouted. Another soldier was with him and they made their way down to her.

"Is that blood?" The other soldier pointed at Aria's feet.

Aria said nothing. She looked up at Rameen, then fell and rolled ten feet down the slope.

ARIA AWOKE IN a darkened room, to the sound of the baritone voices of two men she did not know. At first, she couldn't understand what they were saying. She knew the words they spoke but could not make sense of them.

One of the men noticed she had opened her eyes. "She's up," he said to the other, who replied, "I'll get him."

Behrouz entered, teary-eyed. This embarrassed her, for she knew she had caused him to weep.

"You don't have much time," one of the men said to Behrouz. "She can't stay here."

"Yes, I know," Behrouz replied. Aria sat up. Behrouz held her. "Why did you do this?" he asked, cupping her face in his hands.

"You didn't come back. And everyone left me," she said.

A sound came from the entrance of the tent. It was Rameen. "I can take her home if you like," he said. "I'll carry her on my back."

Behrouz didn't look at him.

"I can go by myself," Aria said. She felt how the sun had burned her face, how her lips were cracked.

Rameen leaned into Behrouz. "I can explain," he said in a low voice. "Please. Let me explain. I'll take her home tonight."

Behrouz stood up abruptly. The other two men took him aside.

"That boy there has been in some trouble," one said, nodding at Rameen. "Thought you should know."

"What kind of trouble?" Behrouz asked.

"There were suits up here. Looking for him. They must be agents."

"SAVAK?" Behrouz asked.

"Think so," said the man. For the first time, Behrouz noted the ambulance insignia on his collar. This man was a doctor, he realized.

The other man spoke up: "We're just being honest with you. And you should know that the village boys are starting to get ideas in their heads, too. We hear all sorts of things about that fellow. And you. I don't care what's going on with you at home, but don't bring your little girl up here again. For her own good."

BEHROUZ GENTLY LIFTED Aria onto his back and stepped into the dusk. Rameen followed and offered him a cigarette, but he didn't take it.

"I'm sorry," Rameen said. "I got busy last night. You asked a favour. I let you down."

"I'm sorry, too," Behrouz said. "And I lied as well. I wasn't in Mashhad last night. I was doing something else."

Rameen took a drag on his cigarette, then exhaled. "What sort of thing?"

"Looking for someone."

"Find them?"

"Not yet," Behrouz replied. He ran a hand through his greying hair and looked at his palms. When had they begun to feel like leather?

Together, the two men lifted Aria onto Rameen's back, and Behrouz crossed her arms around his neck. She was nodding off to sleep.

"I've got her," said Rameen quietly. "You should go. To Mashhad?"

"This time, yes," said Behrouz. "And do you have the address I gave you?"

"Yes."

"When you see her mother, she'll be mean. She'll beat the girl. Like I told you. But there's nothing to be done for now. When you drop her home and my wife closes the door on you, just hang around a bit, see if you hear anything. She hits the child in the face sometimes. That's why her nose looks swollen. It's broken." He gently tapped Aria's nose with a finger. "Listen to see how bad it gets. If it gets really bad, go back in and take her away. If it's not so bad, just leave. My wife will beat her a little and be done with it. I'm figuring out a solution."

Rameen paused and looked closely at Behrouz. "Are you?"

"I'm figuring it out," Behrouz said again.

At this, Rameen took a few quick steps and disappeared into the night. Behrouz watched the white of Aria's dress twinkle in the darkness and fade away.

RAMEEN COULD EASILY have taken a cab. He had a thousand tomans in his pocket and many thousands more in an old wooden box painted with Persian miniatures in his room at home. In the bank, he had yet more thousands—he didn't even know how many. What he knew was that he possessed just as much in guilt, thousands upon thousands of guilt-bills, at once paralyzing him into doing nothing and driving him to change the world. For this reason he could never use the money he had. Each toman was balanced by each token of guilt. He couldn't even buy clothes for himself or a soda at the corner store. The sensation was at its worst when his father took him to the tailor and forced a suit on him. He looked away as his father paid the bill. And then, when they took the long cab drive home, he couldn't look at the beggars they passed, with their children tucked under their arms, hoping the nice men in the taxi would give them a candy or two. Even now, with this poor girl asleep on his back, her arms around his neck, and the road to south Tehran stretching ahead, he couldn't bring himself to hail a cab. He simply walked. Each step negated the guilt, balanced him. And as Aria's weight grew heavier, his body felt lighter. He felt as though he might float above the city, hover over its lights and smells and its misery and mountains.

Aria slept nearly the entire walk. Her head lay against the back of his neck, her arms tight around his collar. But when at last the dawn turned red, he couldn't help waking her.

"Look, Aria. Look at the sun."

She awoke reluctantly, her eyes slowly letting the light in.

"It looks like a cherry in the sky," she said.

"Our own giant cherry," said Rameen.

They walked a little farther down the winding paths of Darband, feeling the gradual heat of morning on their skin.

"How about you stand on my shoulders," he joked.

"I'm too sleepy. And you'll drop me," she said.

"You're just as stubborn as I am. It'll be fun, you know."

"I'll fall."

"But I'll catch you if you fall."

She sighed, readjusted her arms around his neck, and slept on.

Another half-hour into the walk and Rameen remembered he had forgotten water.

"You thirsty? We'll be in the city soon. I'll get you a soda," he said.

"Can I come to your house?" Aria asked.

Rameen took his time to answer. "My house is far," he said. "What's wrong with yours?" But he already knew the answer, and already he was a liar. His house, his father's house, was in the north, closer to the mountain where the wealthy lived, near Niavaran, the Shah's palace. His house wasn't far at all.

"I don't want to go home," Aria said. Rameen kept his silence and swallowed his guilt the rest of the way.

On they walked through the avenues and side streets. At times, they crossed into Pahlavi Street and sped through the crowd. Aria fell asleep again. Rameen's back was starting to ache but he kept on. If others suffered, so would he. At last they entered the South-City and passed the Bazaar. Soon after, they came to the address Behrouz had given him.

Rameen paused and waited outside the door awhile. He thought about what Behrouz had told him about the woman inside. He felt Aria's arms encircling him, her soft, regular breathing.

He couldn't do it.

He turned around, feeling his legs shaking and his feet throbbing. His ankles cracked as he moved them. Stubbornly, he headed north, and the mountains of the city looked down on him. He could almost hear them laughing.

RAMEEN REACHED HOME with Aria on his back. He waited awhile across the street, to be certain the house was empty. He didn't want his parents to see him with the girl, but he knew Belghaise and Bahram, the maid and butler, were likely to be inside. At last, he entered the house, went straight to his room, and put Aria, still asleep, on his bed. He'd explain everything to Behrouz when they saw each other again.

He lay on the floor next to the bed and tried to sleep, but the pain in his legs kept him awake. He had walked the length of the city twice. Over thirty kilometres, he figured. His mind spun, and he thought about how he had only two years to go and his military service would be over. After that, he might never see Behrouz again. He daydreamed about burning his uniform. He knew exactly what he wanted to do. Little by little, he would change things from the inside, so that every captain and soldier would want to burn their uniforms one day, too.

He gazed at the pictures on his wall. His father had painted them. His mother had written some of the books on his shelf and many poems that other parents sang to their children. For the last five years, both of his parents had received death threats. Some came from strangers, but others were from the secret police. Sometimes these people would call the house, and when Rameen answered the phone, he'd hear a voice say, "Your mother's corpse would look nice hung high in Castle prison, wouldn't it?" He would hang up, but these voices would call again and again. For a few months, there'd be a respite, but the calls would start up again as soon as he began to think it was over. Sometimes a dead dog would be left at the front door.

Rameen didn't care. He would write his own book one day, his own manifesto, and those who wished him dead could describe his own corpse to him as much as they wanted. They, like his parents, would have no power over him.

With a quiet resolve he knew he had done the right thing by bringing Aria here. He watched her sleep and wondered what she dreamed of.

6

Aria woke up in a strange bed. Sleepily, she jangled the six bracelets on her wrist, enjoying the noise the beads made when they tapped against each other. She remembered a dream she'd had, or thought she'd had, about a boy running through the alleyways of the bazaar. But when she tried to picture the boy's face, she couldn't.

She rolled over and looked around the room. Rameen was asleep on the floor. Alarmed now, she jumped down from the bed, crouched next to him, and shook his arm. "Why am I here?" she demanded.

Rameen opened his eyes. Aria's voice was as stern as that of the generals who sometimes chastised him. She would have made a good soldier, he thought as he willed himself awake. "You mean business, don't you?" he said.

"You were supposed to take me home."

He sat up. His back ached. Whoever said sleeping on the floor was good for you was a liar. "Yes. And Zahra is at your home. Do you want to go to her?"

"You never do what people ask you to do," Aria said. "Where's my doll?"

"It's here." Rameen stood up stiffly, yanked his coat from the hook on the bedroom door, and fished in the pocket. "What's her name?" he asked, as he handed the doll to her.

"Zahra," Aria replied.

"The doll, I mean. Not your mother."

"The doll's name is Zahra," Aria said. She eyed him carefully.

"I see." He stood up and opened the curtains. The sun was bright but not hot. "It's better here than at your house. Belghaise will make you breakfast. We have a television. Want to watch it?"

"I want to go home," Aria said. She sat on his bed. "Bobo will get mad at you again."

"That's likely," said Rameen. "But you're a little girl. And I know better than a little girl. I'll take you back. I have to return to work tomorrow. I just thought you could rest here for a few days."

"I don't need rest," Aria said.

Rameen grabbed a towel. "Come wash your face," he said, and led the way to the bathroom.

Together, they washed at the sink, and he gave Aria a new toothbrush he found in the bathroom cabinet. Belghaise always bought extra ones when she went shopping. Aria liked the taste of the paste, she told him. Zahra had only ever given her baking soda to use. He nodded, then brushed and braided her hair, carefully following her instructions.

As Aria watched TV, Rameen spent the day thinking of ways to keep her with him, but he couldn't come up with any convincing excuse. Luckily, Belghaise was the only one home, and she didn't ask questions. When he asked after his parents' whereabouts, she told him they were in Mazandaran, resting for the week and enjoying the sea air, with Bahram there to help.

As night approached, he knew it was time to take the child home. He mustered his courage by making a deal with himself. He would simply talk to her, this Zahra. It didn't have to be so hard. He would ask what her problems were with Aria. Maybe Aria did misbehave a little, but if he and Zahra talked about it, they could resolve everything. Many parents beat their children. Even his own father had beat him. In fact, he didn't know of a child who'd never been beaten. It was Aria sleeping outside, in the cold, that bothered him most.

Despite these thoughts, Rameen continued to delay his departure, and so it was near dawn when he and Aria finally left his house. This time, they took a cab. Aria slept through the ride.

Zahra opened the door. "So you've brought the kid back from the damned place. What are you, her father? Replaced the old one? Where has that son of a bitch run off to?"

Rameen straightened his stiff back. "He's in Yazd," he lied. "Then off to Shiraz, I think. Picking up recruits. Doesn't he tell you?"

"Some people aren't worth talking to."

Rameen studied Zahra. She wasn't what he had expected. No veil. No villager's accent. She was dressed in a Western manner, with a frayed dress that came just below the knee. She was wearing heels, even this early in the morning, and her dress and shoes were a matching beige. Her left hand was on her hip and she was chewing gum loudly. The frames of her glasses were almond-shaped, pointed at the ends. They looked like the body of an insect, he thought.

"Well, are you going to take her in?" Rameen asked. He found himself speaking more sharply than he normally did.

"Set her down," she said.

"No. I don't want to wake her. Have you got a couch or something? I can just lay her on it."

"Put that filth with her filthy dress on my couch? You can put her on the floor. Come in."

Rameen entered the apartment slowly, studying this new, undiscovered habitat. It was the world of the Tehran southerner, one he had never seen so closely. He examined the rough concrete floor, cold and uninviting, uncovered by wood or carpet.

"At least put a mattress or blanket down. She'll freeze to death on this floor."

"Why, yes, Mr. Princess." Zahra had perched on a torn armchair. She crossed her legs. One of her beige heels, blackened from her walks through the alleyways of Shoosh, dangled from her toes. "There's a blanket in the bedroom. You can go grab it if you like."

Rameen, still carrying Aria, fetched the blanket. When he returned to the living room, he laid it down with one hand while holding Aria with the other. He folded the blanket three times to thicken its cushioning, then placed her on top.

"You're a piece of shit," he said to Zahra, as he turned around.

"And your tongue is bigger than your brain," Zahra replied. "I told that turd of a man not to take her to the camp. A military camp is no place for a child. A lot can happen to a little girl up there, with all those men. Scum like you will catch her, do God-knows-what to her. But he's an idiot, and she's too stupid to listen to anything."

"She's a child," Rameen said.

Zahra fastened her dangling shoe to her foot. "You know nothing about the world, Mr. Princess. I'm saving that girl. I'm the best thing that could have happened to her."

She got up and walked to the kitchen. Rameen could hear her opening and shutting cupboards. Then the sound of slow running water. "Want some tea?" she shouted.

"No. I'm off."

She came back and stood by the doorway between the living room and kitchen. "Off to what?"

"Important things," he said.

"Saving the world?"

"Maybe," Rameen replied.

"Well, don't try hard. The more good you do, the more you'll be hated. It's the rule of life, Mr. Princess. In my life, I've noticed that it's the innocents who get skinned alive. Whatever good you're doing, mix it with a dash of evil, will you? Just a bit."

Rameen smoothed his hair and uniform. Then he placed his soldier's beret on his head, angling it perfectly. "You're not going to Friday prayers today? I figured everyone from around here would. The girl can have a nice sleep until the time you're back."

"You trying to protect her from me? Don't worry. I'm not as bad as I look. And I told you, I'm the best thing that could have happened to her." Zahra returned to the kitchen. From there she shouted, "Do I look to you like the type who'd go to Friday prayers?"

"I don't know, Mrs. Zahra," Rameen said. "Many in this world are not what they appear to be."

He stepped outside, into the rays of morning light, and closed the door. On the street, he looked back at the place only once. He didn't know if he wished Aria would run away with him up to the mountain, or if he wished to never see her again. From here, at the bottom of Pahlavi Street in the pits of Tehran, the smell of dung and dirt and poverty dazed him. He faced north, where he could see the faint outline of the Alborz range, first Darband and, above it, Tochal. Beyond all of them was the great mountain of Damavand, commanding all of Tehran. The Shah wasn't really their ruler, he told himself as he began to walk. This mountain was, and always would be.

7

Rameen flung open the flap of his tent. It had taken him half the day to get back, and now everything disgusted him. He took off his hat and tie, then stepped outside. He headed to the water pump nearby, filled the basin, and splashed his face. His black hair sparkled. He rubbed his fingers down the moustache he was trying to grow and let water trickle down his long neck. Like the rest of him, his neck was thin, hiding his strength. He took out a handkerchief from his back pocket and dried his face. Squinting, he searched the horizon and fields for Behrouz, without success. It's reading day, Rameen thought. He should be here.

Back in his tent he leafed through the book they'd begun reading together, the one he'd decided Behrouz could learn to read from. *The Good Earth*. It was written by some woman. Along the margins, Behrouz had made drawings with arrows that led to the matching words. So far, his vocabulary was up to one hundred words. Simple words: a triangle over a square for *house*, a circle for *sun*, a shaded circle for *moon*. For *love* and *hate* he had drawn a heart and then a heart split in two. For the word *intelligent* he had drawn the face of a man but made the top of his head larger than it should be. For *China* he had drawn the map of Iran. When Rameen told him it was the wrong country, Behrouz had refused to change it. "It's the only country I know," he had said. "Anyhow, all countries should be home."

Rameen had smiled. "You see the world as though it were made of candy," he said.

Behrouz smiled. "You mean to say I'm stupid?"

"No," Rameen started, but Behrouz didn't let him finish.

"Your problem is that you think you've got it all figured out." He'd taken a drag of his cigarette. "Maybe I've got a feeling that the country in this book is no different from the country beneath my feet."

"Maybe," Rameen had said. "Silly driver."

Now he heard the sound of a truck rip through the mountain dirt. He ran toward it, happy that the silly driver had finally arrived.

The two men who stepped out of the truck were wearing suits, and one of them had sunglasses on. At first Rameen thought Behrouz must be with them. "Where's your driver?" he asked.

"He's in your mother's grave, fucker."

Rameen pumped out his chest. "Where's your salute?" he said. "Who gave you the right to address a captain in the Shah's army this way?" But he knew who the men were. He'd seen their kind before, the same kind of men who'd taunted him about his mother's corpse and left dead dogs at his door. He played the game anyway.

"The Shah himself gave us the right, fucker," one of the men said.

Rameen felt the first blow in his chest. The next was to his back, where a boot dug in. With his face in the dirt, he caught a glimpse of the other man walking out of his tent. The man's feet stopped by Rameen's face and hundreds of pamphlets were dropped on his head.

"These, fucker, mean you're no longer captain. I can put you and your whore mother into whatever grave I want." He kicked dirt in Rameen's face. "Found this, too."

He flung the novel, full of Behrouz's drawings, into the other man's hands.

THE TWO MEN in suits blindfolded Rameen and drove him to Castle prison. Inside, they stripped him of his clothes and gave him a uniform.

He spent the first few nights still blindfolded. The cell was small—he could walk from one end to the other in seconds. He could hear other men in the courtyard and the corridors, so there must be a window somewhere, he thought.

By the third night, he'd lost all sense of spatial orientation. On the fourth night they came for him. He was lying on the floor, trying to sleep. There was no bed in his cell. There wasn't even a toilet; he peed and shat in the corner. Two men opened the door. They held his arms back, and when Rameen struggled, they kicked him.

They dragged him to his feet and made him walk, one man pulling him, the other pushing. In the halls, he smelled what he at first thought was urine but then realized was cleaning detergent, the same kind Belghaise used to clean toilets in his family's home.

They reached a place where the noise from the rest of the prison became muffled. He sensed it was another small room, and although he was still blindfolded, he could feel the heat of lights. The two men held him tight. He heard the door open and more men came in. He wasn't sure how many, but guessed there were three, two of whom placed their hands on him. Then he felt a rope being tied around his wrists and his ankles. The slack on each rope was tightened, as if each man had grabbed his end and wrapped it around something, pulling Rameen's arms and legs far from the rest of his torso.

They left him like that for two days. A guard sometimes came in and stuffed his mouth with bread. Another occasionally forced water down his throat. On the second day, Rameen couldn't stop screaming.

A day later, two men woke him. They lifted him to a chair and took the blindfold off. He couldn't see. The men waited patiently.

When he could make out images, he realized the two men were sitting at the other end of a long table. They looked middle-aged. One had a big moustache. The other was clean-shaven.

"After you, doctor," the moustached man said to the other. But from the way the men were dressed, both in form-fitting suits and thick cravats, it didn't look like they were doctors at all. Rameen closed his eyes and vomited onto the floor.

They gave him a tissue.

"Thank you," Rameen said.

The clean-shaven man spoke. "So, Mr. Emami, been having fun, have you?"

Rameen stayed quiet.

"Do you see where your fun has got you? And there are many worse things it can get you, you know."

"This is just the beginning," the moustached man said. His partner looked at him disapprovingly.

"Now," said the first man, "we want to be very good to you, because it's in our nature to be good. Do you understand?"

Rameen vomited again.

Five hours later, he lay fetal on the floor. Blood was trickling from a cut on his lip. One of his eyes was swollen shut. He held his stomach, where they had kicked him. There was only one man in the room now, the one with the moustache. He was yelling at Rameen.

"Who taught you? Who got you this garbage?" When Rameen didn't answer, the man kicked him again.

"Where are they staying? How many guns do they have?" the man asked. "Wait till I get my hands on your mother. I'll show you what we do with mothers."

Rameen could taste blood in his mouth. His face ached. The other man came back into the room. He was carrying a long wire cable.

This time, they tied his wrists above his head and flung him onto a cold metal table. They removed his shoes, and then his socks, and then they tied his ankles together and tethered them to the legs of the table. The cable was thick at the top, where the clean-shaven man was holding it. It thinned nearer the tip. Rameen felt his ankles pressed together as the men readied him for the whipping. The clean-shaven man told him this was his last chance. They were going to get it out of him even if they had to whip him ten thousand times.

Rameen heard a crack. The cable whipped against the soles of his feet. It sliced them. Blood seeped out. With every whip, the number of wounds grew. His skin began to peel. The moustached man grabbed the skin and tore it off.

But there was nothing Rameen could say. He didn't know anything. No one had taught him anything. He had no knowledge of a secret stash of weapons. He had no ties to other communists, the

Tudeh Party, the Fadayan, or the smaller groups. He swore this over and over until he lost consciousness.

BEHROUZ WAITED FOR hours. He stood in a field in Qasr district, where he could see the rooftops of Castle prison. He tried to un-see his ideas about what they were doing to Rameen inside. He'd tried to get Rameen's contacts, but every captain or colonel he asked refused to speak with him. All Behrouz knew of Rameen's parents was that they were rich and lived somewhere in Niavaran.

He lit a cigarette and smoked it as he walked home. His cravings for opium had become worse, but he knew he had to stay focused. He didn't sleep that night and spent the next three days driving to the outskirts of the prison, watching who came and went, during his lunch breaks. On the fourth day, he was given permission to visit. The guards told him his friend was lucky. Few of the other prisoners got visitors, not until months after they were first taken in. When Behrouz asked why they were allowing Rameen to have visitors, one of the guards said, "The rich get everything." He waited for hours in a lonely room with a man and woman, until all three of them were fingerprinted together. He wondered if they were there to visit Rameen, too, but didn't ask.

"I can sign my name," the man said when his finger was dipped in ink. "So can my wife." He pointed to the woman beside him, who was modestly dressed but without a hijab. The couple didn't look rich, but Behrouz noticed that everything they wore was spotlessly clean.

"We'd rather have your prints," said the warden behind the desk.

"How evolved," the man whispered under his breath.

Behrouz looked away. He had his own fingerprints recorded before returning to his seat.

"Nice uniform," the man said when Behrouz sat down. "Do you know my son?"

"Mr. Rameen?" Behrouz asked.

"Did you know he was up to this nonsense, or was he keeping his love of Stalin a secret from everybody?"

"I don't know, sir," said Behrouz, lowering his head.

"This generation will never learn," Rameen's father said.

His wife touched his leg. "They will, Hooshmand, they will," she said. She sighed heavily. Looking at Behrouz she asked, "Are you a friend? Has he done anything he can't turn back from?"

The warden glanced over at them before returning to his paperwork.

"There is nothing we can't come back from." Behrouz smiled.

"Not always," said Rameen's mother.

She looked just like Rameen, Behrouz thought. Same eyes, same nose. "Your son once told me you write books," he said.

"When they let me," she replied. "My name is Mahnoosh." She reached out to shake his hand. "My husband, Hooshmand." She motioned to her husband.

"Hello, sir. Behrouz Bakhtiar," said Behrouz.

"From the Bakhtiari tribe?" Mahnoosh asked. She seemed pleased by this possibility.

"Only distantly now," said Behrouz. "Sorry to disappoint." He put a hand to his chest.

"You don't roam the plains anymore? Weave your beautiful kilims and carpets?" Mahnoosh smiled.

Behrouz smiled with her. "We should have kept the old ways."

"Some still do, thankfully," said Mahnoosh.

Hooshmand stood up and paced the room. "They could give him life for this, you know. That idiot."

"It will be all right, sir, God-willing," said Behrouz.

"You people and your God. It's always about God, isn't it?"

"Hooshmand!" Mahnoosh warned him. "Sit down and be calm. Your tantrums won't help anything."

"To think we managed to get him this position—as a captain, no less—to keep him away from those lunatic communists. I pulled every string I could."

The warden looked over at them again.

"Better than having him lick the Shah's boots," Mahnoosh whispered, wary of the warden.

"I tried to teach that boy to love poets," Hooshmand said.

"He does, he does love poets," said Behrouz, more passionately than he'd intended. Rameen's parents stared at him. "He's been teaching me about poets," he explained.

A door opened and a guard stepped into the room. "Ten minutes per visit," he said. "Who's first?"

Behrouz watched Rameen's parents disappear down the hall. He thought back to Rameen's description of them, which had been considerably more sinister than the dejected middle-aged couple he'd just met. It was true, though, that the mother was the stronger of the two.

After ten minutes, Hooshmand and Mahnoosh returned, looking defeated.

"Is there nothing you can do?" Behrouz asked, trying to keep the worry out of his voice.

Hooshmand dropped his head. "There comes a time when connections and favours run out. You understand, Mr. Bakhtiar?" He shook Behrouz's hand and left the room.

"He needs time," said Mahnoosh, nodding after her husband. She'd been crying. She took Behrouz's hand with both of hers. Usually, when an unrelated woman touched him, his first instinct was to pull away, but this time he resisted. "Thank you, Mr. Bakhtiar," she said. "You do your ancient people proud. Loyal till the end. My son told me he's been teaching you to read. Be sure to read the right things. In the meantime, we'll see what the lawyers can do."

"You have good ones?" Behrouz asked, still holding her hand.

"Hooshmand's brother is a judge. He has two more brothers, barristers in London. My father was a general for the Shah's father. Now the Shah hates the likes of us, but maybe not all the favours have run out." She squeezed his hand. "Stay in touch, Mr. Bakhtiar."

As she walked down the main hall, Behrouz heard her heels tap against the concrete like a soldier's marching boots. He stared after her straight back, her head held high. He'd seen that walk so many times, mirrored in Rameen's rhythm and stride when he marched up and down the hills and valleys of the mountainside.

"I LIKE YOUR mother," Behrouz said to Rameen when they were finally face to face.

"Do you?" Rameen asked with difficulty. He had a black eye and bruises around his mouth, and he held his stomach as though it hurt. It was hard for him to speak. "She might seem harmless, her type. But she and my father have let the English come and go in this country. They have tea with them while the Brits screw everyone else. Now they talk about poetry and how they hate the Shah."

"Keep your voice down," said Behrouz softly.

"Now they've suddenly seen the light, but do nothing. Poetry will save the world, will it?" He sat back in his chair, as if to ease his pain.

"Does it hurt?"

"What?" Rameen asked.

"Your face?"

Rameen didn't answer.

Behrouz sighed. "I don't think your parents have bad intentions."

"They have no intentions."

"They have good lawyers, to help you. They told me."

"Yeah, uncle so-and-so in London. If you can't be the king, then at least move into his backyard, right?" Rameen coughed and held his stomach tighter.

Behrouz glanced at the clock on the wall. Ten minutes was almost over. "I'll visit you again, I promise," he said.

"You don't have to," Rameen said.

"I believe you, about your parents and the poetry, but maybe—" Behrouz stopped. He felt helpless, and he didn't know how to say what he felt. He stood up to leave.

Rameen looked away and didn't say goodbye.

Outside, Behrouz breathed in the cool mountain air, lit a cigarette, and slowly walked home, thinking of how he would hold Aria in his arms to protect her from the world. Then he imagined the hills and valleys of the camps, and Rameen there marching, back straight, eyes forward like his mother, head-on against the world.

WHEN BEHROUZ TURNED up to see Rameen again, Rameen felt as if he were experiencing a miracle—and he had never before believed in miracles. But Behrouz kept his promise, and for months he visited his friend faithfully.

Then, one day, Behrouz arrived carrying a Quran.

Rameen had been moved to a new cell with no windows, and he'd almost forgotten what sunshine looked like. He had come to feel that time, if it existed, was a stranger whose ways he would have to get to know again. The day Behrouz came with the Quran marked the first time he'd been let out of the cell since the move. Light stabbed his eyes, and noise, even whispers, echoed in his ears and pounded through his brain.

"You going God-lover on me again?" Rameen managed to say. He and Behrouz sat across from each other.

Behrouz smiled at him, his eyes sadder than before. Then he glanced at the guard who was standing beside them—a young boy in a uniform. From between the pages of the Quran, he took out a letter.

"Son, can you read this?" Behrouz showed the guard the letter.

"Get to your business," the guard said, pushing his rifle forward.

"I can't read. I need your help," Behrouz said, holding out the letter again.

"Leave him alone, silly driver," said Rameen.

Behrouz leaned forward toward Rameen's ear. "He can't read. Now I'm sure of it," he whispered.

"No whispering," yelled the guard.

"It's a letter from his mother, son," Behrouz said. "I was hoping you could help us with it."

"Hurry with your business," said the guard again.

Behrouz laid the piece of paper on the table and opened it for Rameen to see. It contained only two lines. They read: "LETTERS TO ARIA. WRITE FOR ME."

Rameen leaned forward. "Why?" he asked.

"I asked one of the soldiers to write this down for me. I've found Aria's mother," Behrouz said. "The real one. I think. And I want to explain things to Aria for when she is older. But as you know, I can't write." He folded the paper and put it in his pocket.

"How did you find her mother?"

"Walked. All over the south part of the city. Stories move down there. Memories transfer."

"You'd think all you South-City folks have one mind."

"One heart, maybe. Please help me do this."

"What good will it do, finding her mother?"

"She might take Aria, and I get the girl away from Zahra."

"What kind of woman would give her up then take her back?" Rameen said. "Didn't you find her as a baby in a dump?"

Behrouz grabbed Rameen's hand. "I've never done anything good in my life."

"Nonsense."

"Not anything I wanted. When I was a boy . . . No, you don't want to hear this."

Rameen took Behrouz's hand. "Talk."

Behrouz paused, then began. "I never knew my mother. She died when I was two." Behrouz played with the pages of the Quran. "I used to pretend I was a mother myself, first with my pillows, then I found this doll, someone had thrown it away . . . I did mother things, fed it, changed it, rocked it. Put it to bed. You know, that kind of thing."

"Yeah," Rameen nodded.

"Zahra was thirty-six when I married her. Her son's two months older than me, you know."

"I understand."

"And we've never done much . . ."

"I know," said Rameen.

"In the bedroom, I mean."

"I know."

"She tried. She wanted . . ."

"You don't have to explain."

"I tried to be a good husband, but . . ."

"TIME!" yelled the young guard.

"We'll only be a minute," said Rameen, loudly.

Behrouz looked into his face and took a deep breath. "When Aria came . . . When I found her . . ." His voice shook.

Rameen held his hand tighter. "Okay. We'll solve it," he said.

THAT NIGHT, RAMEEN gave his cellmate a pack of cigarettes in exchange for a pen. The hundred tomans Behrouz had smuggled in went to a prison cook in exchange for one hundred sheets of paper. And Rameen began to write as Behrouz, each night recalling the driver's voice, the way he would breathe after each drag of a cigarette, the way his forehead wrinkled as his word-drawings came to life in the margins of banned books, the way his jawbone protruded when he clenched his teeth.

One morning each week, Behrouz would visit Rameen and tell him everything he wanted to say. After they parted, Rameen became Behrouz again, writing down everything he could recall for an imaginary daughter, careful not to forget any aching syllable or word.

Sometimes, as he wrote, he thought about his own parents. They had only come to visit that one time after he had been incarcerated. Did they stay away for fear of being implicated? Because they were connected to someone like him? Or were they perhaps really working behind the scenes to free him? His mother was likely justifying her absence by vowing to write a book about his ordeal. She'd claim this was the real way to fight his battle. Nothing had changed, he thought. His mother and all the rest of them wrote their poems while blood flowed in the streets. They would do the same as he rotted in prison.

8

Aria had no idea what she had done wrong this time.

Zahra had locked her in the bathroom, and now Aria could hear her in the bedroom next door, beating the bedsheets to get the dust out. The beating sounded like music, like those drums Aria had seen men play, holding them high in the air and tapping hard with their fingers. When she heard the rhythm stop, she cowered in the corner of the bathroom, where Zahra had lit a candle, even though the sun was shining. In fact, Zahra had lit candles all over the house for some reason.

Zahra unlocked the door and came in, then dropped the dirty sheets in a large bucket beside Aria. She kicked it. "Take this outside. Fill it with water. Wash them," she said. She pointed at the headscarf on Aria's head. "Take that off, wear this." She unfurled a black veil. "Take it."

Aria did as she was told.

"Wash the sheets," Zahra said. "Make sure the veil's covering you or God knows what the neighbours will say. You're already a disgrace. Hurry up, I said." She turned back into the living room, repeating, "Disgrace, disgrace, disgrace."

Aria draped the veil around herself. It covered her head and the contour of her face and ran down the length of her body, hiding her form. She held it closed tight at her chin. The rest of the veil dragged behind her. Every once in a while, she tripped over it, mostly because the bucket was too heavy to lift with one hand and it set her off balance. She decided to drag the bucket instead. When at last she reached the courtyard water fountain, she found the basin was dry. She stood there, staring into the hole from which water usually came. Then she heard the sounds. They were the same sounds she'd thought Zahra was making, beating the sheets. But now she understood it hadn't been Zahra at all. She wondered if it was music from a radio, but as the sounds got louder, a fear gripped her: Was it the sound of bombs going off? No, it wasn't that either, because soon she heard human voices, hundreds of them, maybe thousands. She gripped the handle of the bucket. She wanted to run back inside but feared Zahra's wrath.

"What are you doing?" asked a voice behind her.

She dropped the bucket and turned around. It was Kamran. He studied her with disapproval, then picked up the bucket as though with a great effort.

"What are you doing here?" he asked. "What's this for?" He handed the bucket back to her. "Why are you wearing that? Girls shouldn't be out right now. Only men."

"Why?" she asked.

"Never mind," he said, his tone softer. "You looking for water? It's Ashura. Everybody's been washing all day. Anyhow, can't you hear the chains?"

She looked at him in confusion.

"The flagellators. The mourners?" Kamran sighed. "Don't you know anything? Come see."

She followed him out of the courtyard and they ran down the alley, where the walls of opposing apartments lay close. The alleys were busier than usual, mostly with men, like Kamran had said.

They were dressed in black and carried bundles of fruit or bread. Some had freshly roasted nuts. As she ran behind Kamran, Aria had to fight the temptation to stop and take in the scents around her. They were getting closer to the chanting human voices that Aria had mistaken for drums, and the clanging of a thousand chains she had mistaken for rain.

Finally the maze of alleys came to an end, and she and Kamran were at the foot of Pahlavi Street. It was there that Aria saw the symphony.

"Stand to the side," Kamran said. "If you get in their way, they might trample over you."

"What are they doing?" she shouted as the noise grew louder.

Kamran began to shout too. "They've been doing this for many hours." He pointed at the alley, where the people in the procession were crying and wailing. There were hundreds of women in black veils. "It's a performance," Kamran said, then whispered, "It's not real. But that's a secret."

Aria watched, spellbound. There were ten men out front, one at the head of each line. Each man held a wooden stick, at the end of which were some twenty or thirty metal chains, twenty inches long, hung in a cluster. As they marched, the men swung the chain clusters over their shoulders and whipped their backs. They did this continuously. Then, in unison, they shouted, "Great Hossein!" Although it was hard to see through their black shirts, Aria could tell that a few of them were bleeding.

After some two hundred of these men had passed, there came a line of teenage boys. Many had cymbals that they were smacking together to keep the rhythm of the march. Those who didn't have cymbals were beating their own heads to make a rhythmic sound, adding to the percussion. Behind these boys, another group of men carried a large float on their shoulders, on top of which several ostrich feathers and plumes of different birds had been glued in a linear pattern. The red, yellow, and white plumes provided the only colour for miles, blinding against the black-clothed marchers. At the head of the float were two signs with large green print: "God Is All Merciful," and "Great Hossein." Kamran read these out to Aria.

Then came another procession. Aria was sure this one must number in the thousands—there were too many bodies to tell apart, boy, man, big, small. All faces wore the same expression of mourning, the performance of grief. In unison, the men and boys lifted their arms in the air, like shooting arrows. Then their arms fell back with swelling force as they beat their own chests. Every right hand slapped the left side of each chest and every left hand slapped the right side of each chest. To Aria, watching, mesmerized, it looked painful. Voices began chanting, "Hossein, Hossein."

Kamran began to chant as well, and Aria was amazed by how violent this, too, sounded. But the force of the chant paled beside what happened next. A small group of men with shaved heads came toward them, beating their own skulls with the dull ends of hammers. As the wounds on their heads swelled, they took out pocket knives and cut the wounds open. Soon, blood streamed down their faces.

Aria turned wordlessly to Kamran and saw that he could not take his eyes off them.

HOURS PASSED AND evening fell. As Aria walked beside Kamran, her bucket bumped against the unpaved road. The bottom edge had begun to chip away. Occasionally, boys set off firecrackers, lighting up the road, marking a sudden shift from dark to light and back.

They walked on further, following a procession of mourners and performers. These were called the Army of Mourners, Kamran had told Aria. When the procession finally stopped, Aria realized they had arrived at the foot of an old mosque draped in green fabric and lights. It was as if the night had been lit into a gentle, green hue, like the morning grass when the dew settles upon it.

"What's happening?" Aria asked Kamran under her breath. She always felt the need to whisper near mosques. Something about them made her nervous.

"They've come here for a nazri."

"A what?"

"Nazri. Food! They're giving away free food."

"Who is?" Aria asked.

"Everybody. The people to the mosque, the mosque to the people."

"Why?"

"So they can find out who the nosy kids are," he said and pulled her forward. She tripped on her veil.

"If it's for everyone, do the rich get food, too?"

"For everyone, I said. See those women carrying the big pots? They've cooked all day. My mother was doing it, too. But she doesn't come to the mosques or anything like that. She says the jinns are out tonight, so she hands out bowls of soup and halva from our door. She even gets me to take it out to people. I came to your house today to give you some, but—" He stopped.

"Today Zahra was mad," Aria said.

"I know," he replied. He took her through the crowd, around to the back of the mosque. Aria lifted her veil to avoid trailing it in the mud created by the thousands who'd trampled the ground all day.

"Can we go back now? Zahra will be mad again. And I have to wash these sheets." She looked at the bucket. Everything in it was still dirty. But Kamran was moving fast and didn't wait for her and was soon swallowed up in the horde.

"Kamran, *stop!*" she shouted.

He turned around. "Where are you?" he shouted back. "I can't find you."

She followed his voice and finally saw him after pushing through more people. By then he'd stopped calling to her. There was a man with him now, a man with one bandaged hand. This man was thin and didn't look like he belonged there, amidst the vitality of the crowd. Aria recognized him. It was Mr. Jahanpour, Kamran's father. He was talking to Kamran, who stood on his tiptoes, trying to hear. The two were silhouetted against the lights. When they were done talking, Mr. Jahanpour ruffled Kamran's hair and disappeared into the crowd.

Kamran turned and walked toward Aria. "You all right?" he said.

She took a moment to catch her breath. "Why are they doing this?" She gestured at the people, the lights, the food.

"I told you, the nazri."

"No, I mean . . . why are we celebrating?"

"It's for Imam Hossein," Kamran said. "He died a thousand years ago. I think they tied him to a tree and beat him to death. Or no, that was another saint. They trampled on Hossein with horses. I think."

"Who did?"

"The Arabs. And he died and his men died, and women and children died, and then they cut off his head. I think. I don't know where they put it."

"Wasn't he an Arab himself?"

"Yes. But Persians love him now."

"Why?" Aria asked.

"Because he fought for the true words of the Prophet. Fighting for the truth. He was the Prophet's grandson, so he knew the truth."

"The truth of what?"

"I don't know, just the truth. The truth is the truth." He took her hand and tried to drag her along more quickly.

"So, if we don't tell the truth, we'll get tied to a tree and beaten?" Aria asked.

"No, we don't need to lie to do that. It happens anyway," he replied.

"Is that what your father told you just now, about the truth?"

"My father isn't your business," he said, and would say no more.

They ran through the crowd toward the scent of rice, yogurt, and lamb stew. Aria lifted her veil. In the dim evening light, she imagined a lone figure, lifeless by a tree, his heart pumping out the last of his blood.

ZAHRA COULD HEAR the chants of "God is great" and "Great Hossein," even though the windows were closed. In all her life, even when she thought back to her childhood in Ferdowsi Square, she had never heard Ashura this loud and lively.

Everybody has gone mad, she thought. It was all theatre, whether aristocrats were doing it or those turban-heads. They were all clowns. Even that old wealthy family she'd worked for as a child had found the clanging of the procession comical. Not that they weren't people of God; they were just interested in other things. That much she remembered. Who knows, maybe the old family was still the same, sitting around with their poetry books, discussing things she had never understood. She'd been just a child back then. Those kinds of people always thought they were better than she was. They were Zoroastrian, but had converted. How else could they have become so chummy with the royals? Royal business. Money business. Castles and profits.

Where in hell was that girl? Well, there was nothing she could do to find Aria while the procession was happening. Zahra busied herself with housework, pushing furniture around. She was so busy that she didn't notice at first when Behrouz walked through the door.

When at last she looked up, he opened his mouth to say something, but clearly decided against it after seeing her expression. He glanced around the room for signs of his daughter.

"Do you see what she's like?" Zahra threw a shoe in his direction. "That trash you brought into this house? See what games she plays? Don't think she didn't run off on purpose. Just to cause trouble."

Behrouz put a hand to his chest, calming himself. "Where did you send her?"

"Look at you. I don't have to answer to you," she said. "You, with your fantasies about yourself. You think you have class? You think in *that* world, with all of *them* reading their special books and sending their children away to all those fancy countries, they'd think anything of you?"

He followed her with his eyes as she walked into the bedroom, then returned to the living room with her hat on, and her coat in her hands. She flung it around her body, letting it rest on her shoulders. This was how she always wore her coats, without slipping her arms into the sleeves.

"Where are my gloves? Have you seen my gloves?" she said, before spotting them on the coffee table. Behrouz stood in front of the door, but she squeezed past him and out of the house. The smell of smoke and firecrackers, boiled lentils and halva stung the air. Zahra flew swiftly down the street like a hawk lured by the scent of its prey.

After a moment, Behrouz set out on his own to search for Aria, hoping he'd find her first. And he did. She was asleep beside Kamran on the steps of the old mosque, clinging to a wooden bucket with sullied clothes inside it. He sent the boy home ahead of them, and carried Aria back in his arms while he dangled the bucket off a few of his fingers. As he walked, he thought of Ahmad, Zahra's son. Had she been this way with him, too? And when would the hand of God intervene, rattle the earth and divide it in two, Zahra on one side, he and Aria on the other?

9

The next morning, Behrouz left the house at dawn in the hope of visiting Rameen before starting his next few days of work on the mountain. He had no choice but to leave Aria behind.

Aria ran into the courtyard, and Zahra followed and dragged her back inside.

Kamran was in the courtyard, hanging wet clothes on a line. He could see everything through Aria's half-closed back door, and Aria could see him watching. He'd learned to be ready for days like this by preparing the fort up in the tree, of which they both were now expert climbers. Food and beverages to last them a good two days were placed in the usual secret spot, inside the giant flower-pot, with dirt and roses piled on top.

After a short while, Zahra locked Aria out on the balcony. Aria heard her grab her coat and keys, and listened to the velvet heels of her shoes click-clack behind her as she left the house. She imagined Zahra wearing leather gloves that matched her shoes, and the red glow of her lipstick.

"Guess she didn't like that you disappeared last night. So, are you going to stay up there forever?" Kamran called from the courtyard below. "Why don't we go see a movie? I'm not tired if you aren't."

Aria bent over the railing. "I'll be down in a minute. It's not as easy to climb down as it looks, you know."

She pulled herself up and swung one leg over the railing. She couldn't get it all the way over, so she used her knee to push off and up, and turned partway around. Now her stomach pressed against the railing. From here, she could turn all the way and bring around the other leg. The branches of the cherry tree extended onto the balcony. She grabbed the thickest one.

"Hurry up!"

"I'm coming, I said." Using the branch, Aria slipped down and then clutched the edge of the balcony floor. She dangled there as Kamran ran over and stood under her. She stepped on his shoulders before jumping down.

They ran through the streets for a while before breaking to rest. Neither of them had slept much the night before, but the energy from the chants and prayers had invigorated them. Aria felt as if she was a superhero, indestructible. After catching their breath, she and Kamran ran again until Aria stopped to rub her eyes with her knuckles.

"They sting," she said.

"You haven't washed since yesterday, have you?" Kamran said.

"We don't have water at my house," she replied.

"You liar."

Kamran looked at his watch. Kazem had given it to him so Kamran would know when to be home from work, now that he was the man of the house. He thought of his poor father, who'd been so ill last night at Ashura. Kazem had asked him to collect as much nazri as he could to bring home for his mother and sister. They'd not had a proper meal in weeks.

"We'll have to sneak into the movie," Aria said. "You know I don't have money."

"I was going to pay."

"Maybe I can pay for it with my bracelets." She held out her arm. She had eleven of them now, wrapped one on top of the other halfway to her elbow.

Kamran reddened. "Why would you give those up? Don't you like them?"

"I love my bracelets." Aria winced again and rubbed her eyes.

"Stop doing that," said Kamran.

"It stings. Feels like something's inside my eyes."

"Let me see." He moved in close and gently pulled down the skin under her eyeball for a better look. "Don't move. Silly girl, I don't see anything."

"I don't care if you don't see anything."

"Should we go back home?" he asked.

She made no reply.

"You crying?" He rested a hand on her shoulder.

She sat down on the curb, crossed her arms on her knees and rested her forehead on them. "No," she said, her voice muffled. "You think I'm crying because I'm a girl?"

"Yes, I do. You are crying and you are a girl, so stop it." He pulled at her elbow.

She lifted her head and looked defiantly at him. "It's just my eyes. They're watery." She wiped at the wetness.

Kamran felt a shock rush through his body. He touched the pavement to steady himself. He managed two words: "Your hands."

Aria looked down. Her hands were covered in blood.

Without a word, Kamran took her arm and began to lead her back the way they had come. After a while he heard someone say,

"It will be okay," again and again, but did not recognize his own voice. Toward the end, he pulled Aria so hard she fell and scraped her knee.

Aria looked down to the wound, but there was too much blood in her eyes to see. The world had turned red.

ARIA BREATHED IN deeply. Behrouz's coat smelled of goatskin. She clung to it as he weaved through, in, and around crowds of people. She could feel his anger.

She had been left mostly alone for three days, left to bleed in a corner of the apartment. Zahra had brought her the occasional scrap of food, saying, "It will go away. It will go away."

The blood in Aria's eyes had dried and now she couldn't open them. Pus oozed out of the corners. That was how her father had found her this morning upon his return from three days of work.

Behrouz knew the address of a medical clinic in the north part of the city, one that Rameen had mentioned once. He had set out with Aria to reach the clinic on foot, calculating that navigating through the traffic would take longer. But now he was getting tired.

"If I ask you to walk, can you?"

"I'll try," Aria said.

He set her down. Eyes still closed, she walked beside him, holding his hand. She could feel the film beneath her eyelids.

The further north they walked, the more the bustle of commerce turned into a waltz with the clatter of cafés, greetings, and conversations calm and regal. It was as if they had travelled between two cities, each with a very different tale to tell.

Behrouz had walked this path many times but only in the

dark, after coming down Darband. He hadn't known what it was like in the daylight. He wondered how many times Rameen had seen it this way, this beautiful. The buildings, hidden at night, now rose monumental before him. Figures moved behind the windows he had so often peered up at. Behind glass, men in suits spoke into telephones as they paced back and forth, loosening their ties. Figures sat on interior window ledges, others at their desks. More than anything else, the women in this area of town seemed strange to him. They held their heads high and their shoulders back. Not one of them looked at the ground, away from the gaze of men.

Behrouz glanced at Aria, who had come from the belly of the other world. She held his hand tight so as not to fall. She could see none of the things he did, but he wanted her to. And the more he wanted it, the awful knowledge that she might never have such a chance grew within him, a fearsome monster.

"TRACHOMA," THE DOCTOR said. "Has she not been washing properly?"

"I'm not at home much to see," said Behrouz.

"No wife?"

"Yes, but . . ."

"Well, have her wash the child, or they'll take her away. Neglect doesn't go unpunished in this country, you know."

The doctor sat at his desk, scribbling something on a pad. He'd hardly looked at Behrouz after their first hello.

"I understand. But my wife isn't her mother," Behrouz said.

"Your wife isn't her mother?"

"No. I'm not her real father, either. I've adopted her but . . ." He looked at Aria, who sat at the edge of the examination table with an unopened lollipop in her hand. The bottom of the bandage wrapped around her eyes sat just above the tip of her nose.

The doctor continued: "Mr. Bakhtiar, I must be very clear with you. Now . . . the conditions . . . Well, I understand that it's not easy for you, but this disease occurs when proper hygiene is not kept. It's especially problematic for children, you see—"

"When I'm around things are fine," Behrouz said.

The doctor adjusted his glasses and his tie, then cleared his throat. "Mr. Bakhtiar, a child needs constant care. If your wife can't do it, then you have to."

"Understood, doctor, but . . ."

The doctor leaned back in his chair and put his hands behind his head. He looked out the window at the half-erected building on the other side of the street. "It's interesting what's out there," he said.

Behrouz followed his gaze. A large portrait of the infant prince had been painted on the building. The doctor rocked back and forth in his chair.

"Some people dote on their children, see? They put up a portrait of their kid even before the building is finished. It's like our monarch has something to prove now that he's got his heir. And then there are people like you. Of course, you say she isn't really yours, so perhaps she means less to you. Worst case I've seen. From all that lice in her hair. I'm surprised you hadn't noticed. What is it you do again?"

"I drive a truck, sir," Behrouz replied.

"No matter," said the doctor. "A man should really take care of his children. They're our future, are they not? Though with *him* around, an ego like that, already erecting portraits of his son, who knows what this country's future will be. You aren't a royalist, are you, Mr. Bakhtiar?"

Behrouz didn't answer. He didn't know what the doctor wanted to hear.

"Of course not; look at you. You're from the South-City, correct? I'm sure they've got everybody down there believing how great things are. But just look at what they did to that poor man on house arrest at his farm."

"Mr. Mossadegh?"

"Of course." The doctor smiled. "I'm surprised you're familiar with the matter. Well done. But back to your situation, Mr. Bakhtiar. As I've said, and I'm aware that sanitary conditions might not be as readily available to you, but this sort of disease generally occurs from excessive flies. I'm sure you know what flies are, yes? Well, these flies eventually make their way into the eyes, and their presence leads to gross infection, as you can see with your daughter . . . or whatever she is." He tapped his pen on his writing pad. "She's got to come in for treatments. The risk of blindness is high."

The cadence of his speech was broken by hums and haws, as though voicing his thoughts were a disruption to his life. Behrouz hunched forward in his seat to listen, ignoring the muffled clang of construction from the building site outside.

"She must come in three times a week for cleaning and disinfestation. This sort of thing can take months. I'm very troubled by the circumstances that have led to it. But if you promise to bring her in for every appointment, I'll make a deal with you and not report it. I'll have my secretary make some sort of contract. Don't worry about writing your name. We can just fingerprint you. Let's get a better look at the girl now. This might not be easy."

Behrouz lifted Aria onto his lap, and the doctor whispered in his ear, "You're going to have to help me."

"How?"

The doctor whispered, "Just do what I say," and then spoke aloud. "Okay, my girl, your eyes still sting? We'll make that go away soon."

Behrouz watched as he removed the bandage and pinched the top of Aria's left eyelid, pulling it away. Aria squirmed.

"No, no, sit tight. Mr. Bakhtiar, please help."

Behrouz held Aria tightly. He was close enough to the doctor now to read his name tag: Vaziri. It was the first word he'd ever read on his own, without Rameen's help. *Vaziri*, he thought. *The judge.* Dr. Vaziri took a single, rectangular razor blade from inside a napkin on his desk. He flipped Aria's eyelid inside out and, with the sharp edge of the blade, began to cut at the dried pus, shaving a small layer off. Once he had the hang of it, he dug deeper. Another layer, thicker this time, rolled off. He did the same thing with the other eye. "May have more trouble with this one," he mumbled, but Behrouz hardly heard him.

Vaziri shaved away, little by little. But this time, instead of layering off, the pus crumbled into Aria's eye, which began to bleed again. Vaziri blew into it. Then he wiped the sweat on his forehead. "We'll try one more time," he said, and cut into the infected area once more. A thin layer came off. He wiped his forehead again. When he was done, he threw the blade into the trash.

"Keep her eyes closed," he said. "Wrap them up until the infection subsides." He whispered into Behrouz's ear, "And Mr. Bakhtiar, I have to tell you again, there's no guarantee here. We won't know how bad the damage is until we've stabilized the problem. You know what *stabilized* means, right? There are brochures I could give you, but what's the use if one can't read, right?"

"True, sir," Behrouz said.

"Of course. Well, it's not your fault. I'll give them to you anyway, good man, and maybe you have a friend who can read them for you?"

"My wife can read."

"Ah, good. Not to worry, Mr. Bakhtiar, my wife's smarter than I am, too."

10

Eight weeks had passed since Aria's first visit to the doctor, and not much had changed. Aria still couldn't see. She couldn't walk on her own, either. Zahra had to carry her. With Behrouz working at the barracks, there was no one else to do it.

Aria knew that Zahra had agreed to this in order to save face. "I guess if I don't take her to the doctor and she drops dead, then the whole town will blame me for it?" This is what Aria had heard Zahra say. Aria had watched her fight with Behrouz for hours. "I'll be damned if the vermin around here get to whisper to each other about me. That's what you wanted, wasn't it, Mr. Bakhtiar. All along, it was about getting back at me."

Behrouz sat silently for the entirety of this rant. Zahra had hurled at him every vulgar word Aria had ever heard, but in the end she had given in. She concluded her performance by reminding Behrouz how grateful he should be to have a wife like her. And since then, except for the two times when Behrouz had been home on leave, Zahra had walked with Aria to the clinic in North-City. This had become their routine. It was also the only time Aria was able to leave the house.

Aria had always known that Behrouz was afraid something would happen to her, but now she felt Zahra might be, too. If Aria didn't reply the moment Zahra called for her, she would run into the room calling Aria's name in a voice that sometimes shook. Aria had become good at hearing that quaver. There were things she could hear now that she had never been able to before, and Zahra's shaking voice was one of those things.

Still, Aria wished someone else could take her to the doctor. "What about Kamran?" she had suggested to Behrouz one night when he was home. She hadn't seen Kamran in weeks.

"Kamran's only a boy," Behrouz had said.

"Yes. He's a boy. He can do anything," Aria replied.

She hadn't been able to convince Behrouz. Still, she hoped a solution would present itself. Now, as Zahra blasted through the apartment, searching for her makeup and her keys and purse before heading to the doctor again, Aria waited quietly on the balcony, listening for a sign from Kamran. She'd heard him at the door a few times, asking Zahra if he could see her, if her eyes were all right. Zahra always told him to get lost. But today Aria heard a sound she hadn't in a long time. It was Kamran, she was certain, playing with his ball in the courtyard, bouncing it off the wall and jumping high to catch it before it hit the ground.

"You're not going to throw it up here?" Aria said, her voice raised a little, hoping he might hear her.

After a moment, Kamran answered. "You've got no interest in talking to me, so why should I?"

"It's not my fault the monster told you to get lost," Aria said.

"You don't even come out to the balcony anymore," he said.

"I'm not allowed. And Zahra's not supposed to put me here."

"Why?" Kamran asked.

"Because I'll fall off."

"Why?" Kamran asked again.

"Because I'm blind."

"Well, you're not stupid. You can feel the rails, can't you?"

"Zahra can't be shamed," said Aria. "Because the vermin around here must not talk about her."

"What vermin? What are they going to say?" said Kamran.

"It'll all be her fault if something happens, and everyone will know what a bad mother she is."

"Everyone already knows that," Kamran replied.

Aria sat down against the railing. "You don't understand anything," she said.

"Stand up. I can't see you," said Kamran.

"I can't see you either, so we're even," Aria said.

Kamran threw his ball against the wall a few times. "So are your eyes still bleeding?"

"Not anymore. But they're glued shut because of all the disgusting stuff."

"But will you see again soon?" Kamran asked.

"I have to go and get it cut off, with blades, all the disgusting stuff. Zahra takes me, on her back. I told them you should take me, but you're a boy and you can't, so they said no."

"I can do anything," Kamran protested.

"That's what I told them," said Aria.

They were quiet for a while.

"So, when will you see again?" Kamran asked again.

"I don't know." Aria could hear Zahra opening the balcony door.

"Well, you'd better be able to see soon. I don't plan on spending the rest of my miserable life carrying miserable you around."

Aria stood up. "I have to go now," she said.

"Stop talking to that cockroach and get inside." Zahra grabbed Aria's arm and pulled her in.

"When you're better I'll take you to the cinema again!" Kamran called after her.

—

ZAHRA SQUATTED SO Aria could wrap her arms around her neck, then she piggybacked the girl, even though it was hard to do in heels. That husband of hers owed her new ones even if it killed him. Still, she loved walking along the upper part of Pahlavi Street. It was nice to see the neighbourhoods again. There were newer things in the shop windows now. When the Shah had married Farah, his new queen had brought tastier things into the city, Parisian-style things that Zahra loved.

New trees had been planted, rows of them, on each side of the street. To hell with those who didn't like it. What did those fools from the south know, anyway? Most of them had never been up here. She was admiring all this, the boutiques and the trees and the cars, when she felt Aria squirming on her back.

"You awake?" she asked.

A man walking past yelled at her, "Your daughter's eyes are bleeding!"

Zahra ignored him but the man came closer. He set down his briefcase and loosened his tie. "That kid got a daddy, lady? You looking for a daddy for her?"

"They should have your testicles chopped off," Zahra said. But the man kept coming toward her. "Where are you from, lady?"

Another man intervened. "Leave her alone," he said.

The first man pushed him and grabbed his arms.

"I can take care of this trash myself," Zahra said, wedging herself between them. She grabbed the first man's tie. "Want me to choke you with this?" she asked.

He slapped her.

Her cheek felt hot but she stood her ground. "So your answer is yes?"

"Lady, get out of the way. Can't you see this guy's crazy?" the second man said.

"You probably are, too, asshole," Zahra replied.

The first man grabbed her arms; the second man walked away. Zahra tried to free herself, but the man was holding her too tightly. Now others rushed in, and it was only when she escaped after an exchange of blows that Zahra realized Aria was gone. In the commotion, the girl had fallen off her back.

"Where did that shit of a child go?" She searched through the crowd, calling Aria's name. "You good-for-nothing trash!" she said loudly, but Aria was nowhere to be seen. She searched for some twenty minutes before the heat of the sun weakened her. No one was paying her any attention. The debate over her dignity, the dignity of a woman, had turned political, and now she heard snatches of heated discussion about everything from the ayatollah, whose works were banned, to the state of oil production, to the greatness of the Shah, the King of Kings, to the flashy new President Kennedy.

A few feet away, a newsstand was closing for the day. Her eyes drifted to the magazines, lined up side by side. Sophia Loren smiled out from the cover of one. Zahra walked over to the stand and ran her fingers over the photograph.

"Closing," the vendor said.

"Just looking," she replied, then added, "Have you seen a white-skinned girl, white dress? Dirty girl. Reddish hair?"

"Never seen no girl, miss. Closing. Don't touch, please."

"Asshole," said Zahra. She looked around. The crowd of men had dispersed. As her gaze wandered, she heard a voice. It was a voice as familiar to her as the air she breathed.

"This one?" The voice was broken, emerging from the cracks of history. Zahra turned around. A little woman, covered head-to-toe in a blue flowered veil, held a large basket of fruit in one hand and a large basket of flowers in the other. She was pressing the baskets against her belly; her large breasts fell over them. At her side, Aria had buried her face in the veil's delicate fabric.

"Don't tell me this is one of yours?" the woman said. "I would have thought yours would be much older than this, you good-for-nothing mule."

That Esfehan accent. Unmistakable. Zahra grabbed the woman by the shoulders, her heart pounding.

"Found her standing right up against a wall. Saw her on your back before that. Couldn't tell at first if it was you, but it sure as hell was. Then that vermin came by. Figured I'd grab your little girl for you while you dealt with him. Shit people, no? Look at you, thinking you could handle the likes of him on your own. Fool. Well, well, well."

Zahra couldn't take her eyes off the woman. "Look at how fat and ugly you've gotten, Massoomeh."

"How are you, sister?" Massoomeh said. She giggled, and her breasts bounced against her belly, and her belly pressed against Aria's face.

"You old hag," Zahra said, smiling. "After all these years."

AN HOUR LATER, Aria was fast asleep on a luxurious couch, and Massoomeh sat across from Zahra at a long kitchen table, slicing celery for dinner. There was a dimpled smile on her round face, which, despite her increase in girth, still seemed too big for her short stature. Massoomeh had been sixteen the last time Zahra had seen her. She hadn't kept her looks; Zahra almost didn't recognize the person in front of her now. She wondered if her old friend thought the same about her.

"World's a small place. God wanted us to meet again, sister," Massoomeh said. "Remember when we used to run through the streets swiping apples and treats off them vendor carts? Never did pay the price for that business, so maybe something's waiting for us round the corner. What you think?"

"Your tongue seems to have stayed intact over the years. I always wondered if you'd get yourself into a mess after I was gone."

"I was taken care of fine. Did my job, made my wages, never bothered no one—and never swiped nothing the way you did. Monsieurs and Madames have always been good to me. Haven't done too bad for myself."

Zahra studied the familiar kitchen. Brass pans hung from nails on the wall. When she and Massoomeh were working here as children, there'd been a rumour that the pans were leftovers from the Queen of England, the old one, sent over from the palace in London as a special thank-you to Mr. Ferdowsi for his "remarkable talents and magical hands." But who knew if all that rubbish had ever been true. Now there were refrigerators and ovens beside both of the brass sinks at each end of the room, and the finest set of cutlery she'd ever seen was piled haphazardly beside the porcelain plates, which had the name Qajar, the old monarchical family of Iran, embossed neatly along the edges, and the peacock symbol marked underneath. All were remnants of the old dynasty, the one that disappeared around the time she and Massoomeh had been born. Now she picked up one of the Qajar plates.

"The old royalty were much better back then, if you ask me. More like the English kings. There's something a bit too American about this new Shah. European movie stars are even better than monarchs, though. Why do you still insist on working for these vile people?"

"The Ferdowsis are fine. Good people."

"Is that so?" said Zahra.

Massoomeh pressed four purple eggplants against her breast and carried them to the sink. "Life is easy here."

"Even better than it was before?" Zahra leaned back on her chair and crossed her legs. She twirled a strand of hair around her index finger.

Massoomeh focused on the pot in front of her, with its stew of diced vegetables and spices, her shoulders hunched forward, her head lowered. Zahra studied her old friend's stump-like hands and wondered if her own would be the same, so wrinkled before their time, had life gone differently and she too had stayed on the Ferdowsi compound.

Massoomeh asked questions as she washed more vegetables.

"So, the little girl is yours, you say?" She removed her knife from an eggplant and pointed it at Zahra, her elbow resting on the familiar tabletop.

Zahra folded her arms and then unfolded them. "Something like it. The old mister found her in some dump somewhere, and you know me, I agreed to raise the poor thing."

"Something like it?" Massoomeh jabbed the knife into the eggplant. "You really found her on some street somewhere or did you get into trouble from some other fellow? Or more likely, your old man go off and get some poor girl in trouble?" She laughed, the same uproarious, vulgar laugh Zahra remembered from their childhood, unfiltered and untamed. "Course, she looks nothing like you. Must be that, then. He go off with another woman, sister? Get himself a second wife? Third even? Oh, Imam Hossein, don't tell me there's four of you."

The repetitive beat of Massoomeh's knife against the chopping board began to grate on Zahra. She started a mental list of the things that were irritating her: the light through the window reflecting off the mirror on the opposite wall, the many brass pans, the running water that Massoomeh had forgotten to turn off, the large rooms, the smell of oak, the steam from the boiling pot, and above all Massoomeh's lowered head, drowned in some judgment in the air between them. This judgment settled into the weak spot in her stomach, which was tied to every facet of her life, anointing her with a distaste toward all things, and reminding her of her loathed childhood, when she'd been brought by some great-uncle, orphaned and penniless, to wipe the feet of those who drank the blood and sweat of others and were awarded brass pans by the fat old Queen of England.

"Didn't I already explain the girl to you, you empty-headed woman?" Zahra retorted. "Who knows where the bitch that had her is? And as for the mister, I've had about enough of him."

"Well, you're still taking care of her. Nice of you."

Nice wasn't a familiar word to Zahra. Not even in their child-hood could she recall Massoomeh using that word to describe her. It had always been Massoomeh who'd stepped in to save Zahra, taking the blame for this and that. And the Ferdowsi sib-lings, especially the oldest sister, had never hesitated to punish Massoomeh. Zahra remembered it well. Sometimes, even now, she felt bad for how she had hated them, had stolen from them so many times. But mostly she felt bad for not having had what the Ferdowsi sisters, Molook and Fereshteh, had—girl things, pretty things, things she'd hated destroying. Still, when she thought about it, there'd really been no other choice.

She got up and walked to the door to look in on Aria, who was still asleep on the couch.

"She's a tired one," Massoomeh said, "with those bandages. Lucky she's not gone blind. My brother is. Same sort of thing. Trachoma is it? Flies in the eyes, can you believe it? Bastard ended up hit by a mule wagon when he was just shy of thirty. Never had a chance. Couldn't see it. Life, sister. Life!" Now she was kneading a slab of ground beef with her knuckles. "You and the girl are staying for supper, I hope. Madame will be happy to see you. Funny how the old master left this place to her and not the brothers. But they got lots of homes, these people. Just a strange thing, this old place, in the heart of the city. And he leaves it to a daughter, not a son. Funny, ain't it? They're good stock, these people. You did a shameful thing, leaving when you did. Could have had a good life here."

Zahra narrowed her eyes at the brass pots as if they were gusts of fire from the sun. She felt the old anger boiling up in her again. How easily people forget, she thought. But perhaps even the most horrific of memories could be dimmed by time.

11

Fereshteh Ferdowsi basked in the dim glow of her once-bustling life. Her household maintained its own brand of reality. Now was the time to sleep; now, to awaken; now, to pick berries; now, to stoke the fires in the chimneys; now, to paint the gates green. Over the years, life had grown more and more mundane. When she walked north, and the grounds and the apartments on the estate came into view, she couldn't help feeling that it wasn't as grand as it used to be, back when everyone had wanted to live there and the opulence of her family's mansion was the talk of the square. Now, how many rooms lay empty? It had been so different back when maids and gardeners and cooks had kept the homes as their own and filled them with their extended families. There had even been carpenters to renovate and expand the house, a barber for the boys, and soldiers who used to stay when on break from the barracks. But Fereshteh's home, a monument to the past, had been unable to maintain its aristocratic flair against the onslaught of modernity, especially as the highrises and lowrises outside its gates multiplied. She had decided long ago that she would resist change.

Inside the house, only she and Maysi remained. Sometimes her oldest brother, Jafar, came for an extended stay if her other brother, Mammad, got too tired to look after him. Maysi, who'd been there since their childhood, was like family now—not quite a sister; perhaps a secret cousin from far away, the kind one didn't talk about much.

Today Fereshteh walked home in the sun's faded burnished glow. The pavement was cracked beneath the thick soles of her leather flats. She'd never been able to pull off heels. They were too tied to sexual allure, which she had always felt so distant from. She felt sexless, even genderless sometimes. She was certain that the husband she'd once had must have been an accident. Accidents were rarely repeated, and now the rooms in the house of the past lay empty. Nothing there but Maysi, who must have supper ready by now.

She passed by her friend Mr. Safai's flower shop, as she did every evening on the way back from the shelter where she took the little cakes and biscuits Maysi made to give to the poor. God would be the judge one day. Best to be prepared for it.

"Just in time," Mr. Safai said, lining up some geraniums in a box. The metal door of the tiny shop was pulled halfway down. The newspapers he also sold had been placed in a pile on the ground outside to make room for the next morning's delivery. "What will it be today, Mrs. Ferdowsi?"

She studied the offerings. "You have hyacinths out. How odd." She felt the surface of a petal. "In this heat?"

"You'd be surprised how long they last through spring. They just don't want to die."

"How strange." The way she spoke, with a slight tremble in her voice, wasn't due to any illness, but rather a simple misalignment of the vocal chords that she'd had since childhood, and which made her sound like an old woman even when she was young.

She brought the flower to her nose. "Extraordinary, aren't they?"

"Indeed they are, madam."

"Maysi would like them, don't you think?"

"Indeed she will, ma'am." Mr. Safai said.

Ma'am? Had she become *ma'am* already? At times she forgot her age and the change in appearance that came with it. She had never been a beauty. Though not unkind, genetics hadn't favoured her; not in the outward sense, anyway. Still, she was one of the fortunate ones, given what her family had offered her. That's all that really mattered. Perhaps her looks were the result of all that intermarriage, or the Zoroastrian blood. She had once walked in on their tailor telling his apprentice that the whole family looked like crows. He'd been horrified when he saw little Fereshteh, not more than five at the time, standing at the doorway. She imagined him worrying for days that he'd lose his job. But she'd never told her father.

When she got home she hooked the key in the lock, but the door was already open. A draft lingered in the entryway, which branched into the living room on one side and bedrooms on the other. She kicked off her shoes, eased into her slippers, and studied her familiar home. The black crystals of the French chandeliers hung like droplets of melting coal in the great hall that served as the living room. Four chandeliers lined the perimeter of the ceiling. At the centre hung a bigger fifth, only this one was clear crystal bejewelled with pearls carefully arranged in swirling patterns to follow the cuts on the glass. It was all so grand. Most days she didn't notice it. But for some reason, today everything looked both familiar and strange. The grooves of oak that formed the walls of the living room rose, plateaued, and curved down again to meet the crown moulding over every door. One of the doors led to the study, one the dining hall, one the kitchen, one upstairs. Armoires holding books and antique Russian china and old portraits were pressed against each wall. Soft, dim light came through the clear glass doors that slid open to the long balcony overlooking the garden. At the other end of the garden, her garden, was the home's other half, almost as big as the first, but not quite.

She suddenly wondered why her parents had built the house this way. It was nearly dark now, and only a faint light illuminated the great living room. Her eye was caught by the shimmer of the thousand dots of silk woven into the Persian rugs that spread across the entirety of the mahogany floors. The rugs around the perimeter were hued in dark blue and green and accented with brown, which crept from the floors into the furniture. Only a small dark-green rug that served as a centrepiece stood out from the rest.

As Fereshteh walked across the hall she had such a strange feeling. She could hear Maysi singing quietly to herself in the kitchen. The thirty steps it took to get to the sofa in the centre of the living room seemed to take a lifetime. On the mahogany cabinet beside the sofa, a small lamp lit up the dark room. It made barely visible the outline of feet and legs, and the rise and fall of breath from a small body that lay on the sofa. Fereshteh bent low for a better look. The little girl was sleeping with the tip of her thumb in her mouth, a bloody cloth wrapped around her eyes.

Fereshteh turned her head toward the kitchen. She was close enough now to hear that Maysi wasn't singing, but instead quietly talking to someone. She was telling one of her stories again: "And so I says to her, I says, 'Lady, mind your business with that religious trash-mash. If I don't want to go to mosque I don't have to.' Course I did though, always do. But can you believe it?"

A male voice laughed. "But she threw the shoe at you anyway?" The man was sitting at the kitchen table while a strange woman at the other end gazed around at every crack in the room.

"Can you believe it? Right at me. Crazy woman. Took it right off, like that. Not a bad arm either. Was pretty strong, the little bastard. What world she came from God knows but—"

Maysi had spotted Fereshteh at the door. "Oh, my, Madame, come in, come in. We got company for dinner. Look at this, look. You remember Zahra? Zahra Miladi. And this is her husband, Mr. Bakhtiar. We had to phone the grocer round the corner from his house to tell Mr. Bakhtiar to join us. Miracle we reached him, wasn't it, Miss Zahra?"

Behrouz quickly stood and bowed his head. His right hand went to his chest, and he made sure to keep his feet perfectly together. "Missus Ferdowsi," he said. "Behrouz Bakhtiar. Deepest honour." He bowed again.

"You remember Zahra?" Maysi prompted again.

Zahra stood up and flung her purse over her shoulder, then unzipped it and removed her leather gloves. "How are you, Miss Fereshteh, eh?" she said. Then she turned to Maysi. "But really, Maysi, I must be going. So much to do. All day busy this, busy that. Buy this, buy that."

Massoomeh looked surprised. "You didn't say you'd be leaving so early."

"Mr. Behrouz can stay for a bit and take care of the girl. How fabulous it was to see you though, Massoomeh. Truly wonderful. If I need some help around the house, I'll think of you. And not to worry, the mister will pay you well. Lovely to see you, Miss Fereshteh." She lightly shook Fereshteh's hand. "So sorry we couldn't speak more."

With that, Zahra walked past the ghost from her old life, and without a glance at Aria on the sofa, left the Ferdowsi home.

"Now, why'd she up and leave like that?" Massoomeh said.

Behrouz turned his attention to Fereshteh. "Madam, it is an honour to meet you. My apologies for intruding on your home like this."

"No formalities needed here, Mr. Bakhtiar. Please think of this as your own home. Please, sit down. I take it that's your little girl asleep out there?"

Behrouz stood up. "I'll wake her right away."

"Sit down please, Mr. Bakhtiar. Let the poor child sleep. Maysi, get a blanket for her."

Fereshteh leaned against the counter and looked more closely at the sickly appearance of the man before her. He reminded her of workers she had played with as a child on their farm. There were cracks in his face and hands. But she could tell from the way he moved that he was younger than he looked, prematurely aged. "Married to Zahra, you're just as good as family now, Mr. Bakhtiar," she said.

"You're too kind." Behrouz bowed again.

"You've known Maysi long?"

"Never met her before. I confess Zahra hardly ever talks about her days here." He reddened slightly.

She moved to the kitchen window that looked out over the garden and for a moment watched the sprinkle of stars in the limitless Tehran sky. Of all the places she'd seen, even at the northern tip of the Swiss Alps, where her father had taken her as a child, she'd never seen stars like these: bold, intrusive, as though they wanted to penetrate the lives of the humans under the cloak of their shelter, rain down their constellations, and dictate the stories of their lives. To warn? To guide? She wondered. Or was it simply to amuse themselves with the errors of men?

"Beautiful night," said Behrouz, behind her.

"It is," she said. Then: "Mr. Bakhtiar, forgive me, I've neglected to ask: What do you do, sir? Your line of work?"

He dropped his head, and she saw how shy he was.

"Oh not much. Nothing special. In the army."

"You are ranked?"

"No, nothing like that. I'm a driver. Oh, some twenty or so years now."

From the living room, Aria called his name, and he quickly excused himself and went to her. Fereshteh could hear him whispering to the little girl. What was taking Maysi so long? It was uncomfortable to be around Mr. Bakhtiar by herself. All these years of solitude, surrounded only by a few people and her sister and brothers, had made her forget how to speak to others, especially to people like Mr. Bakhtiar. Of course, she didn't dislike such people. In fact, she thought them better than most. It was just the little things that discomfited her—the way they moved and talked. It was the things they said, and how they didn't seem to know that some things should never be done. Like bowing. And of course, there was their ignorance of the world. All these people needed to do was pick up a newspaper, turn on a TV. Yet they wouldn't know where England was if you asked them. It was all these little things. What would she ask the child? She had nieces and nephews, but there was always the filter of their parents between them. So much to consider.

"See? Mrs. Ferdowsi is a very nice lady," Behrouz was saying as he and the child came into the kitchen.

"Is she all right, Mr. Bakhtiar?" Fereshteh asked, noticing the girl's bandaged eyes again.

"A small problem. Zahra was bringing her back from the doctor, you see, when she came across Massoomeh. Massoomeh called me at the barracks, from your telephone. I hope that's all right."

"I see."

"Aria, say hello."

"Hello," Aria said, half awake. She raised a hand as if to rub the bandage over her eyes, but Behrouz gently flicked her fingers away.

Fereshteh lowered her voice. "And what is the small problem, Mr. Bakhtiar?"

He lowered his eyes. "An infection," he said. "But we must be going. Kind of you and Maysi. Thank her for me."

"She's very beautiful, your daughter, Mr. Bakhtiar."

"Yes, very much. Thank you."

"Beautiful colouring. Such redness to the hair. And these are some lovely bracelets she has."

"Yes. She won't be parted from them."

"My friend leaves them for me. I know he does." Aria yawned.

"You have a wonderful friend," Fereshteh said to her, then turned to Behrouz. "Please, do stay for dinner."

"No. We really must go," Behrouz replied.

"Is there a problem, Mr. Bakhtiar?" Fereshteh asked.

"Everything is fine." Behrouz found himself struggling. A strange feeling had come over him, as if he was about to open a door into an unfamiliar space. He mumbled, "It's, uh, Mrs. Zahra. She finds the housework difficult at times, and with the child around . . ."

"The girl has trouble with her mother?"

"Zahra's not her real mother," Behrouz blurted. "But Maysi can explain that to you."

Fereshteh looked at the little girl. She'd begun to whimper against the side of her father's leg.

"You know, Mr. Bakhtiar, we have lots of space here. If things are difficult for you. She could even invite her friend. What's her name?"

"He's a boy called Kamran,"Aria piped up. She turned to Behrouz. "Can we bring him?"

"I wouldn't think of it, madam, but thank you."

"Maysi would love the company. She loves her chatter, as you know."

"Really. But thank you for your kind offer." Behrouz bowed.

As he and Aria walked down the lane and into the heart of the city, the grey brick of the mansion vanished behind them. He stopped and looked back. Lights were on in all the rooms—probably Maysi, he thought, searching for the blanket she had never come back with. He was relieved to be out of the house. It was too much to talk to a woman like Mrs. Ferdowsi. It was even more difficult than speaking to Rameen's mother. He breathed in the air of the city, a city that felt smaller to him now. Aria walked at his side, holding his hand, and he pressed it softly.

A WEEK LATER, Aria dug a nail under one eyelid, held it open, and tried for the third time to push the pus out of her eye. The infection had not spread, Dr. Vaziri had told her and Zahra in his office that morning. She had begged him to let her take the bandage off, because without it, as she explained, she could at least see colours, even in her blindness. Dr. Vaziri relented.

Now, back at home, Zahra was trying to teach her to cook.

"Take this," Zahra said, and Aria felt the contours of a metal stake, the length of which exceeded that of her arms. "We're roasting kabobs. The meat's right here, ground and salted. You chop the onions. Peel and slice them. Stick them on the stakes when you're done. You know how. Hasn't your darling father shown you a thousand times when you interrupt him at work?"

But Bobo had never shown her, Aria thought, and she had never interrupted him. Aria listened to Zahra's footsteps as they shuffled against the concrete floor.

"Have it done by the time I get back."

Keys jangled, a purse was zipped, and Zahra left so quickly that

Aria wasn't sure if she'd really gone. The door hadn't slammed or creaked. It was as though Zahra had evaporated, like a thunder-shower that leaves as suddenly as it came.

Aria felt for one of the stakes on the tabletop, then followed along its length with her fingers until she found the onion resting close by, and the knife beside it. Carefully, slowly, she peeled the onion's soft skin until she came to the thick inside layer.

A tight grip on the knife didn't help much, but she clenched it in her hand regardless. With the other she held the round belly of the onion. She hoped it was the centre and not an edge. She pressed down hard, but the knife was dull. Again she tried, this time piercing the onion a little, but it still wasn't enough. Her arms were weak. She'd have to try with both hands this time.

When the knife went through, it hit the counter so hard the blade jammed into the wood. Pulling it out with difficulty, Aria moved to cut the two pieces of onion into four. Then the onion had to be shredded down into thin strips that could blend into the meat. Her eyes had begun to sting. Zahra had surely known this would happen. Water burned through the slits where her lashes met.

As uncontrollable tears welled up, the dried pus turned liquid and dripped down the corners of her eyes, down her cheeks and nose. Still, she sliced some more of the onion. Her fingers slid back as she felt the blade at its tip. Yes, it seemed as if the pieces had been shredded smaller.

She lifted a hand to wipe away the tears and pus around her eyes. It now hurt to breathe, but the burning wouldn't stop, so she wiped at her eyes again because she didn't know what else to do. She began to cry the way people do when they don't care if anyone else hears. For all she knew, Zahra was still there, sitting on a chair, watching her.

Aria reached out an arm and looked in the direction she was pointing, hoping to make out the image of a body through the colours she saw in her mind. And to her surprise, she did see the colours, the reds and yellows and purples, but no bodily form emerged. Then she heard a door open, and a voice calling out.

Aria held the knife close to her chest.

"Heavens, child!" Maysi said.

"Who are you?" Aria asked.

"Who am I? Some memory you have." She pulled Aria into her arms. "Don't cry now. God laughs at girls who cry."

"I am not crying. It's the onions."

"Why do you have that knife in your hand? Thank the Lord I listened to Madame when she said I should come check on you."

"Zahra told me to."

"Zahra told you to what? Stop rubbing your eyes." She gently smacked Aria's hand away from her face. Aria could feel a rush of air, as if someone were fanning her.

"Can you see? Can you see my hand? I'm holding it up. See?"

"I see colours," Aria said. "I feel them, too."

"Is that Zahra crazy? Get your things together. You're coming with me. Get your things, I said."

"I can't."

"I'll do it for you, then. Where's your room?"

"She'll come back."

"To hell with her. Massoomeh's known her long enough. I'll pack for you, then, and let's be on our way."

part two

FERESHTEH

1959—68

12

Fereshteh Ferdowsi's great-great-grandfather was the son of a silver merchant. He had travelled widely, and among other treasures, he'd brought back silk lace from Marie Antoinette's corset, encrusted with the royal insignia, to Persia from Versailles, before the people beheaded her and the king. This souvenir made him famous. When Agha Mohammad Khan Qajar, Iran's castrated Shah, decided to make Tehran the capital of Persia and build his palaces there, he asked Fereshteh's great-great-grandfather to serve as the palace silversmith. That's how the Ferdowsis became who they were. "I've never allowed a Zoroastrian through my gates," the Shah told him. "You're the exception."

The family hadn't always been known as the Ferdowsis. They had been the son of the son of the son of the Silversmith, and like everyone in Persia, had no surname. It was Fereshteh's own father who chose Ferdowsi, not after the poet but the square they lived in. "They call it a last name," the registry clerk told him when he stepped up to pen the word in a thousand-page notebook. Fereshteh's mother, Arnavaz, was pregnant with her. "*Last* name?" she said. "As if it is the last name this family will ever have. There is doom in that."

"I believe they also call it a surname. A top name," Fereshteh's father replied. "It's the English way of keeping stock of things. So when that baby is born everyone will know he belongs to me." He pointed at her belly.

"And me, Hormoz? The baby's not mine?"

"Oh, how unjust the world is to women," the newly named Hormoz Ferdowsi said, touching his wife's belly. "If only I could make it better for you, poor lamb."

Hormoz had still been a boy when he'd started his silverwork for Nasser al-Din Shah. His great-grandfather had laid all the silver in Golestan Palace, and his grandfather and father had maintained it, polished it, chiselled it, added rubies and jades to it. Walking through the palace halls, Hormoz had promised the Shah that his work would be great, too, as great as that of his predecessors. "It'll make even the Russian Tsar jealous, your majesty," he said.

But later, when the Tsar visited Tehran, he wasn't impressed. "Despite your country having kings longer than most, you still don't know how to be a royal," the Tsar joked with the Shah. After hearing this, Hormoz fell ill for thirty days. He lost fifty pounds and forgot his own name for a while. He refused to play with his newborn daughter, Fereshteh, and accidentally knocked her out of her pram when he fell from dizziness. At his worst, he drank alcohol for twenty-four hours straight, and the doctor told him his liver was failing. But he recovered. He started making silver again. There was a difference in him, though. "The colour of your eyes has changed, husband," Arnavaz told him one day. "I see blue streaks in the brown."

"I have failed the Shah," Hormoz replied.

In the following years, the Ferdowsis had three more children, a boy, a girl, then another boy. Palace courtiers told Arnavaz it would have been better if the children had been born the other way around: boy, girl, boy, girl. But Hormoz Ferdowsi was perfectly happy. "I am a modern man," Hormoz said. "I would have kissed the hand of England's Queen. Would have let her knight me. A first-born daughter is no shame. And if the Tsar can have four daughters before a son, I can too."

He began to take Fereshteh on trips to Golestan Palace. He showed her the family legacy. "One day when you are old enough, my angel, you will carve the silver into these walls. And you will build more palaces for more kings and carve the silver into them. You will make Tehran shine and your children will, too." He lifted Fereshteh toward the ceiling filled with diamond-encrusted silverwork. "It looks like there are stars up there, Baba," she said, reaching out to the sparkles.

"Yes," Hormoz said. "Man can make stars if he wants to. The Tsar will see my stars one day. One day he will see what you see."

Fereshteh was seven when Hormoz left for Russia to see why the Tsar had not liked his stars. That day, he played with her and her younger brother Jafar, tossing them a ball while the two youngest watched from their prams. He gave each child a kiss on the cheek. He gave wooden dolls to the girls and wooden horses to the boys. He was supposed to be gone for a month, but he was never seen again.

When the month came and went, and there was no word from Hormoz, when she realized he was never coming back, Arnavaz did not leave her room for thirteen weeks. The wet nurse fed the infants, and Fereshteh watched as maids rushed in and out of her mother's room. For weeks she did not see her mother, till one day, through the crack of the door she caught a glimpse of a maid spoon-feeding her. Arnavaz, once a dark, Parsi woman with a chiselled jaw and the long face of a Zoroastrian, was now pale and paralyzed, food spilling from her mouth. Eventually, she recovered some of her health, but she would never talk again.

The Russians searched for Fereshteh's father for three months before giving up. Two years later, a letter came.

Dear Madame Ferdowsi, it has fallen upon the head of the Bolshevik Party of Leningrad to inform you that the Soviet Republic can no longer seek the remains of an imperial aide. Your husband was last seen in the Winter Palace. Regards.

It was after the arrival of this letter that Hormoz Ferdowsi became a legend in the neighbourhood. After her first day of school, two years after her father's disappearance, Fereshteh ran into the kitchen as the maids were making dinner and declared, "Father is going to be the new king of Russia!"

"They've already got a king—a king they're trying to kill," the wet nurse replied, pulling the youngest child away from her breast and handing him to Arnavaz. Fereshteh's mother smiled and nodded. Then she made two circles with each hand and placed them in front of her eyes like they were binoculars. "Your mother says he's a spy," said one of the maids. All three of the servants had learned how to read her mother's new language. Arnavaz was convinced that Hormoz had been sent by the Shah to spy on Russian communists in case they had plans to come south to Persia. She made a fist and pounded it on the table. "He'll come back," the maid said, interpreting. Arnavaz smacked her forehead, then made a cutting gesture at her throat. "After the Bolshevik is dead, your father will come back," said the maid.

But the Bolshevik, Lenin, did not die, at least not soon enough. Arnavaz suffered and ignored her children until Fereshteh was twelve. Then one day she packed a bag. Without a goodbye, she walked into the deep night, up Darband, through the winding road that led deep into the great mountain of Damavand. Somewhere beyond, she met a goatherd who took her to the Soviet border and pushed her across it, into Fereshteh's memories.

With both parents gone, the Ferdowsi children had to fend for themselves. A courtier from the palace had an idea. Their home would become a compound. Peasants could come and work in the gardens or build more rooms, and in return they would have a place to live. Within a year, everything was prepared, and as the oldest, Fereshteh was appointed the matron.

In August of 1921, the doors of the Ferdowsi compound opened. No one came.

"The people are lowly, Mademoiselle Ferdowsi," the palace aide said. "They think in the old ways. They think your kind, Zoroastrians, do magic and worship fire because the devil worships it. They think you do hocus-pocus."

Fereshteh had not understood what the man was saying back then. She only wanted to play dress-up with her sister, Mahnaz. A few days later, dead lambs were left at their door as a sacrifice. From across the street an old peasant man yelled, "The Prophet save you, or save us from your villainy!" Fereshteh watched as blood poured from a lamb's throat down the road and into Ferdowsi Square. Two days later, the sacrifices were repeated. The Ferdowsi compound turned red.

One day the four children arrived home from school to find the words "House of Sinners" scrawled across the front doors. Mirza, the youngest, had just learned to read. He was keen to read the words over and over. "House of sinners, house of sinners," he repeated all day.

Finally, the Ferdowsi children converted. When choosing their Muslim names, the girls argued. "I want to be Fatemeh!" Mahnaz yelled. But as the eldest, Fereshteh thought it appropriate that she herself be named after the Prophet's daughter. "You get Khadijeh," she said to her sister. "The Prophet's wife. The nine-year-old one."

The boys didn't fight. Fereshteh gave the oldest the name Jafar and the youngest one, Mohammad. None of them had planned to be called by their Muslim names, but Mirza liked his so much he demanded the others use it. Mohammad was better than Mirza, which reminded him of a food dish.

"It's too hard," Mahnaz said. "Arabic names are strange."

"Then we'll call you Molook instead. That's an easy Arabic name," Fereshteh told her.

Soon Mohammad became Mammad because it was easier for her to say. And after a while Jafar kept his Arabic name, too, because somewhere through the years he forgot his Farsi one and wouldn't respond to Jahangir. In the end, all three siblings got accustomed to their new names. But Fereshteh's name remained. That's what she had always been to them.

THE FIRST PEASANT to arrive at the door of the compound was a sweet-faced girl named Massoomeh. Her father kissed her cheek, then turned to Fereshteh to ask if he could have monthly visits.

Fereshteh smiled. "Of course. Any time."

"Her name's Massoomeh. She's a good cook, my mother taught her. Please send half of what she makes back to us. The other half she can keep."

"We don't pay," Fereshteh explained. "She'll get to live and eat for nothing. But we don't pay."

"Fair enough," her father said. "But if you ever do . . ."

"We'll send what we can," Fereshteh said.

Over the next several months, more peasants came. A few were from the South-City, but most came from the villages. One of the peasants was an old man. He brought his niece. "Got two boys. They will do my work and be my heirs," he said. "But she's no use." He pushed the girl through the door. "Though she can scrub floors real well." He slammed the door and left. The girl had a dirty face and matted hair that looked as if it hadn't been washed for months. Her nails were black. Tears had drawn lines on her face. She breathed heavily as she tried not to cry.

"What's your name?" Fereshteh asked. She turned the girl around. A note was pinned to the back of her coat. *Zahra*, it read.

Fereshteh took her inside. "You'll like it here," she whispered. "There's a nice girl your age. Her name is Massoomeh."

FOUR MONTHS LATER, a boy, Mahmoud, arrived at the door wearing clothes too big for him. They had been his father's. He was dirty and his clothes were filthy. His eyes were the bluest she had ever seen. They looked like sapphires against his soiled face. He was thirteen, a year younger than she was. "I can garden," he said, and showed her his hands. The lines on them proved it.

"We already have three gardeners," Fereshteh said.

"I'm better." Mahmoud smiled.

It was true that he worked hard. He would spend six hours at a time in the gardens, and three mornings a week he ran through Tehran buying soil and seeds or tending to other things. He could run faster than anyone else at the compound. The cooks gave him more food.

He would run into the house sweating, bags of soil in each arm. "Miss Fereshteh, where do you want this? Do you want bigger hyacinths or bigger poplars? We must choose." Fereshteh always chose the poplars, but with a heavy heart.

"You're not betraying the flowers," Mahmoud would say as they laid the soil together, pushing it into the earth with bare hands. "Trees are more important. No trees, no flowers." He smiled and she didn't feel so bad.

One day, she got home early from school, before Mahmoud had returned from his errands. She watched as he arrived, took off his shoes outside, and prayed before entering the house, placing both hands in the air with the palms facing him. He mumbled Arabic words Fereshteh did not understand, although she knew she was supposed to have learned them when she converted.

"Come into the courtyard. I want to show you something," she said. She grabbed his hand. "Look there," she said, pointing.

At first, Mahmoud couldn't make out what she was pointing at in the wildly overgrown garden. But then he spotted it. "Is that a bicycle?"

Fereshteh nodded. She had seen men riding them through the streets, and had once spotted Mahmoud at a magazine stand poring over pictures of them.

"Where did you get it?"

"I bought it. This afternoon in the square." Fereshteh couldn't stop smiling.

"Do you know how to ride one?" Mahmoud asked.

"I don't need to. It's not mine."

"Whose is it then?" He rang the bell three times.

"Yours," Fereshteh replied. "Go on, get on it."

"I can't," he said. "Why did you do this?"

"Don't cry. Are you going to cry?" she teased. "It's so you can get around the city easier. So you don't have to run. Look there." She pointed to two baskets leaning against the fountain. "You can mount one in front and one in back. You can carry everything in them."

Mahmoud played with the bell again. Then he hopped on the bike. He wobbled a little as he circled the courtyard.

"Don't fall!" Fereshteh shouted, and he almost did, throwing her an angry look. Then they laughed together.

"Do you think you'd fit in those baskets? Maybe I can take you with me," he joked.

FERESHTEH DID NOT mingle much with the servants, other than Mahmoud. For the first three weeks after he arrived, Mahmoud occupied much of her time. She would watch the others at work, though, and sometimes asked Jafar to look after them. Her younger brother tried his best but had begun to develop an odd habit that occupied him as much as the new boy occupied her. Fereshteh would see him sometimes, lining up his coins on the kitchen table, and polishing them one by one with a small cotton handkerchief no bigger than a sugar cube.

Massoomeh, she noticed, was always on time and did whatever the family asked of her.

"She's with that other girl all the time," Molook said to Fereshteh one day. "Zahra. That girl gets Massoomeh to do all her work for her." She was gazing out the long window in the great hall as she said this.

Fereshteh opened the latch on the window and stepped out onto the balcony. She looked at the gardens below. Massoomeh was moving along the path, weeding, shuffling along on her knees. There was no padding laid out for her. Zahra stood above her, watching.

"Surely, there must be something for that other one to do," Fereshteh said.

"She scrubbed the front stairs this morning," Molook said, nodding. "But that doesn't mean she should do nothing the rest of the day."

IN THE GARDEN, the girls were laughing. Massoomeh had made a dirty joke again. They were always about penises or vaginas, and Zahra always laughed at them.

"Don't let the family hear you laugh," Massoomeh said. "They'll kick us both out for indecency."

Zahra played with the bark of a fig tree. "What's indecent about our jokes?"

"These families don't talk about it."

"About what?"

"About *it*. Nobody has a penis and nobody has a vagina and foul words don't exist. I saw it myself once. One of them older maids said something about her pussy being itchy and one of those brothers slapped her hard. I think it was the shorter one."

Zahra laughed again and watched as Massoomeh moved slowly from weed to weed, pulling them out by the roots with her fists clenched tight.

"How'd you end up here?" Massoomeh asked.

"My uncle brought me," Zahra said.

"Oh yeah, I remember now." Massoomeh laughed a little. "Pushed you right through the door. Couldn't wait to be rid of you." She laughed harder. "Did he give you up on a holy day? Just like that? Thought he'd drop you here on the way to mosque?"

Zahra remained silent.

"Well, you're better off here," Massoomeh said. "My Baba dropped me off. Madame Fereshteh up there, she told him that we just make our food and board here, but that if I ever do make money, she'll send him some. Too many kids back home, right?" She looked up at Zahra, hoping she would agree. Still Zahra said nothing. "You do much work today?" Massoomeh asked.

"Washed the stairs. Out front," Zahra said.

"Want to give me a hand?"

"My back." Zahra arched her spine and looked away.

Massoomeh shuffled forward to the next group of weeds, her

bent knees moving quickly beneath her. "Well then, whenever you feel better. I got lots for you to do."

"Can you read?"

"Reading? What for? Nah. If I want stories I just ask people to tell me about their messes. Heh, sometimes I just listen in on other peoples' conversations. They never know."

Massoomeh finished her work without help, but the company was a nice change. Her hands hurt from pulling at the weeds all day. She asked Zahra to go to the kitchen with her, where she boiled tea and mixed it in a bowl with hot milk, soaked an old rag in the mixture, and held it between her hands.

"Makes your hands strong again." She smiled at Zahra. "My aunts in Esfehan always did this after butchering goats all day. Where your folk come from?"

"Shiraz," Zahra said.

"Well done. You're pure Fars like me."

Zahra watched as she squeezed the milk out of the rag and then soaked it again.

"You know how to cook?"

"No," Zahra said.

"You'll learn tonight. We'll make celery stew for these fine people. Just don't say nothing about the celery looking like Mr. Mammad's wee-wee. They'll slap you." She laughed loudly again, waiting for Zahra to join her. But this time, Zahra did not laugh.

That night, when the cooking was done and the Ferdowsi children had all gone to bed with full bellies, Massoomeh and Zahra snuck away to the building on the other side of the garden and climbed up to the attic with two bowls of celery stew. There, they ate and gossiped about the day, trying but failing to keep their voices low.

"You'll wake the boys up when they're having their sex dreams," Massoomeh said. Zahra kept her eyes low. Massoomeh sipped her stew noisily. "If you can climb, I'll take you somewhere real nice," she said.

"Where?" Zahra's eyes glistened in the gentle light of the wall lamps.

Massoomeh pointed a finger vertically. "Up there."

She took Zahra up a short flight of stairs, then another even shorter one, to the attic she had found only days after arriving at the compound. Moonlight shone through a small window in the corner. There was another window on the ceiling. Massoomeh opened this one wide, like a door. "You have to pull yourself out," she whispered. "Pull with both arms."

She did it first, hanging in mid-air for a while as her arms, strong from the years of work, kept her suspended. She pulled up her knees.

"Push me," she said. Zahra did as she was told.

"Pass me the bowls," she said when she was standing on the rooftop.

Then it was Zahra's turn.

"I'll pull you," said Massoomeh. She held out her hands. "But you need to try to lift yourself." Zahra grabbed a hand. She threw her other over the opening of the door, onto the rooftop. She pulled up a knee, then caught her ankle on the ledge. She dangled upside-down a moment, until Massoomeh caught her and pulled as hard as she could until Zahra was finally over.

"The moon is full," Massoomeh said, after they had caught their breath.

"Yes, it is," Zahra replied.

That was the first time Massoomeh saw Zahra truly smile, her face reflecting the light of the moon and her eyes turned to stars.

—

"I WANT TO read the Quran," Mahmoud said to Fereshteh a year later.

"I can't read Arabic," Fereshteh said.

"Then teach me the Farsi version first," he replied.

After instruction, it took him a day to read a page.

"It's hard for me to read, too," Fereshteh said. "Even the scholars find it hard."

"Which scholars?" he asked.

"The ones in Qom city. The mollahs and ayatollahs. It takes them years to read the Quran."

But Mahmoud was determined. And one day Fereshteh saw him riding home with a book in both hands.

"You're going to die doing that," she shouted. "You aren't even watching the road."

"The road should be watching me," Mahmoud said. He hopped off the bicycle and leaned it against the wall. They sat on the front steps, watching the daily life of Ferdowsi Square go by.

"I went to mosque today," he said. "I read for the mollah. He said if I get better I can study. He'll teach me himself."

"Why do you want to know the Quran so badly?"

"Because all the rules of life are in there, all the wonders. It teaches to not harm. If you'd ever been harmed, you'd understand."

"I have been harmed."

"You? With your blessed life? Tell me, master of the house, who ever harmed you?"

Fereshteh took the Quran from his hand and browsed the pages. "My mother and father. They left us."

"That's not harm." He laughed. "It's a blessing. If only my mother and father had left."

He rolled up his pants. A long scar ran up his leg, from ankle to thigh.

"A rake," he said. "Pure steel. I wasn't raking fast enough. I was seven. My father ran after me, and when he couldn't catch me he threw the rake at my leg. Mother was watching. After that, he kicked me in the stomach for a good five minutes. Mother was watching that, too. She said nothing. After that day, it happened all the time. No matter what I did, he'd come at me with the rake." He rolled up his shirt and showed her a scar there, on his stomach. "A God-fearing man would never have done it."

Mahmoud stood up and walked over to the rushing water in the gutters that ran down Shah Reza Street. He followed the gutter to Pahlavi Street, and Fereshteh trailed after him. "The new ruler has named the long street after himself," he said. "I guess he plans to be king one day. It's a wonder how man thinks he can put God's creations in his own name. He'll never be a real king, anyway."

"Be careful. They'll fry you for saying that," Fereshteh said.

"Does your family know him?"

"My father worked for the old king. He would have hated this one."

"The old one was just as bad. They're all bad. They believe they're gods on earth. They really do, you know? The English one thinks so, too. And the Russian one. All of them."

"Some of them try to do good." Fereshteh joined him beside the running water and looked down along Pahlavi Street. "I hear the new one's building trains."

"He's also forcing women to unveil! It's unfair. Women shouldn't walk around like that."

"I'm unveiled," Fereshteh said.

"You people are different."

"I don't want to fight with you," Fereshteh said. She held up the

Quran. "Do you want to go practise some more? Maybe by week's end you can go back to the mollah."

"I'm not supposed to see you anymore," Mahmoud said hesitantly. "The mollah was angry with me. 'Where did you learn to read, son,' he asked me. 'From the mistress of my house,' I said. 'She teaches me every night. She's a high-class girl. Speaks French and German, too.'"

"What did he say to that?"

Mahmoud came close and turned his cheek so she could see it.

Her eyes widened. "He hit you," she said, touching the mark there.

"Well, he's right. It's a sin to speak to girls. And I shouldn't have taken the bicycle from you." He looked away. "The new ruler named himself after the greatest warrior in the history of Persia. Would you ever call yourself Pahlavi?"

"My father named us Ferdowsi," Fereshteh said.

Mahmoud raised his eyebrow, questioning.

"He's the poet who wrote about the warrior Pahlavi," Fereshteh explained. "I think that's worse."

Mahmoud laughed. Then he turned around, heading back to the compound. "I need to speak with your oldest brother," he said.

"What for?"

"Because you have no father. Who else can I ask to marry you?"

MAYSI AND ZAHRA spent most of their time at work on their knees. Some days they would scrub the cobblestone path that led to the front stairs of the house. Other days they tended to the garden. Zahra hated the work, but Maysi felt at ease in the garden and didn't mind. The house was kept up in this way. The other maids, who were a little older and therefore closer to the age when they would be married, did most of the cooking, even if

Massoomeh liked to help. The scrubbing and washing was always Zahra's job.

"I hate to cook," Zahra said to Massoomeh one night on the rooftop as they watched the stars. It was their habit to come up here now, while the house slept. "I hate that we make such good food but can't have any ourselves."

Massoomeh lay comfortably on her back and munched on the walnuts she'd brought up with her. "Who says you can't? We eat their food all the time."

"It's stealing. We're not allowed to."

"It's not stealing when you've made it yourself," Maysi said.

The night was warm. Summer had set in and it was impossible to sleep inside. The girls slept under the sky on blankets soaked in cold water, just as they had back in Shiraz and Esfehan, far from the mountains, where the season burned through the skin. Night flies buzzed around them, but they didn't care.

"Do you think we'll be married soon?" Zahra asked, holding the cold blanket to her neck.

"I'm never getting married," Massoomeh said. "You think I'd do the same for a man as I do for these folk? Once a day is enough."

"But you wouldn't be working here anymore if you were married."

"Bet you I would. Plus, I wouldn't move out of a place like this. Got my own rooms, nice kitchen with bronze pots and all, a nice garden. You'd move out of here to a tiny chamber in the South-City?"

Zahra rolled to her side, away from Maysi. "Who said I'd move someplace small? I'll marry a rich man. Maybe we'll meet some working here. The Ferdowsis know tons of rich folk."

"And those men will marry you? A maid?" Massoomeh laughed.

Zahra flung herself around to face her friend. "Aren't I pretty enough?"

"That you are," Massoomeh said. "But pretty means nothing.

Haven't you seen this family? The prettiest in the lot isn't half as decent as you."

Zahra took some walnuts from Massoomeh's hand. She chewed them slowly. "It's all about love, anyway. Once a man falls in love with me, he won't care who I am."

Massoomeh closed her eyes. "I wonder if the crows will ruin my garden tonight. This morning they ate all the cherry roots."

"My mother used to call them black-jinns," Zahra said. "She said they sat on rooftops like jinns and watched you. And when you aren't looking they steal your life away."

"Was she sick?"

"My father beat her to death." Zahra rolled back over and got up. She walked to the edge of the roof and lay down on her belly there. "If we sleep at the edge, they'll think we're watching them. They'll be too scared to take your cherry roots then."

Massoomeh did not reply. For a while, she watched Zahra looking down at the garden. Then she joined her. They lay, side by side, watching the garden through the darkness. They lay like that for a time, until a beam of light flashed through the shrubbery and slowly moved toward the flower beds, where that morning Massoomeh had laid the monkey flowers, *mimulus guttatus*. That's what she'd heard Madame Fereshteh call them.

Mahmoud had come to plant scarecrows into the soil. He had spent all day making them.

"You don't like him, do you?" Zahra said after they had been silent some time, watching him.

"Like him? God kill me if I do. Anyhow, I think he's spoken for. Haven't you seen him with Madame Ferdowsi? She talks of nothing but him."

"Why do you call her that? Madame? She's only fourteen, and she's not French."

"These folk live the French way. They say *merci* for thank you and kiss the air at each cheek. Too scared to touch their lips to skin. You find the same kind in Esfehan. My father worked for them there. My mother, too. I just call them what they call themselves."

"But she's not a madam. She's no different from you or me."

Massoomeh watched as Mahmoud heaved his body onto a scarecrow, pinning it down as hard as he could. "I wonder if he knows we're up here?" She could barely make out his face.

"You do like him," Zahra said. "Let's hope your madame never finds out."

"Or what?" Massoomeh asked.

"Or you'll have to move to that chamber after all," Zahra said.

"Don't be mean." Massoomeh leaned a little farther over the edge, searching for the boy with the help of the moonlight. "I hope he puts those scarecrows in the right places. If the crows see they're not real, they never fall for the trick again."

Zahra watched the boy now too, hardly hearing a word Massoomeh said. In the moonlight she had caught a glimpse of the side of the boy's face, his hard jaw and strong neck. She could even see a bit of his shoulder peeking out from his loosened shirt. For the first time, she noticed how big and powerful his body was. While Massoomeh wondered about the scarecrows, Zahra wondered if a gardener boy could possibly fall in love with a girl like her.

FERESHTEH FERDOWSI BECAME a bride at seventeen. It had taken her two years to convince her family to let her do so. In the end, she had threatened to never marry at all if it couldn't be with Mahmoud. She had also threatened to donate the house to the mollahs, who would tear it down and turn it into a mosque. It was this thought, of their sudden homelessness, that persuaded her siblings.

Fereshteh and Mahmoud were married in the courtyard beside their garden. Maids held a silk sheet over their heads while Fereshteh's sister, Molook, ground two great blocks of sugar onto it, providing sweetness for life. When the mollah told them to, they dipped their pinkies into honey and fed it to each other.

"Now you can teach me anything," Mahmoud said.

"Our ancestors were peasants once," Fereshteh told Mahmoud that night, after they had made love.

"I'm only sixteen," he said. "Once I'm a mollah, no one will remember I was ever a peasant."

"After I teach you to read, I'll teach you numbers. I'll teach you French."

"I don't need to know that language," he said.

She was pregnant a month later. Four months in, she could feel the baby kicking. She asked Mahmoud to feel it, but he didn't want to.

"I have to memorize ten surahs for the mollah," he said. He finished packing his bag and rushed out the door. He didn't come home that night. He had fallen asleep at the mosque beside a shelf of books, every one of which was a Quran.

The next morning, when he came home, his face showed his confusion.

"I have to go," he said. He ran to the bedroom. He threw clothes in a bag, then took them out. He talked to himself. "It doesn't matter. They're to give me robes. I'm getting my own robes."

"Who is giving you robes?"

"Please move." He pushed Fereshteh away. "Where is my Quran? Do you have it? Have you taken it from me?"

"It's under your pillow," she said. "Where you always leave it."

He took the Quran. "Don't ever steal it from me again," he said. He put the Quran in the bag. It was the only thing he packed.

"Where are you going?"

"Qom. The ayatollahs have accepted me there. In three years I will be one of them." He paced around the room, not once looking at her. "One day I'll teach sinners."

"Will you be back in time for the baby?"

"I told you, three years!"

"Three *years*? The child will be here soon."

"That child is a sin," he said. He paced back and forth in front of the window, looking out.

"Are you waiting for someone? And what do you mean our baby is a sin?"

"Why didn't you tell me?" he shouted. "Why did I have to hear it from others in the mosque? I've married a Kafar. You worship fire. You have evil gods. Fire belongs to Satan, and I have married you."

He kicked the wall, and his foot made a dent in the plaster. He kicked it again and this time made a hole.

When he was gone, Fereshteh cried for a week.

"I told you not to marry a peasant," said her sister. "Their heads are filled with rubbish. Everything is a sin. Tying your shoes is a sin. Doesn't matter if they're Muslim or Zoroastrian. If they're peasants, they see the world through black lenses."

Fereshteh's baby came early. It was a boy, smaller than her hand. He grew anyway, but slowly. She named him Ali.

"A true Muslim name," she wrote in a letter to her husband.

"Names never helped us before," said Molook. "Our brother is named Mammad, but they still call us fire worshippers."

When Ali was three months old, Fereshteh put him down

for a nap and decided to garden again. She remembered the hyacinth seeds Mahmoud had bought her before leaving. She raked the soil bed, poured water, and planted. By spring the seeds would grow. She spread them all around the garden, imagining how they would circle and loop. They would go over the little brook and around the fountain, and rise up to the balcony. She closed her eyes and envisioned it. She breathed in the air, then exhaled. If she became a good Muslim, a real Muslim, maybe her husband would come back. She promised herself that in the morning she would visit the orphanages and hospitals. She would give them money, and instruct her maids to make them food as nazri, to please God so that God might help her. If she did all this, surely he would come back.

When she returned to the baby's room, she lifted him for his feeding. He made no sound. She placed a finger in his mouth to wake him, but felt no breath.

He lay in a coma for three days.

She begged and pleaded and swore she would help heal the world if he lived. She would be the greatest Muslim, if only he lived.

"Please, God, please my Sultan, my prophet, my Mohammad," she cried.

Ali died in her arms, his face blue.

FERESHTEH BURIED HER son in the garden with the hyacinths. Massoomeh and the other maids watched, silent, from the kitchen.

"Your son is dead," she wrote Mahmoud. "He died of grief. There are worse things than a father who leaves and a father who beats. There is the father who was never there to begin with, for like Kings he believes he is God. Or maybe God killed this son because his mother was not a Muslim. His mother gave nothing, and helped no one, and this is her punishment."

She burned the letter without sending it, then tried to stab herself in the heart with a knife.

She had miscalculated and missed. God let her live.

A clerk from the lawyer's office arrived with her father's letter the next day. "It's a will he wrote before he left," the clerk explained. "He knew there would be a coup. He had heard the British talking. He left the house to you. All of it. As the oldest. Forever."

Fereshteh tried hard to concentrate and understand what the clerk meant. But the wound she had made in her chest the night before ached and burned. Her vision blurred. She fought to keep her head up and speak calmly. "What about the boys, my brothers?" she asked.

The clerk unfolded the will again. "I am a modern man." He read the line and gave the will to her. She read it herself to be sure. "Do you have children? Read further down."

"It says I need a child."

"You need to make heirs. That's the one condition. You'll have the gardens and farm in the north. You'll have this place."

"My brothers will hate me," Fereshteh said.

"That's the business of family. We tend to hate our own kind the most. If they're smart, they'll learn to share. But first, make a baby."

FOR THE NEXT ten years, Fereshteh felt nothing. And she did not mention the will to her siblings. When she was thirty, her sister married. Mammad soon followed.

"You'll prune and ferment soon, sister. Better get a move on," Molook said, three nights before Mammad's wedding to an aristo-cratic girl called Nasreen. "And you'll have to move out as soon as Jafar gets married. He'll want his home for his own family."

That same night, Mammad confronted her: "We'll be turning

this place into lease-lets. I think the English call it that. Then we'll divide it up and sell the units off."

"You can't do that, brother," Fereshteh said. "Those places the English lease have their own bathrooms and kitchens. We haven't got that here."

"The sooner you leave, the sooner we can build them," Mammad said.

On Mammad's wedding night, Fereshteh showed him the will. He was so angry that he didn't read it through.

"You'd better find a man and bear his children soon, sister, or I'll have the law on you."

Mammad did not stay long enough at his own wedding to exchange honey with his bride. He stormed out of the house as soon as the vows were made. Jafar and Molook followed him. It would be another ten years before any of them talked to her.

During that time, Fereshteh gave away as much as she could without leaving herself homeless. "I want to give you what my father left me," she said on the phone to the local mosque. "Think of it as nazri."

She asked Massoomeh to cook thirty meals a day. "The other workers are getting angry, Madame," Massoomeh insisted. "You're giving everything to the poor. The gardeners and landscapers and bricklayers come in here and I've got nothing to give them."

"Then they can go home," Fereshteh said. "They can run away like Zahra did."

After a few years, the house began to empty of workers.

"There won't be anyone left to keep this place up," Massoomeh said one day, when only two other workers were left. "It'll decay, all this. The pool will stop working. You can't keep that garden up yourself. The wall's already crumbling."

"My people turned silver into flowers and welded them to walls. I can manage stone."

BY 1955, WHEN Fereshteh was in her forties, almost everyone was gone. Only Massoomeh was left. "I can finally start paying you," Fereshteh said. She and Massoomeh were alone in the living room. Massoomeh was knitting scarves for the winter. "You can give half to your family and keep the rest."

"My family's all dead, Madame," Massoomeh said.

"But your father?"

"You were busy mourning your own child, Madame. No point in telling you about my grief."

"I mourned my child for many years."

"That you did."

"Do you have anywhere else to go?"

"This is my home now."

"Then I need another child," Fereshteh said. "So you can keep your home."

"You're too old to give birth to a child now. But the angels will bring you one," Massoomeh said. "If not, I'll find you one myself, I promise."

13

On their way to Ferdowsi Square, Maysi had kept Aria pressed to her side. For the first time in thirty years, she wanted to weep. She allowed herself only a small groan, the kind that always lumped in her throat when she knew she could not say the things she wanted to say. It was a skill she had learned from her childhood, from those days in Esfehan when the adults had watched for any wrong move and then promptly slapped her face. This was why, she'd always thought, she had such a thick neck. So much was hidden there.

She thought back to those years with Zahra long ago, and to all that Zahra had done. The food she had stolen, and the jewellery—especially that diamond-encrusted gold necklace. It was Maysi who'd taken the fall for that. Madame Fereshteh had been heartbroken. "Go on, Maysi, keep on with your work. Maybe a jinn took it. Maybe it's the will of God. Although I don't think I believe in either of those things."

Maysi had slithered away, even though Zahra was the real snake. Maysi tried not to think about what had happened after that, but still the memories rushed back. She remembered that necklace on the baby—the baby the whole family had later excised from their memories. She had seen the necklace so many times, delicately placed around his little neck, the way rich folk liked to do, showing their babies off to whoever was looking. It was after the jewellery was stolen that bad things had started to happen. *Zahra*, Maysi thought. It had always been Zahra who brought trouble.

The necklace had been made of gold, and the face of Imam Ali was etched onto its surface. On the other side was the Imam's name, the man who had married the prophet's daughter, the king of the Shias. Maysi knew the Ferdowsis were converts, and she had never understood why a Muslim necklace mattered so much to them. Maybe it was because of the baby's father, the gardener boy.

She remembered further back, to that night on the rooftop when she and Zahra had first watched Mahmoud. Afterwards, Zahra could not stop talking about him.

"He's almost the same age as you," Maysi said to Zahra one night. "It's not right for you to like a boy his age. You need an older man."

"Who says I want him?" Zahra had replied, and ran off. But later, Maysi noticed that whenever they were in the room with Fereshteh, Zahra wouldn't look up at her mistress. She answered when spoken to, but always with her head down and quick, sharp words.

"Who made her God?" Zahra said to the others after Fereshteh had remarked upon the fact that she hadn't finished the washing.

"You're living in her house," Massoomeh replied.

"They're rich because they steal from the rest of us."

A while later, Maysi saw Zahra deliberately break the household china for the first time. She dropped one of the old Qajar plates, the ones that were made just like the Tsar's.

"I'm sorry. My hands. They hurt from working all day," Zahra muttered.

Fereshteh hadn't been angry. In fact, she had barely cared.

"You need to come up with something better next time," Maysi told her that night before bed. Zahra didn't reply, but moments before Maysi fell asleep she could have sworn she heard Zahra crying.

The grudges went on, and only became worse when it became clear the gardener boy was in love with Fereshteh. He would disappear on cycling trips with Fereshteh, and Zahra would find something new to break, something new to take.

Remembering all this now, Maysi could feel the lump rising again in her throat. She looked carefully at Aria to see if the child was aware of her crying.

After Fereshteh's marriage to the gardener, Zahra had started disappearing from the house during the day. Massoomeh would cover for her, and search for her for hours, to no avail. Then Zahra would turn up again at night, without excuse or explanation. Then, months later, Zahra started disappearing in the night, too. Maysi caught her sneaking out the window.

"Where you off to? You got a lover or something?" Massoomeh whispered from her bed.

Zahra stopped halfway out. "None of your business," she said.

"You're always disappearing," Maysi said. "And you've changed," she added. "Your face."

"It's the face of an angel, and it's mine," Zahra had replied, and hopped out the window onto the stone gates below, then onto silent Pahlavi Street.

It was the very next day, Maysi remembered, that Fereshteh had told them she was having a baby.

◇

FERESHTEH STARED AT the bloodied bandage wrapped around the girl's head. Aria lay asleep on the couch. From the kitchen, she could hear Maysi explaining.

"She might go blind, I said," Maysi called, repeating her words.

"Is that really what Mr. Bakhtiar said?" Fereshteh asked.

"As God is my witness. Heard it myself from the doctor's mouth!"

"You talked to the doctor, Maysi?"

"Sure did. Sure did."

Maysi was a bad liar. This had been true all her life, even when she was a child caught stealing from the Ferdowsi children's rooms. Fereshteh stared her down until she relented.

"All right, maybe I never talked to the doctor. But Mr. Behrouz did, and he knows that the doctor said the girl's gonna die."

"I thought you said she's going blind?"

"What's the difference? You go blind you may as well be dead."

"And Zahra. What does she say?"

Fereshteh took a coverlet out of the hallway closet and laid it over Aria. Its silk layers fell gently over the little girl's body. Fereshteh thought about resting, too. It had been a busy day. Prior to her stop for flowers, there had been the charity—thirty-odd children, motherless. There had been lunch with this attorney and that banker. What best to do with the assets . . . store them? Sell them? Combine things. Why not get married again?

"Isn't it time Mrs. Ferdowsi?" these men had said. "It has been so long." It would make things so much easier, they told her.

Then she'd had brunch with Mammad and Molook, who lived side by side in two English-style mansions near the mountains, houses their father had built. Her siblings had started talking to her again a decade ago, thank God.

The cool late-winter light flooded the room and sat discreetly on the silk sheets. Fereshteh sighed. Had it only been a week ago that the child had visited?

"Zahra says nothing," Maysi said. "I haven't heard from her, no peep no yell no shout no scream."

"We can't just keep the child without hearing from her mother."

"Zahra says she's not her mother," Maysi replied. "And you yourself said Mr. Behrouz was fine with her staying here."

"Yes, but she needs a mother," said Fereshteh.

"I never had a mother, you never had a mother. We're still smart and happy, aren't we? Maybe me more than you, Madame, but still."

A MONTH PASSED, Aria remained at the Ferdowsi house, and Zahra had not visited.

One afternoon, Fereshteh spotted Aria sitting outside on the doorstep, staring down the street. Her eyes were normal again, finally healed from their infection. Blue-green and pebble-like, they looked beautiful when they caught the sun.

"Looking for someone?" Fereshteh asked.

"Is Zahra supposed to come today?"

"No, but your father will."

At first, Behrouz had come to visit Aria a few days a week, taking leave of work, rushing down the mountains. But now he had settled into a routine of visiting on Thursday evenings, before the Friday weekend. Fereshteh thought about waiting for Behrouz with Aria, but there were seeds to buy for the garden. She was keen to plant a less organized new section, more Persian in its pattern; something wild and feral, bountiful, without compromise; virile yet deceivingly calm. She felt a compulsion to go. As she walked away, she tried to grab hold of the right thing to say as desperately as she sometimes yanked out weeds. But nothing came to her. So she walked away without a word to the child.

Aria, indifferent, watched her leave. The old woman in the house, Madame Ferdowsi, was still a stranger.

Behrouz eventually arrived on foot. To Aria he was a mighty giant, and she ran to him and jumped just enough so he could lift her. She did not notice how this made him lose his breath, how weary he was.

"Can I show you everything?" she said as she pulled him through the door. She was used to the house now, was learning its secrets, and she wanted Behrouz to attain the same familiarity with the old place. She knew where all the rooms were, even the forbidden ones. She knew the pool was always empty, the balcony was twenty-five feet long, the garden wrapped around the house. She showed him the kitchen, where she helped Maysi chop celery, sage, mint, and basil. "It's supposed to go into some stew, with beef and goat meat, potatoes, garlic, saffron, and onions," she told Behrouz. He nodded approvingly and laughed. "Good, my girl," he said.

They stayed in the kitchen with Maysi awhile, and helped her until she had enough of them.

"Get out. Get out of my kitchen," she said, and she snapped a tablecloth in their direction. "And you with your red eyes. The girl can see and suddenly she thinks she's queen of the kitchen."

In the living room, Behrouz inspected Aria's eyes. "Let me have a look," he said, pulling open the lids. "Still a little red, but I see those beautiful blues again."

"My eyes are green," Aria said.

"Sometimes they're green, sometimes blue. What luck."

"Zahra says they're devil eyes."

"Superstition," her father said. "What stories we invent, our people. Isn't that so, my darling?"

Aria felt moved and a little uncertain. Behrouz had never called her darling before. It was such a fancy word. A word that people like Madame Ferdowsi used. Not people like Bobo and Zahra.

"Is she coming?" she asked.

"Is who coming?" said Behrouz.

"Zahra. To see me. I can show her how my eyes are getting good."

Behrouz was slow to answer. "Zahra is busy," he finally said. "But she'll come the moment she can. You're with Madame Ferdowsi now. Is she nice to you?"

"She never talks to me. Almost never. She puts plants in the dirt instead. But she's nice."

"Well, plants are pretty things," Behrouz said.

He spent the evening with Aria, taking her to the vendors near the market and buying her a skewer of liver and, after that, some faloodeh, which was almost as good as ice cream. As the sky got dark, he brought her back to the Ferdowsi home to sleep, but returned early in the morning.

"You haven't been to hamaam yet, have you?" he said.

A new bath had just opened near his house, in Shoosh, in the Molavi district not far from the Bazaar, leaving the area as yet unaffected by the new Western way of bathing. Behrouz held Aria's hand and walked her to the women's section. He paid for them both. "Take the nice lady's hand," he said, gesturing at an attendant. "One hour." He held up his index finger and walked in the opposite direction.

When they were done he said, "Clean and perfect," and smiled. He, too, was nicely clean and coifed. He took Aria back to the Ferdowsi home and hugged her goodbye.

When Maysi saw Aria, she slapped her own head and said, "Well, now we'll have to worry about the boys." She turned to Fereshteh. "See, Madame? We'll have to worry about the boys."

Fereshteh said nothing, but it seemed to Aria that she approved.

"My skin is so white," Aria said, marvelling.

"You won't be staying too clean," said Maysi. "You have to help with the cooking. Next week your father'll need to come back and get you scrubbed all over again. Did that man suddenly find a pot of gold somewhere to get to those fancy baths?"

THE NEXT NIGHT Aria cooked with Maysi in the kitchen. In a giant pot atop the stove, four cups of rice steamed, stretching out into thin, separate grains. The rice was from India, but Maysi said the Indians had stolen it from *them*. She also said they'd stolen tea and every spice known to man. Maysi said that without the Persians, India would be an empty desert, but she loved Indian movies anyway, especially Raj Kapoor, who was the best of them all and made Clark Gable look like a peasant.

"Are you listening to me?" Maysi said. "Children who don't listen get beatings. In this house you're out as quick as you're in. Be careful. I can ask Madame to send you back."

"You dropped one of the celery sticks," Aria said. "Also, you don't know how to be mean. You don't scare me. Zahra does it much better." Aria kicked the celery under the kitchen island. "Do servants go to school?" she asked.

"What? Of course not. Why are you asking?" Maysi said.

"If I'm supposed to be a servant, why does Madame say I'm to start school?"

"What? When, in God's name? In the name of Imam Reza and Saint Maryam, I don't know what you're saying," Maysi exclaimed.

"Madame Ferdowsi told me yesterday. She came into my room and put a notebook and two pencils on my bed."

Maysi placed her knife on the counter, dropping a carrot as she did so. Aria kicked that under the island, too.

The schooling would be in French. "It's the best language to know," Madame Ferdowsi told Aria the next morning. "Farsi's good for poetry," she added. "The only language for poetry. One should speak it in dreams, never elsewhere."

"But we do speak it," Aria said.

"Yes, we do."

"Does that mean our lives are dreams?"

"I suppose it does."

Later that day, Aria joined Fereshteh in her garden. "What should I call you?" she asked. "Do I have to call you Madame the way Maysi does?"

"What about calling me mother?" Fereshteh asked. She picked a ripe plum and opened it. "Always check to see there are no worms. I don't mind if you call me mother."

"Zahra will be mad."

"Zahra? Well, is there anything else you'd like to call me? Maybe we can replace that word with another one, just between us. So Zahra won't find out. Did you call Zahra mother?"

Aria shook her head. "Just Zahra."

"So why would she be angry with you?"

This was too complicated a question for Aria to answer. She thought for a moment, then said, "I accidently called my baba Bobo once, and now I call him that forever."

"And you'd like to call me Bobo?"

Aria laughed. "No."

"But I think I understand. You could call me something similar to Maman."

"I could say Mada, or Mara? Or Maya, or Mana."

"Would you like half this plum? We can share it."

Aria took the fruit and let the juice flood her mouth. "Which do you like?" she asked Fereshteh, as the juice trickled down her cheek. "Maybe I can call you Mana?"

"I do like that."

"And Zahra won't get mad?"

"Not if she can't figure out what it means."

They walked over to the cherry trees, where tiny green balls hung from leaves; only a few had begun to blush red.

"Maysi says I'm not really going to school. She says you just made that up," Aria said. "She says I'm lying. That I'm here to work for you like Zahra used to, and that girls like me don't go to school."

Fereshteh searched for words again, the right ones that she could never find. "You should go to your room," was all she could manage in the end, even though she knew she should have said something else entirely.

AFTER THEIR EXCHANGE in the garden, Fereshteh didn't speak again with Aria for another week. Several times she passed the little girl in the hall, but when she opened her mouth, nothing came out.

Every night Aria helped Maysi make dinner, usually a stew: a night of lentils, a night of eggplant, a night of beef, a night of chicken. And every night Aria helped chop things, kicking vegetables under the island when they fell.

It was another two weeks before Aria met the rest of Fereshteh's family at Friday tea. First came Madame Nasreen and Mr. Mammad. They arrived with their twin sons, Hossein and Hassan, who both ran past Aria without a hello. Mr. Jafar arrived next. Maysi had told Aria that Mr. Jafar spent hours washing his hands, that it was his favourite thing to do, and that he also liked to spend hours washing coins and bills and pencils and forks. He hung his bills from a string to dry after he washed them. When Mr. Jafar walked into the living room, he bowed to Aria, then sat down in an armchair, took a walnut from his pocket, and began wiping it with a handkerchief. Madame Molook was next. She arrived half an hour later than the others, at exactly four o'clock. She told Aria that this was what the English did, and that if Aria was going to live with them, she had better be prepared, which meant being properly dressed at four o'clock every Friday, and that she had better learn her etiquette, quick, so she could be just like the English. Madame Molook was accompanied by her two daughters, Shahlah and Shahnaz. They were lanky girls with dark hair, one a year younger than Aria, the other three years older, proper ladies who sat discreetly on the sofas. It was clear neither could see the point in greeting, much less welcoming, a peasant girl.

"Do we have to say hi to her?" Shahlah asked her mother.

"Don't mind the boys, Aria dear," Madame Molook said, referring to Hassan and Hossein. "They haven't the patience for anything."

What about your own stupid girls? Aria wanted to say. Instead, she smiled and bowed her head.

"What's wrong with her, Maman? Why is she bowing her head?" Shahlah asked.

Madame Molook replied by smacking the back of her daughter's head.

A little later, from her nook in the kitchen, where Maysi had told her to chop more things and not speak to the family, Aria listened; and whenever she entered the living room to serve fruit or tea or sweets, she watched. Madame Nasreen had a way of pressing her lips together whenever she looked around the room. And each time she did, she would say, "Well, what can you do? What can you do?" followed by a sigh. Mr. Mammad, Aria noted, did nothing but sip his tea.

"So what's that girl doing for you, sister?" Aria heard Madame Nasreen say. "I imagine she'll be a help around the house. You start training her well now, you'll have a good one in some years." She spoke between sips of tea and presses of lips. "Lord knows, Massoomeh will need the help. She'd better appreciate this."

"Yes, yes. Good thinking, sister," said Mr. Mammad, speaking at last.

Mr. Jafar took another sip of his tea. "Yes. Good thinking, sister," he echoed, but the conversation had moved on.

Aria returned to the kitchen, but curiosity got the better of her. She tried to slip off her stool and go back to the living room. "What are you doing?" Maysi asked.

"I want to watch Mr. Jafar clean a walnut."

"Don't you dare."

Moments later, Madame Nasreen joined them. She walked to the stove, where the kettle was set to boil, poured herself a cup of tea, and set it down. She lifted an eggplant from the pot where it was soaking, smelled it, and dropped it.

"This is horrid," she said. "And that tea there." She pointed at the cup she'd left on the table. "It's cold. I want it hot." She looked directly at Aria. The pitch of her voice was high, and became higher with each word. "Pass it to me, please."

Aria reached over, picked up the cup, and placed it in front of her.

"I can't drink something this cold," Madame Nasreen said. "Do I have to tell my husband how incompetent you are?"

Aria closed her eyes. She tried to shut out the noise around her. When that didn't work, she began to hum.

"Stop that, child," Madame Nasreen said. She turned to Maysi. "Why is she doing that?"

"You sound like my mother," Aria said. She kept her eyes shut.

"Keep your place, child," said Maysi, for the first time with anger in her voice.

But Aria ignored her. "Zahra. You are like Zahra." She felt rage fill her insides, and her heart raced. Something uncontrollable was about to happen.

"You dare talk to me like that! This child, she dares?" Madame Nasreen looked at Maysi. "Who is Zahra?"

Maysi turned and walked to the other side of the kitchen. There was only so much of Nasreen she could take. The child would have to cope on her own.

Aria finally opened her eyes. No, Madame Nasreen didn't look like Zahra at all. She lifted the kettle. "You want it warmer?" she said.

"What are you doing?" Madame Nasreen said. "How dare you speak like that to an elder."

For a moment, Aria hesitated. What she was about to do might affect the course of her life, and maybe send her back to Zahra. But some unknowable force willed her toward her destiny. Aria flung the kettle at Madame Nasreen, splashing water on the woman's face and body. The water wasn't hot, but Nasreen screamed anyway.

Vaguely, Aria was aware that Maysi had begun to chant, "God forgive me, God forgive me," while smacking her own head.

Fereshteh came running into the kitchen, followed by Mr. Mammad and Madame Molook, and finally by Hassan and Hossein, and Shahnaz and Shahlah. The children were laughing. Only Mr. Jafar had remained in the living room. Perhaps, Aria thought madly, he was still cleaning his walnut.

"Calm down," Fereshteh said firmly.

"I'm sorry, Mana," Aria said, but she wasn't, not really. Whatever had happened was out of her control. When she'd thrown the kettle, she thought she knew why she was doing it— but the reason escaped her now. "I'm sorry, I'm sorry," she repeated numbly.

"See the kind of creature you've brought into our home?" Madame Nasreen shouted.

"I'll cut off her fingers myself," Maysi said.

The twins and Shahlah and Shahnaz continued to laugh, until Fereshteh sternly told them to stop. Then she slapped Aria's face.

She stepped back, then looked around the kitchen at her family's faces to see their reaction. Her act of revenge settled them.

Later that night, after the family had left and Aria had been sent to her room for the night, Fereshteh sat on the edge of Aria's bed, woke her up, and asked for forgiveness.

"You're sending me back," Aria said.

"No," Fereshteh said. "But not everything will be up to me."

Aria watched her leave the room. She sunk into her bed, thinking of what would happen if Madame Ferdowsi did send her back. Would Zahra take her in, or leave her outside to freeze to death? What if Zahra never fed her again? Maybe she could sleep on the front steps, or on the balcony like before, and Kamran would bring her food. She knew Kamran was still her friend—at least, she hoped he was, even if she was living in this big house now. She turned in her bed, faced the window. A breeze cooled her face. She wondered if Kamran missed her. Did he still wait to catch sight of her on the balcony, or throw a ball into the tree so that he could call out to her? She wondered if Zahra was lonely without her, alone in the house while Bobo was far away on the mountains or travelling to other cities, Esfehan or Shiraz or Ahvaaz. Before, if Zahra was angry, she had Aria to yell at. But now, Aria thought, the only person Zahra could scream at was herself.

It was with these images of a lonely and screaming Zahra, and an anxiously waiting Kamran, that Aria fell asleep.

THAT NIGHT, HUDDLED outside the Ferdowsi compound, Kamran watched and waited. When he saw Aria's new family leave, he sighed and clenched his fists. He made a quick calculation: If he made a run for it, he could jump high enough to get onto the first stone gate and, from there, jump onto the second, which would take him to the railing that led to Aria's new window.

When he reached the windowsill, he bent his knees a little and took the bracelet out of his pocket. He pushed gently against Aria's window. It opened easily and silently. He read the word spelled out by the beads on the bracelet one last time, making sure he had spelled it correctly: *Remembrance.* He slipped it inside.

14

Within a month, the extended Ferdowsi clan had relented, agreeing to accept Aria into their family, despite Madame Nasreen's continued resistance. Mr. Mammad had been the one to talk her into it.

"Fereshteh has no children. Let her have this one," he said to his wife. "Besides, when our dear sister gets older, it won't be us looking after her. The kid will have to do it."

It was the latter proposition that nearly convinced Nasreen, barring one final caveat. "The money. This means Aria will get all the money," Nasreen said to Mammad.

"When my sister dies, *I'll* get the money. Don't you worry about that," Mammad replied. He pointed to his chest. "Real blood is what matters, not bastard blood. The law sees to that."

With that, Nasreen was appeased, and Aria became a Ferdowsi, in everything but name. But the name didn't bother her. When Fereshteh told Aria the news, she nodded and said, "I like Bobo's last name. I'll keep it."

Acceptance into the family meant Aria could now do what other Ferdowsi children did. In September, she started school. Lycée Razi was located at the top of Pahlavi Street, north of the Vanak neighbourhood, to which only the privileged had access. There was a British school nearby, but Mana told her that the

French were better at everything. The Shah and the Queen wanted to send their children to Aria's new school, too, Mana said. The Shah was fluent in French, English, and German, she added, aware that Aria was looking at her with rapt attention. He had learned German because his father had loved the Nazis and because his former wife had a German mother, and he loved her way more than he loved his present one.

There were fifteen boys and girls in Aria's class. Aria knew that some mollahs had tried to shut the school down because they didn't like the sexes mixing, but all the foreigners in the city, even the Germans, sent their children here. Madame Dadgar introduced Aria to everyone. In each classroom, long tables seated four children each, two boys, two girls. Aria took her place by the window. At the other end was the strangest-looking boy she had ever seen. He was leaning on the table with his hand under his chin, gazing out through the open window at the wide courtyard at the front of the school. He barely noticed her.

Beside him was a girl, sitting as still as a guard dog, nose pointed at the blackboard. Her eyes blinked. She turned to Aria and held out her hand.

"I'm Mitra," she said. "This is Hamlet." She poked the boy and quickly pushed back the glasses that were about to fall off her nose. Aria extended her hand but Hamlet still didn't notice. Mitra punched his side.

"What?" he said.

Madame Dadgar made the introductions, mostly in Farsi so that Aria could understand, but threw in the occasional French. "Hamlet, Mitra, this is Aria Bakhtiar. *Hamlet, s'il vous plaît, changez de place.*" Hamlet moved beside Aria.

Mitra threw her hand up. "Madame, he copies me," she said in Farsi, forgetting to use her French.

"What's so special about you that I'd want to copy what you say?" said Hamlet. "Anyway, you're blind. You can't even see with those glasses on."

Behind her, Aria could hear a few girls giggling. Madame Dadgar approached the table. "Mitra, dear, will you help her the next few weeks?" the teacher asked, nodding at Aria.

"Why not me?" Hamlet said, half-heartedly pounding a loose fist on the desk.

"I'm smarter," Mitra said.

"Mitra lives near Aria. It'll be easier for her to visit," Madame said.

Mitra agreed. "You know," she told Aria, "there are one hundred French words in Farsi. You understand them already. I'll show you."

At lunch that day, Hamlet and Mitra stood in a corner of the courtyard, unaware of Aria nearby. "Why did you offer to help the new girl?" Hamlet asked.

"Because she's stupid, and stupid people need smart people to help them."

"She didn't look stupid to me," said Hamlet.

"Her accent," said Mitra. "You can always tell from their accents."

"I have an accent," Hamlet said. He kicked at a jump rope lying in the courtyard.

"You're just Armenian," Mitra said. "She's South-City. You can always tell when they're South-City. My father says so because he's a communist."

"Is that what you're going to be, too? My father helps people. He gives them jobs, then takes the jobs away. He says that's the best way to help people."

"How is that helping?" Mitra asked.

"He says it gives them life lessons."

For a few moments, the two children silently watched the action in the courtyard. Other children were running about, and the click-clack of shoes smacking against the smouldering pavement rang in Mitra's ears. "Your father gave my father a job," she said, finally.

"But that was a long time ago. Your father works for the government now. And gets into trouble with them," said Hamlet.

"He works for the oil company."

"Everyone knows that's the government. My father says that if your father hadn't gone to work for the government like so many others, all the trouble wouldn't be happening. My father says the Shah gives everyone extra money for the new year, and anyway he doesn't understand why everyone is making such a fuss about the Shah."

"Isn't your father friends with the Shah?" Mitra asked. She took the jump rope Hamlet had been kicking, wrapped it around her waist, loosened it, and wrapped it again.

"Are they bad people in South-City?" Hamlet asked, changing the subject quickly. "My father says I'm never to go. Are there Christians there?"

"There are monsters there!" said a voice from behind them. They turned around, but no one was there.

"Up here!" said the voice.

Aria sat on the branch of a large tree, her legs dangling. She said nothing else.

Hamlet whispered, "How much do you think she heard?"

"I don't know," said Mitra.

"Do you think she hates us now?" Hamlet asked. "What do South-City girls do when they're angry? My father says South-City folk are the most dangerous, since all they do is believe in God and go to mosque and pray for everyone else to die."

"My father says God is dead," Mitra said.

Hamlet placed a hand on Mitra's shoulder. "I'll watch her in class. If she's praying, we'll know she's dangerous." He glanced up at Aria, then took Mitra's arm and walked away.

ARIA DIDN'T TALK to Hamlet again until just before Christmas.

It was snowing heavily, but Hamlet and Mitra were sitting on the stairs at the entrance to the school, eating ice creams. Winter had settled over the city, and the snow in the courtyard was so deep, it reached above their knees. The other children looked at Hamlet and Mitra strangely.

Aria crept up behind them. "Where did you get those?" she asked.

Hamlet stood up, surprised. "At the cafeteria. But you have to pay. Want some of mine? Look. Put snow on it." He held up his cone so the flakes covered the top.

"You're not normal. But yes," Aria said. And she thought of Kamran, who for so long would bring her the chocolate Zahra never allowed her to have. It would be so nice if she could return the favour, she thought. He had made her happy when no one else would. And once, he had wiped blood from her eyes.

The three children stood under the falling snow. They tilted their heads up, closed their eyes, and stretched out their tongues.

"This is God's number two," Aria said, and all three laughed. The grey of Tehran fell over them.

Aria smiled. As the snowflakes fell on her tongue, she stole a sideways glance at her new friends. Hamlet and Mitra were holding hands.

She left school that day feeling light. She kicked at the snow and the powder exploded into the air. Perhaps the snow brought luck, she thought. But then she corrected herself. Having friends at school wasn't what had made that day perfect. The perfection had begun the night before, when Mana had received a call and told her to come downstairs.

"A friend," she had said, holding out the phone.

Aria spoke into the receiver fearfully. She was wary of an unknown voice answering back.

"Mana, is it Zahra?" she asked. Fereshteh shook her head.

"Are you there?" a boy's voice said quietly.

"Who is this?"

The voice sounded a little heartbroken. "You don't recognize me?"

And then she did. Her eyes widened. "Kamran," Aria said. She tried to control her voice so it wouldn't quaver.

"Want to see a movie tomorrow? It's Thursday."

"I—Bobo is coming for his visit," she said.

"I asked him. He says it's okay," said Kamran.

ARIA ARRIVED HOME from school the next day, tornado-like, flinging off shoes and school uniform and untying her hair. "I have to go now, bye!" she yelled to whomever.

"Slow yourself and all the godforsaken jinns that have possessed you!" said Maysi. "Where are you going?"

"I can't talk. Movie. Have to go."

She slammed the door so hard it drowned Maysi's yells. Aria ran as fast as she could, along Pahlavi Street for a while, then past the boutiques and vendors. She ran past Café Polonia, where the foreigners went to smoke and sing, and neared Goldis Cinema with her heart pounding, and not just from the running.

There he was: Kamran. Standing there shyly, watching the people pass.

"You're so tall now," she said.

"And you're still a pain."

He tried to pay for the movie, even though she had brought a bundle of cash. "Mana gave it to me," Aria said.

"Is that the new woman you live with?" he asked.

"Yes. She never talks but is so nice. She doesn't hit me like Zahra, except that one time. But like you say, I'm a pain." She smiled as she gave the man in the ticket booth her money.

At some point during the first half-hour, Kamran slipped from his seat, then reappeared. Aria tore her eyes away from the glare of the screen. He was handing her a chocolate bar. "Take it," Kamran said.

"I can get them from Mana now," she said. Kamran's face crumpled. She reached over, took the bar, and thanked him, thinking about the ice cream she hadn't been able to save for him. "Where are they?" she asked, returning her attention to the movie screen.

"Paris," he said. "Now be quiet and watch the movie."

Later, as they walked down an alley outside the theatre, she said, "You're acting different from before." Kamran said nothing. At the next crossing, they held their noses as the smell of dung rose from a gutter. Further along, the scent of roasting walnuts masked the stench and it was safe to breathe again.

"Your accent is strange," she said. This was another thing she noticed now. "Why do you speak like that?"

"I don't talk any different from you," Kamran said. "You're such a pain." He pinched her cheek. "Wipe that silly smile off your face, lady. Since when did I say you could tease me?"

Aria brushed his hand away. "I only said you sound different. And don't touch my face if I haven't asked you to."

Kamran fell silent after that, but Aria asked question after question. "How is your school? When do you finish? Will you become a doctor when you grow up? Can you drive a car?"

Kamran didn't answer. He kept his head down for a long while. Finally, he looked up. "You still talk all the time," he said.

"You don't," responded Aria.

It was true. Kamran didn't chatter freely anymore. Not like before. Perhaps he was growing aware of his deformed lips. Aria noticed how he would touch them all the time and try to hide them behind his hand. The doctors had stitched them up and brought them back together, but they still looked different from other people's lips.

"The boy, the one in the movie, looked so sad," Aria said.

"His mother hates him," Kamran said.

"How do you know?" She gave him a little push, as a joke.

"Stop asking so many questions, you goat," he said.

"If Mana ever hates me I'll put shit in her food," Aria said.

Soon they reached Mellat Park, where all the families with money went. Kamran had never been before. He wasn't paying attention to her. He had caught some people staring at his lips and was now hiding them with his fingers.

"Antoine Doinel," he told Aria. "I want to cut my hair like him."

It had begun to rain, and they decided to run the rest of the way home. They ran side by side. The thin scarf that covered Aria's hair fell to the nape of her neck. Her auburn bangs flew off her forehead in the wind. She closed her eyes. She didn't need to see. She trusted Kamran would lead her, like he always had.

"Faster, Aria, faster!" he yelled, and as she opened her eyes, he lifted his arms, pretending to be a plane. She saw he was older now, taller. He could stretch his arms far out.

She copied him, watching the sway of his hips, the tilt of his neck. "It's a long way from the South-City," she said.

They turned into an alley and stopped just short of Aria's new home. Kamran sat on the curb and Aria joined him.

"Want to go get some ice cream?" she asked him. "Me and my friends were having ice cream at school the other day."

"What friends?" he asked.

"Mitra and Hamlet."

"Are they nice to you?"

"They help me with homework."

"That's good then." He kicked a pebble. "I can't. Have to go back. Don't have any money, anyway."

"I can get us some. From Mana."

"I don't want her money. People like her get their money from the Shah. Everybody knows. But thanks, anyway, kid. Why do you call her Mana?"

"Just a nickname. Her real name is Banoo Fereshteh Khanoom Ferdowsi."

"That's some name," he said. He picked up another pebble and flicked it across the pavement. It disappeared into the running water in the gutter. "I used to like to sneak into movies, but not anymore. Feels wrong to steal. Movies mean something, you know? You shouldn't steal them."

"How do they mean something?"

"You keep talking the whole way through and never learn anything," he said.

"Not true," she said. "You'll teach me, anyway."

"What can I teach you? Now that you've got all those fancy people. Go ask them questions."

"Why are you yelling?" Aria grabbed one of the pebbles he'd thrown. "I stole something once. Zahra found out."

"What did she do?" Kamran asked.

"She hit me. Right here." Aria pointed to her upper-left cheekbone, where it met her eye. "And then she hit the other side."

He snatched the pebble from her, winked, and ran off. She yelped and pulled at the silk scarf around her neck and ran after him. A minute later, they ran into another alley. It was unlike the others they knew so well. There were no mules or opium sellers on bicycles. There weren't even fat women in black veils carrying food home. This alley was lined with mulberry trees, one bigger than the rest, and surrounded by the neighbourhood garbage.

"We're in Youssef-Abad, I think," Kamran said. "What an odd place to plant trees."

They sat down and were quiet awhile. Kamran stared into the distance. Aria watched him. "Do you hate your mother, like the boy in the movie?" she asked at last.

He didn't answer.

"Maybe it's better to scare people than to hate them," Aria said. "Then they'll never hurt you."

"They'll never love you, either," Kamran said.

"Well, I love you," Aria said. She kissed him. They both giggled and turned red. They sat there in silence as the sun over Tehran began to set, and the scents of kabobs, heated butter, spinach stews, and boiling rice filled the air. Heavy smoke from shishas and steam from black tea wafted through the cafés. And from the mosques came the call to prayer.

THE NEXT DAY, Kamran returned to the Ferdowsi home. Nasreen, who happened to be visiting her sister-in-law, opened the door, and he yelled, "I brought her chocolate!"

Nasreen stared at him in silent disapproval.

"I brought her chocolate," Kamran said again, quieter this time.

"Brought who chocolate?" she asked.

"Is Aria here?" he asked.

Nasreen shook her head slowly. "So you're the type she spends her time with. No one here wants your filthy chocolate. With your filthy hands and your diseases. This country's still in the dark ages because of your kind."

Kamran held out the bar of chocolate and spoke almost in a whisper. "Aria is not here?"

Nasreen glanced at his lips, then looked away. "Miss Aria wants nothing to do with your kind. Go on. Get lost."

"I want her to have this," Kamran said. He tried not to cry.

"She doesn't want it, I said." Nasreen closed the door.

Kamran walked down the house's steps. When he reached the bottom, he placed the unopened chocolate bar there and put the beaded bracelet he'd made at work on top of it. He'd made sure to buy the darker kind. It was what Aria liked best.

He walked home slowly, stopping only when he came across a crowd of people waving banners. They were shouting, "Death to the Shah! Long live Khomeini!" One of those names Kamran knew, the other he'd never heard of. He continued on his way.

15

Aria waited for days and then weeks to hear from Kamran again. But he never called, and eventually her thoughts of him faded. Meanwhile, her days with Mitra and Hamlet went along as usual. Then, one Saturday, Mitra didn't come to school.

"Do you know if she's okay?" Aria asked Hamlet as they ate their sandwiches on the stairs. "She was supposed to help me today. I brought her some sweets that Maysi made."

"Her father went to jail. The Shah sent him there. She's gone to visit him with her mother and brother," Hamlet said.

"You're lying," Aria said. "Is he a robber?"

"I don't think so. But he did say that the Shah is, which is why I think he went to jail. But I live near the Shah. I've never seen him rob anything."

"What did her father say he robbed?"

"All the oil."

"That's stupid," Aria said. "If I could steal something it would be the ice cream shop on the corner of Ferdowsi and Shah Reza Street, the one that has all the colours. They have the homemade kind."

"Haven't you stolen before? All people from the South-City steal."

The next moment, Hamlet was on the pavement. Aria had slapped him so quickly he hadn't seen her hand coming at his face. He lay there, dazed.

"You'll probably get suspended again," he said.

"Good," Aria said.

She didn't talk to him for the rest of the day. It was foolish to think she could have any friends here.

After school, Hamlet saw her outside the gates, walking home fast. He yelled after her. "I didn't tell anybody."

She didn't stop.

He yelled louder: "I didn't tell anybody you hit me! But you need to stop hitting people!"

Parents and children stopped and stared. Aria stopped, too. Hamlet caught up to her.

"You hit like a boy," he said. "Are you going home? Do you want to go to that ice cream shop you were talking about? I have money."

Aria refused to answer, but he took the bus with her the rest of the way home anyway.

A week later Mitra was back. "Hamlet says you hit him," was the first thing she said to Aria. But she didn't seem to disapprove.

"If boys aren't shoved they never learn anything," Aria said. She and Mitra both laughed. "So, is your father out of jail?"

Mitra looked around uncomfortably, then nodded. "Hamlet needs to shut up," she said.

Aria changed the subject. "Want to come see my house? It's big. My mother will be there. But she never talks."

"And I'll help you with homework," Mitra replied.

That afternoon, as they studied, Aria noticed Mitra biting hard into her thumb. She even saw a bit of blood, but Mitra quickly sucked it up. They worked into the evening, conjugating verbs, until Mana came into the kitchen and told them Mitra's father had arrived to take his daughter home.

Mitra looked quickly at Aria, clearly surprised he had come. She got up, put on her coat, and shoved her hand into her pocket to hide her wounded thumb.

"It is true that my father works with oil people," Mitra told Aria quietly, as they walked to where he waited by the door. What she didn't tell Aria was that she still remembered the first time the English men in suits had come to their house and threatened him.

"Mr. Ahari, there was no coup. The Iranian people simply wanted their king back," one of the men in suits had said.

Mitra remembered how angry her father was. He had pushed the man hard against the kitchen table, which had come crashing down with its assortment of tea and sugar that her mother had laid out. The other man in a suit had grabbed her father and held him immobile.

The first man adjusted his tie. "There was never any need to nationalize the oil," he said. "The company has always paid its employees."

"This isn't about employees," her father said, lunging at the man again. This time Mitra's mother also held him back, while Mitra and her brother, Maziar, watched in terror from the kitchen corner.

"It's been nearly ten years since your so-called coup, Mr. Ahari, and this country is better than ever."

"Half my men can't feed their children while that shit for a king sits between his walls of silver and gold," Mitra's father said. Speaking these words had been enough to land him in prison.

After that, the lycée sent Mitra and Maziar home for a week. Word had got out about their father. He came back home a week later, only to be arrested again. The second time the men in suits came, they weren't as friendly. "No reason to form a union, Mr. Ahari. As of tomorrow, your contract with Anglo-Iranian is terminated."

"What's a union, Mazi?" Mitra asked her brother.

"When the workers all get together and tell off their boss."

"But Baba's the boss," Mitra said.

"No, they tell off *his* boss, who's some English man."

The next day, Mitra started biting her thumb. At first it was a kind of gnawing, but over time the wrinkled skin on its curve became so numb that she no longer felt her teeth cutting through it. When a wound opened, she let it heal for a few days, then bit it open again.

"Baba's joined the Tudeh!" Maziar exclaimed one day a while later.

"How do you know?" Mitra asked. She was covered with a veil. She'd been preparing for evening prayer, as her mother had taught her. Her prayer-stone was placed at the centre of a small, embroidered rug; she had already performed her ablutions.

"I saw the paper he signed. On his desk. With their name on it. He's off with the Russians now."

With the new money he made, their father bought guns. One day Mitra had walked into her room to see him sawing through the wooden floor. Then he lifted out some concrete, threw the guns inside, and nailed the wood back on top. He patted her head and gave her a candy stick. But instead of sucking on it, Mitra spent the rest of the day biting her thumb.

Now Mitra greeted her father in the hallway of Mana's home. He was tall and heavily built, with one of those giant moustaches that always amazed Aria, with long bristles that fell down over the upper lip, making it hard to guess what its owner was going to say next. She made a note to tell Kamran the next time she saw him to grow a moustache like that. That way, no one would ever know his lips were different from those of other people.

16

Three weeks earlier, Fereshteh had spent several days walking down and up Pahlavi Street in the South-City. She had become intimate with it, and with the avenues and alleys that crossed into it. Turning in her mind were the words Aria had spoken to her: "Aren't you my mother now?" the girl had said. And was she not? And if not, what was she? These questions, and her confusion, plotted against her. If this city, this Tehran, were a chessboard, she would need to find her own moves.

The first time she walked the route, she arrived at a mosque. It was like any other mosque she had seen, beautiful and quiet and intimidating. She had never learned the prayers properly—the salaat, with its Arabic words and musical rhythm, was too hard to memorize. She wondered how others did it. She had watched Maysi recite the prayers all these years, but the words had never burned into Fereshteh's mind enough to be remembered. Perhaps the words themselves sensed her Zoroastrian-ness.

The mollah, or akhound, as the common folk called him, had been so kind. He'd gently ushered her into the mosque without touching her, for she was a woman after all. He motioned to an old woman, older than Fereshteh, to lead her to where the women prayed. "I've always been useless, haven't I?" she said under her breath. And then she whispered the only words of the salaat she could ever remember: "Bismilla al Rahman al Rahim." She said it with the Persian accent, dropping the *al* before each name of God. "In the name of God, the Most Gracious, the Most Merciful." For those were God's other names, of the ninety-nine. His name was Gracious. His name was Merciful. He had other names: He was Muhaymin (Guardian) and Salam (Peace). He was Noor, (Light). He was Shaheed (Witness). Fereshteh wondered if he was witnessing her now, or using his other names to judge and condemn her. But she only used the two names and hoped some answer would arise. None did.

"May we see you with joy and light in the days to come, sister," said the mollah as Fereshteh exited the mosque. She smiled, knowing a man like that would have seen right through her.

But she did go back, this time wearing a darker veil that imbued her with a strange confidence. She found the mollah and told him, "I have a girl. I am not her mother but may have to be."

The mollah nodded and thought for a moment. "Does the child choose us or do we choose the child? Think of the Imam Ali. As he says, you have two ways to live. In a person's heart or a person's prayer. We are happy to pray for you here."

After the visits to the mosque, Fereshteh walked some more. She saw how the city was growing. There were more cars and men in suits. But the poor were still there, too. They were everywhere, without homes or food. She saw them lined up on the street corners and jammed under makeshift roofs. "No one where I come from sees this world," she thought.

The farther she got from South-City, the fewer mosques she saw. She passed by a Christian church, unsure if it was Armenian or Assyrian. There was another church nearby, one where the

Polish immigrants gathered every Sunday. She liked all these buildings, all these homages to God, but in the same way she also liked the current films or fashions. They were pleasant parts of life but without great meaning.

It was quite by accident that she came across the temple. She wouldn't have known what it was if she hadn't seen the men dressed in white, with white hats too, standing outside. By chance the entrance doors were open, and she glimpsed a flicker of fire.

She waited outside until the others entered, and then it was easy to go into the courtyard, and just as easy to knock on the door. She heard humming from inside, or maybe chants. The men were singing. It was a language she didn't understand, but it still felt faintly familiar. She had heard it as a little girl. She pushed the doors open. In the grand hall she could hear the hypnotic, almost atonal chanting even louder.

"What are you doing here, my lady?" a woman said, rushing toward her. The woman was dressed all in white, too. "You cannot be in here. Have I ever seen you before? Are you a Zartoshti?"

"A what? No. I mean yes," Fereshteh said. But that infinitesimal *no* was enough to paint the picture.

"Please, ma'am, if you will."

The woman ushered her outside. But before she left, Fereshteh turned around and caught sight of the fire again. At that moment she felt a burn in her belly. Heartburn, she thought. Or maybe not. She walked away from the Zoroastrian temple, quietly. She didn't look back.

THAT SAME DAY, Behrouz came to see Fereshteh. He had a secret he'd been keeping for too long. "I think it's time to tell you," he said. "But I fear. I fear . . ."

"What do you fear?" Fereshteh asked.

"That you'll give Aria up. That you'll send her away. It's not what I want. But knowing this secret may help you. And Aria."

That was when they had made their plan.

"Maybe," Fereshteh said to him, "this will be a good thing for her. With God, I mean. So much of Islam is about charity is it not? And charity can lead to heaven? She will be saved, she will be a real Muslim, and she will never suffer, right?"

She'd waited for Behrouz to answer, maybe to teach her.

"I'm no expert," he had said. "Or so I've been told."

But now here he was, with Aria. She watched him from the kitchen as he bent his knee and talked to the child.

A WEEK LATER, Behrouz led Aria down an alley, deep into South-City. The overwhelming smell of human waste here was mixed with the waste of stray dogs left to starve and die because the Hadith said they were untouchable and haraam.

They reached an old building with an ancient door that opened to a flight of stairs. They walked down them until they reached a landing lit by a single hanging light bulb.

"Are you sure Mana wants me to meet these people?" Aria asked.

"Don't talk," Behrouz said. A man appeared on the landing and gave him a short brown stick in exchange for money. Aria knew it was opium.

"Let's go," Behrouz said, and they walked back up.

Now they walked through a wider alleyway, down another flight of outdoor stairs, and down yet more stairs into what seemed to Aria to be a dark hole. It was as if the city in this area were no longer horizontal, but a vertical maze with no end. They walked in darkness until they reached a light, then descended more stairs. Then, still in darkness, they climbed for a long stretch. When at last they got to the top and looked at the street before them, a broken old home awaited them.

Its grey, mortared walls were crumbling. Its front gate, made of sheet metal, was held together asymmetrically with tired screws and painted green, giving the place its only colour and differentiating it from other houses down the road. Beyond the gate was a patch of open space filled with dust and dirt and bits of the crumbled wall that had turned to rubble. Aria could see small footprints scattered about as she and Behrouz walked through—children's footprints, she figured. She paused before entering the house. A wooden roof sat atop its concrete frame. Shattered windows along the perimeter were nailed in place to rotten plywood. She smelled decay—perhaps rats? She could see worms and insects crawling about; a cockroach climbed a wall, trying to get in through a window. The front door was made of wood painted green and like the gate, it squeaked as Behrouz pushed it open.

Inside, there was a kind of living room, with a wood block as a table and an old metal chair painted the same green as the gate outside. In the corner was a single-burner stove that looked to be a hundred years old. A wooden staircase wound crookedly upstairs, from where she could hear pattering feet.

Then she heard a child say, "Don't. Fara, don't," until it sounded like someone was smacking her. A large, unshaven man with dirty clothes, his belly exposed, walked out of another room. He smelled like sweat and rosewater.

"Hello," he said. He shook Behrouz's hand. "Hello, young lady," he said to Aria, shaking her hand, too. "Come this way."

"Don't speak a word," Behrouz warned her, as they followed the man.

The man led them into the kitchen, where a table was laid with broken plates. There were no utensils beside the plates, but exactly five cups, each marked with different coloured paper. A small woman was sitting behind the table.

"I want to leave," Aria said quietly to Behrouz, but he ignored her.

"Hello, missus," Behrouz said. The woman was wearing a veil printed with flowers, like the kind Maysi wore. She calmly said hello. Upstairs, the sound of the children had ceased, as though they were secretly listening in.

Behrouz removed a small envelope from his jacket, placed it on the table, and sat across from the woman. When she didn't move, he picked up the envelope and removed its contents: photographs, a dozen or so.

"That's when she broke her nose," Behrouz said, pointing to one. "She's four there," he said, pointing to another of Aria standing beside Zahra and barely reaching her waist. Behrouz flipped through the photographs and said something about each one.

Aria, still standing beside Behrouz, fidgeted. "Why are you showing those pictures?" she asked.

"Want to sit down?" the large man asked.

"No," she said.

"This is my favourite one, Mrs. Shirazi." Behrouz held up one of the photographs.

Mrs. Shirazi. So that was the woman's name. Aria badly wanted to ask her father what they were doing here. But Mrs. Shirazi looked intrigued, and the large man, who Aria assumed was her husband, looked even more so. Mrs. Shirazi reached out and took the picture. Her fingers curved along the edges.

"She can come once a week," Behrouz said. "I get her on Thursday afternoons and can drive her down the next day to spend the day with you, on the Fridays."

Aria could not contain herself. "Wha—"

Behrouz shushed her.

"That's great. Isn't that great?" said the large man, nodding at the woman.

Behrouz continued. "I was thinking she could help your girls to read, Mr. Shirazi. Her guardian is sending her to some special school. This way she and your girls will get to know each other. That's always a good thing, isn't it, Aria?"

Aria remained silent. She looked about the small kitchen, dust-filled and grey, and wondered what girls her father was talking about.

Mr. Shirazi's eyes lit up. "What do you say, wife?" He rubbed his belly. Mrs. Shirazi hadn't looked up from the last picture she'd been given; her eyes were steady and focused.

The large man, whom Aria now knew as Mr. Shirazi, shook her father's hand. "This is so kind of you. So kind. And give our best to Missus Ferdowsi."

"I will."

"With the help of God," said Mr. Shirazi, and shook Behrouz's hand even harder. Aria tried to speak again, but Behrouz took her hand in his and squeezed it. All this time he had not spoken to or looked at her once.

As they were leaving, Aria heard the children's footsteps running up the stairs. She caught a glimpse of one of them, a little girl younger than her by about five or six years. The girl, small and fragile, had auburn hair and green eyes.

BEHROUZ ASKED ARIA to wait in the truck. It was parked at the end of an alleyway, far from the home they'd just left. It had taken them half an hour to walk back to it, up and down the winding labyrinth of stairs and shanty homes. Now Behrouz grabbed a small bag from the glove compartment and walked away.

Aria waited for a while, just as he had asked, but agitation soon got the better of her. She quietly followed the path she'd watched him take. He had walked back into one of the dark underground staircases, where there was nothing but a small bulb to light the way. And there he was, sitting on one of the bottom stairs. She slipped into a shadow so he didn't notice her close by, watching. He removed an object from his bag. It was the thin brown stick he had bought earlier, and he was grinding it into a pipe. She had seen sticks like this before, up at the barracks. He lit the pipe and smoked. It didn't take long for his body to go limp, and soon he had fallen asleep, the pipe falling to his side. After watching him for a while, Aria ran back to the truck and locked herself inside.

FERESHTEH WAS HOME when they got back, waiting in the kitchen. She sent Aria to her room while Behrouz reported on the day. "Everything went well. God has gifted you," he said.

Fereshteh thanked him and watched him leave, sensing the reluctance in his departure. Then she walked slowly upstairs to Aria's bedroom.

"Why did I go to that house today?" Aria asked her.

Fereshteh didn't answer. Instead, she went to the closet and got out some clothes for Aria to wear. "You've got to dress properly for dinner. Go put these on with your new black shoes. And ask Maysi to do your hair. And remember, you'll be going back there again soon."

"Where?" Aria asked.

"To the home you visited today. The Shirazis'."

"Why?" Aria asked.

"Because it's good for you." Fereshteh left, agitated, and went downstairs to the kitchen. To her surprise, Behrouz was there again.

"I thought you'd gone," she said.

"I have a question. Do you think it is right? For her to be there?"

"Things like this are always right," Fereshteh said. "Did she look happy?"

"Who?"

"The mother?"

He shook his head. "It was like talking to a ghost, madame. There's nothing there. I have to go. I don't know if what we are doing is right."

"What is the matter, Mr. Bakhtiar? You should be happy. It is right for Aria to do this. And then God will help her."

"Do you believe that, madame?" he said. "I used to think such things, in my dreams. But I feel now that dreams somehow belong only to the dream world." He stood up again, lifted his hat to her, and once more quietly left.

17

A week later, Fereshteh filled a large suitcase with cleaning products and several pieces of cloth. She had told Behrouz to bring his truck that morning. Everything would have to go in the back. Maysi had stayed up through the night, cooking rice and lamb. Lamb was the most expensive thing you could get these days. The Shirazis would be grateful. Fereshteh had also given Aria the Quran, and told her to wrap it up nicely. It had to look good when she presented it to them. A few days previously, Fereshteh had taken it to the calligrapher and asked him to write the names of Mrs. Shirazi's daughters on special paper and place it in the book. The Farsi names would have to do for now, she thought. She would add the Muslim ones later and give Mrs. Shirazi a proper family Quran.

Aria was waiting for Behrouz at the front door. "You'll have to help your father with this," Fereshteh said, hauling the luggage down the stairs. "My knee is getting worse."

"Bobo's no Hercules either."

"But you are," Fereshteh said.

Aria sat cross-legged on the bench in the entryway. "I don't want to go back there." She found a mark on the wood floor and stared at it. "They're disgusting. There's dirt on their floor and rat droppings and worms. Her daughters smell."

"I thought you didn't see the daughters," Fereshteh said.

"I could smell them all the way from downstairs. And they don't have couches, and just one table."

Fereshteh said nothing.

"One of the girls has something growing around her lips. They smell."

"That's *enough*," Fereshteh said sternly.

"But they do."

"I don't care if they're made of manure. You're going to help them. Your father and I have decided. This is a path to heaven. I've been to the mosque and talked to the mollahs and this is what they told me. So you will clean that floor and give them food. You'll even bathe the little one if they ask you. I didn't take you in so that you'll look down on people. Money doesn't make you better than anyone."

"You sound like Zahra," Aria said. She could see Fereshteh's chest rise and fall, but all her guardian said was, "Your father's here. Take good care, the ride will be long. I will see you this evening."

MRS. SHIRAZI HAD three daughters: Farangeez, Roohangeez, and Gohar. Aria said hello to each one as they came downstairs. The little one, Gohar, ran to her mother, and Mrs. Shirazi took her into the kitchen, leaving Aria to fend for herself. One of the older girls, Roohangeez, said hello, but the other folded her arms. Aria gave them each a bottle of spray detergent and a cloth. "Clean," she said.

Roohangeez, who was the middle child, sprayed some detergent in the air. "What is it?"

"It cleans," said Aria.

Farangeez, the eldest, disdainfully dropped the bottle Aria had given her. "That's your job. Mother says you're here to work so you'll go to heaven when you're dead and rotten." She pushed Roohangeez out of her way to peer in the suitcase. "What else is in there?" she asked, seeing the Quran's sleeve.

"That's what they'll use to pray for you when *you're* dead and rotten," Aria said.

Farangeez picked up the Quran. She slid her hand over the cover. She opened it and looked inside. "What's here?" She found the paper where the calligrapher had written the girls' names.

"Spells," Aria said. "Magic spells. Voodoo."

"What's voodoo?" Roohangeez asked, still fiddling with her spray bottle.

"It makes your enemies drop dead," Aria said.

Farangeez threw the Quran at her.

Aria caught it. "Don't do that!" she said.

"Why not?"

"Because it's a perfect creation, and perfect creations aren't supposed to be thrown. And I have to give it to your mother."

"She doesn't need it. She doesn't need these, either." Farangeez pointed to the bottles of detergent.

"She does. She's filthy," said Aria. "Just like the two of you."

"You mule!" Farangeez shouted. She took Roohangeez's bottle and sprayed Aria in the face. Aria slapped her.

"Stop it," Roohangeez protested.

Mr. Shirazi ran into the room. "You, young girl." He pointed at Farangeez. "No dinner and five lashings." He took off his belt. "Get upstairs." Farangeez shot a look at Aria and ran to her room.

Aria picked up the Quran and held it out. "Mana said to give you this."

Mr. Shirazi took the book. He opened the cover, flipped some pages, and read a few lines. Then he shut it quickly. "Very well. Thank you," he said.

"Your daughter's names are in—"

"That's all very well," he said. He took the book upstairs, swinging his belt as he went.

"What is that book?" Roohangeez asked softly.

"It's a Quran," said Aria.

"Yes, but what is a Quran?"

Mr. Shirazi had returned, and there was no time for Aria to explain. Instead, she showed her hosts the rest of the detergents and cleaning supplies.

"There's one for washing your stove, one for your floor, one for the tables, and one for the toilet. Mana says you can keep the suitcase for when you travel."

"What's travel?" Roohangeez asked.

"Quiet," said her father. He looked at Aria. "Think this place needs cleaning, do you?" He was smiling, but something about his smile confused her.

"No. I don't. Mana gave it to you because—"

"My girls will do the cleaning. Good exercise for them. They should be strong, right, my love?" He stroked Roohangeez's hair and pulled her into him. Roohangeez hugged her father's leg. "They'll do the cleaning at night," he said. "But I want you to do something else for us."

Aria waited.

"You go to school, girl? You read?" he asked.

"Yes," she said.

"Mr. Behrouz suggested . . . Well, what sort of things do you read? Storybooks? News about the world?"

"I can read anything," Aria said.

"You read those poems folks always talk about? Rumi and such?"

"Those aren't easy for my age. We learn to read them when we're older."

"Older, hey?" He looked at his daughter. "Can you teach this one to read?"

"How old is she?" Aria asked.

"How old are you, child?"

"Six," Roohangeez said.

"That's when everyone at my school starts. But I didn't start till I was seven," Aria said.

"Well, she'll be smarter than you then, won't she. If you start teaching her now."

"I suppose," Aria said.

"Now, go home," he said gently, handing her the Quran she'd given him. "Mr. Behrouz will be waiting for you at the end of the alley."

"It's a gift," Aria said.

"Take it, girl," he insisted.

For a moment, Aria waited for Roohangeez to say something or for Mrs. Shirazi to come out of the kitchen, where she had lodged herself the moment Aria arrived. But taking the book was all there was left to do. She held it tight under her arm and walked the narrow hall through the courtyard to the front door. It was as dirty as the first time she'd seen it. The smell of rat dung still hung in the air. The front door was still that ugly green, the same colour as the gate. She pressed the Quran hard to her chest so it wouldn't fall, and searched for her shoes.

"Where are they?" She turned around and faced Roohangeez, who had followed her. "My shoes. Where did you put them?" Aria demanded.

"I didn't take them," Roohangeez said.

"Yes, you did." Aria pushed her so hard that Roohangeez stumbled.

Across the hall, they heard laughter. Farangeez was standing there, smiling.

"You took them, you took my shoes," Aria said.

"Prove it."

Aria ran down the hall, then darted upstairs. The girls' mattresses lay on the floor, covered in green and white sheets. Aria flung these in the air and dust showered down. She kicked a lone chair against the wall. "Where are they?" she shouted.

Farangeez and Roohangeez, now joined by their younger sister, Gohar, were standing at the door. A few broken toys lay scattered about the room, and Aria picked these up and smashed them against the wall and broke them even more. She tried to rip one of the sheets in half but couldn't, so she shoved it into Farangeez's arms instead. "I'll kill you," she said. Tears washed down her face. With only socks to cover her feet, she ran through the muddy courtyard and pulled at the green door with one hand while clutching the Quran with the other. The door was too heavy. She dropped the Quran, pulled with both hands, and at last ran into the busy street.

A voice cried out after her. "Come back. You forgot!"

Aria turned around. It was Roohangeez waving her down.

Aria slowed her pace but kept walking. Soon, Roohangeez caught up to her. She held out the Quran. "You forgot your book."

Aria stopped and glared at her. "I dropped it already, so I'm going to go to hell now. I don't want it anymore. It's shit. And it has your names in it."

"It has beautiful drawings," Roohangeez said.

"Those aren't drawings. They're words in another language, so they look funny. And if they're so beautiful, keep the book then." Aria started walking again, then stepped on a pebble and winced.

"Your feet will hurt." Roohangeez pulled on Aria's sleeve to stop her. She bent down and removed her slippers. "You can have mine." She held them out.

"They're too small for me," Aria said.

"But you won't hurt all the way home."

"Why did your sister do that? Do you know why I'm here? My mother made me come. For her charity. I'm supposed to help you."

"Yes, Baba told us," Roohangeez said.

Aria paused, realizing how fragile this sister was, too. Her face was all bone, with dark, solemn eyes.

"My sister is like that," Roohangeez explained. "She's always been like that."

"Well, I'm supposed to teach you to read, so don't be so mean about it."

"I won't be mean to you. Take my slippers."

Aria did and squeezed her feet into them.

"And take this, please. I'm not allowed to have it. It's pretty but you shouldn't have brought it here." Roohangeez held out the Quran.

Aria finally took the book. She opened the cover and turned the first page. She looked at the foreign words that ran across the pages as if they had been written by the wind. Roohangeez was right. They were strangely beautiful, almost like Farsi words yet completely different in meaning, and Aria could not make any sense of them.

"Is this the pretty part you mean?" Aria pointed at the words. Roohangeez nodded.

Aria tore out the page. "I'm going to hell anyway so it doesn't matter. Here. Don't tell anyone," she whispered.

Roohangeez took the page and folded it, making it so small that it would fit in the tiny pocket of her skirt. She smiled. "I don't hate you like my sister does. I promise."

"Good. Then I'll teach you to read first. I'll teach her all the wrong things."

Both girls laughed.

"Is it really true that if you help us you'll go to heaven?" Roohangeez asked.

"That's what Mana says. She says a mollah told her so."

"A what?"

"A wise man."

"If I learn well, I'll be wise, too."

"Yes, you can be wise and I'll go to heaven."

Roohangeez laughed. Aria walked away with the slippers tight on her feet and the book heavy in her arms, aware that another pair of dark eyes followed her from the bedroom window of that rat-filled tumbledown home. They were the eyes of an eldest daughter who had resolved to do everything she could to keep Aria out of heaven.

18

Shortly after Aria's second visit to the Shirazi home, it was time for her and Hamlet and Mitra to start middle school. A lump formed in Aria's throat when she learned that, for the first time since she had started at Lycée Razi, Hamlet was not to be in her class. She soon forgot her own sadness, though, when she saw Mitra's desperate eyes watching Hamlet, her best friend, walk down the hall to a different classroom.

"His father took him out of our class," Mitra said, quickly wiping a tear from her cheek. "He doesn't like people like me or you. But mostly people like you."

"Non-Christians?" Aria asked.

"No. People without money," Mitra said. "And if you could only learn to pronounce words properly and not talk the way you do sometimes—"

"Talk how?" Aria asked.

"I said the way you do *sometimes*, not all the time. And I've taught you how to sit properly a thousand times. And you're not supposed to touch food with your fingers, even if you're picking it off the floor."

"When have I done all that?"

"Always. Always," Mitra said. Her face had turned red from

chastising Aria. "Now we just have to deal with it," she said sadly.

Hamlet's classroom curved round to the other side of the school, on the other side of the courtyard. It was also the biggest room. Mitra and Aria could look out the window of their own class and see it across from them. In the distance they saw Hamlet walking in, led by his new teacher, the one who had never bothered to learn Farsi because she believed French was the language of the world. The other children stood up to greet him.

"All of them have houses made of diamonds," Aria whispered to Mitra.

"They do not," said Mitra.

"Fine. Houses made of gold," said Aria. "If they have a cavity, they break off a light switch and fill their teeth with it."

"*Venez, les filles*," said their teacher, Madame Dadgar, and pulled the girls away from the window.

Later that morning, Aria whispered to Mitra, "Look." She pointed at Hamlet's classroom. There, etched in the dust that covered the window beside Hamlet's seat, was the letter *M* written in the clumsy hand of a pubescent boy, its curves and long stems slightly crooked. It was hard to see the letter for what it was at first. But Aria was sure of it. It was an *M*.

For the rest of the day, as Madame Dadgar talked, Aria furiously took notes she was never going to look at again, and Mitra scribbled the letter *H* on every page in her notebook, neglecting her academic diligence, her perfectionism, her duty, her fear that she would never amount to anything. She told Aria she was trying to think of all the words she knew that began with an *M* and ended with an *H*, and then all the words that ended with an *M* and began with an *H*.

"Those are some good names," Mitra said. "One belongs to a Danish prince and the other to a Persian God."

Aria looked up from her mangled notebook. She had given up taking notes and was now trying to draw a sparrow in a tree. "I think they hate each other. Gods and princes."

"Why?" asked Mitra.

"Because one always curses the other," Aria said. "It's in every story ever written." She tapped the end of her pencil on her desk.

"But Gods make princes, don't they?"

"Yes, and princes hate their Gods."

Mitra returned to her notebook. "*Mah, meh, ham*, and *hayaam*, the moon, the fog, together, and I," she said. She rearranged the words on the page. "I, together, the fog, the moon." Then she rearranged them again. "Together, the moon, I, the fog." As the last bell rang, Mitra slowly collected her papers and pencils, as if under a spell, but Aria was impatient. She wanted to run home.

"Come on, Mouse," she said. That's what she and Hamlet had recently started calling Mitra. "A new episode of *Bonanza* is on!" She pulled on Mitra's shirt.

"I told you not to act so vulgar!" Mitra shouted. She walked to the window to watch Hamlet's new classmates. On the window, the M remained. And written under it, accompanied by a sad face, were two words, *Hokm-mam* (my sentence).

A MONTH LATER, Hamlet was still complaining about his separation from Mitra.

"I have been sentenced by my father to live in eternal shame, in the fiery pits of damnation until the day I die—or at least until I go to university," Hamlet said.

"Is that why you wrote those words?" asked Mitra.

"Wrote what?" said Hamlet.

"Last month. On the window, the first day of school."

"He can't even remember what he had for breakfast today," said Aria. She lay on the bench opposite her two friends in the middle of Melli Park, pretending to do her homework in case Maysi or Mana walked by. Hamlet and Mitra leaned against each other's backs doing homework, which Aria thought was the oddest thing. Her friends had been doing their homework, and she had been pretending to do hers, every day at Mellat Park, which everyone shortened to Melli, for the past month. She wasted her time by strolling around or sketching cartoon characters in her books, always from four in the afternoon until eight, when everyone went home for supper. Nothing had changed in this routine except for the girls' heights as they sprouted, Mitra a little faster, while poor Hamlet remained closer to the earth and felt bad about it. He looked in the mirror every morning, searching for a moustache, yet not even the smallest of follicles had opened above his lips, nor on his chin, nor beside his ears, and while for most Armenian boys this would have been strange, Mitra assured him that, being light-haired, for him these things would take time.

She knew it was said, years ago, that the Qajars had built the park. But then after a while everyone said no, it was Reza Shah, the old shah, the new shah's father, who'd built it to look like the parks in Paris. Now everyone came here. Even the opium dealers. Aria was glad to be with Hamlet and Mitra. She didn't like being in the park alone because she remembered how Bobo would pass through here sometimes, on his walks back from the mountain, moving through these trees.

"We should go away to the sea," Mitra said, as if reading Aria's mind.

"My father says the real sea is the one in the south of France. He says the Caspian isn't real," Hamlet said.

"Your father says too many things," said Aria. "Anyhow, my father said he'll take me up to the Caspian one day."

"We used to go every summer," Mitra said. "Don't your people come from there?" She looked at Hamlet.

"North. More north," Hamlet replied. "And then west."

They were still talking about the sea when they heard the noise. They stood up from their benches for a better look. A crowd was following a bald man with a thick black moustache and a belly that moved independently from the rest of his body. He wore cheap black pants and a white collared shirt that reminded Aria of the kind the men wore in South-City. In the crowd behind this man, Aria could see two other men wearing black suits as well, but unlike the first man, they weren't wearing shoes and their suits had no ties. With these men were three women. All wore black veils.

The man at the centre of the group moved quickly, leaving the others struggling to catch up. It seemed as if the men in bare feet were trying to help the first man, while the women in veils were trying to stop him.

"Mister, don't!" one of the women begged. "In the name of Imam Reza, don't!"

"Think what the Prophet will do if he finds out!" screamed the other woman.

"The Prophet is dead," shouted the bald man, which made the women call out and beg the Prophet for forgiveness. Then all three men, the two barefooted ones and the bald one, stopped and stared in the direction of Aria and her friends.

Before Aria could register what was happening, the men ran toward them.

"Those are your people," said Mitra accusingly, turning to Aria.

The bald man had undone two buttons on his shirt, revealing a tuft of hair that sprang out like grass. For a moment, the children were too scared to run. The man lunged at the three of them, and grabbed the one he wanted. Hamlet went up in the air, and soon he was hanging upside-down by his ankles, where the bald man had a painfully secure grip.

"Run, run, Jamsheed!" one of the barefooted men yelled. The women were screaming again, and now the bald man ran, and Aria and Mitra ran after him, watching Hamlet hang and spring up and down, kicking and yelling.

"Let him go, let him go," Aria shouted as she ran. Mitra was crying too hard to shout. They hadn't got too far before exhaustion set in and the three men were too far off to catch.

"Stop," Aria said then. "Just stop." But Mitra couldn't stop crying. She tried to tell Aria this, but she could not do it. Aria yelled, "I mean stop running. One of them is coming back."

It was one of the women, panting as she neared. And running alongside her was Hamlet, clutching her hand tightly.

"Children!" the woman shouted. "Go tell this boy's father, the Armenian, what happened. Go tell the boss who is friends with the Shah. Hurry, quick! He hasn't paid them in ten weeks. That's why they tried to take the boy. But I can't let them do it. I convinced them to let him go. This time, at least." Her face was beautiful. Aria noticed her eyes were as blue as Turkish tile.

"That's not true about the pay," Mitra said, her voice returned at last. She grabbed Hamlet's arm and pulled him to her side. "Hamlet's father is a fair man."

"He goes to Paris for lunch, with the Shah's wife. Everyone's seen it." The woman's voice was as beautiful as her face, but her accent made Aria wince.

"Anyhow, the Shah is a good man," Mitra continued.

"The Shah put your father in prison," Aria said quickly, turning to her.

"You shut up," Mitra said.

The woman wiped sweat from her forehead and adjusted her veil. "I don't care who is good and who is in prison," she said, glaring at Hamlet. He stared at her wordlessly, still in shock. "Go home to your father, go home to the Armenian." Then she turned back toward the South-City.

Aria and Mitra each took one of Hamlet's arms and ran with him further up North-City. By the time they got all the way north, the sun was setting. They climbed the narrow, cobbled roads of Darakeh up to Niavaran. This was where the Shah had his palace; it was also where the Agassian home was waiting for them. Hamlet hadn't said a word during their journey, but now he broke into a run. The lights were on outside his house and along the endless yard, but inside everything appeared dark. As they neared the front door, they heard it creak open. A tall man, who'd been silhouetted against the vast arched doors, stepped out. His gold wristwatch shone in the night. He quickly walked over to Hamlet and took him in his arms. The boy broke into sobs. The girls shuffled back, afraid, but Mr. Agassian caressed their heads and Aria felt the fear leave her a little for the first time in hours.

"Are you okay?" Mr. Agassian looked at Mitra. "And you?" he said to Aria.

"You know what happened?" Mitra asked.

"Of course I know. Those men phoned my secretary to threaten me before they did it. I told the police to find you kids, but they thought you were at school, not in some park. You shouldn't be in that park anyway, child." He stroked Hamlet's hair and searched the darkness. His voice cracked. "Then they went to the park and you weren't there."

"We were running here," Aria said.

"I can see, child." He sighed. "It will be all right."

"It's those people who work for you. My father says you always have to watch out for the workers," Mitra said.

"Your father has bigger problems, my child," said Mr. Agassian.

"Those men said you haven't paid them for ten weeks," Mitra said.

Mr. Agassian sat on the stairs in front of the door, hugging Hamlet to his side. "Come here," he said to the girls, and pulled them both to his knees. "They haven't even worked for me for ten weeks, my girl." He looked into the darkness. "They want something else."

"They say you spend your money on going to lunch in Paris," Aria said. "With the Shah."

"Not with him, no. But with his sister, his brothers, yes. And sometimes his aunts. Is it wrong to enjoy the money you slaved for?"

"My father says it's wrong," Mitra said.

"Your father has caught the plague of benevolence. Your father also grew up in a house with food in it. Unlike me. If a man works hard he must have the right to reap the rewards, no?" He pulled the girls closer to him. "And I suppose he must also pay the price. But no, girls, I wasn't serious. I don't have lunch in Paris. Maybe his people up there," he looked at the lights that fell over Niavaran Palace and its gardens, "maybe they do such mad things. I go to Paris for business. And it's never him I have lunch with there. Don't let anyone make you believe it. Never the man himself. Each moment that man is away from his country he cries. He flies a plane, all by himself, only to see it from the sky, then settles right back on the soil. He likes feta and bread for lunch, with cucumbers. What garbage do they teach you at school? What nonsense runs through the streets of this country? Folk tales, fairy tales; they've been around for the ages, haven't they?"

The girls liked listening to him, and when he had stopped talking they felt a penetrating emptiness.

"I'm from South-City!" Aria shouted.

Mr. Agassian laughed. "Are you? Well bless the heavens you don't have to sleep there tonight."

"There's nothing wrong with South-City," Aria said.

"Isn't there? All right, I believe you." A light had turned on inside the house. "There's your mother," he said to Hamlet quietly. "Go tell her you are here safe." Hamlet glanced at Aria and Mitra, then nodded at his father.

"Bye," he softly said to the girls, and went inside.

Mr. Agassian waited a moment, then took the girls inside and gave them tea and sweets made from sesame, rosewater, and flower petals.

"Armenians eat the same sweets we do?" Aria asked when he had left the room to check on Hamlet.

"I think so," Mitra said.

They had just finished their third cup of tea, served by Kokab the maid, when Fereshteh walked through the door.

"Mana!" Aria cried.

Mitra's mother was right behind Fereshteh. She clutched her daughter and hugged her. "God be great they didn't take you girls," she said.

Mr. Agassian had returned to the room. "They will do nothing to the girls. With them, they do nothing. If they ever try anything, I'll have their arms broken."

As the adults shared news of the day's shocking events, Aria noticed that Mana mostly kept her silence while Mr. Agassian and Mitra's mother talked rapidly. "We have to go," Mana said after a polite interval, motioning Aria toward her. "Mr. Agassian, please know that if a court matter were to arise over what happened today, I would attest to your character."

Mr. Agassian thanked her. "And apologies that my wife has not joined us. She's staying close to Hamlet." He looked at Aria and Mitra, and said gently, "I'm sure he'll be fine in a day or two."

Fereshteh and Aria left the house hand in hand, and began the walk home. Fereshteh had never learned how to drive. Mitra's mother had offered a ride, but Fereshteh insisted it was unnecessary.

"Will you ever learn to drive, Mana?" Aria asked as they followed the winding roads and descended the hills.

"No," Fereshteh said. "There are some things one doesn't learn on principle."

Aria held Mana's hand, and slowly began to swing it back and forth as the lit trees of Niavaran Palace twinkled behind them. She was reminded of her walks with Bobo, and Aria wondered if right then, at that moment, the Shah was in his bed and if, in his sleep, he was flying over the land and crying while he did so. Or was he maybe somewhere in Rome, dining with beautiful women, his thoughts as far from this place as could be? She weighed the options, the probabilities, the proofs and explanations well into her own dreams, and even there, where all answers and solutions are found, she could not find a single one to solve the riddle.

19

Mrs. Shirazi tried to scrub the plates clean, but her hands ached. Someone had told her she had a disease of the bones, a disease called arthritis. She couldn't remember who had said this. But she did have a faint memory of her own mother with hands and fingers that didn't look normal. She'd been so little then. She wasn't even sure the memory was true. Maybe her brother had told her about her mother's hands. She wondered if Farangeez could clean the dishes, but her daughter had so much to do already. Maybe the other child would come visit again, the one called Aria. In all her years she had never known a girl with that strange name, which Persians often gave to their boys. She sighed. She sometimes forgot her own name these days. When she wasn't called "mother," it was "Mrs. Shirazi." Her husband called her "wife," except when he was angry, when he called her "woman," and when he was kind, "darling." She liked that he addressed her with the plural pronoun. It was so polite. So Persian.

He had endured a great many things, her husband. Things most men had not. He'd waited a long time for her divorce from her first husband. And then he'd been brave enough to marry a woman without a family. The matter of her being previously married was bad enough: she was spoiled and not a virgin. But Hadar had forgiven her transgressions, so maybe she did have some luck in life after all.

When the rich woman came to the door, it had been a great surprise. She had never met a woman like that before, so well spoken, so well dressed. Yes, she had seen wealthy people and had even spoken to them, but Mrs. Ferdowsi was a different breed. Dignified.

When she'd asked Mrs. Ferdowsi how she'd learned about her family, the rich woman had vaguely mentioned the mosque, had said someone there knew about her and her daughters and thought they could use help. But she'd known immediately that Mrs. Ferdowsi was lying, so the two of them had sat down and spoken the truth. And that's why this girl, this Aria, was to come visit her family now and teach the girls to read. It was how she liked to think of it. *I am a poor woman, called Mrs. Shirazi, and I am grateful for your help. You are a good child of God.* Yes, that's how she had decided to think of it. Still, she wondered how the girl, Aria, had found her way to wealth and how Mrs. Ferdowsi had come to possess her. But she did not ask. It was best to not know so many things.

She went upstairs to rest. Her hands ached too much. Her body did, too, from all the children she had birthed; her heart did for other reasons. She stood by the bedroom window for a while. She could see the endless rooftops sprawled across Tehran. The city was becoming more beautiful, even in these parts. So many new trees had been planted, and small creeks still ran through the city with fresh water from the mountains to the north. Sometimes, on good days, the beauty was enough to mute the poverty surrounding them.

She watched the sky and city a while longer until she spotted one of the neighbourhood boys, the Jahanpour child with the cleft lip. Kamran was his name, she remembered. The boy was always in and out of his house, running errands at all hours. He left in the early mornings and she was certain he must work at the Bazaar to help pay his family's way. He was the only child from his building whom she saw regularly. The doors of most of the other apartments were round the back and she never saw people coming or going. She watched him now go inside and then, a few minutes later, come out dressed all in black. She knew he wasn't in mourning, but for some reason he wore black once a month. On those days, he didn't return home until the early hours. She never saw him in the darkness, but she'd notice the light shine through his front door when he opened it. Such strange ways they have, these people, she thought. But she had grown up alongside them, nearly her whole life, and for the most part they were always pleasant and friendly. They seemed to do everything out of kindness. This was true even of that Mrs. Ferdowsi. "We can help you with whatever you need, Mrs. Shirazi," she had said. And the neighbours would offer food at Ashura, saying, "Would your girls like some halva, Mrs. Shirazi?"

She hoped the Jahanpour boy wasn't mixed up in the wrong things. There was too much goodness there to waste, goodness that could be lost so easily. This had been the lesson of her life.

KAMRAN LEFT THE mosque early. He had heard the sermon before, and it bored him. "I work early in the morning," he said to the mollah, who put an understanding hand on his shoulder. This was the same mollah who once suggested he change his name to something more Islamic, something Arabic. "I'll ask my father about it," Kamran had replied. He hadn't, and thankfully the mollah had forgotten the whole thing.

As was his monthly habit, he strolled through the uneventful night, took two buses up north, and walked pensively, with his fists jammed in his coat pockets for warmth. His fingers were stiff, but he held tight to the bracelet all the same. This time he had chosen purple beads. He'd heard somewhere that girls liked purple. The bazaaris did not like it at all. It was the colour of royalty, they said, and spat.

He walked more slowly the closer he got to Aria's home, but when he was twenty feet away he broke into a run, careening at full speed toward the stone gate. The wind whistled past his ears, his chest heaved as air entered and exited his lungs, and he almost crashed into the stone. But at the last moment, with a touch of his right foot, then a lift and a final jump, he swung his arm to grab the top of the gate. It was easy now, and within moments he was at Aria's windowsill. When he peeked inside she was asleep. He wondered what she dreamt about.

He stayed there awhile, back bent and feet balancing on the ledge. The moonlight was about to fall on Aria's face. He remembered their past, how he had taught her to climb trees so well that she had surpassed him and was forever better at it. That was a good thing, he thought. The moonlight inched closer. He took out the bracelet, blowing on his cold fingers. "What would my name be if I were a prophet?" he whispered. "Should I be an Ebrahim or a Mehdi?" Looking at Aria one last time, he said, "You choose. Maybe your dreams will tell you."

He left the bracelet where he always did, half inside the sill and half out, with the window set gently against it. He read the word the beads spelled out one last time to be sure it was correct. "Empress," he said aloud. Maybe she would be an empress one day. Or maybe she would be an actress and play an empress, like in the Indian movies. He said a prayer for her. Just a short one that he had learned at the mosque. He went to mosque more now. Only because the other bazaaris did. They liked to buy and sell and go to mosque and feel angry with the king. He never questioned their frustrations. He knew how hard they worked. They didn't believe the Shah when he told them he'd better their lives with his new idea. The White Revolution, he called it. He would take land from the landowners so that poor people, like the bazaaris, could buy some too. But at the mosque everyone complained about the Shah. "He's only pretending to care about us," they said.

"Maybe if you were Empress you could fix it all," he whispered to Aria.

He lingered there for a few seconds longer before disappearing into the night, his black clothes shielding him from the eyes of the world.

20

Despite the fact that she now had new friends and a home with Mana, Aria remained convinced that nothing good would ever come her way. She played with the new bracelet she'd found on the windowsill that morning. It was her first-ever purple one.

Earlier in the day she had returned to the Shirazi home for one of her scheduled visits, and everything had gone wrong. Mrs. Shirazi had decided to not speak to her. And Farangeez had thrown her out.

"My mother's sick and you're a pain," Fara said.

Aria's frustrations with the Shirazis were only mounting, but nothing would convince Mana to let that family go.

Aria had spent the week before the visit begging her guardian. "Mana, please. They don't want me there."

"Just that one daughter, the one whose heart is heavy. I've talked to Mrs. Shirazi. She's happy to have you. Why don't you speak to her more?"

"She's a mute. She only talks to her daughters and sometimes herself."

But Fereshteh had made her decision. There'd be no arguing. The next Friday came, and Behrouz arrived in the morning to drive her to the Shirazi home.

"They seem like nice people," Behrouz said as they drove.

"I'm the only kid who does this on her day off, you know. And I've got homework. Mitra's gone shopping. Hamlet takes guitar lessons," Aria said.

"The Shirazis seem like nice people," Behrouz repeated, as if he hadn't heard her.

"One of them is. But the oldest girl is evil, and the mother is dirty. The father is stupid."

"We shouldn't speak about people like that, Aria," Behrouz said.

But Aria refused to say another word to him.

When Aria arrived, Roohangeez was waiting with her pencil and two sheets of paper she had borrowed from a neighbour. "Can we write?" she asked as Aria walked through the door. Aria said nothing. Instead, she opened a paper bag and took out the slippers Roohangeez had given her some time ago.

"Here," she said, holding out the slippers. "I still expect my own shoes back one day."

They sat down on the floor of the kitchen. It was the only place with a hard surface that didn't wobble. Roohangeez laid out her pages. She placed her pencil in a perfectly vertical line between them.

"As if she knows anything to teach you," Farangeez said. She'd been standing at the door, silently watching.

"Come learn, Fara," said Roohangeez.

But Farangeez walked away.

Aria began with Roohangeez's name. She spelled out the letters and told the younger girl to copy her.

"No," she said, at the girl's clumsy marks. "That's so wrong. Do it exactly like I did."

Roohangeez tried again, but her mistakes were the same.

"Forget that. Let's start with the alphabet," Aria said. "Aleph,

Beh, Peh, Teh . . ." She wrote the first four letters. "With these two you can write two words. First, *aab*." Roohangeez, watching closely, wrote the word *water*. "And *baba*," Aria said. Roohangeez wrote the word *father*. "Good," said Aria. "We're done." She stood up.

"That's it?"

"I'll teach you more later," Aria said. "If I teach you too much . . ."

As she spoke, Farangeez reappeared and pulled the page out of her sister's hand. She read the words out loud: "Water, father, water, father, water, father." Then, in a mocking voice, she mixed them up. "Wather, fater, wather, fater." Roohangeez began to cry.

Farangeez looked at Aria. "You think helping her write two words is teaching? She won't learn anything." She held up the page and tore it in half.

Mrs. Shirazi entered the kitchen. Aria had hardly paid attention to her on previous visits, and now it felt strange to have her standing so close.

"She was just teaching me how to write," Roohangeez said to her mother, wiping her eyes. Mrs. Shirazi said nothing, but walked over to the counter, where some diced vegetables sat in a bowl. A pot of water was waiting on the stove. She dumped the vegetables into the pot and set it to boil.

"Why doesn't she talk?" Aria whispered to Roohangeez, but Farangeez overheard.

"She doesn't talk to you because you make her sick," Farangeez said.

Roohangeez scowled at her sister. "Mama's pregnant," she said to Aria.

"Is that why she won't talk?" Aria asked.

"I said she's not talking to you because you disgust her," Farangeez said.

Mrs. Shirazi appeared not to have heard. She lowered herself slowly onto the rug on the floor.

"I learned how to spell two words, Mama." Roohangeez ran over to her mother. "I wrote them on that paper." She pointed to the torn pages.

"Good for you," Mrs. Shirazi said. She smiled. Then she looked at Farangeez and smiled at her, too. "My girl, can you please throw those papers in the trash."

Farangeez picked up the papers.

"But she's the one who tore up the paper," Aria said. "And Roohi worked so hard."

Mrs. Shirazi ignored her.

"Do you understand?" Aria tried again. "She tore it up because she hates me. I was only helping. I'm helping because Mana told me to."

Mrs. Shirazi looked at Aria in her quiet way. Then she turned and spoke to Farangeez. "Love, keep your eye on the pot. The water will boil soon." Farangeez nodded. She sat beside her mother and put her head on her shoulder.

"I'll write those words for you again," said Roohangeez, trying to regain her mother's attention. "*Water* and *father.*"

"Of course you will," her mother said with a weak smile. "You've always been my smartest girl. Gohar is my little helper. The baby will be my spirit, and this one is my saviour." She stroked Farangeez's deep black hair. "My little brain is going to read and she'll be amazing at it. Won't you?"

"Your little saviour is trying to stop her from reading," Aria said loudly.

Again, Mrs. Shirazi ignored her, looking down at the floor.

"Shouting isn't helping you," Farangeez said. Her head remained on her mother's shoulder.

Soon the sound of boiling water came from the pot. Farangeez rose to take care of it. She had just turned off the stove when Aria stopped her. "Wait," she said softly. "You're right. Shouting isn't helping. Can I serve that to your mother, please?"

"The bowls are in that cupboard," said Farangeez. "There's a spoon beside the sink."

"Thank you," said Aria. She walked the heavy pot to the counter, fetched a bowl from the cupboard, and poured the soup into it. With the spoon she stirred, then blew onto the surface. "Shouldn't be too hot," she said, looking straight at Mrs. Shirazi.

But Mrs. Shirazi was still staring at the floor.

Aria walked the bowl toward her. "Hope you enjoy, missus," she said. Then she took a deep breath, stepped back, and flung the bowl at Mrs. Shirazi.

Instinctively, Mrs. Shirazi looked up and tried to catch the bowl mid-air. She held out her hands, but as the object came closer she seemed to change her mind. She turned her head and used those same hands to cover her face. The bowl crashed and shattered beside her feet. Pieces of clay flew across the kitchen, and the hot soup covered her hands, making them burn, then blister.

Farangeez grabbed a cloth and ran outside to the water basin in the courtyard. She pumped dirty water onto the cloth and sped back inside. Mrs. Shirazi was breathing heavily but made no other sound. Farangeez threw the damp cloth over her mother's burnt hands and Roohangeez ran forward to help, too. She tried frantically to blow cool air over the cloth, but her sister pushed her away.

"Stop it. That won't help," Farangeez yelled.

Aria stood unmoving. "I hope you burn just as badly in hell," she said stonily. Then she waited for the hands of justice to deal her punishment. But nothing happened, and no one paid her the least bit of attention. Mrs. Shirazi now wept quietly as her daughters ran back and forth for more water to cool her raw skin.

Eventually her rage left her, and Aria became aware of the depth of villainy that had come from within her, without reason or cause. And so, she ran. She ran out the green gates, through the alleyways, past beggar families and opium dealers and tin-can sellers, until she found Pahlavi Street and ran through its chaos. She ran as fast and far as she could, up, up, up toward the mountains of Alborz, heading north. She ran until she couldn't anymore, at which point she spotted a bus stop across the street, and hopped on as others were shuffling past, hoping the driver wouldn't see her. The bus took her most of the way home, and as she sat still, her hands trembled. An old lady smiled at her, but Aria didn't smile back. When at last they reached the centre of the city, she hopped off and ran some more, trying to shed the fever of the day. She ran past Amir-Abad Square, the police station, and the cafés. As she skirted the edges of Lycée Razi, for a split-second her thoughts shifted into French before returning to the thousand spiteful words that had left Zahra's lips, describing so thoroughly all the ways in which Aria was wicked and foul. These came tumbling back to her in her mother tongue, and so she ran even farther and faster for what seemed like hours until she reached Ferdowsi Square and saw the familiar old French doors, and the brick and silver of Fereshteh's hundred-year-old compound.

Once inside, Aria hurried upstairs and closed the door to her room. The echoes of traffic, car horns and angry screams, filled her room. She slammed her window shut. Then she paced for a while, until her anger boiled over again and she kicked the wall. She stood back and fixed her eyes on the hole she had made. There was a piece of plaster clinging to it. She finished it off with another kick.

Fereshteh knocked on the door.

"I made a hole in the wall!" Aria shouted. She didn't open her door. Maybe Mana would throw her out, and she'd be back on the streets again, or sent to live with Zahra or even Mrs. Shirazi, whose hands she had just burned. There was a silence, but Aria knew Fereshteh was still outside in the hall. She locked her gaze on the door and drew a deep breath. "I burned her hands," she shouted. "I threw boiling water on her."

"No one could have deserved that," Fereshteh said. But her voice was gentle.

Aria sat on her bed, thinking for a minute. Then she stood up and opened the door.

"There's a hole in the wall," she said, and pointed at it. She slumped on her bed again.

Fereshteh stared at the wall, then turned to look at Aria.

"You're going to kick me out now, aren't you," Aria said.

"Tell me, whose hands did you burn?" Fereshteh asked.

"I'm never going back there again. I don't care what you say."

"Did you hurt the children?" Fereshteh persisted.

"I might next time. If you send me back there. This time it was Mrs. Shirazi."

"Well, I am certainly sending you back there," Fereshteh said. "First thing in the morning. You're not to go to school. You're to go back there and apologize. This is nazri, Aria. Which means: Do good to those who hurt you. In this way, God will always protect you. And nothing bad will ever happen to you."

"I burned her. Her hands turned red and blistered," Aria said. Her eyes welled with tears. "I hate her, Mana."

Fereshteh walked to the door, then stood for a moment without moving. Slowly, she turned around. "That's why you're not to go to school for a week. Every morning you are to go and beg for their forgiveness. Those poor souls, those poor souls."

"No!" Aria yelled.

But Fereshteh was calm. And calmly she said, "I will not lose another child." She shut the door and walked away.

EARLY THE NEXT morning, Aria rang the broken bell of the Shirazi home. The green gates to the courtyard were open and so she entered. It was cleaner than the day before; someone had been sweeping. She walked up the few stairs to the front door, but before she could knock, Farangeez opened it. She looked at Aria, spat in her face, and slammed the door shut.

Aria wiped away the spit. A moment later, Roohangeez opened the door. "Hello, Ari," she said. Her voice was so faint that Aria could barely hear her. Her dark eyes and olive skin looked even darker in the sunlight, and like Farangeez, she had a fold of skin under her eyes that made it look as if she were smiling all the time. For the first time, Aria noticed she had a dimple, too, at the corner of her mouth. "Mama's okay but she can't touch anything," Roohangeez said.

"Can I come in?" Aria asked.

But Farangeez had shoved her way in front of Roohangeez, holding little Gohar's hand. "No, you can't," she said. "And Roohi, hurry up." She grabbed her hand, too, and led both sisters down the courtyard. Roohangeez turned and waved. "We're going shopping. Because Mama can't touch anything. Bye." The three sisters disappeared beyond the gates, wearing only slippers for shoes.

Aria waited, unsure what to do. After a moment, she tried to peek through a nearby window, but it was too high up. Another window to her left had a wooden board nailed to its frame, blocking her view. Broken glass clung to its edges. She knocked on the door, at first softly, then more boldly. Then just as she was about to give up and leave, Mrs. Shirazi opened it, using a cloth to hold the doorknob. Her hands were bright pink, and a layer of skin was peeling off them.

Aria could not look away. *What have I done?* she thought.

With her foot, Mrs. Shirazi opened the door wider and retreated inside. Aria followed.

Mrs. Shirazi sat on one of the dusty rugs in the main room. A bowl of peeled and diced cucumbers was at her side. She dipped one hand in. Moments later she switched hands.

Aria sat down, as far from Mrs. Shirazi as she could. "Mana told me to come apologize," she said. "She says I have a temper."

Mrs. Shirazi said nothing, and her eyes were as quiet as the day before.

"Do your hands hurt?" Aria asked.

Mrs. Shirazi did not reply.

"I only got angry because Roohi is really smart and Farangeez was teasing her, and . . ." She stopped. Mrs. Shirazi was looking away, not even listening to her.

"You teach my girls to read," Mrs. Shirazi said at last. "You teach them how to leave this life." She was not looking at Aria, but gazing into the courtyard.

"That's what I was trying . . ."

"Not about books. Not about words. About people. Teach them about the kind of people you're with now. Those upper-crust sorts of people. Teach them to read those people."

Aria looked into the courtyard now too, wondering if something was out there. She could see nothing unusual. "Those people aren't any different from anyone else," she said.

"Teach my girls to read people," Mrs. Shirazi said again.

Aria turned her gaze back to Mrs. Shirazi, taking in how pale her skin was. Her body was small, but it was hard to get a sense of her real shape under her thin veil. The veil itself was flower-patterned and fragile, like the ones Maysi wore, and not at all like the thick black ones other women in the area wore. She breathed heavily, as though she was trying to force life out of herself, but life kept forcing itself back in. "There isn't any other use for you but that," she said, and her voice was cold, full of nothing.

Aria felt a sudden pain in her chest. This time she couldn't keep her tears from falling. She cried as Mrs. Shirazi spoke: "So many other babies die. They die all the time. Dogs eat them. Eagles carry them away. They starve. But my babies have lived. So they might as well learn how to read, how to figure things out." She sat silent for a while. Then she turned and finally looked at Aria. Her eyes were like daggers. "I bet you could have died, too, like so many others, but like the rest of us you've been left here to infest and fester, like a maggot, no?" She stared at Aria until a smile broke on her face and she began to laugh. Then her laughter turned into a cackle, hard and loud.

As if released from a spell, Aria shot up and once again raced out the door. She pushed the metal gates so hard they flew back and beat against the brick walls. She ran down the alley, but at the end of it, confused, she pulled up short. For a moment she had thought Mrs. Shirazi was going to kill her. Now she wiped her tears and turned in her spot, unsure what to do. Behind her was the house, its green gates still swinging. In the alley, she felt a thousand eyes upon her. She spotted a mulberry tree across the road and went over to it, dodging a motorcycle that was bearing down the alley. It swerved and just missed her. She tucked her small body behind the tree, and there she sat and cried, deep into the day.

In the late afternoon, still hidden in her spot, she saw a figure step out from behind the gates. It was a woman cloaked in a veil

with the same flower pattern, blue and white, that she had seen on
Mrs. Shirazi that morning. The woman was looking at the ground
as she walked, as if ashamed to face the world.

Aria followed her, deep into the city centre. They moved
through the bazaar, navigating its maze-like pathways, dodging
the merchants and shoppers. She caught sight of a boy with a cleft
lip and, thinking for a second that it was Kamran, almost called
out. But the boy disappeared quickly from sight. Minutes passed
like hours. Finally, early evening light broke through the clouds
and Aria could see that Mrs. Shirazi had found a way out of the
bazaar. Again she followed, and soon realized they were on Pahlavi
Street, and that Mrs. Shirazi was headed north.

Aria shadowed Mrs. Shirazi for an hour longer, walking past
Behjat-Abad, and then north-west, all the way to Youssef-Abad
Square. Something about this place felt familiar to Aria. She
searched her memory, and at last came the story Behrouz had
often told her: it was here, near this square, where he had found
her among the trash, beside a row of mulberry trees. Was this the
first time she'd come back after all these years? Aria looked
around at the roads and the shops and the old buildings, testing
her memory to see if anything from her infancy remained. But
nothing was familiar.

Nightfall was close now. Mrs. Shirazi walked along a side road
and turned onto an older street. Aria looked up to read the sign:
15th Street. At last, Mrs. Shirazi stopped before what looked like
the oldest building on the street. It stood separate and bigger from
its neighbours, and didn't look like a house at all. Its mortar, brick,
and stone were crumbling. Iron gates clanked and squealed as
Mrs. Shirazi opened them and went inside. Others were entering,
too. Aria spotted gold letters written above the gates: "Kenisah
Sukkot Shalom." She didn't recognize any of those words. Maybe

they were words for students older than she was. She waited a while after Mrs. Shirazi had disappeared into the building before walking inside with a group of others.

She found herself in a great hall, its floor covered in Persian rugs, some of them twenty-feet long. She counted twelve large chandeliers, each with thirty crystal bulbs hung in a perfect pattern from the golden ceilings. The walls were decorated with old mosaics, hexagons and octagons, painted in gold leaf. At the head of the hall were giant wood doors, as tall as the walls themselves, with large iron hinges. As Aria took in the sights, she realized she had lost Mrs. Shirazi. She was scanning the hall for a glimpse of a blue-and-white flowered veil when a man tapped her shoulder.

"Upstairs," the man said, pointing.

Aria smiled. "Thank you." She turned her head to look upstairs but still didn't see anyone she knew. When she turned back, the man was gone. But then she understood: On the floor of the hall, everyone was either a man or a boy. She looked upstairs again. Yes, that was where the women were, watching patiently from the seats, gazing down on the chaos below.

Aria climbed the stairs, and when she reached the mezzanine, she saw Mrs. Shirazi sitting in the farthest corner, all alone. Aria went to the edge of the balcony and looked down. She chuckled a little when she saw the strange hats the boys and the men were wearing. Half-hats that covered only the middle of their heads.

"Why are they wearing such silly hats?" she said aloud. A woman nearby shushed her. At just that moment, a man down below with a long beard and blue-white robe walked to the head of the hall. The building fell silent. Then the man began chanting in a language Aria did not understand. But she knew that whatever he was singing, it was a kind of prayer, and it was not a prayer from Islam.

—

WHEN ARIA GOT home a little later that evening, she ran immediately to the kitchen. Maysi and Fereshteh were sitting together at the table.

"I followed her!" Aria said, almost out of breath. "She goes to a temple. That's why they wouldn't take the Quran as a gift." She felt as if she had discovered a lost treasure. "Mana, I followed her . . . Mrs. Shirazi. I followed her to a temple."

"What do you mean, child?" Fereshteh asked. Her face had fallen.

"Mrs. Shirazi . . . I went to Youssef-Abad. The place where Bobo found me when I was a baby. There's a temple there . . . Something Shalom."

Fereshteh glanced up at the old English clock on the wall, another gift from the previous queen. "Is that why you're so late? It's dark out. We were worried."

"It's half past eight, Madame," Maysi said. She turned to Aria. "How many times have we told you? It's far too late for you to be wandering around, child. Did you even have anything to eat?"

"But tell me again," said Fereshteh. "Where did you go?" Her voice was shaking.

Aria had sped home and was still breathless, and now she was confused by this strange reaction to her news. "I told you," she said. "I followed Mrs. Shirazi. She went to a temple, the big one in Youssef-Abad. Kenisah Shalom–something. A Kenisah is a temple, right?"

"A synagogue," Maysi said, and she picked up a knife and began to chop celery.

Aria glanced at Fereshteh. The colour had left her face.

"Synagogue, synagogue," Maysi said again, shaking her head and chopping a stalk each time she said the word.

"What's wrong?" Aria asked.

"You're not to go back to that family again," Fereshteh said, her voice sharp.

"Why, I thought you wanted me to—"

"I said: You are not to go back there again. I don't want them teaching you their religion. You must be a good Muslim. That is all."

Fereshteh stood up stiffly and her chair legs screeched on the floor. She came toward Aria and knelt in front of her. "Look at me." She took Aria's face in both her hands. "Let me see your eyes." She studied Aria's face, from her nose to her lips to her chin, to the forehead and curve of her cheeks.

"We're going to mosque tomorrow," she said. She combed her fingers through Aria's crimson hair. She cupped Aria's face again and shook it. "Do you hear me? First thing tomorrow. Understand? And you will never go see those people again. I will not lose another child."

21

"If the mother's a Jew, the daughters are Jews. It's all over them, like skin on bone," Maysi said as she cleaned the rice. "Lucky for them, it's easy to turn Muslim. Not much fuss to it."

"What is a Jew?" Aria asked.

"A soul. Like any other soul," said Maysi. "But doomed."

"Mrs. Shirazi and her daughters are doomed?"

"Everybody's doomed." Maysi shuffled through the kitchen. Her mind was elsewhere.

After Aria helped prepare dinner, Maysi sent her off to find something else to do. Upstairs, in the old music room, Mr. Jafar was tinkering with the piano. It had become his new obsession. He would lightly tap a key and tune a string until it sounded right. He had been on this one key, D flat, for twenty days. This obsession, thought Aria, was almost as bad as when he took to cleaning coins and washing dollar bills.

Usually, Aria didn't spend much time talking to him. Sometimes he'd stay with Mana, other times with his younger brother. But lately, given his fixation on the piano, he had been living here. Now she watched him from the doorway of the music room. His hair was beginning to whiten, and his pants were too big. He had grown skinny because the days would pass and he'd forget to eat.

"I think it sounds good now," she said, leaning against the doorway.

Startled, Mr. Jafar turned around. "Oh yeah?" he asked. "Listen well." He tapped on his one key over and over. "You sure?" He brought his right ear close to the ivory. "I feel like—"

"It sounds fine," Aria interrupted. "I have a question. What's a Jew?"

"What's that, now? A Jew? Here we have a different name. *Kalimi*. We call them Kalimis in this country."

"Why?" she said.

Mr. Jafar shook his head. "Don't know. Started somewhere in Shiraz or Yazd, I think. Could be a Yazdi dialect. The children of Esther." He tapped the ivory several times. "You know any?"

"I might," Aria said.

For a moment Mr. Jafar forgot about his perfect note. He looked around the room, reached into his pocket, and pulled out a coin, one toman. It was big. He took his handkerchief from his chest pocket and began to polish it. "Well, hmm. I don't know what to say," he said.

"I only wondered," Aria said, "if you know anything else about them? Who's Esther?"

"A princess, from long ago. The Kalimi have been in this country for a long time, longer than the Muslims. The only people who've been here longer are us."

"Us?" Aria said.

"My family's kind. Oh, but we can't talk about that. Fereshteh hates all that. God is God at the end of the day." He returned to his ivory, polishing the same black D-flat key before tapping it again.

"What kind? What does she hate?" Aria asked over the noise, but he ignored her, and she left him to his quest for perfection.

◇

A MONTH LATER, school broke for the New Year. From her bedroom window, Aria listened to the sounds of car horns and the
hum of engines. In her mind, these were now mixed inextricably
with the smell of cherry blossoms. The extended family came to
celebrate: Nasreen and Mammad and their twin boys, Uncle Jafar,
and Molook and Shahlah and Shahnaz. Maysi had set the Haft-
Seen, the Table of the Seven S's: vinegar, sumac, coins, garlic,
wheat-germ samanu, grass, and the fruit of the senjed tree—also
known as the Russian olive. All these had been set out with hyacinths, apples, and objects that began with the letter S. There were
goldfish, too, in a giant fishbowl. A mirror, almost as big as Aria,
sat at the head of the table, reflecting it all. This, she knew, was all
part of the old Zoroastrian religion. She had learned about it at
school. But hardly anyone was really Zoroastrian anymore.

"Why do we still celebrate this way if everyone is Muslim
now?" Aria had asked Maysi while she cooked.

"Because everyone is still secretly Zoroastrian. Just don't let
the Prophet know it." Maysi winked.

"Hamlet's celebrating, and he's Christian," Aria said.

"Don't matter what you are."

"Would Kalimis celebrate it?"

"Everyone. They have their own New Year, too. Kippur. Kippur,
I think."

"Even Mrs. Shirazi and her daughters?"

Fereshteh was across the room arranging a vase of flowers.
When she heard that name, she paused. Aria caught her eye.

"Don't talk about them anymore," Maysi said softly.

At dinner, Aria noticed that Nasreen and Mammad sat close
together, whispering. Nasreen was angry about something. She

finally broke away from her husband and addressed Fereshteh. "You know," she said, "there's apparently something in the law that says a woman can't adopt without a husband."

Mammad stepped in. "That's right, sister. How do you plan to adopt the girl when you have no husband?"

"There's time yet. Don't rush the woman," Maysi said, as she placed food on the table.

"The Shah's changing all that anyway," Molook added. "With his White Revolution."

"We learn about that at school," Aria said. "The White Revolution." She looked around the table and everyone stared back at her.

"Very good," Fereshteh said.

Aria wasn't finished. "One thing we don't learn about, though, is Jews and Zoroastrians. Anybody know about that? Because I hear you're all Zoroastrians."

A breath would have cracked the room like thunder. The children stared at Aria with open mouths. Nasreen and Uncle Mammad put down their forks. Madame Molook stared at her plate. The only person who kept eating was Uncle Jafar, as if he hadn't a care in the world.

Fereshteh sent Aria to bed without dinner and without the gold coins she was supposed to receive for the New Year.

"You should have slapped her hard on that rosy face of hers," Nasreen said, after Aria ran upstairs in tears. "Who is Zoroastrian here? I want to know. My husband's name is Mohammad; his brother over there is Jafar. Who is Zoroastrian? You women of this family may have your stupid Farsi names, but who?"

"Nasreen, don't be silly. Your name is Farsi, too," Uncle Mammad said.

"It is not. It is not at all," Nasreen said. "Both of you close your ears," she admonished her children, but Hossein and Hassan laughed at their mother. "We're going to mosque first thing in the morning. Wrap it up, wrap it up, maid." She looked at Maysi and motioned to the Haft-Seen. "Take that nonsense off that table."

Maysi rolled her eyes and left for the kitchen. "When the head is wrong, all hope is lost," she mumbled.

"There is no way I will let that child have this house," Nasreen said. She looked at Mammad. "You tell your sister that, husband. We're getting lawyers. In fact, we've got them already. My sons will have this house if it kills me."

THAT NIGHT, FERESHTEH had two nightmares. In the first, a man with a top hat and cane and the legs of a goat walked backward into her room. He peered over his shoulder and smiled. Soon, his smile turned to laughter. A second later, he was standing on the mattress at the foot of her bed. A second after that his face was leaning into hers as she looked up at him.

"I will eat the eyes of all your children," he said.

She tried to scream but couldn't. The goat-man jumped to the window ledge and threw himself off. When she got up to see where he had fallen, he popped up behind her, then disappeared again. Back in bed, she looked across the room into her vanity mirror and saw his face looking back at her.

In the second dream, she was walking down a path on a cool autumn day, wearing her nightgown. Leaves, green and yellow, flew about her in the wind. On each side of the path was an endless row of mulberry trees. She looked as far down the row as she could, and there she saw Aria, walking toward her, smiling. In her arms, Aria carried something—a bundle. As Fereshteh got closer, it was clear the bundle was a baby. She finally reached them. Aria held the baby out.

"It's yours," Aria said. "Your son, Ali. Remember him?"

Fereshteh felt a terrible pain in her chest. She took her son. He was just as she remembered him, his round face full of life. Then that same face began to turn black as charcoal. It happened so fast it burned Fereshteh's hand. She couldn't hold on and dropped the bundle. The baby fell to the earth and caught fire. Fereshteh looked to Aria for help, but the little girl had turned into charcoal, too, then burst into flames.

"Told you," a voice behind Fereshteh said.

She turned around. It was Mahmoud. But he was not like he'd been when he left. This was the same boy she remembered from her youth, the boy riding his bicycle, sweating hard, and smiling when he saw her.

"Told you it would happen," he said again.

She reached out for him, but he shuffled back. When she looked down, Fereshteh saw his legs. They were goat legs. Mahmoud laughed, then turned and galloped off as far down the path as she could see.

THAT SAME NIGHT, while Fereshteh was having her nightmares, Aria climbed out of her bedroom window and hopped down the single storey onto Shah Reza Street. She took a bus as far south as she could, walked through the Bazaar, then took another two buses when she couldn't walk any farther. Finally, she arrived at the Shirazi home. There, she waited at the green gates for the sun to rise.

When it was light enough, Aria walked through the gates without fuss. She tried to look inside the cracked window by the door, but once again the board hid too much. She went around the back, and there she saw a small shed with a tin roof. The door of the shed was open, and as she went toward it a rat ran out. She reached up; she could just touch the roof of the shed. She managed to climb up and, from there, hopped onto a ledge where there was another broken window. This was the window to the girls' room. She peeked inside and saw little Gohar, asleep under a thin blanket. Aria fiddled with the window and soon freed it from its seal. She slowly slid it open. Gohar murmured in her sleep but did not wake.

Mattresses and sheets were sprawled across the floor. Aria stepped onto them with her muddy shoes, rationalizing to herself that they were already dirty. She could hear the rest of the family downstairs. She crept to the edge of the stairs and tried to peer into the main room. She could only see a corner. It looked like they were having breakfast, huddled around a blanket. She could see Mr. Shirazi's back, and one of the older girls' elbows. She climbed down a few stairs, but one creaked and she stood very still. The voices didn't stop. She stepped onto the next stair carefully. In the corner, beside the door, several feet from where the family was eating, she saw the Haft-Seen. It was all there—the correct herbs, plants, even the gold coins. Aria wondered how the Shirazis had managed to find gold. They even had the necessary goldfish. She counted seven—but that was too many. There was supposed to be one goldfish for each person in the family, Maysi had told her. But here there were seven, one more than was needed. She stepped down again, nearing the bottom stair. Because the staircase was winding, she remained out of view—which also meant she couldn't see the Shirazis anymore. They were eating in silence. She walked quietly over to the Haft-Seen, dipped a finger in the goldfish bowl, and made a spiral in the centre. The fish scattered.

"What horrible lives you have," Aria whispered to them. She cupped one in her hand, but the fish flopped frantically. She examined the rest of the table, feeling calm as she inhaled the scent of the hyacinths. She picked up the cup holding the gold coins and realized her mistake. These were simple rials; someone had painted them yellow. She smelled the garlic and drew her face away. She'd forgotten how hungry she was.

"What are you doing?" an angry voice said. Aria whirled around.

It was Farangeez. "We have a thief in the house," she said loudly, so the others could hear.

Eventually, after exclaiming over her and asking questions that Aria refused to answer, they offered her breakfast.

"I'm okay," she said. "Full." She tapped her belly. But minutes later, sitting around the spread, she said, "Mind if I have a piece of bread?"

Roohangeez passed her one.

"I just wanted to see you all. It's been a while," Aria said breezily. She snuck a look at Mrs. Shirazi's hands. The skin was pink and wrinkled, but the burn mark was still there. Mrs. Shirazi's belly was also much bigger. Aria understood what that must mean. She imagined the tiny baby floating inside.

"How did you get in?" asked an amused Mr. Shirazi, sipping his tea. "You're a confident one, aren't you." He had a cube of sugar lodged into his cheek to sweeten his tea, and this made his voice sound deeper than it was. It scared Aria a little.

"Through the window," Aria said. "I stepped over Gohar."

At the mention of her youngest, Mrs. Shirazi lowered her eyes.

Her husband fidgeted and said, "She just has a little cold. She'll be over it soon."

"Will she come down for breakfast?" Aria asked. She put the bread back on the table.

"Go ahead and eat it, child," Mr. Shirazi said. "Gohar has no appetite right now. Maybe she'll be down for supper."

Aria slowly drew the bread back to her lips and took a bite. It hurt her as it went down, but not in the throat. It hurt her somewhere deep in her chest, then deep in her stomach, even though she knew the bread itself had not reached that far.

"I'm sorry," she said, when she had finished eating.

Mrs. Shirazi looked away.

"One doesn't apologize for eating," said Mr. Shirazi.

"No. I meant . . . I'm sorry . . ."

"This is your home," he said. "One doesn't apologize for breaking into one's own home."

Aria turned red. Mr. Shirazi stared hard at his wife, and then at Farangeez. Mrs. Shirazi looked away again, wrapping her veil around her face.

"One also doesn't stay away from one's home for so long," Mr. Shirazi finished.

"Where did you go?" Roohangeez asked.

"She hates us," Farangeez said, waiting for Aria to agree.

"Are you poor because you're Jewish?" Aria asked quickly, and regretted her words the moment she spoke.

Mrs. Shirazi stood and walked upstairs without a word. Her two daughters watched her.

"You're Satan," Farangeez said, and ran after her mother.

"Is that why we are poor?" Roohangeez looked at her father.

Mr. Shirazi took another sip of his tea and allowed it to combine with the remaining sugar-cube crumbs in his mouth. He shook his head calmly, then spoke. "Doubt that has much to do with it." He stroked his daughter's hair.

"Mana told me she refused to have another dead child. She told me not to come back here," Aria said, looking from father to daughter.

"Well, if anyone's going to have another dead child, it is us," Mr. Shirazi said. His voice was heavy and sad, and his eyes flickered toward the stairs, but he willed them back to focus on Aria.

"Is your daughter sick because you are poor or because you are Jewish? Maysi says you're lost souls."

Before Mr. Shirazi could answer, Mrs. Shirazi returned downstairs, alone. Farangeez had stayed in the room with her sister.

Mrs. Shirazi walked slowly to the kitchen. A plate of feta cheese was on the counter, and this she cut into blocks. She sliced some cucumber into a bowl, then dropped a few walnuts on top. She placed bread beside the blocks of feta, then set the plate and the bowl in front of Aria. "Eat," she said.

She walked around the spread and sat directly across from Aria. "Eat," she said again. Her voice was hard.

Aria didn't move. "I have to teach the girls," she said. "They haven't had lessons in a month."

"Eat first, girl," said Mr. Shirazi.

But Aria turned to Roohangeez. "I'll teach you how to spell the S words on the Haft-Seen," she said.

22

As the next few years passed, Hamlet would walk home from school carrying Mitra's books for her, and as he walked, he sometimes remembered the day he had almost been kidnapped from Melli Park. He laughed at the thought, but also developed a habit of cocking his head sideways and checking behind himself.

The books he carried now were the ones needed for the second year of high school. They were heavier than last year's books, and he reflected that this was the price one paid for being fifteen, and old enough to drive, although neither he nor Mitra did drive, yet.

"Did you see your father at the prison again?" he asked Mitra. She noticed him struggling and took two of the books to carry herself. He steadied himself. "Thanks," he said.

"He got out last week," Mitra said.

"Why didn't you say so?"

"It's not a big deal. And he always gets arrested again six months later," Mitra replied. But her voice wavered and she looked as if she might cry.

"It is a big deal. Maybe this time it'll be different."

"You don't know my father. He can't keep his mouth shut like yours."

"I don't think my father has any reason to open his mouth," Hamlet said.

"True. All is well in the Agassian world. Diamonds aren't oil. Nobody pays attention to them."

"The smart people do." Hamlet smiled, and Mitra shoved her two books back into his arms.

"Is your servant taking you home, Mouse?" Aria said from behind them.

Mitra turned around. Aria was the only one who still called her Mouse. She knew this was Aria's defence against the other girls, who called her Rat. Mice were cuter, Aria always said when Mitra protested. Mitra had learned to live with it.

"As a matter of fact, he is," Mitra said, looking at Hamlet.

"Shut up, you two," Hamlet said.

"Carry mine, then?" Aria tossed her lone book toward the pile in his arms. Hamlet moved to catch it, dropping the others. The girls laughed.

"Let's help this poor kid, Mouse." Aria stooped to pick up the books, and Mitra reluctantly did the same. "My hands are dirty now," she said.

"Not as dirty as your mind," Aria said.

"You're disgusting. Hamlet, she's disgusting," Mitra said.

"Hey, if you're going to come to my place today, you can't talk like that," said Hamlet.

"She's coming, too?" Mitra asked.

Hamlet shrugged.

"He invited me," Aria proclaimed, a wide grin on her face.

Mitra shoved her books back into Hamlet's arms. "Glad you let me know." She walked ahead of him and Hamlet ran to catch up. Aria trailed behind. She liked how Hamlet teased Mitra. It reminded her of Kamran and the insults he and she would hurl at each other.

A lot about Hamlet reminded her of Kamran, even though the two of them looked nothing alike and didn't even practise the same religion. Kamran was thin and frail, and his dark skin had an olive tint to it. Hamlet was fairer, and his hair was straight and perfectly cut. His walk was different, too, with its bouncing steps. Kamran's feet had landed so heavily that sometimes Aria thought he might break the pavement. But so much in his manner was similar to Hamlet's. She laughed as she watched Hamlet circle Mitra, who was always nervous, always upset with something or someone. Her face hinted at some kind of upset even now. Aria watched Mitra's lips move, and crept closer to try to decipher her whispers.

"I can't believe you're letting her in your house," Mitra was saying in a low voice. "She'll embarrass us."

"It'll be fine. My parents are in Paris anyway. Only Kokab and the gardener are home. Anyhow, you're obsessed with being embarrassed. Embarrassment embarrasses you. Is she not your friend?"

"Yes, but . . ." Mitra walked faster. "I'm just saying she says things. Wrong things."

"It doesn't matter. You know, for someone whose father is a communist, you sure don't live up to your family heritage."

"Shhh, shut up." Mitra looked around. "People will hear you." She caught Aria's eye. Aria winked. Mitra turned to face Hamlet again. "Fine, invite her over. But we've been trying to teach her manners for years and she still can't say a proper hello."

"Hey! What's that?" Aria called out suddenly.

Mitra whipped around. "What's *what*?"

"That." Aria pointed.

The three of them stared across the street, at the point where Ferdowsi Square merged with Shah Reza Street. It was a busy intersection with criss-crossing cars that, in the absence of clear rules, always looked as if they were about to crash into each other.

Today, a lone figure, dressed head to toe in red, was trying to cut in front of the vehicles. Even her purse and shoes were red, and her brown hair flew out behind her. For a while, the cars refused to stop, but they were forced to come to a screeching halt when the woman held up a hand.

"She's mad," Aria said. "They're going to kill her."

"No, they aren't," said Mitra. "Let's go."

Aria grabbed her friend's arm. "What do you mean? Look at her."

"She's been doing that for years. She lives in that square. If she hasn't died yet, she won't die now."

"Have you seen her before?" Aria asked, turning to Hamlet.

Hamlet nodded. "A few times, with Kokab. I told you about her once. But we were always in a car when we saw her."

Aria stared at the woman again. "She's really mad. Why is she doing that?"

Now Mitra shook her arm free. "Let's go. We'll be late. You can't be late to Hamlet's house. Or did he not tell you that?"

"I want to talk to her."

"No," cried Mitra. "She's crazy. Can't you see? She'll hurt you."

Cars honked in unison and slammed on their brakes. The woman had decided to stand in the middle of the road.

"She's looking for something," Aria said.

"She does that a lot. We told you." Hamlet pulled Aria away. He eventually hailed a cab and the three of them rode in silence the rest of the way to his home.

AT HAMLET'S HOUSE, Aria said little and refused to eat dinner.

"What is wrong with you?" Mitra demanded. "You can't act like that here. It's fine to sulk at your own place, but not here."

Aria looked around the room, trying to think of something nice to say. "They're pretty," she said, pointing to the marble columns. "And those are nice, too." She gestured at the gold flowers that were carved and etched into the walls, running along the halls and winding into the rooms. She glanced a moment at the pool outside, its water turning deep blue as night settled in. But not the blue of the water, the gold on the walls, nor the pearl white of the marble could make her forget the woman she had seen.

"I want to know why that woman was in the square," she said to Mitra after dinner, when Hamlet had gone to fetch something in his room.

"It's not important," Mitra said. "You nitpick over the silliest things but never worry about how you behave at school or in a place like this. You're a mystery, Aria Bakhtiar."

"At least I don't look like a wet mouse," Aria said.

Mitra managed a laugh. "I wonder, too, about that woman sometimes," she said. "But she's mad, very crazy. No use talking to her. People say she speaks only gibberish."

They were laughing again when Hamlet joined them. He passed Mitra a notebook. "Here. I finished it for you."

"You're doing her homework for her?" said Aria. "I was only kidding about you being her servant, you know."

"It's just grammar. A stupid waste of time," Mitra said. "And Hamlet offered."

"She's never in school on Thursdays when we have that class," Hamlet explained. "She's missed all the work."

Aria was unimpressed. "Yeah, I know she's visiting her father in prison. Maybe I should get arrested and you can do my homework for me?"

"That's not funny," Hamlet said. "I'd like to see your parents in prison."

Aria grabbed a book from the pile on the table. "Sorry," she said. But Mitra was busy writing something and paid her no attention. It was only later, when Mitra left the room for a moment, that Aria could sneak a peek. And what she saw, in bright red ink, wasn't writing at all, but a portrait of the woman from earlier that day, with brown hair blowing in the wind as cars charged her like bulls at a matador's cape.

THE NEXT DAY it was raining hard when four men came to the door of Mitra's house. Mitra looked out her bedroom window and saw them standing below, on the front stairs. She summoned Maziar, and her brother ran to the front window.

"I see them," he called up to her.

Mitra ran downstairs. "Where's Baba?"

"In the kitchen," Maziar said.

"It's bad this time. There are four of them." Mitra peeked through the curtain for a better look. All four secret agents were wearing suits. She ran to her father.

"It's the SAVAK. They're outside again. What did you do this time?"

"It's all right, love." Her father dried his hands with a rag. He straightened his shirt collar as he looked at his reflection in the kitchen window.

"I haven't shaved yet," he said wistfully. "Bring your brother to the kitchen, and stay here." He opened a drawer, pulled out a box of sweets, and took the lid off. From beneath a layer of biscuits he pulled out a plastic bag.

"Money's all in here." He gave it to Mitra. "Your mother will be a while coming back. That's good. You may not be able to see me for some time." He kissed her forehead, and Maziar ran to him. He grabbed his son and hugged him hard.

The agents pounded on the door.

"Be careful with the money," Mitra's father said, then he gently opened the door. Within seconds the agents had pulled him to the ground. Then they took him away in a van.

Mitra ran out into the street, and north toward Hamlet's house. He was the only one who could heal her. When they had been smaller and she cried, he would hold both her shoulders and shake her, saying, "It's okay, Mitty, it's okay, Mitty. Smile, Mitty, smile." She would try and fail to smile, and he would say a few words in Armenian, hug her, and bring her his colouring books. They would colour for hours. After a while, she'd yell at him for colouring outside the lines and he would snap back, "It's modern art. I can do what I want." Her drawings would turn out perfect, colours matching, while his were unruly, colours vibrating. But he would have healed her, and nothing else mattered.

Mitra ran as fast as she could while the rain beat on her face. She had worn the wrong shoes. Somewhere along the way her glasses fell off, but she didn't realize she could hardly see until she arrived at Hamlet's house. The maid opened the door, and Hamlet popped up behind her. "You're soaked," he said.

He took her inside and the maid lit the fireplace. Hamlet threw a towel over Mitra's shoulders.

"I lost my glasses," she said. Her tears were mixed with raindrops.

Hamlet brought her a cup of tea, but instead of drinking it, she threw her arms around him and cried until she couldn't anymore. "They took him again," she said then. "And I hear they're . . . they're executing people."

"I know," he said.

"You know?" she said, through tears. "But how do you know, Hamlet Agassian? How does a rich boy like you, who is a neighbour of the Shah, whose daddy gives the Shah his pinky rings, know if they're executing or not executing?"

"Because I hate my father," Hamlet said. He lifted the tea to her lips. "Drink. It has nabat in it. And the sugar has saffron. You need it." He wiped the tears from her face and held her in his arms. "One day we'll change all this," he said.

23

On her way to the Shirazi home, Aria bought loaves of bread and several bags of nuts at the Bazaar. Despite Mana's pleas and warnings and fears, she still visited the family regularly.

Fereshteh had years ago decided to turn a blind eye, but still asked Maysi to pray that Aria not go to hell.

"Madame. The Prophet sat at dinner with the Jews—have you never read the Quran?"

"I know *you* never have, Maysi," Fereshteh would say, reminding the maid that she knew she could not read.

When Aria arrived at the Shirazis' this time, it was Roohi who answered the door. "Are we celebrating something?" she asked.

"No. I'm hungry," Aria said as she walked inside.

Mrs. Shirazi was sweeping the floor slowly, in fits and starts, until finally Farangeez took over and finished the job herself. Meanwhile, Aria sat with the younger girls on a rug in a corner. They ate the bread and nuts and washed the food down with water that Roohi had boiled in the kettle.

"Are you keeping up with the work I gave you?" Aria asked, her mouth full. The girls nodded.

"I even did extra," Gohar said, putting up her hand as if answering a question.

"Well, fetch it and show me," Aria said. She was aware of Mrs. Shirazi and Farangeez watching from a distance. Farangeez was holding Tooba, the baby, tight in her arms.

She looked over Gohar's work and then Roohi's before giving them more words to learn, demanding they write ten sentences for every new word they learned. As usual, she let them stay in the corner and work with their backs to each other while she sat three feet away and looked through a magazine or did her own home-work. Aria liked being here. Mrs. Shirazi never bothered her, although sometimes Aria wished she would. She sensed an aversion, perhaps a kind of disgust, as if there was something fundamental about her presence that Mrs. Shirazi did not like.

An hour into their lesson, Gohar asked a question—and Mrs. Shirazi's reaction was immediate and volcanic. The question was too innocent to cause such a reaction, thought Aria, especially when asked by Gohar, an unspoiled child.

"Can we come do lessons at your house, one day?" was what Gohar said. And this was enough for Mrs. Shirazi to slap Gohar's face and command that she go upstairs—which Gohar did, crying.

Aria's heart beat fast. The idea hadn't occurred to her before, but why couldn't the girls come to her? Was there a reason they had to be sequestered here, away from everyone, as if they were diseased? But when she thought about it some more, Aria realized it was impossible. She tried to explain: "It wouldn't be comfortable for you, would it? Mana—my mother—makes everyone keep the house perfect. You can't touch a thing in that house. Not even me."

Farangeez and Roohi weren't buying it. They looked at her like an audience that had seen this play a thousand times.

"I have these friends," Aria tried again. "You don't know them, Hamlet and Mitra. They can be tricky. They're not even nice to me half the time."

Mrs. Shirazi had remained quiet throughout this explanation, but now she spoke haltingly. "Gohar shouldn't have asked," she said. "My daughter is young. She is sorry."

Farangeez snickered derisively. "Are your friends the tricky ones, or you?" she said to Aria.

"I like it when you come here," Roohi said. "You make it happy here."

Aria smiled gratefully. She stayed long enough to correct the girls' spelling mistakes and give them more homework, then took her leave without saying goodbye to Mrs. Shirazi. On the way home, halfway through Ferdowsi Square, she stopped at Mitra's house.

"Am I evil?" she asked Mitra when her friend opened the door.

"Well, anyone can be," Mitra said.

"I'm coming inside and I'm not going to cry, but I feel like shit and I don't want to talk," Aria said.

Mitra held up her hand. "You can't. There's a big problem."

"Problem?"

"My dad had people over today. I'm not supposed to let you— or anyone, really—see them."

"What kind of people?"

"His—his people."

"Commies!" said Aria.

"Just leave." Mitra pushed her gently.

"Really? Commies?" Aria asked.

"They're Mujahedeen. Muslim commies. They have Shariati readings."

"What?" said Aria.

"He's some philosopher. I don't know. I'm just not allowed to—"

"Come with me, then."

"Absolutely not. I have to study."

"No, you have to come with me. I'll teach you all about studying."

Aria pushed open the door and ran up to Mitra's room before her friend could stop her. She picked up a coat and Mitra's books, ran back downstairs, grabbed Mitra's arm, and whisked them both out the door.

"Aria, I said no," Mitra protested.

"One more no and I swear I'll go back in there and make a scene. Tomorrow I'll tell the whole school that your father wants to kill the Shah." And with that, Aria forced Mitra to walk alongside her the half-mile to the Ferdowsi home.

Maysi gave them dinner and warned them not to make any noise. "I'm done with changing your diapers, you hear?"

"You never changed my diapers, Maysi," Aria said.

"You know what I mean."

"Where's Mana?"

"Minding her own business, I imagine," said Maysi. "And where were you this afternoon? I needed your help. At the Shirazis' again?"

Aria reddened. She glanced at Mitra. "Who?" she said dismissively. "We don't go to school with any Shirazis, Maysi." She got up from the table. "Come on, Mitty. Adventures await."

Mitra followed Aria like a trusting child.

"Zahra once told me there is magic in this house," Aria said.

"Zahra?"

"My aunt. A great-aunt," Aria replied. "Come on. I'm going to show you some rooms you've never seen before."

They walked through the living room into a long hall. At the end of that hall was the smallest of the servants' rooms. And on the ceiling of that room was a window—a skylight that let in the light of the moon. "Can you believe that Americans might walk on that moon?" she said to Mitra, and Mitra gazed out the window too. Their entire class had been discussing this in school, debating whether it was possible or not.

The ceiling was low enough that Aria could touch the bottom of the windowpane.

"I think it opens," she said. "Help me?"

Mitra wrapped her arms around Aria's knees and lifted her. Aria tried to push the window open. "It's jammed," she said.

Mitra set her down for a moment, and then they tried again. This time, Aria pushed harder, and when the window still wouldn't open, she punched it. It cracked at the edge, and with a little more pushing finally loosened and flipped back like the cover of a book. Aria wondered if she would ever be able to bring the Shirazi girls to this place. What would they think, to see a house as big as this?

"Maybe you can be a guinea pig," Aria said, half-voicing her thoughts.

"What?" Mitra was confused.

"A lab rat. A tester. Do you think anyone else would like to come up here?"

"Hamlet?" Mitra said.

Aria shook her head. "Hamlet doesn't notice beauty."

And beautiful it was. She climbed through the window and carefully walked away from the skylight, circling the vast roof. From here, even in the darkness, they could truly appreciate the size of the compound. Below, there were at least thirty rooms in two parallel buildings joined by a single long balcony, like a bridge. Underneath it, instead of a lake, was Mana's garden and giant pool. The moon was full and glowed back at Aria like an illuminated apple. She clambered onto another, smaller rooftop, then pulled Mitra up to join her. From here they could see Tehran's skyline and the great Mount Damavand, which stood over it like a guardian.

"You can see all of the Alborz from here," Aria said, pointing out the mountain range whose shadows hovered in the night.

They sat on the roof in silence, neither of them wanting to admit they were cold for fear of disturbing the magnificent sight before them.

"I wonder if the ancient gods saw all this," Mitra said. "Mitras, and Raman, and Faravahar."

"How do you know those gods?"

"They're from Zoroastrian times, and even before then. My father told me their stories."

"I bet Rostam saw this because he came from Mount Damavand," Aria said.

"Rostam wasn't a god," Mitra said. "Well, maybe he was half god," she corrected herself.

Aria had been reading about Rostam in school, in *The Book of Kings*, and now she recited for Mitra what she knew. He was a warrior, part man, part god, who had brought the Iranians peace after eons of war. His lineage stretched back to the beginning of time. His forefathers were the great jinns who ruled the universe and the heavens at the formation of the cosmos. Rostam had brought the Iranians together and unified them, the Persians, the Kurds, the Azeris—maybe even the Jews, she thought, if Jews had existed back then. Some said he was brought to earth by the great phoenix, the Simorgh, who lived on Mount Damavand and whose wings expanded from one end of the universe to the other. Its wingspan was so vast that all the Iranians—the Arians, they were called—could have gathered beneath, to be cradled by the universe itself.

"There would be room enough for all of them," Aria recited, seeing the wings in her mind's eye.

"What are you on about?" Mitra asked.

"The Simorgh. The phoenix," Aria said.

The crickets in the garden chirped, and beneath the lamps that lit the fountain, hundreds of goldfish flashed in the water, turning it gold. Aria breathed deeply. The air was clean, and she could see doves flying by.

"Have you seen Hamlet lately?" Mitra asked after a while.

"At school, like usual," Aria said. "Have you seen him?"

"Sometimes after school." Mitra paused before adding, "He talks about you."

"Does he?"

"Yeah. He says your people are like this or like that."

"What people?"

"South-City people."

Aria looked away.

"Hamlet likes South-City folk," Mitra said.

"What does he say about them?"

"He says, 'They're tough, like Aria, and smart, like Aria, and scary, like Aria.'"

They laughed a little before falling quiet. Then Aria said, "Everybody says South-City folk are stupid. Nobody likes South-City folk."

"Hamlet thinks you're all geniuses."

They laughed again.

"So who is Mana, anyway?" Mitra summoned the courage to ask. "Is she your rich aunt or something?"

"Yeah, something like that. Mana's the rich aunt. Zahra's the poor aunt. Or maybe they're both my mothers, not aunts. I don't know."

"Sorry for being nosy. I've always been shy about asking you." Mitra tried to think of something else to say, but Aria abruptly changed the subject. "Why does your father talk to communist Muslim mollahs?"

"I don't know," Mitra said. "My father says mollahs are worse than the devil they hate, and my mother says they're angels."

"What about you?"

"What *about* me?"

"Do you think the mollahs are devils or angels?"

"I don't know what I think," Mitra said.

"That's because you make others think for you," Aria said. "You don't even want them to hear you thinking."

"That's not true," Mitra said.

Aria continued. "I, however, do think. And what I think is that strange things happened here." She surveyed the rooftop, and peeked back into the small room they had climbed out of. She deepened her voice. "Ghost things, with jinns and spirits, and dark shadows human eyes can't see."

"Stop it," said Mitra.

"I can feel it. Can you feel it? In fact, right behind you I see something moving through the trees." She pointed past Mitra, who resisted looking in that direction. "Maysi told me stories of dead beings rising from the rooms we just passed. She told me they climb up here. They walk to the last room along the corridor and come up to this window because they worship the moon, since the moon raises the dead."

"Stop it," Mitra said again. She closed her eyes and covered her ears.

"Some of the dead become angels and some become demons, whether they were mollahs or women or children, or even dogs. You never know what they will become."

Mitra backed away from Aria, edging higher on the roof. "Why are you doing this?"

"Because you must choose." Aria deepened her voice dramatically. "You must choose, Mitra Ahari: What do you think is evil and what do you think is good? Choose, choose!"

She walked toward her friend, and Mitra backed away until she had nowhere left to go. Aria laughed. Her voice returned to normal. "You're so silly," she said.

Mitra opened her eyes, angry at first, but soon she too was laughing, a bit embarrassed. "Don't do that anymore," she said.

"Your imagination is too strong," Aria said. "My stories wouldn't work on anyone else. You only see bad things, but the world isn't going to fill up with monsters."

They both laughed again, and Aria stepped forward and reached out her hand. "Come, let's go look at Damavand," she said.

"I see it. Right behind you. And Rostam's phoenix is rising out of it," Mitra said.

Aria turned to look, and for one fleeting instant she believed magic did exist. In that moment, she thought about Zahra screaming at her long ago, and Mrs. Shirazi screaming at her daughter that afternoon. They were like characters from the legends, fighting back against persecutors, and against their own children. She felt the weight of myth settle upon her from the skies, and she trembled at the excitement of it, at the thought that those imaginary beings, written into eternity by the great poets, might be real enough to touch, their beauty anointing the world with their goodness, their truth. And as she turned, she lost control. Her ankle, always so reliable, twisted, and she found herself fumbling, tripping, toppling over the clay-tiled rooftop, and she heard her body crack onto the concrete of the garden below, and then there was nothing.

24

When Aria lifted her head, her world turned red, as if it were the day of Ashura, when blood streams through streets, when everything dies and is resurrected into the silent lull of the next day.

She woke up in the hospital. Mana was there, in one corner. In the other corner, Bobo was sitting in a chair, cradling a bouquet of lilies.

Maysi was there, too. "You've been here since the sun showed its face," she said. She had arrived with food after diagnoses were made and the doctors left.

The moon appeared over the mountains again, and Mitra came with her mother and brother, full of apologies. Hamlet, too, stood in a corner, having arrived by himself. He had bought flowers at the hospital shop, flowers that now stood in a vase on Aria's bedside table. He stole glances at Aria's father, who was sitting in the opposite corner and had the distinct look of lower-class folk, the kind who worked for his father on building sites.

Now all seven visitors were gathered around Aria. They looked like disciples before their prophet, Aria thought. She wished she could excommunicate them. "None of you have to be here. I'm not dead or anything," she said with difficulty, pulling the bedcover up to her chin.

"Well, if I'm not wanted I'll get dinner ready in case you decide to come home and devour it," Maysi said, but did not budge.

Aria turned to look at Behrouz. He stood up, walked haltingly over to her bed, and laid the flowers he'd brought on her blanket.

"You have a limp," Aria said. She'd seen her father walk like this before, but now she noticed he was breathing heavily and his steps were slower than usual.

"Why did you go and hurt yourself, girl?" he asked. He kissed her forehead and coughed, leaning against her bed to steady himself. He had a book in the hand closest to her.

"What book is that?" she asked. She managed to open the flap and saw a word written there: *Rameen*. Vaguely, she remembered knowing someone with that name. Was it the soldier who had carried her home once when she was a child?

"It's all right," said Behrouz hastily. "I can carry it."

"Is your leg all right, Mr. Bakhtiar?" Fereshteh asked.

"I slipped on the way here, when I heard the news, madam." He tucked the book into his coat pocket.

"He did slam the phone down mighty hard when I told him," Maysi said. She turned to Behrouz. "I told you she was fine. Just a bump on the head."

"More than a bump, I'd say," said Fereshteh. "Sorry for worrying you, Mr. Bakhtiar."

"Thought you'd leave her with us and all her troubles would be solved, hey?" Maysi said, laughing. When no one else laughed, she frowned. "Just trying to lighten the mood," she said, staring at Fereshteh.

Behrouz coughed again.

"Sit down, Mr. Bakhtiar, sit down," Fereshteh said.

Behrouz touched Aria's leg lightly. "We should climb back up to the mountains one day, me and you, for old times' sake," he said.

"You shouldn't be climbing anywhere," Maysi said, helping him back to his chair.

"You promised me the Caspian," Aria said, and she closed her eyes again, giving in to the overwhelming urge to sleep.

She was just dozing off when a nurse rushed in and shook the bed. "Wake up! You've slept long enough." As Aria opened her eyes, the nurse turned to Fereshteh and whispered, "You must try to keep her awake."

Hamlet overheard this and sprung into action. He tore a flower petal from one of the bouquets, rolled it up, and flung it in Aria's face. "Hey Mitty, why don't we see who can hit her harder."

Mitra looked away, embarrassed, but her brother laughed. "I'll play," he said.

"No, don't you dare," Mitra replied.

Hamlet flung another petal, and Aria had just enough strength to catch it. "You're a madman," she said.

"Maybe. But I wouldn't have let you fall off the roof."

"I didn't let her fall!" Mitra said.

"You were too scared to help. Like always," said Hamlet.

Now Behrouz stood up, a hand on the chair. "The Caspian," he said. "I will take you there, I promise." He coughed. "You can come, too," he said, looking at Mitra and Hamlet.

"Mr. Bakhtiar, you ought to have a doctor look at you," said Fereshteh.

"I really must get going," Behrouz said, shaking his head and suppressing another cough. "Zahra is waiting."

"Does she know I'm here?" Aria asked.

Behrouz put on his hat and kissed her cheek. "I'm sure she'll ask about you, my girl."

"Will she come, then?"

Behrouz cleared his throat. "I'll give you a ring in the morning," he said to Fereshteh. To Aria, he said, "No more climbing up roof-tops, my girl."

Aria nodded, and Maysi walked Behrouz out. Soon the others left, too. Hamlet paused at the door. "If I had been there, I would have caught you," he said again.

"I believe you." As impossible as it sounded, Aria did believe him. Perhaps Hamlet was Rostam incarnate.

At last Fereshteh was the only one who remained, and she was so quiet, her silence soon lulled Aria to sleep, try as she might to remain awake.

IN THE MORNING, Mitra returned with Hamlet while Aria still slept and Fereshteh kept watch. Hamlet whispered in Aria's ear, still upset. "Stupid girl."

Fereshteh looked over at Mitra. "What were you doing up on the roof?" she asked quietly. She had needed an entire day and night to think through what to say.

"We were trying to see the Simorgh, the phoenix," said Mitra, in the serious way she said everything.

Before Fereshteh could think of what to ask next, Maysi walked into the room carrying a heavy pot.

"Abgoosht," she said. "Took me all night to make it. My hands hurt. Mashed beef, beans, herbs, garlic, onions, potatoes, tomatoes, salt. That'll wake her."

She placed the pot near the foot of Aria's bed and eyed Fereshteh. "Last night's dinner. You can eat it now for breakfast."

"Massoomeh, get that pot off her bed," Fereshteh said.

Maysi didn't budge. "I'm not cooking anymore until this is eaten," she said. She lifted the lid. "Children, use your hands, like we do in the villages."

"What do you mean, *hands*?" Hamlet asked.

Fereshteh laughed. "Like this," she said. She rolled up her sleeves and threw her hand into the pot, scooped just the right amount of stew between her thumb and fingers, then used her thumb to shovel the food into her mouth. After a moment, Hamlet and Mitra did the same.

As the others ate at her bedside, Aria had a dream in which she and Mana were holding hands while standing in the middle of a road, the end of which they could not see.

"It is the road that leads nowhere," Fereshteh said. "I've been here before."

"Then show me what nowhere looks like," said Aria. But when she looked up at her third mother, she didn't recognize the Mana who stood before her. Here was Mana young, with long hair flowing, still not beautiful, but quiet and steely.

"Nowhere looks like every land you've ever seen," Mana said. She wore a vest over a dress. On the vest, the letter *F* was embroidered in silver silk.

"But I have not seen all the lands," Aria replied.

"You have seen some land. Some land is any land," her third mother said. Then she said, to Aria's surprise, "I am not your third mother. Stop thinking that. I am your only mother. And any mother is every mother. You never had three mothers; you have always had one."

Aria let go of Fereshteh's hand, and it was in that moment she knew she was dreaming. Yet she allowed the dream to continue.

"Go on," Aria said in the dream. She was trying to make Mana walk on ahead and leave her, but instead, they walked down the road together—or maybe it was up the road. "Are you sure we won't get somewhere?"

"I have tried so many times," Fereshteh replied.

When they had walked awhile, they turned back. The road

behind them disappeared. "It does this all the time," Fereshteh said.

Aria pleaded. "But I swear it was there."

"No," said Fereshteh. "You only thought that. But it's never there."

They walked on, and with every step the road behind them vanished, its bends and turns appearing only in the traces of Aria's memory. "This is heartache, Mana. It hurts my heart," Aria shouted, still aware that she was only dreaming.

"A heart is meant to ache; that's why it's made of flesh," said Fereshteh, and she began to cry.

She was still crying when Aria awoke, unsure whether the sobs she was hearing were in her dream or were real. She looked over to see the real Mana alone in the room, and she was indeed crying, the Mana who had grown old.

"I didn't know you could cry," Aria said, and touched Mana's hand.

Fereshteh took Aria into her arms.

"Where is Mitra?" Aria asked.

"She and Hamlet were here for a long time but it is late now. Hamlet stayed longer than anyone else. You've scared him, you know." Fereshteh looked long and hard at Aria. "What made you think the Simorgh was behind that mountain?"

"The poet said so," Aria replied.

"That's the sad thing about poets," Fereshteh said. "They write beautiful words, and people get killed."

25

Aria came home from the hospital a week later, stiff and bruised, her head swollen, but otherwise without lasting damage, or so the doctors promised. Fereshteh helped her with everything, including the schoolwork she had missed. "I didn't finish school, you know," she said the first day they sat down together over Aria's books.

"Girls didn't go to school back when you were young?"

"No, it wasn't that. I had this place to look after when my parents died." Fereshteh glanced around the large living room. "These days there is no one here, but back then . . . My younger siblings, they all finished school."

"Were you sad about not going?"

"Oh, back then I was. But I'm not anymore. Sometimes it is good to forget the past."

"Is that why the roads kept disappearing?" Aria asked, remembering her dream.

"What roads?" asked Fereshteh.

"Nothing. I . . . I just wish Zahra had come to visit," Aria said, and turned back to her books.

It was during these days, as Aria recuperated, that Mana talked to her more than she ever had before, and for the first time, shared a little of herself. Many years later, this was what Aria would remember most about Mana. Other memories would disappear, like the vanishing road in her dream, but Aria would recall being at home with Mana while her own swollen head slowly returned to its normal shape. She would think about how Mana had shared her heartache, and would realize that it was a lie to say you have no regrets, that in fact, most of life was filled with regret, and at road's end you might well feel that things would be much better if all your former acts disappeared. Yet despite midnight pleas to gods or deities, nothing could ever be changed. Regret is the fire of the soul, Aria would think one day. But that was a day far distant from this one, when she was still a girl sitting quietly with a third mother, a mother who also understood the lies of life.

THE WEEKS PASSED, Aria healed, and Fereshteh grew quiet again.

When did I lose myself? she whispered one day to her reflection in the hallway mirror. She went to the kitchen and found Maysi there.

"Massoomeh, do you really think that mirror needs to be in that hallway?"

Maysi ducked her head out of the kitchen. "Which mirror?"

"The mirror in the hall," said Fereshteh. "It's a rather redundant thing."

"I don't know that word, Madame."

"It's vulgar, truly vulgar," Fereshteh said. "No one ought to see herself before going out into the world. It'll bring nations down."

"What do you want me to do about it?" Maysi said, waving her cutting knife as though it were an extension of her hand and her words.

"Give it to the neighbours," Fereshteh said.

"The neighbours have their own mirrors," said Maysi.

"Give it to Aria," Fereshteh said, and left the kitchen. She walked out her front door and stood on the step. "I am too pale," she said, looking at the skin on her hands. She considered the garden for a few minutes, and decided she would buy gardenias today. The garden had not had gardenias in some time, and she struggled to think why.

"It must have been because they reminded me of him. He used to plant them often," she whispered at last. Here she was, speaking to herself again. She had to stop that. "I should never have bought him that bicycle," she said, louder this time.

She wondered if, from the room above, Aria could hear her talking.

Fereshteh took her usual path to the flower shop, past the sweet vendors and bakeries, and then the row of mosques that had been the very first buildings in Tehran, long before the Qajar kings had made the city their capital, back when it was little more than a village with an illiterate population, where children never went to school, and where coffee shops were the meeting place for traders and merchants from every corner of the nation.

She watched as women in black veils poured into the mosques, following their men. What did the world look like from behind those veils, Fereshteh wondered. She had never worn a scarf, not even during Qajar times, before the Shah's father, Reza Shah, had ordered all the women to unveil. She remembered how, as soon as the old Shah abdicated, his young son—who, come to think of it, was nearly fifty now—had said the women could go back to wearing veils if they wanted to. The son had never been as forceful as his father, and, like the whitefish in the Caspian Sea that return each season to the place they're from, the women—or most of them, anyway—went back to their veils. Fereshteh had never understood it. But the girls these days, the ones Aria's age, they didn't care for it much. She hardly ever saw them veiled. Perhaps it was finally a thing of the past.

She watched the doorways of the mosques fill with people, and, forgetting about her flowers, felt an unfamiliar urge to follow them. She waited until the last person had shuffled through the door of one of the mosques and walked in after them. The smell of goatskin was overwhelming, as was the scent of the homemade leather shoes and wool coats. She stood hesitantly just inside the door and watched the people pray, the men to one side, the women to the other. Some fifteen minutes later, a mollah spoke from his high chair atop the stage, at the head of the mosque. His robes made him look bigger than he was, and although Fereshteh couldn't know it, his turban hid a mop of thick red hair that the mollah, who was from Qazvin, had inherited from a great-grandmother from Babol, who had inherited it from her great-grandmother, who had come from near Moscow. The sermon covered the usual topics: the sins of the West, the importance of chastity and honour at times like these, and the usual praise for the Shah.

"The White Revolution will bring equality to our people," the mollah said. "Once again our great king, like all great Iranian kings, has felt the pulse of his people." The congregation clapped. "How lucky we are," the mollah said, "that we have such a benevolent leader." Again the people clapped.

Fereshteh left the mosque and inhaled deeply. The smell of hyacinths told her the flower shop was near. As she turned the corner toward the shop, she came upon a wedding. The bride and groom were running toward a car as a few people threw rice at them, and then water, making sure to miss. Some of the guests were beating pots, making a ruckus that could be heard all the way down the street, and then she heard the frantic flapping of wings. Someone had brought along a chicken, and was holding it by the neck. It was trying to fly away, but a man in a suit—maybe a brother or an uncle, or the bride's father—grabbed the chicken more firmly, and with a pocket knife sliced its neck in half. He splattered the blood that poured out of the animal onto the water and the rice and the car where the couple were safely tucked away, smiling and waving back at their audience. Someone played the traditional wedding song on a battered old record player and the couple drove off.

Fereshteh walked quickly over to a gutter and vomited. She wiped the sweat from her face and looked back at the road and the dust, turned red with blood.

She reached the flower shop moments before it closed. "I tried to get here earlier, Mr. Safai," she apologized.

The florist held up his hand in protest. "As long as we see you, madam, our days are brightened." He bundled up her usual order: hyacinths, lilies, jasmine, baby poplar, daisies, roses.

"I'll be taking some gardenias today, too," she said.

He paused, and Fereshteh remembered how, as a boy in his teens, the florist had helped his father in the shop. Sometimes back then she would come in for gardenias—but it had been years.

"We've got a new kind of food for the flowers," the florist said as he added the gardenias. "With new minerals. Makes them grow bigger. It has dead bees in it and good bacteria. More natural. The Shah's florist uses it, they say. The queen is a gardener, I hear. Lovely woman."

How strange, Fereshteh thought. She had so often heard people speak ill of the queen and of the Shah. But twice today, in the mosque and in the flower shop, she had heard how loved they were.

"He's a good man. A good man, the Shah," Mr. Safai said, as if reading her mind.

"Ah, but what about his thoughts on women?" Fereshteh asked, thinking to stump the florist. "With his new revolution he says women can be judges. Would you let a woman judge you?"

"Oh, that won't last, madam." The florist shooed the idea away with the flip of his hand. "But he's a good man. And he keeps the women happy, I guess."

"Do you go to mosque, Mr. Safai?"

"Mosque? No, madam. No mosque for me."

"Too early in the morning?"

"No, madam. Mornings aren't a problem." He lowered his voice and moved closer to her. "We're Bahá'is," he said. He was whispering now. "The wife and me. Bahá'is." He smiled.

"I see," said Fereshteh. She returned his smile, took her flowers, and left.

AT HOME, FERESHTEH went upstairs to Aria's room and placed a daisy on her bed.

When Aria heard Fereshteh ascending the stairs, she had closed her eyes and pretended to sleep. Now she pretended to wake up. "It's beautiful," she said, taking the flower.

"A Bahá'i man gave it to me," said Fereshteh. "I wonder how many times people like that have changed their religion, become something different from what their people were in the past."

"What's a Bahá'i?" Aria asked. Mana didn't answer. Sometimes it was so hard to understand what Mana meant. Aria felt as if she was somehow meant to decode Mana's words, to get at the truth of things, yet she always felt that Mana didn't really want her to know the truth, either.

Fereshteh gently put a hand on Aria's head and searched for the scar where her head had split open from her fall. "I saw a chicken have its throat split today," she began to say.

"Must have been a sacrifice," said Aria. "Cheaper than a lamb. Did you see it in South-City? Zahra used to do it all the time." Zahra liked the blood, Aria thought. She liked the feeling of taking life.

"Zahra never lifted a finger to do anything like that when she worked here."

"Why do they sacrifice animals?"

"To deflect blame, I imagine. To throw their own sins onto something else."

"Poor chicken. It's a good thing Abraham didn't kill his son in the end. Everybody would be killing their sons now."

"Who says they aren't?" Fereshteh laughed in a subdued way. "South-City folk are all happy," she remarked.

"That's because they can't wait to take your land." Aria laughed. "That's what the White Revolution will do, right?"

"It's not just my land. Some of it is your land. One day." Fereshteh didn't look at Aria as she said this. "You can pick the part you want to keep. And then we need to let the family know."

Aria laughed again, until she realized Fereshteh wasn't joking. "You're giving it to me?"

"When I'm dead. Hopefully not soon." Fereshteh smiled. "Of course, Nasreen is still a problem."

Aria played with the daisy. "Nasreen is Abraham," she said at last.

"No, Nasreen is God," Fereshteh replied. "Ruthless. And she hates her children equally."

"Why are you giving land to me?" Aria asked.

"Maybe I'm the Shah. I like to help the poor." Fereshteh winked.

"I'm your charity into heaven," Aria said.

Fereshteh said nothing. After a moment, she got up and left the room.

"I don't want your land!" Aria shouted after her.

But all she could hear was footsteps descending the stairs.

THAT NIGHT, FERESHTEH watched Maysi pray.

Maysi prayed five times a day. She fasted during Ramazan, gave two percent of her pay to charity, and always said, "Peace be upon him," before uttering the Prophet's name. Maysi was almost the perfect Muslim. All that was left for her to achieve perfection was to go to Mecca.

Now Fereshteh watched Maysi bend forward and back, kneel, then stand up, kiss the floor and touch her forehead on the rock in front of her. After each one of these gestures she held her hands open to the air.

After a few moments, Fereshteh retrieved a veil, wrapped it around her head and body, and joined Maysi. When Maysi bent, Fereshteh bent alongside her, and when Maysi kissed the floor, Fereshteh kissed it, too. But she stopped before Maysi finished her routine, put the veil back in the wardrobe, and left the room.

In her own room, she sat on her bed and admitted to herself that she hadn't felt anything at all. God had not entered her or spoken to her. This was exactly what she had felt when she was sixteen and had crept into Massoomeh's room when the young servant was praying, and copied her movements. She had even tried to startle Maysi out of the trance of her prayer, but Maysi was always far away when she prayed, disengaged from the world of suffering, somewhere flying with birds—or so Fereshteh had thought. That was the place where Fereshteh the Zoroastrian could not go. Or perhaps it didn't matter the religion. God wasn't in her. The world as Maysi saw it, as the people in the mosque saw it, was plain, unmoveable. So long as there was God, they could breathe.

Fereshteh returned downstairs. Maysi had finished her prayers and was now cooking supper. She was making abgoosht again.

"They say those who pray do so because their sins are great," Fereshteh said.

"I agree," Maysi replied. "This one here," she tapped her chest with her thumb, "this one's bad to the core. Soul's all crumpled up, got dirt all over it. I pray He cleans it." She pointed at the ceiling. "I get dirt on it again, he cleans again. The best you'll ever know, He is. Better than good old Maysi."

"What do they teach you in those mosques?" asked Fereshteh.

"Maysi doesn't go to the damned mosques. They pile even more shit on you. Sorry for the language, Madame, but they pile it and then He has to clean you all over again. Only their shit is heavier than all the other shit. Pardon the language. So He has a harder time washing you. Do you follow, Madame? All they talk about is save this imam, or save that one. Imams don't need saving. God does the saving."

"Today, I went into the mosque and they were going on about how much they love the Shah," Fereshteh said.

"One minute they love the Shah, the next minute they hate him. Makes life interesting, I guess, Madame. I'm not interested in being interesting, Madame. Maysi stays at home. Maysi would read the Quran if she could, but I can't and that's all fine."

"I should have sent you to school when you were young," Fereshteh said.

Maysi chopped a carrot. "Life is as it should be. God knows why you went to mosque today. Were you searching for something? Maysi sees everything, as does that child upstairs."

Before Fereshteh could speak again, she heard the sound of Aria descending the stairs. She didn't like how fast Aria was running, seeming not to care at all about her injured head. The girl rounded the corner into the kitchen, looked at the two women with eyes full of wonder and said, "I heard on the radio they're going to the moon! The Americans are going to the moon!"

In the distance, the sound of the day's final call to prayer broke the sudden, shocked silence. Fereshteh looked at Aria and closed her eyes, and for once, simply took in the music. She felt that thing called a soul inside her, beating against her body as it slowly came alive and took her, for the first time, to the same land as those who prayed, the land of the free, or perhaps the land from her favourite story in childhood, about the Persian princess who told stories full of wonder and enchantment to soldiers and kings to free her city from tyranny.

part three

MEHRI

1968–76

26

Mrs. Shirazi remembered clearly the address her old friend had given her over the phone the other day. This was one of the benefits of illiteracy: You developed great recall. Her friend now lived in a tall building, one with floors so high up that when you stood on one of the balconies, you felt eye-level with the Alborz mountains, Darband and Damavand and Tochal.

She had to knock a few times, and when her friend finally did open the door, Mrs. Shirazi saw the undeniable shadow of grief over her face.

"Come in, Mehri, dear," her friend said.

Mehri sat carefully on the brown leather sofa. She had never sat on anything like it before.

"You look all right," said her friend. "Not as bad as I expected."

"And you look . . ."

"Worse than hell," her friend interrupted. "It's all right. You don't have to be polite. Grief does funny things to us. I'm different from you now, aren't I, Mehri?"

Mehri was silent.

"Well, I'm sorry I made you come all this way," her friend said. "I wouldn't have if it didn't matter."

"I'm so very sorry for your loss," Mehri said.

Her friend gazed out the window at the mountains. "I should have known," she said, "given his age. I should have known he would go long before me. He worked so hard, hours and hours. Especially after the shop became so popular. We had people lining up down the block, and sometimes round the corner. The money he always wanted, he finally got."

"He was very good," Mehri said.

"In spite of himself," said her friend, nodding. "More good than you even know."

"I never thought he had any badness in him, ever," Mehri replied.

"I don't want to keep you long," said her friend. "You've got to get back to your children. Does your husband still work?"

"Yes. I help him sometimes."

"Do you? Is that really right for a woman with children?"

"You worked in the bakery," Mehri said.

"I had no children, and those were different times," her friend replied. She sighed. "Well, I'll be quick about it," she said. "My husband . . ." She hesitated. "My husband has left you something. Money, in his will. The lawyers told me to tell you. That is all, really."

Mehri held her breath. She found she could make no sound.

"Oh, you don't need to act so surprised, dear Mehri. I wasn't. It was all in the stars, from the beginning. Here's the letter telling you all about it. It's sealed, as you can see. I can't open it. Only you can. Since you can't read, the lawyer is willing to do so. Take a taxi there. He will pay for it. Show the driver this address." She handed Mehri a slip of paper. "I think that's all, then," she said.

MEHRI'S FLOWER-PRINTED VEIL flowed behind her as she walked along the street. It took her some time to hail a taxi. Perhaps the drivers didn't want to pick her up, she thought. Maybe they could tell she didn't belong in this part of town. When one finally stopped, she showed him the address on the piece of paper. He drove her there and waited as she stepped inside the building. A lawyer greeted her, paid the driver, then sat her down and explained about the small fortune that Asghar Karimi, the man who brought her first daughter into the world, had left her.

Mehri remembered Karimi's hands, how they had turned red with her blood. She took the money without a word. As she walked the long way home, she held her sudden fortune close to her chest and resolved what to do with it, as hard as it would be to keep secret. Sounds from that long-ago night came back to her, strengthening her resolve, and she remembered the cold and wet and snow. She breathed deeply and took in the sounds around her now, the weight of the Tehran streets with their geniuses and madmen.

Her decision made and her heart certain, Mehri swiftly headed back south from whence she had come.

TODAY, ARIA HAD something important to do at the Shirazi home.

She had just returned from the mosque, where she had covered herself, especially her miniskirt, with a veil. Nothing much had happened at the mosque except prayers, although some of the women had cried for their dead husbands, or for the ones they said were kept in the prisons by the Shah and his secret police. Aria listened to all the tales about corruption and secrets, but she didn't go to mosque for those stories. She went in the hope of seeing her childhood friend Kamran, the bracelet-maker. She would wear all the bracelets he had left for her years ago, jangling them and holding them up to the brilliant light that crept through the high windows and reflected off the mosaics, hoping that her bracelet-maker would see their sparkle and find her. But he never had, not once in her months of going there. So she had tuned her heart to the music of prayer instead. Whether there was a god she did not know—she knew even less now that she was fifteen. But Mana didn't mind her going to mosque once in a while, and the prayer stirred her, so she listened to the sad songs of the Quran, and secretly cried along with them.

Now, at home, she took her veil off, which meant she had only her cream-coloured overcoat to hide the miniskirt. There was no way she could let Mana see her like this. She buttoned the coat and tied its belt loosely at her waist. The coat fell below her knees and covered everything except her neckline and the collar of the green blouse Mana had given her for New Year's, a nice spring colour.

Maysi hollered from the kitchen. "Don't forget the sweets for Mrs. Shirazi's birthday!"

"I know!" Aria hollered back. She hoped Mana wouldn't hear the two of them—or at least wouldn't know what they were up to. She quickly packed the sweets and set out at a brisk walk.

At the bottom of the stairs that led to the Shirazi home, Aria hesitated. She removed a folded piece of paper from her coat pocket and scanned the poem she'd been given in class the previous day. She'd been ordered to memorize it for tomorrow, and now she was running out of time. She scanned it, then stuffed it back in her pocket as Gohar opened the door.

Inside, Aria removed her shoes and carefully nudged them onto the shoe rack. Mr. Shirazi had recently made the rack for the girls, since each had her own pair of shoes now, instead of the slippers they used to wear.

"You aren't taking your coat off?" Gohar asked.

"No," Aria replied. "I can't stay long."

They walked to the far end of the living room, where Aria glimpsed, in the room adjacent, a motionless Mrs. Shirazi beneath wool covers. Gohar whispered into her ear that her mother had been sleeping there all day.

In the corner of the living room were some twenty cushions, arranged to suggest a sitting area. Aria sat, cross-legged, thinking how nice it was that the Shirazis had a place for gathering now.

Gohar knelt next to her mother in the adjacent room. "Aria's here," she said softly.

Mrs. Shirazi sat up and put her hands on either side of Gohar's narrow face. "Look at you," she said. "So pale, and black under your eyes. You've no iron, my girl."

"Aria won't take her coat off," Gohar said.

"Well, never mind that. Call your sisters."

"They're in the courtyard."

"Doing what?"

"Washing the clothes, I think."

"Call them."

Gohar crossed the living room, stepped out the back door, and soon returned with her sisters. The girls sat beside Aria and silently ate the fruits and treats she had brought.

After a short while, Mr. Shirazi arrived home from work. Aria watched as he touched something bolted to the door frame and whispered under his breath before entering the home. Aria knew Mr. Shirazi was a full-time bazaari now, but had to pretend he wasn't a Kalimi, a Jew. He had bought a rosary, making sure it was green so that no one would confuse it with a Christian one. This he always kept around his wrist. And he had recently bought his own shop with the money he'd saved for years.

"Well, well, look wife, our sweet Aria is here." Mr. Shirazi kissed Aria's forehead in the same way he kissed his daughters'.

"She brought sweets for mother's birthday," said Gohar.

"Aria, are you staying for supper?" he asked.

"No, sir. Exam tomorrow," Aria said.

"Is that so? Look, wife, our sweet helper already writes exams. Good for you, my girl."

"It's only an exam about a poem."

"A test is a test. Which poem is it? Who's the poet?"

Aria played with her folded paper. "You wouldn't know it. But here." She handed him the paper, then remembered. "I'm sorry, I forgot you couldn't . . ."

"It's all right, child. Read it for me." He lowered his head and waited.

"I will, but not the whole thing. It's too long," Aria said. She began her recitation:

> I am a Muslim
> The rose is my Qebleh
> The spring my prayer-carpet
> The light, my prayer stone
> The field my prostrate place
> I take ablution with the heartbeat of windows

"Do you understand?" she asked. The girls looked at her with blank stares, but she continued:

> My Ka'ba is beside the brook
> My Ka'ba is beneath the acacia
> My Black Stone is the light of the garden

Aria glanced again at the girls. "See, I told you you wouldn't understand," she said, and folded up the paper.

"It's a Muslim thing," Farangeez said dismissively.

"It's about the real Islam, and the real God. And the real everything. That's the point. We're learning it in secret."

Still, it seemed the Shirazis did not understand. After a pause, Mr. Shirazi said lightly, "I had many Muslim friends as a boy. We used to skip pebbles down the street, not too far from here. Ever try controlling those tiny things such a long distance? We'd chase them into every gutter. They rolled everywhere." He laughed at this, and his belly shook. His daughters' eyes glistened as they watched their father tell his old story again. "My mother used to yell at us to get back inside. Threatened to take the pebbles from us. Ha! I kept them hidden under my kippah. Imagine! Ten Muslim boys and then me, wearing the kippah. What fun we had."

Aria didn't know what a kippah was but didn't dare ask. Instead, she changed the subject and said she would stay for supper after all, promising to help Roohangeez with homework.

After dinner, the two found a place away from the other girls. Aria had brought a magazine with her, and after she set Roohangeez to work on some lessons, she opened it. Roohi looked up from her work and pointed to a photograph.

"Who is this?" she asked.

"How can you not know?" said Aria.

"What are you fighting about?" Gohar asked, moving closer.

"Don't you know who this is?" Aria showed Gohar the photograph too. "I'll give you a hint. It's a movie star."

Roohangeez shook her head. "We don't ever see the movies."

"Baba says Hollywood's filthy," Farangeez chimed in.

"And the Shah gives them money and has Hollywood people come to his house. So he's also filthy," said Gohar.

"He's not filthy," Aria said. "He's very clean and proper, and can fly a plane."

"He's a bad man. He hurts people. Baba hears it all the time at the Bazaar," Farangeez said.

At this, their father glanced up sternly and shooed the girls away so that Roohangeez and Aria could finish their lesson.

Before she left for the evening, Aria went looking for Mrs. Shirazi to wish her happy birthday. Mrs. Shirazi had disappeared again immediately after dinner, almost as if determined to hide.

"Mrs. Shirazi!" Aria yelled up the staircase. "Are you up there? Where are you?" She hummed a tune as she looked around the house, then stepped through the back door and into the small courtyard. The water basin there was empty, and she wondered if the family had had their water cut. In any case, Mrs. Shirazi was still nowhere to be seen, so Aria gave up her search. She said her goodbyes to the girls, retied her coat tightly so there was no hint of the miniskirt beneath, and headed home again.

27

The next day, Aria and Fereshteh headed to Ferdowsi Square to do some shopping.

Aria noticed that the city seemed less noisy and bustling than usual—but then again, she thought, it was a Friday. Ever since the riots in Qom, more people than ever before had been heading to Friday prayer. Qom was where the famous cleric Khomeini, whom everyone called "the Indian," had been arrested and exiled from the country. Now people went to Friday prayer begging for the Indian's return. Earlier that day, when Aria asked why he was called this, Maysi said, "It's 'cause of his mother. Came from the five waters, they say."

"You mean the Punjab?" Aria asked.

"That's it."

"Grandfather," came a voice from the living room. It was Jafar, who explained he had read the news about the cleric with the Indian grandfather in the very newspaper he'd been carefully cleaning that morning with dried soap. He had recently started washing newspapers and hanging them to dry in the living room from a wire strung across the mahogany tabletops. He would then iron them and only read them once the cleaning was done. While he waited for the newspapers to dry, he would wipe a napkin with another napkin.

Fereshteh didn't think much of the cleric. "Doesn't matter if he's Indian, Arab, Turk, or Yugoslav," she said. "People aren't idiots. They can go to Friday prayer all they want. They'll never receive mercy from the clerics."

"His grandfather's from India," Jafar said, ignoring Fereshteh. "His father died in Najaf. That's the story. He makes noise. A ton of noise."

"You mean he talks and talks?" Aria asked.

"Yes, about things that'll get him killed. Ah, but the Shah wouldn't dare," said Jafar.

"Why won't he dare? Why?" Aria said, moving closer to him.

But Uncle Jafar was distracted. "Where's my napkin? Have you seen my napkin? I had a napkin here."

Aria found it lodged between the sofa's seat and body. "Why won't the Shah stop the Indian?" she asked again, giving him the napkin.

Uncle Jafar wiped his seat with the napkin. "Because, just like the mollahs, the Shah thinks he's been touched," he said.

"Touched? Touched by what?" Aria asked.

But Uncle Jafar did not reply, and walked upstairs to his room.

ARIA THOUGHT ABOUT what Jafar had said for the rest of the day, as she and Fereshteh walked through the strangely quiet streets around Ferdowsi Square. They went to nearly every store before finally stopping at Mr. Amiri's tea shop. It, too, was eerily hushed, and Aria had the strong sense that something important was about to happen.

Shouts erupted out of the silence. Aria left Fereshteh in the tea shop and ran toward the noise. It was coming from the small park across the intersection from the tea shop.

A woman was sitting on a bench in the centre of the park as a gang of boys, none of them old enough for their voices to have broken, circled around her. A strand of the woman's long, grey hair lifted in the wind. But she didn't move. Even from a distance, Aria could see that the woman was dressed entirely in red.

The boys yelled and whistled at her, infuriated by her silence. *"Little old lady, little old lady, sitting on a bench, turning to gravy. Forget the trash, forget the dead, there's nothing more rotten than a lady in red!"*

Aria crossed the intersection, picked a few rocks off the ground, and threw them at the boys. "Turn around, bastards!" she yelled. The boys spun around and looked at her. One tried to throw a stone but the others stopped him.

"Want to see the crazy lady?" another shouted at her.

Still another boy said, "She'll kill you, you know. She'll cut your throat."

"I'll make sure she cuts yours and feeds you to pigs!" Aria shouted back.

Reluctant to make a scene, the boys moved away. Aria caught her breath and sat on the bench beside the woman in red. She searched for something to say. "I like your dress," she said at last. The woman said nothing, but folded her hands on her lap.

"Can you speak?" Aria said. "Those boys were cruel."

The woman in red shook her head. "Walnuts," she said.

"I said they were mean to you," Aria spoke slowly and more loudly. "Walnuts?" You want walnuts? I don't have walnuts."

The woman grabbed her arm. *"She can cut your throat. She can cut your throat,"* she sang, repeating words the boys had been singing.

"My name's Aria."

"That's a boy's name," the woman said. "You shouldn't have that name."

"I know, but I have it," Aria said nervously. "And I'm not a boy. It means 'Iran,' and it also means 'song.' In Latin, I think. It's a kind of song that people sing."

"Here, it is a boy's name," the woman said again. *"There's nothing more rotten than the lady in red.* That's a song," she said. *"Walnuts, walnuts.* Your suitor will want them. I've eaten all the bad ones. Take the good ones. Be sure your suitor knows you. Take the good ones. The good ones." She pointed across the street. Aria followed her gesture and spotted a walnut vendor. She looked back at the woman in red and saw that a single tear swam in her eye.

"You want me to know that there's a man over there who sells walnuts?" Aria asked, pointing at the vendor across the street. "I'll get some for you."

"I've eaten all the bad ones," the woman said.

Aria crossed the street and bought a small bag of the nuts. They were roasted and warm. She walked back to the bench and placed the bag in the woman's lap.

"Do you sit here all day?" Aria asked.

"Take the good ones, take the bad ones. Yes. Yes, I wait here," she said.

"They're warm," said Aria. "If you eat them now, they're all good."

The woman laughed. "If I wait long enough they'll become bad."

"Don't wait, then," said Aria. "See?" She opened the bag and took out a walnut. "Eat them now, they're fresh. I can get you something else. Would you like something else? Do you have a place to sleep?"

The woman nodded. "Yes, yes."

"Where?" Aria asked.

"Yes. Yes," the woman said again.

"All right. Well, if those boys come back again, you scream loud and I'll find you. I know how to punch boys."

"Take it. Take it." The woman held up the bag.

"I thought you wanted walnuts?"

The woman took out one nut and put it in her mouth. "Mmm, good. Take." She gave Aria the bag.

Disappointed, Aria took the nuts and walked back to the tea shop. Fereshteh was still browsing and hadn't noticed a thing.

THAT NIGHT ARIA badgered Maysi with questions about the woman dressed in red.

"It's a long story," said Maysi.

"But I want to know," Aria said.

"You shouldn't have talked to her."

"I was bored. Now tell me before Mana comes inside." Aria looked out the kitchen window to the garden, where Mana was hunched over a bed of soil.

"Her morning glories are out," Maysi said. "That's all she'll be concerned with for a while." She waddled back to her station at the sink.

"So?"

"So nothing!" said Maysi.

"What's wrong with that woman? One of the boys said she could kill somebody."

"You have too many questions, child."

"Why does she wear all red?"

"You know, when I was a child, we got a beating for each question."

But Aria wouldn't stop, and Maysi finally put her knives down, threw her hands in the air, wiped them with a cloth, and told the story of the woman in red.

"They called her Yaghoot. But who knows if that's really her name. Those who have been living in Ferdowsi Square long enough can remember her as a girl. She fell in love back then, and he was a young one, too. He loved her, they say, or at least he made her think so. She was beautiful and he liked to see her in red. Then, one day, he left. Some say he went to Russia because secretly he was a communist. Others say he was close with the Americans, and others say it was something religious that took him away. But it makes more sense that he was a communist. Reza Shah didn't like communists, just like his son hates them now. He didn't like all sorts. There was a story about the old Shah, how one time he went to a village, to a baker's shop. He didn't like the look of the baker, so he threw that fellow into his own firepit. The baker had done nothing wrong."

"I heard that story," said Aria. "At school. The teacher told us the baker was hoarding wheat during the war, while the country was starving. A boy at school, his grandfather was a general—"

"Oh general this, general that. I don't know those stories. What do I know? All Maysi knows is that the old Shah scared everybody. And he really scared the communists. So Yaghoot's lover ran away. He promised to come back for her, but he never did. The end."

"That's not the end. There has to be more," Aria said.

Maysi smacked a rag on the counter. "Fine. He liked how she looked in red. Always used to tell her how beautiful she was. So now she sits on a bench or walks every corner of the square, from one end to the other, thinking that if he's back in Tehran this is the only way he'll recognize her. Love is a terrible thing, not what dreamers say it is. And hope is just as bad. Hope will turn you mad."

LATER THAT SAME night, Aria phoned Hamlet. "You didn't tell me the real story about the woman in the park. The one in red. You lie. You keep things secret."

Hamlet remained silent on the other end of the line.

"You lie and keep things from me," Aria said again. In the background, she could hear Kokab calling Hamlet to dinner. "I met her today. She talks to herself."

"I told you she talks to herself," Hamlet said. "What do you mean you met her?"

"I talked to her. I bought her walnuts," said Aria. "Maysi told me about her, about her life. Bet you knew the whole story and kept it from me because you have no heart. It's a love story. A love story, Hamlet Agassian, and you said she is mad and crazy."

"She *is* mad," Hamlet insisted.

"She's mad like Majnoon. It's different, you idiot. You heartless, empty . . ." At a loss for words, Aria slammed down the phone.

An hour later, near midnight, Hamlet knocked lightly on the Ferdowsis' door. Aria, who had been half expecting this, opened it. "What?" she said.

"Can I come in?"

"No."

"I didn't know all those things about her," Hamlet said.

"You're so unaware of the world around you. You live in that big house with your big maid who shoves food into your mouth, and your world is perfect." With this, Aria slammed the door shut. Light from Fereshteh's room fell on the stairwell.

"Sorry, Mana. Go back to bed," Aria called up in a loud whisper. "It's just Hamlet."

Fereshteh stepped slowly down the stairs, a shawl wrapped around her. "What is that boy doing here this time of night?"

"Begging," said Aria, but she opened the door again. Hamlet was still standing on the step. He waved to Fereshteh.

"Boy, come in, phone your parents so they won't be worried, and spend the night. I'm not letting you go back in this dark. Come in."

"No," Aria insisted. "He's going back."

Hamlet laughed. "Sorry, Auntie. Aria wasn't well, so I came to see her."

Fereshteh ushered him in. "I'm not so sure she needs to be checked at this time of night, my son."

Maysi came down a minute later. "Why do these kids hate us, Madame?" She wore a goatskin coat over her veil and her slippers smacked against the floor.

"Get the boy some soup," Fereshteh said. "Or no, that's all right, Maysi. Go back to bed and I'll do it myself."

"I'll get it, I'll get it," Maysi said. "Though that creature ought to be doing it." She pointed at Aria. "Girl, in my day if we had a boy visiting us in the middle of the night, our bare asses would be red from beatings. Instead, this one here gets soup."

Hamlet smiled and Aria scowled. "He's a shallow, selfish mule," she said.

"Aria is mad at me," Hamlet told Maysi, "because I didn't know about some lady who wears a red dress."

"So, that's what this is about?" said Maysi. "The child drilled me all day about that little tale."

"The Yaghoot woman?" asked Fereshteh. She sat at the kitchen table, and Hamlet seated himself beside her. "And why did this matter bring you here in the middle of the night?"

"That one says I lied to her about it." Hamlet pointed at Aria.

"And that one has no heart." Aria pointed at Hamlet.

Maysi shoved bowls of soup in front of both of them. Hamlet ate his quickly, but Aria pushed her bowl away.

"Rumour has it she waited for him by the Caspian Sea," Maysi said. "That was before she came back to Tehran. She waited for him by the Caspian Sea for a decade, camped out with them fishermen up there."

Hamlet slurped as he finished his soup. "I don't see why you're so interested," he said to Aria. "Mitra's seen that red lady loads of times and she's never cared."

"Did you tell her the real story?" Aria asked.

"I told her the woman is crazy."

"And Mitra believed you?"

"Sure."

"Mitra just went along with whatever you said. She never bothered to ask the truth? Just like that?"

"Yeah, like that," said Hamlet. "She didn't give me a headache like you do."

"I give you a headache because you deserve one. You know nothing about the world. It's full of so many things, and you know nothing of it."

"What did I do?" Hamlet turned to Fereshteh. "Auntie, really? What is wrong with her?"

It was Maysi who answered. "There is so much wrong with her," she said, and gently slapped the side of Aria's head. "I've tried to train her, but no luck."

"I'll go get your bed ready," Fereshteh said. "Have you called your father? He'll think you've been kidnapped again."

Hamlet stood up from the table. "No, thank you, Auntie. I'll take a taxi. My mother's heart will stop if I'm not in my bed in the morning. I just came here to be diplomatic and apologize to the princess over there."

"You're the princess," Aria retorted.

Hamlet thanked Maysi for the food and turned to Aria. "Why do you have to be so strange, Aria Bakhtiar?" He followed Fereshteh to the door. "I apologize, anyway," he called as he left the kitchen.

"I don't accept your apology!" Aria shouted after him.

HOURS LATER, AS the sun came up, Maysi and Aria were still in the kitchen. Fereshteh was asleep, and Hamlet had called hours ago to say he'd arrived home and was nicely tucked in bed.

Aria leaned against the kitchen window ledge. She played with the bracelet on her wrist, turning each bead. Then she brushed her fingers against them all, and the beads spun, each in its private orbit. As the beads spun she felt her head spinning, too. She hadn't slept and her eyes closed involuntarily now and again. "Why does Fereshteh call you Maysi?" she asked, turning around. "I've never asked you that before."

"Happened accidentally," Maysi replied. "Madame started yellin'. Tried to say my name as she was yellin' and it came out halfway . . . Maysi."

"Why would she be mad at you?" Aria asked.

"I don't want to tell you that story. All these damn stories today!" Massoomeh shook her head. "Anyway, it's one of those stories that shouldn't be told. It's a secret, but you'll open your mouth to Madame and we'll all go to hell."

"No, we won't. Tell me."

Maysi placed a bowl of the previous night's soup in front of her. "Eat."

"I'll starve myself until you tell me," Aria said.

"Well, good, then we'll be rid of you. You stubborn mule," Maysi said. "All right, in the name of Imam Reza. It was because I stole something. Or Madame thought I did. Still thinks so to this day."

"You stole from her?"

"I told you, it wasn't really me. It was that lizard, Zahra. But I never found that out till later."

"Why did you steal from Mana?"

"I told you, I didn't. You deaf, child?"

"Then why did Zahra?"

"Never you mind. We're done here. Finish that soup."

Aria could tell Maysi meant it this time, with no playfulness in her voice to encourage Aria further. She quietly ate her soup and left at last for bed.

As Aria slept, her mind swam with the story of the woman in red and her Russian lover. When she awoke, hours later, she realized she'd been crying in her sleep, but she could recall only scraps of her dream. The sky had been red, and the clouds in the sky, and Bobo had appeared, holding her hand and walking alongside her on a red road. A strange wind had lashed at them and Bobo's greying hair blew along with it. He steadied himself as he walked, taking careful steps from one red rock in the road to another. In the dream, Aria had asked him where he was taking her. "To the Caspian Sea," he said. "I will show you where the blood of your country comes from." He picked her up and carried her. But in the dream she didn't know if she was small Aria, the little girl he used to carry up and down the mountain, or the Aria of today. If it was today, how could his aging body bear her weight? He hummed a song as he walked, and she curled herself into his chest and slept. When they reached the Caspian, the sun had turned red, too, and the sea, which should have been the blue-green of Aria's eyes, just as Bobo had described to her many times, was now crimson. "It is blood, Bobo. Real blood," she said, and her father wept. "I don't know what happened," he said as he wept. He placed her on the ground, and together they cupped the red water in their palms. Suddenly, the water cut into their hands and she could see it enter their wounds, red as rage, moving through their veins and up their arms, until she felt it enter her heart, making it beat faster. "Is this the real Caspian?" she asked her father. But he was silent, until finally he said: "I have wronged the great sea of life; the heart has turned into a wound."

The moment Bobo spoke those words was when Aria woke up, crying.

Now she went downstairs. The house was calm. Maysi and Fereshteh must still be sleeping. She picked up the phone and called Behrouz, but it was Zahra who answered.

"You don't need anything, do you?" Zahra said. "Because I don't have anything to give you."

"How are you, Zahra?" Aria asked.

"As if the world cares," Zahra said.

There was silence on the line for a moment, then "Hello?" said a gentle voice. It was Behrouz. "I have missed you, my girl. How is your head? Are you all better now?"

"Yes, I'm better. But I want to ask you something. Will you take me to the Caspian?"

"Yes, of course, someday—"

"No, now. It has to be now. I met a woman who went there years ago. She wears a red dress, and she's looking for someone. I want to help her find him."

It took a while for Behrouz to answer. "On one condition," he finally said. "If anyone asks, we are going to the barracks up there. Which we are."

"Okay," Aria said.

"And one more thing," said Behrouz. "I am feeling just a little unwell these days. So someone else must come with us."

28

The next day, Behrouz idled his truck outside the Ferdowsi compound so that the cab would stay warm. It had been a nightmare convincing the captain to let him take it. First, he had promised that he'd work two extra Fridays, and when that wasn't enough, he'd promised two more. In the end, as luck would have it, the military needed him to take a delivery up north anyway, to Masuleh, one of the seaside villages that a general had told him looked like it was right out of Italy. Behrouz knew nothing about Italy except that Sophia Loren lived there. He figured that if he could show Aria the village of Masuleh, maybe it would be as good as showing her Italy.

Aria jumped in the truck and Behrouz drove to Mitra's home, where Mitra was waiting outside. "If you hadn't hurt your head I would not be doing this," she said, throwing her backpack and a thin blanket into the cab. "But don't think you have any sway over me. It wasn't my fault you fell. That was an accident."

"I don't deserve you, Mitty. I don't," Aria said.

Behrouz drove up the mountain road, the girls bouncing in their seats like unhinged marionettes. Aria, remembering her dream, asked, "Is there a part of the Caspian that is red?" Behrouz and Mitra laughed. "It is as green and as blue as your eyes," Behrouz said, as he always did.

The spring Tehran air was crisp, and up here in the mountains it felt like a new weapon: clean, fresh, a little dangerous. Aria, who was wedged close to Mitra on the passenger side of the truck, rolled down the window. It was a strange kind of wind on this road, she thought. "You will see, toward the Chalus Road, how the wind changes," Behrouz said, as if reading her mind. "It is different, like the wind of another planet."

AS BEHROUZ DROVE he thought of Rameen, how the authorities had allowed him to come back from Shiraz months ago but refused to let him have visitors. Behrouz thought guiltily of Zahra, too, hoping she wouldn't be angry when she learned he'd left without saying a word. But she would understand he was with Aria. After all, Zahra knew everything about him. In the distance he could make out ant-sized military buildings. Beneath his tires was dirt and mud from the rough road that took them away from Tehran and into the valleys and trees. Soon, they would pass new soldiers heading back from their morning march.

Beside him, Aria was planning out the day for Mitra, explaining how there would be introductions to the soldiers, describing the different ranks and who did what and who came from where, elaborating on how life was lived up here, and even suggesting a trip to the pomegranate garden at the other end of the hill. Behrouz listened to the conversation, intrigued, as Aria asked Mitra why she was always angry with her. He noted how the girls argued over who could have the closest seat to the window on the way north, and how they fought over the Armenian boy Hamlet.

Behrouz glanced at Aria. Through the years, he had noticed

changes in her, and certain complexities. Now he saw that she had somehow acquired the ability to be two things in one, two Arias: one was smiling graciously at the view of her beloved pomegranate field; the other was angry with her friend. Her face was like the Mona Lisa's, full of elegant kindness and calculated contempt, both in a single glance. Years ago, Rameen had read to him about the Mona Lisa, saying the reason everyone cherished the painting so much was because of the duplicitous nature it depicted, containing, within the curve of a half smile, love and hatred, good and bad. Now he was beginning to see all of life like this, too.

"I want you to look at something," he said to the girls. "To the west."

The girls gazed at the horizon where he was pointing.

"Do you see the valleys before the mountain rises again?"

"Yes," Mitra said.

"Are you looking, Aria? Look beyond the Alborz and beyond those valleys, girls, to the west. Look beyond what your eyes can show you. Far beyond, and even beyond that, lies the Alamut."

"I can't see beyond what my eyes show me," Mitra said.

"Imagine. Try to imagine," said Aria.

Behrouz continued. "At one time there were fortresses throughout that land. They call it the Valley of the Assassins."

"Assassins?" Mitra said.

"Yes, named after the Hashashins. They were followers of Hassan-e Sabbah, an ancient leader of Persia. I'd like to take you there. You too, Mitra. There are beautiful things to see."

"Do they kill people there?" Mitra asked.

"Used to," Behrouz replied.

"Assassinate them?"

Behrouz nodded. "Assassinated, executed. It was a valley of fear. Wherever there is immense beauty there is immense fear— of losing that beauty, perhaps."

"Did they kill out of fear?" Mitra asked.

"Is there ever another reason?" Behrouz said. "The valley is endless. Like a sea of hardened sand. If you journey through it long enough, you begin to think all the world is like it. You begin to think the earth is red. But just when you're certain of your space, certain that nothing around you will change, suddenly everything moves and shifts. The valleys fall into rivers. They stream down from the well of the Caspian, like flattened water-falls. The more you walk, the farther north you go, the more you realize that nothing you were certain of is true. A world that seems fixed one way suddenly becomes another. The red valley turns green, mountains grow, cloaked with trees more beautiful than you can imagine. You reach the slopes of Mazandaran, from the tip of which you can see the Caspian Sea, way out there, and you can taste the salt of its water as the clouds carry it to you."

"But it's really a lake, not a sea," Aria said.

"Yes, it's really a lake, not a sea at all. But it can make you believe it's a sea. And its water is salty. That is the Caspian: the great deceiver. It is two things at once. That's where its beauty lies."

BY NIGHTFALL, THEY had set up camp. The grudges and offences between the girls had been forgotten and were replaced by the teenage distractions of outfits and the broad-shouldered boys in uniform, who were playing a soccer match to capture the girls' attention. Aria and Mitra talked about the boys, about what kiss-ing them might feel like. They wanted to talk about sex, too, but neither could—although each imagined which soldier she would do the deed with. Later, after dinner, they lay quiet on their blankets and looked at the stars.

"What kind of boy will you marry?" Mitra asked.

"I'll never marry," Aria said.

"You're mad. All women marry. We have to," Mitra said. "I'd like someone fun, handsome, maybe a little dumb so he'll do what I say."

"Hamlet would be perfect for you," Aria said.

"I'd never marry Hamlet," Mitra said.

"You haven't thought about it?" Aria asked.

"Never. Not once." Mitra turned on her side, away from Aria. Aria could hear the lie. "I bet he'd marry you," she said.

Mitra was silent.

"I'll be an astronaut, and maybe go up to the stars," Aria said.

After a while, the girls moved to their tent. Mitra fell asleep, and in her dream a boy held her to his chest, so close that she could feel his hardness. Aria remained awake and thought of other things, of a mother who left her, a mother who beat her, and a mother who loved her but couldn't say so.

The girls had been set up in a side tent on the military grounds reserved for the odd visitor. Two oil lamps lit their little room. When Behrouz walked in to say good night, he found Aria sitting on her bed, awake. He'd forgotten his satchel in the tent, and she had removed its contents and was flipping through the pages of his secret books.

"What's that you're reading?" he asked. *"Les Misérables?"*

She looked up. "How do you know what it's called when you can't read?"

He sat on the bed and tapped his finger on the book. "The picture on the cover."

"Oh," she said, studying the design. Behrouz noticed another book at her side, an unfamiliar one. Behrouz picked it up and opened the pages. In the margins, he could see lightly pencilled notes in his daughter's handwriting.

"This one's yours," he said.

"Yes," she said.

"Is it for school?"

"No, not this one. I just like it."

"The heart of a poet, I see."

"How do you know it's poetry?"

"Pushkin," he said, pointing to the letters on the cover.

"But you can't read it!"

"I know the shape." He couldn't think how to tell his daughter that someone had been teaching him to read, someone now wasting between prison walls.

"Have you ever tried to learn?" she asked.

Behrouz didn't answer. "You should get to bed now," he said, collecting his books.

"Does Zahra ever ask about me?"

He stopped and looked into Aria's eyes. "Yes. Sometimes."

"To be sure I never go back to her? So that she's rid of me?"

"No, that's not why." He stood at the entrance to the tent, his eyes downcast. "My girl, there's a lot you still need to learn about this country, about its people. It is seven thousand years old, maybe more. When something is that old, it begins to crack. It begins to rot. The oldest tree is the first to burn. Right?"

"Does Zahra hate me?" Aria asked softly.

Behrouz started to cough, so hard that he bent over, covering his mouth. Aria could hear the squeeze of air in his lungs. When he straightened, there was blood on his hands.

Aria grabbed them, terrified.

"Let go, my girl," said Behrouz hoarsely. "It's all right."

"Does she not take care of you?" Aria searched her father's face.

He cleared his throat. "Zahra's my wife. She has not hurt me. And she's your mother. Go to bed, my girl."

IN THE MORNING, Behrouz drove on through the valley.

"Look there," Behrouz said, pointing ahead, but all the girls could see was endless land and mountains beyond.

"On the ground, the dirt. See it?" The girls shook their heads. "The lines," explained Behrouz. "The railway lines. Reza Shah built those. Know who he was?"

Aria shook her head, but Mitra said, "The Shah's father. The King before the King. There is always a King before a King, and a King after a King."

"Maybe," said Behrouz. "He was the one who had those lines built, from all the way down to all the way up."

"Down where?" asked Aria.

"Down the country, dummy," said Mitra.

"You're the dumb one," said Aria. She turned to Behrouz. "Down to the Persian Gulf?"

Behrouz nodded. "From down to up, west to east. He saved this country. People hate him—I hear the generals talking this way, sometimes—but I don't know. He's the one who got the trains going here." His voice became thoughtful. "And then there was Mossadegh. I think he was trying to use the trains, too."

"My father hates all the kings," said Mitra.

"I understand," Behrouz answered. "Maybe he should, maybe he shouldn't."

"With the trains we can go anywhere, can't we?" Aria said.

"We can. And food can travel, and oil. A lot of things can travel."

"My father says the British took the oil, using the trains."

"Indeed." Behrouz nodded. "Then we had a prime minister who—"

"Why don't we just kick the British off the trains and ride them ourselves," Aria said. "Pow, pow, pow. I'll punch them." She laughed, but Mitra frowned.

"I think we tried to do that, my girl," said Behrouz. "It's what I am told, anyway."

"My father uses the trains. For work. He puts the oil on them," said Mitra.

"So he did punch the British!" Aria pumped her fist in the air.

"No, dummy. He's trying to punch the Shah. I think."

"What happened to the British then?"

"I don't know."

The girls quickly tired of talk about the British and trains, but as they drove, Aria couldn't keep her eyes off the rails that had sparked the conversation. She stared at them until, with a few turns and meanderings of the road, they disappeared from sight. She and Mitra drank their sodas in silence for a while. Earlier, they had seen a van by the side of the road with its back door open and a sign that read: "Pepsi-Cola 5 cents – America's biggest nickel's worth." They had stopped and bought six bottles, the girls choosing between the Pepsi and another brand with James Dean on the label, saying, "Get Kist Today! Kist Kola, 5 cents a bottle!"

As the girls drank, Behrouz breathed in the cool breeze of

the north, a breeze like that of another planet, and veered off the unpaved road to head for the main one, Chalus Road. This would take them to the giant lake, to the Caspian. The girls put their heads out the window, and the faint taste of salt settled at the backs of their throats. They passed farmers pulling mules, and Aria could see little girls out in the fields, their hair covered with flower-printed scarves. Like all gypsies, they wore pink silk trousers, puffed at the sides, above bare feet.

"It doesn't look like we're in Iran anymore," Aria said.

"Iran is different in different places," said Behrouz. He pointed to where a group of people were gathered at the side of the road. "Tabrizi carpet sellers. Turks from Tabriz. Their rugs and carpets are the reddest of all."

Aria studied the rugs as the truck drove by. On several she saw the figure of a bird by a pond, with twenty-nine other birds surrounding it.

"That's the Simorgh," Mitra said. "Remember the story?"

"Yes, as if I could forget. I fell off the roof because of it," Aria said.

"Father told me that story," Mitra said. "The Simorgh was really a hoopoe bird, and twenty-nine other birds flocked with it, to go looking for God. And they found him in a lake."

"I don't remember that part," said Aria.

"I was going to tell you before you fell and cracked your head," Mitra replied.

"How can the great phoenix be only thirty birds if it's supposed to be as large as the universe?"

"Maybe they're giant birds?" Mitra replied.

"The universe is full of mysteries, my girls," said Behrouz. He drove on, listening quietly as the girls discussed everything from apparitions to saints to monsters to love. He listened to their wonder and longed for the days of his own childhood, when he would marvel over the myths, too.

Finally, they reached the water. Aria breathed deeply when she saw that neither the sky nor the sea was the red of her dreams, only blue and green, as Behrouz had always told her. They camped in the tent under the stars that night, and Aria and Mitra quickly fell asleep.

Behrouz stayed awake for a while longer, his body aching. His thoughts became fixed on his opium and sneaking a few smokes before joining the girls in sleep. But when he crept out of the tent and searched the truck, he found no trace of his drugs. He had forgotten them at home—or maybe Zahra had taken them? Yes, he was certain he'd left some in the truck. He kicked the dirt. *Zahra*, he thought. She must have taken the opium. For a moment, he hoped that it was because she loved him, but twenty years had taught him that all she felt for him was spite. Now Zahra's sharpened malice cut him like a lance that burned through his heart and organs, all his muscle and bone.

He returned to the tent and willed himself to sleep. But after dozing briefly, he awoke and left the tent again, desperate. Maybe she had left something in the truck, maybe just a little of the drug. His body hurt and his arms and legs were stiff, as if locked into position at his sides. His neck throbbed, as did his head, and his heart was beating fast. Somehow those beats drove him to cry out in pain.

The girls awoke a while later, to the scent of moss and lilies. They sleepily exited the tent and were staring at the sea when Behrouz cried out again. He was standing by the truck, holding his chest.

"I'm fine," he said when they ran to him. "I'm just not as young as I once was."

Aria looked up at him with wordless fear. "I'm fine, my girl," he said again. "Was getting some air before you two woke." But even as he said these words, his body went numb. He tripped over a rock and landed, hands outstretched, on the hard earth. His chest tightened with each breath and he heard, as if from a great distance, the faint sounds of the girls' voices calling out. He could no longer see what was in front of him; instead, he saw a screen in his mind's eye. On that screen were three faces. The first was Aria's. She was a little girl wearing the white dress he had bought her. Beside her face was Rameen's. He was holding Aria, and they were waving at him.

Far away was another face. As it slowly came into focus, he could see it was Zahra's. She was the age she'd been when he married her, after they'd met at an old opium bar thirty years ago, when he was so young and she'd told him the story he already knew, about her life and her son, Ahmad. He should never have married her. But if he hadn't, what mirror would there have been left for him to look into? Back then, so many people had been talking about him and his delicate ways, spreading rumours that were killing his father. And he had found himself unable to leave Zahra all alone, husbandless, betrayed by the world.

Now he could feel Aria holding him, hear her calling his name. His body felt limp. He touched his chest and tried to breathe in the air, but it felt different. It was not like air he had breathed before. The wind here moved differently. The wind was hurting him. He felt his body shake and then convulse. Making a great effort, he looked into his daughter's eyes.

"Aria," he said. "Aria, the wondrous. I found you under the moon." And then he felt the last beat of his heart, and there was nothing but a beautiful darkness.

29

The body was lowered slowly, in silence. It was only when it slammed against the earth that Zahra's wails filled the air. She threw her own body on the ground and beat her fists against her head, then into the mud and gravel. She shrieked and begged Imam Ali to resurrect her husband.

Aria turned her face away from Zahra, crying quietly, Mitra and Hamlet at her side. Molook took her hand and held it. Maysi cried too, tears rolling down her face as she recited the Quran beneath her breath. Fereshteh could not cry; she could not even fake it. Worse, she could not give Aria a reassuring look or gesture. She could not fake that either. But Molook had done it for her, her younger sister who'd always been more comfortable in the world.

Fereshteh watched as Behrouz was hidden beneath the earth forever. Then she and others slowly left the graveside—even Zahra, who had succumbed to the exhaustion of her own drama. Finally, only Mitra remained to comfort her friend. Aria stood unmoving, her back straight, wiping away each tear before it fell.

Just outside the gates of the cemetery, a figure lingered, and when at last Aria turned away from the grave, she caught sight of him. He was too far away, and her eyes were too liquid-filled to see clearly, but the way he moved reminded her of someone.

"What are you looking at?" Mitra asked.

"Nothing," said Aria. "For a second I thought I saw someone I know."

KAMRAN COULD SEE a female form staring at him, but could not tell, from his spot just outside the gate of the cemetery, if it was her, Aria. All the women at the burial had been veiled, and so Aria's auburn hair was hidden. Now only two women remained in the graveyard, but even their identities were secret.

Both women looked in his direction, holding each other. Kamran peered again, but it was hopeless; he couldn't make out their faces. The one thing he knew for certain was that the man in the ground had been a titan of his childhood. And now Behrouz Bakhtiar was the first person Kamran admired who had died. As he watched Behrouz being lowered into the earth, Kamran had imagined that somehow the man would crawl back up, digging fingers into the mud and pulling himself out. The image had momentarily filled him with terror, before his reverie was interrupted by Zahra's extravagant performance.

"You haven't changed a bit, have you, woman?" Kamran muttered. "As godly as a kafir. No better than Jews, no better than Christians." He watched as Zahra threw herself on the ground, pretending to follow Mr. Bakhtiar's body in its descent, until soldiers, friends of Bakhtiar's perhaps, caught her. Kamran bit the edge of his lip near the spot where he had grown a moustache to hide his deformity. "Knew they'd catch you, didn't you?" he mocked. He spit in the dirt, and watched with amusement as the soldiers carefully pulled Zahra away. Soon, most of the others followed, and now here he was, trying to make out the obscure faces of the two women—or girls (he couldn't tell).

What Kamran did know was that one girl, probably one of the two whose faces he could not see, had a tight grip on his heart near the right ventricle, at the centre of his chest, and the pressure from that grip was so heavy with sadness that it reverberated down to the pit of his belly, and there it throbbed and ached and wept and hollered through all the echo chambers of his body.

He decided that tonight, despite the years that had passed, he would try to see Aria again. And this time, when he leapt onto her windowsill, instead of leaving a bracelet he would step inside her room, sit at the head of her bed and stroke her hair. Maybe he would tell her a joke from their childhood, maybe he would instruct her, the way he used to. It would be like it was before.

The veiled figures turned and walked in his direction. He slipped behind an olive tree, hoping its bends and branches would shield him. He dipped his head but kept the figures in his line of sight. The cemetery was filling with mourners who had come to see their dead, and sinners who had come to see their future. Somewhere amongst the sinners and the broken, Kamran thought, Aria was walking with a friend—but even as he thought this, he lost sight of the figures he'd been following. He stepped out from behind the tree and looked past the rows and rows of stones and death, but the black veils that shrouded the cemetery were effective camouflage. There was no way to find those women now.

MITRA CLIMBED INTO a waiting car with her mother and brother. "I am so sad, although I didn't know your father well," she said, as she hugged Aria.

"Me neither," Aria said sadly.

Maysi and Fereshteh were waiting for Aria beside a taxi, a black Mercedes that suddenly struck Aria as incongruous. It belonged in the streets of Paris or London, or some extravagant land where sad things did not happen.

"Do you mind if I go for a walk?" Aria asked. "I'll join you later."

Maysi pulled her into a hug, kissed both her cheeks twice, and then a third time. "Anything, anything," she said.

Fereshteh simply nodded.

"Thank you, Mana," Aria said, and instinctively headed south toward the Bazaar and the old city. Soon she realized that Shoosh, and the Shirazi home, wasn't far.

She knocked on the Shirazis' door and walked into the house before anyone could invite her. The house was unusually quiet, and there was no sign of the girls. Aria found her way to the back, and from the window she saw Mrs. Shirazi outside in the courtyard.

As if attracted by Aria's gaze, Mrs. Shirazi looked up. She turned away quickly, went over to the courtyard basin, and washed her face. Then she looked over at the window again. Aria raised her hand in greeting.

"They're not home," Mrs. Shirazi called. "My girls. Come back later, they're not home."

But Aria did not move, and soon Mrs. Shirazi approached her. "They're not home," she said, stepping inside.

"I didn't come to see them," said Aria.

"Then why did you come?"

"I don't know." Aria hesitated. "Did you hear? My father. He died."

Mrs. Shirazi was silent for a long moment. "Madame Ferdowsi didn't tell me," she said at last.

"I'm sorry if I bothered you. I just walked here from the cemetery."

Again Mrs. Shirazi said nothing. Instead, she slowly circled the room, tidying blankets and pillows.

"Can I help?" Aria asked.

"Why aren't you with your family?" said Mrs. Shirazi.

"I don't know. I started walking and I ended up here."

"Well, you shouldn't be here." Mrs. Shirazi picked up some of the girls' clothes, thrown carelessly on the floor, and went upstairs. Aria followed, watching as Mrs. Shirazi folded the clothes and placed the appropriate garment on the exact spot where each girl slept. Aria turned to the window, where the sun was streaming in.

"It's nice up here," she said. She looked outside. "You know I used to live nearby." As she gazed down on the neighbourhood, she recognized some of the houses. When she stretched her neck, she could even see her old house. She could make out part of the courtyard, and the balcony where she had sometimes slept. She wondered if Zahra had arrived home yet.

"Did you know I used to live there? Right there." She pointed, but Mrs. Shirazi did not look.

"I don't know anything," she said.

"If you had known me back then, you could have seen me from this window. It's so strange." A sudden thought struck her. "Did you not really know me? I used to play there. On that balcony. You can see the corner." She waited for Mrs. Shirazi to look, but the woman ignored her. "There was a boy who lived in my building, too," Aria continued. "Kamran Jahanpour. He has a cut on his lip. Like a twisted lip. You ever seen him, Mrs. Shirazi?"

Mehri rearranged the sheets on the mattresses and said nothing.

"Does Kamran still live there?" Aria said.

Mehri patted dust from the sheets and turned away. "I don't see anything," she said, and went downstairs.

Aria followed her into the kitchen and sat at the table. "Are you sure you didn't know me before? Or Kamran? He was good to me. He made jokes when I was stuck out on the balcony. But I have other friends now."

Mrs. Shirazi chopped vegetables silently.

"I'll help you," Aria said. She grabbed the knife and began working away. Mrs. Shirazi gave up and sat down across the table from her.

"Your knife is almost useless, Mrs. Shirazi," Aria said. "I'll tell Maysi to get you a new one."

"No more charity," said Mrs. Shirazi. She looked Aria in the eye for the first time that day. "And my name is Mehri," she said. "You can call me Mehri."

Aria stayed at the Shirazi home for a short time, chopping food with her dull knife until the girls arrived with their father. They had been helping clean the shop at the Bazaar, all four of them. "God forbid people say we're dirty," said Mr. Shirazi.

"Do they say that?" Aria asked. "That you're dirty?"

"No, my child," said Mr. Shirazi. "Only sometimes. Only some people. Here and there."

"Mrs. Shirazi said that her name is Mehri," Aria said quietly to Mr. Shirazi as he saw her to the door.

"She told you that?"

"Yes," said Aria. "And I told her that my father has died. He was buried today, and then I walked here."

"My wife doesn't tell anyone her first name," Mr. Shirazi said, his voice full of wonder, his eyes sad. "And I am so sorry about your father, my dear girl."

—

INSTEAD OF HEADING to Ferdowsi Square, Aria made the short walk from the Shirazi house to her old home. The lights were on, and she could see Zahra through the front windows. It was strange to see Zahra like this, truly alone. Aria watched for a long time, as Zahra flitted about the kitchen and then sat in the living room, looking through her magazines. She was no longer wearing black. Instead, she wore a tight dress with a short burgundy cardigan. She didn't look sad, but there was something singular about her, as though she were the only figure in focus in a photograph that was otherwise blurry. Or maybe Zahra was the one out of focus while other figures were perfectly in view. Whichever was true, Zahra was the focal point, the main attraction. Aria couldn't tell if Zahra wanted it this way; maybe it was an undesired thing.

After a while, Aria went to the door and raised her hand to ring the doorbell. She tried to bring her finger close to the button to press the alarm, but paused. She could hear no rustling or movement, nothing but utter silence on the other side of the door. Maybe Zahra had felt Aria's presence. And maybe that was just enough.

Yes, it was best to leave it at that. Aria lowered her hand and walked away slowly, wondering which movie star Zahra was reading about now.

It was late by the time Aria arrived home, and everyone was asleep. She knocked gently on Fereshteh's door and woke her up.

"Mrs. Shirazi told me her real name," Aria said quietly.

"Did she tell you anything else?" Fereshteh asked, now fully awake.

Aria shook her head, and Fereshteh kept her silence. She led Aria to her room, tucked her in like a child, and went back to bed.

In the morning, Hamlet and Mitra dropped by to give their respects for Behrouz again. Both of her friends solemnly hugged her, and this time as Hamlet leaned in, Aria could smell his scent.

It was different than it used to be; there was something heavy about it, something new and masculine. He was wearing aftershave, and as Aria pulled away, she could see that his face was freshly shaved. Only dark spots, small and insignificant, remained on his skin—but no, she thought, they weren't insignificant at all. They made all the difference, these spots, and the tiny spikes of hair that grew out of them. They would give him his authority. From now on, he would always be the victor and have the last word, the final say.

Aria wanted what he had, this new scent, and she breathed him in. She stared at his neck. It reminded her of a poem, although she forgot by whom, a poem about boys' necks, how they were lean and strong and there to be caressed. She almost touched it, but caught herself at the last moment and glanced quickly at Mitra, hoping she hadn't noticed anything.

After breakfast, Hamlet left to do errands with his father, and Aria and Mitra sat by the fountains in the garden and splashed water with their fingers. Fereshteh watched them through an upstairs window.

Soon the girls started hopping from the smaller fountains to the larger ones, trying to balance on the edges but failing, and falling ankle- or knee-deep into the water. Despite her grief, Aria smiled a little, and for this Fereshteh was grateful. Upon seeing the girls' smiles, Fereshteh felt the same shape forming on her own face, her lips curving, her eyes narrowing, gentle pain in the cheeks. Her eyes filled with tears. It was the greatest pain she had ever felt.

30

A year later, the whole world watched a great change happen. Fereshteh could do nothing but smile in spite of herself as she, Mitra, and Aria sat on the sofa, staring at the television and watching a man walk on the moon. Hamlet and Kokab had come to Fereshteh's house to watch, too, because once again his parents had left him for the delights of New York. He sat next to Kokab and stole secret glances at Mitra and Aria in the glow of the TV screen.

"The world will never be the same," Hamlet pronounced.

"So true." Mitra nodded.

"Do you think we'll all end up moving to outer space?" he asked. "I think life will be so great because of this."

"You're so right. The world will evolve," said Mitra.

"Nonsense. It won't change a thing. How will this feed anybody's belly?" Aria scoffed.

"Who needs their belly fed?" Hamlet said.

"Out there, out there." Aria pointed out the window vaguely. "Landing on the moon won't change that."

"You're blind," Hamlet said.

Mitra nodded with him. "Yes, Aria, you're blind."

"And I'm nearly deaf!" Maysi yelled, and Hamlet and Aria stopped their bickering.

They watched in silence as the man in the spacesuit hopped his way across the terrain, and the dust under his boots rose, suspended, particles floating off into the abyss. As the grainy images on TV filled her eyes, Aria squinted, looking for the face of the Prophet somewhere on that moon surface. All her life, people had told her that his face would be there. What she couldn't know was that Fereshteh was searching the moonscape, too. She was searching for the face of God, any god, the God of Islam or the God of the Jews, Jesus, or Ahura Mazda, and when no face revealed itself, she prayed it would stay hidden, somewhere underneath the moon dust, unwilling to come out.

LATER THAT EVENING, Fereshteh walked the children home, even if they were sixteen now. She made sure to stay a polite twenty steps behind them, and the two maids walked another ten steps behind her, gossiping and giggling, arm in arm. The three teenagers in front of her did much the same, though Hamlet kept a slight distance between himself and the girls.

Then Fereshteh saw him, or least she thought she did, try to hold Aria's hand, but Aria quickly moved her arm out of reach. How funny that was. Over the years she had always thought it was Mitra whom the Armenian boy was closest to. Then again, Fereshteh reflected, children do change. They grow and bend and break and remake rules; they lose their way only to find it again. She had watched her younger siblings do this, and she had watched Maysi do it, too; and despite all the contortions, they had smiled as much as they had cried; laughed as much as they screamed. Yet she herself had never been able to do these things. She remembered how, as a child, she had watched Chaplin on the movie screen yet not once had she laughed, smiled, bent forward with excitement, thrown her head back with anticipation. Even back then, Fereshteh had remained fixed, a pillar holding up all her rejected emotions. No one knew, she thought, what depths lay beneath her surface.

The children walking in front of her now fell into each other clumsily as they laughed, and again she saw, for only an instant, the Armenian boy grab Aria's hand.

IT SEEMED TO Aria that Mehri was always asleep, and unwell with an unnamed illness, when she visited the Shirazi home these days. Mr. Shirazi now regularly took his girls with him to the Bazaar, and Aria sometimes watched over their mother, studying by her bedside, when they were away.

The Shirazi girls worked hard alongside their father, and the reading lessons Aria had given them were an asset at the Bazaar. "They could go to school," Aria had suggested once. But Mr. Shirazi didn't see the benefit.

"What else do they have to learn?" he said. "My girls can read and count numbers. They are more educated than half the men I know."

Aria, unconvinced, confided in Hamlet. She had been forced to reveal the existence of the Shirazis to Mitra and Hamlet when they'd insisted on knowing why Aria was often absent on Fridays. She rarely brought up the topic, though, and most such conversations happened at the library, where Mitra insisted they go to study every afternoon.

"I don't know," Hamlet whispered, for fear of Mitra overhearing. "Anyhow, you never tell me much about this family you visit."

"Just answer the question without being an ass, will you? Their dad says he needs them at work," Aria said.

"Young girls at a Bazaar, with grown, ignorant men?"

"I thought you were a broad-minded man of the people, Hamlet Agassian."

"I am. But those bazaaris are getting some twisted ideas in their heads."

"Will you two be quiet?" Mitra said, her head behind her book.

"Yes, the bazaaris." Hamlet whispered. "They're completely lost in that guy's ass. The one who was kicked out of the country."

"The Ayatollah?"

"Yeah, him."

"Khomeini. Everyone says he's a saint. I hear the Shirazis talking, and according to them he's good and gentle and noble. Don't get carried away by your father's love of the Shah, Agassian."

"I'm not!" Hamlet said, angry. "And Khomeini sure writes some strange things for such a noble fellow. Maybe those girls should go to school after all."

"What things does he write?"

"Reza showed me."

"Who is Reza?" Aria asked.

"Funny you should ask. I asked him to meet us here. He's coming over now."

A tall boy strode purposefully toward them. "You three trapped in here?" he said loudly. Mitra sank deeper behind the cover of her book.

Hamlet stood up. "Girls, this is Reza. A family friend. Reza, this is Aria, and that one with the book is Mitra."

Reza shook Hamlet's hand, then Aria's. "Our fathers work together. Unfortunately. And you? Hello." He poked Mitra.

"*Enchanté*," Mitra said, without looking up.

"Mitty's busy," said Hamlet.

"Keep your voices down, please," Mitra said.

"Do you go to our school? I haven't seen you there," Aria said.

"Reza's at college," said Hamlet.

"I'd rather not be," Reza said. He was a year or two older, and wore a black turtleneck with a brown leather jacket. He was taller than Hamlet.

"Reza's the one who showed me the writing from that ayatollah," said Hamlet. "What the bazaaris are talking about."

"I have the source itself," Reza said. He sat, one arm behind his head, right foot on left knee. His legs were long and lanky, and his bent knee tapped against the table as he rocked in his chair. He smiled at Aria and pulled a small green book from inside his jacket.

Hamlet's eyes widened. "Where did you get that? It's banned."

"Read it and weep. Or laugh. Whatever," Reza said.

"Can you people not be quiet?" hissed Mitra, popping her head up from her book.

Hamlet took the book from Reza. "He writes one mad thing after another," he told Aria. "About sex. How to have sex. How to not have sex. Women's periods and how they should have sex when they bleed."

"Try to be more vulgar, would you?" said Aria. She took the book and flipped through it. "This is just mollah stuff. The clerics all say this, too. It's the laws and rules of Islam. Nobody takes them seriously." She put the book on the table. "Reza, you should know better."

Reza covered the book with his hands. "Careful," he said. "The bazaaris are taking it seriously."

Aria stood up. "But they can't even read."

"Somebody who can is reading it for them," said Hamlet. He turned to Reza. "Let's have a crack, man."

"Not here," said Reza.

"My place, then. Mitty, get up," said Hamlet.

"I'm studying," said Mitra, looking up at them. Her glasses had fogged and she held her book too close.

"You don't need new glasses, do you, Mouse?" Aria asked.

"I'm fine. I need new friends is all."

"Let's be off," said Reza. Hamlet gathered his books and papers, and he and Reza stood near the entrance, whispering as they waited.

"I don't want to go with that guy," Mitra said to Aria. "Who is he, anyway?"

"Some college guy whose ass Hamlet likes to kiss, I think."

"Shut up," Mitra said. "Walk with me then, so I don't have to talk to him."

"I'm kidding. And I can't. I've got to run." She hugged Mitra goodbye. "Bye, maniac," she said to Hamlet as she passed him. "You too," she said, reaching up and pinching Reza's cheeks.

"She's not coming?" Reza asked, turning to Hamlet.

"She's worse than mercury. Can't catch her," said Hamlet. "But I know where she's going. South-City."

"Why is she going all the way down there?"

"Something about girls needing to know how to read," he said lightly. He stuffed Mitra's books in her bag and threw it over his shoulder.

BACK AT HIS house, Hamlet sat on his bed and wrapped himself in a blanket. He was reading Khomeini's book.

"What's it about?" Mitra asked. She had given up any attempt to study.

Reza sat at the other end of the room, coolly watching.

"Let's entertain you, Mitty, shall we?" Hamlet exclaimed. "Reza, will you please do the honours?" He threw the green book across the room.

Reza read, "*Young boys or girls in full sexual effervescence are kept from getting married before they reach legal age of majority. This is against the intention of divine laws. Why should the marriage of pubescent girls and boys be forbidden because they are still minors, when they are allowed to listen to the radio and to sexually arousing music?*"

"Hear that, Mouse? You should have married me back in first grade," Hamlet said.

Reza laughed and tossed the green book back to Hamlet.

"Why wasn't I aware of these glorious rules before?" Hamlet asked.

"I don't know, comrade. Thank goodness we're not in the dark anymore."

Hamlet read now. "Mouse, listen: *A woman who has contracted a continuing marriage does not have the right to go out of the house without her husband's permission; she must remain at his disposal for the fulfillment of any one of his desires, and may not refuse herself to him except for a religiously valid reason. If she is totally submissive to him, the husband must provide her with her food, clothing, and lodging, whether or not he has the means to do so.*"

"Dammit, son, I could be in complete control of her right now," Hamlet said to Reza, who could not stop laughing. Hamlet shouted, "Did you hear that, Mouse? Our situation here could have been very different. I order you to stop running away."

Mitra shouted back, "That book is illegal, you know. The Shah has banned it. If they catch you . . ."

"The Shah can kiss my ass," Hamlet said. "He can kiss his ass, too." He pointed at Reza.

"I don't want that man anywhere near my ass," Reza protested, and he and Hamlet laughed some more.

Mitra frowned, grabbed the book, and began leafing through its pages.

31

At the other end of the city, near Niavaran, a man pushed open the prison door and bent his body toward the ground, as though afraid of the air. He took off the sunglasses he had been given, but as soon as the light hit his eyes he put them back on. He coughed a few times and walked several feet before looking back at the building that had imprisoned him for so long. Then he turned away, vowing never to look at it again.

He headed for a café he knew was close by, not far from the Shah's palace. Once there, he picked out a table, sat down, and placed his bag on the chair next to him.

"Tea?" asked the owner.

"And dates," the man replied. "Do you have a washroom here?"

"In the back," the owner said. "I'll just bring your order, then. Name?"

"Rameen," said the man.

Rameen took his bag with him to the washroom. He locked the door and removed the contents: a shirt and pants, a toothbrush, a small mirror, and a box of sweets one of the prison chefs—a friend—had given him as a parting gift. He opened the box, took out a sweet, ate it, tucked the rest of the treats in a plastic bag, and placed them in the pocket of the trousers. As he emptied the box, the money, covered with the white powder of the sweets, came into view. It smelled good. He folded the bills as tightly as he could, then took off his shoes and placed one bundle into each. When he slipped his feet back in, they felt tight. Walking with some discomfort, he returned to his table, where he popped a date into his mouth, washed it down with hot tea, then ate a second. "Thank you," he said to the owner, and left the café.

Even though it was autumn and the sun was weak, Rameen left his sunglasses on. The first place he headed was the one he had dreamed about since Behrouz had stopped coming to see him at the prison years ago. That silly driver had disappeared from his life as quickly as he'd appeared in it. Rameen walked the length of Pahlavi Street, all its twenty-some kilometres, until he reached the bazaar, his feet aching. Behrouz lived somewhere nearby, if he remembered rightly from that time he had taken the little girl home, likely still with his old hag of a wife. He walked through every avenue and alley near the Bazaar, hoping his memory would be triggered by a familiar sight. The door to Behrouz's house was a light blue, he remembered. He stopped a veiled woman and her child, and asked, "Mother, do you know where the Bakhtiar family might be living? Behrouz Bakhtiar. Has a wife, Zahra." But the woman covered her face even more tightly with her veil and fled, dragging her little boy behind her. He continued in this way for nearly an hour until an old man recognized Behrouz's name. "That man in the uniform? Hasn't lived around here in years. Saw his wife for some time, vile woman, walking around without a veil, and those stockings and miniskirts of hers. A disgrace. Wanted to be like those damned Americans."

"Is she still around?" Rameen asked. "Was her name Zahra? She had a flat face? Wore makeup?"

"Yeah, that's her. But she's been gone some time. Some say she got a visa and left the country. But I bet you she just went back to the village she came from. She was no high-class woman, to be heading off to Europe or wherever. God will be the judge of her." The old man adjusted his cane. Rameen moved to help him but he whacked his hand away. "Leave me alone, boy. You look like they've sent word of your death. What hellhole did you just come from? I don't want your diseases on me."

"Thank you for your help, father," said Rameen.

"The hell with you," the old man replied.

Now Rameen walked to the Bazaar and stood at its centre, gazing around at the many alleys, which spread outward for blocks. Here were carpet sellers, nut sellers, jewellery sellers; here was the smell of hot liver, as people bit chunks of it off thin metal spikes. For a moment, it was the Bazaar it had always been, as if from his boyhood memories. But then Rameen noticed something different. The usual framed pictures of the Shah had disappeared. He couldn't spot a single store displaying one. He picked an alley at random, and began to stroll with the crowd, looking inside the shops. No Shah. But what he did see surprised him. Each store had a framed photograph of an old mollah, a man Rameen recognized from the old days, when he had first gone to prison. It was the same mollah who had roused a protest and been deported. Well, that was a nice fuck-you to the Shah, thought Rameen, even if he'd never liked the clerics. He stopped at one of the jewellery shops, thinking he would buy something for his mother, and watched as the vendor came toward him with a box of bracelets made of gold beads. "Is that old Khomeini? Am I remembering the name?" Rameen asked.

"God save him, it is." The bead-seller took out the bracelets, placed them on the counter, and retrieved another box full of necklaces. "If he tells me to dance for him one hundred times a day, brother, I will," the vendor said. He took out the necklaces and displayed them. "If he tells me to give him all my wealth, I will." He polished one of the bracelets and lifted it up. "If he tells me to turn my back on my family, I will, brother. And if he tells me to kill, God forgive me, I will."

Rameen nodded. His eyes flitted between the vendor and the bracelet's gold shimmer.

"That man will save us, brother." The vendor thumped his chest. "I will give my life for him. You should do the same."

"I've heard he's a great man," Rameen said carefully. "By the way, did you ever know a man named Behrouz? Bakhtiar? With a daughter named Aria."

"Aria's a man's name, brother."

"This one was a girl."

The bead-seller clicked his tongue with disapproval, and shook his head.

OVER THE NEXT few days, Rameen tried again, asking vendor after vendor in the bazaar about a man named Behrouz and his daughter, Aria. Finally, he walked into an old bakery and laid down his bag, about to give up. "Three loaves of sangak," he said. The owner, a plump woman, folded long loaves of bread with black sesame seeds across the top, placed them in a bag, and handed it to him. "Fariba" said the name on the tag pinned to her chest. Some flickering hope inside Rameen compelled him to try one last time. "Excuse me, Mrs. Fariba, did you ever know a man named Behrouz with a daughter named Aria?"

"Depends on how you look at it," Fariba said. "I know the child's mother, Mehri."

◇

AT MOSQUE, KAMRAN often watched the women in their black veils, all the same, as if they were one organism, moving and praying in identical steps, melting into a black-clothed mass. Even Aria, the girl he had once so wanted to talk to, had dissolved into this imagined collective. He remembered her father's funeral, and how he had resolved to visit her that night and, instead of giving her another bracelet, offer her his heart. But that was the night the bead-seller caught him sneaking out of the shop and dragged him to the mosque, smacking his head all the way there, saying God would punish him on the day of judgment.

That evening at the mosque, Kamran and the bead-seller, along with a dozen mollahs and some younger boys he didn't know, sat together on the floor and, instead of praying, read the writings of a man named Khomeini. It was the night his new life started. Afterwards, his life was about two things: the holy book, and the holy man from Khomein.

Now the bead-seller, Mr. Sohrabi, was always talking to him at the mosque. "There are important things for you to do," he told Kamran one day. "Can you help the music seller? He recorded some tapes and needs you to distribute them."

"Tapes?" Kamran asked. "Tapes of what?"

"He recorded songs on a tape, then cut other things into them. Speeches. I need you to make copies. Hundreds. Maybe thousands. Then I need you to deliver them."

When most of the congregants had left the mosque, Mr. Sohrabi led Kamran to a spot on the floor beside some men who had stayed behind to study. The mollah was teaching them about the achievements of Imam Hossein, the martyr, the saint.

"Whose speeches are on the tapes?" Kamran asked when he was seated.

"You'll know when you hear it. I need you to deliver them. You'll be paid."

"Deliver where?"

"To the mosques, all of them, and give them to your friends, too. That group you have. That boy Ahmad and the others."

Kamran thought about that for a moment. Ahmad and his friends had changed. Gone were their days of petty thieving and small fights. Recently, Kamran had been trying to get away from them. But now he nodded and said, "Okay."

"The tapes will be very different than *him*," Mr. Sohrabi said, pointing to the lecturing mollah. "You'll hear how a real mollah, an ayatollah, moves the people."

KAMRAN MET WITH Ahmad and his gang the next afternoon. They had been using heroin—all except Ahmad himself, who had sold it to them—and were thirsty.

"You should come to mosque," said Kamran. "It'll be good for you."

"Will your mollah make me rich?" said Ahmad.

"He'll make it so you're never poor."

"Maybe, but it's bad timing, Jahanpour," Ahmad said.

"Why?"

"I've got business to take care of. I owe someone money. You're no good to me anymore, unless you have money for me. Or drugs."

"Drugs?" Kamran said. "From me?"

Ahmad's friend Saiid yanked his arm. "Let's go, Ahmad."

"I don't do that kind of thing anymore. And you shouldn't be selling that junk. I told you, come to mosque and the bazaaris will take care of you," Kamran said.

"The bazaaris do shit," Ahmad shouted. "I make six times more selling drugs than what I can get from their little charity."

"Well then I'll pay you. That's why I came. I'll give you money and you can help me with something."

"Can I?"

"I need to make copies of some tapes, then you'll deliver them, get them to as many of your friends as you can. The more people you get the tapes to, the more money."

"Who's paying?" said Ahmad.

"The bazaaris. You'll get your money. But first, help me."

"What's on the tapes?"

"Songs, with messages in between. Secrets," Kamran said.

"Is it illegal?" Ahmad looked at Saiid and the others as they lay on the ground, still weakened by the heroin. "We should all have knives, if you ask me," Ahmad said. "That's even more important than money."

"You can have both. I'll get you both. Money will get you knives, and knives will get you more money. Right?"

Ahmad found a lamppost and leaned against it. He took out a cigarette, lit it, and took three hard drags.

"Things are finally making sense," he said. "Tell me, what is with the bazaaris? What secrets?"

"If you came to mosque more often you'd know," said Kamran. "Our time is coming. Why should the Shah have all the wealth?"

"He shouldn't, should he," said Ahmad.

Kamran shook his head. "And nor should the North-City and those godless vermin, with their suits and ties and gold watches and their women who dress like sluts, with short skirts and hair blowing in the filthy wind of this place. Change is coming. Will you help?"

Ahmad flicked his cigarette away. He took out his pocket knife and flipped open the blade. The light it reflected crossed Kamran's face, like a scar. Ahmad eyed him for a while, then said, "Brother, I will go where the money goes."

THAT NIGHT, KAMRAN and Ahmad made a master tape, and the first song they recorded on it was ABBA's "Dancing Queen." The next song was by Julio Iglesias, and then there was another by ABBA, and then one by the Beatles. It was after the fifth track, an Iranian pop song, that they spliced in the tape Mr. Sohrabi had given them, sent directly from Iraq. It contained a sermon by Khomeini. Calls to revolution, he called them.

"Never heard of the man," Ahmad said, after listening. But by the end of the week, after dubbing six hundred copies, Ahmad knew Khomeini's voice the way he knew the voice in his own head.

"It's a good start," Mr. Sohrabi said when the delivery was made. He gave a fistful of cash to Kamran, who gave half of it to Ahmad. Ahmad divided among his gang, keeping thirty percent. That's how their enterprise started. The more tapes they made, the more money they got. After a month, all the gangs in the area wanted to work for the bazaaris. Soon after that, some wanted to *be* bazaaris. But that wasn't so easy.

Six months after Kamran and the gang began copying tapes, four men in suits kicked down the door of the Jahanpour home. They smashed all the chairs, opened all the kitchen cupboards, flipped mattresses over, and pinned Kamran to the ground. One of the men pulled his arm so far back that it broke. Kamran's mother held her daughter tight and screamed. His father, who had been resting in the other room, limped out to see his son on the ground. He yelled, "I'm the one. The tapes. I made them. I told the kids to make them. They work for me because my hand is bad. See?" He held it up.

Before Kamran could stop them, the men threw his father into the back of a truck and drove away. Ahmad, Saiid, and others were already there, their faces bruised. The truck drove all the way to North-City, to Evin prison.

Kamran would never see his father alive again. Kazem's heart simply stopped that night—or so the SAVAK wrote to the family. They delivered the body to the cemetery, and Kamran endured the pain of his broken limb, and a pain far worse in his heart, as he helped two men lower his father's body into the earth. Years later, when Evin came under his power, he would remember this pain, and it would propel him into a future he had never imagined.

32

In the university lecture hall, Mitra took frantic notes as Professor Saberi rushed through his lesson. Aria, on the other hand, sat back, her arms folded across her chest. She sometimes followed the notes the old professor wrote on the board, but for the most part, her eyes strayed to Hamlet and Reza. They were sitting together again, rummaging through some book, this time a red one. Sometimes they would laugh, reminding her of schoolgirls crushing on boys. Reza had a thick moustache now, and Hamlet was trying to grow his own moustache but failing. It was coming out red, and people laughed at him.

Beside her, Mitra was frustrated about having missed one of the professor's points. "What did he say? What did he say?" she asked. When she saw Aria wasn't taking notes she turned to the boy on her other side. "Did you catch that part about the land rights?"

"Shh," said the boy.

"Why aren't you taking notes?" Mitra asked Aria.

"Because there are no rights. The rich own the land, so who cares?" Aria said.

"You'll fail your exam," Mitra said.

"What do you think they're talking about over there?" Aria looked at Hamlet and Reza.

"That book, and the mollahs and the Shah. And apparently every being that's ever betrayed any Iranian. You're all obsessed with that stuff. I'm staying out of it," Mitra said, as the boy beside her shushed her again.

When the lecture was over, Aria lost sight of the boys in the crowd, so she and Mitra headed to the cafeteria. It was there that she saw Hamlet, walking up the stairs to join them. A group of third- and fourth-year girls followed him. She could sense Mitra's disapproval.

"You're lucky those aren't Hezbollahi wives following you," Aria teased him. "You'd get charged with trying to convert them."

"Shut up. There could be SAVAK all over this campus." Hamlet sat down. "Ladies, there's a party tonight. Will you follow me, like those girls? Don't worry, Mouse, there won't be any alcohol. We're righteous people."

"Where is it?" asked Aria.

"At Reza's. North-City."

"I'm not associating with fanatics," Mitra said.

"What time?" Aria asked, and pulled her chair closer. She pulled Mitra's chair closer too, but Mitra pushed herself back. "And who else will be there?"

"Everybody. And of course you two. We need more women. It's you we're fighting for. Mostly."

"My ass, you're fighting for us," said Aria.

Mitra looked around anxiously and tapped her foot against the leg of her chair. "You two can go if you want."

"Come, Mouse. Don't break my heart," Hamlet said.

"It's violent, what you talk about," Mitra said.

Hamlet lowered his voice. "Who said anything about violence? You've got some strange ideas in your head, woman."

"Could be. All because of some fantasy in those books you read," Mitra said.

"It's not a fantasy. It's real. Change can really happen this time. We're backed up. We've got France, England, even America . . . We've got backup, kids. There's talk about bringing Khomeini from Paris. As crazy as he is with that book of his, at least we can get things moving forward."

"He says he doesn't want to rule," Aria said. "He's just paving the way. He wants what is good."

"Where did you hear that?" Mitra asked.

"Everybody's talking about it," Aria and Hamlet said at the same instant.

"Imagine if they let him back into the country. Mayhem. Mayhem and momentum, Mouse," said Hamlet. He made a fist.

"We'll be done with this backward country. Finally things will get better," agreed Aria.

Hamlet patted Mitra's head and left. The girls finished the rest of their lunch in silence, hoping the wrong people had not heard them.

The walk home from the university took an hour, but Aria preferred it. Driving or taking buses reminded her too much of Behrouz. When she got home, Maysi had set out snacks on the table for her. Study-snacks, she called them. Two slices of lavash bread, a block of feta, some chopped cucumbers, parsley, and soaked walnuts. Water for the tea was boiling in the samovar.

"I can't eat much," Aria said. "I'm going out later."

"Again?" Maysi asked. "What do you do all night? Talk about things you shouldn't be talking about?" She shoved the plate toward Aria.

Aria placed a walnut in her mouth. "Maysi, are you happy?"

"Happy? Didn't anybody ever tell you there's no such thing?"

Maysi moved from the counter to the table and back to the stove, wiping every surface. Then she stopped for a moment. "I used to know someone who was always searching for happiness. It was the biggest mistake she ever made. Don't ever dare search for happiness." With that, she went upstairs to call Fereshteh down for dinner.

AT REZA'S HOUSE, the girls stood in a group at the back of the room. Aria had forced Mitra to come after all. Tall men in front of them blocked their view of the man who was speaking, but they could hear him clearly. He was talking about dividing and conquering.

Mitra watched Hamlet as he chatted with Reza and some of the other boys. She wished he would just take her away.

Finally, the speaker wrapped things up, saying, "God is great!" Most of the crowd cheered, but Hamlet was one of the few who didn't. He looked over at the girls and shook his head.

Aria made her way toward him. "You didn't say you were bringing us to a religious thing," she said. "Feels like it's Ashura."

"It's fine, it's fine," he said over the din. "I'll explain."

"Some communist you are, Hamlet Khan," she said.

A new speaker had made his way to the front of the room now, speaking in a louder voice than the man before him. "The Shah is Satan!" he proclaimed. He pointed his finger in the air, then made a fist with one hand and slammed it into the other. Aria moved up to see, but so did others, and in the press she became separated from Mitra and Hamlet. As she got closer, something about the man's face drew her in.

"How many people has he tortured?" the speaker said, his face turning red. "Five thousand? Six thousand?"

"More like five hundred, sir," said an old man standing close by. Aria recognized him, with surprise. It was Professor Saberi, head of the law school, whose lecture she had attended earlier that day.

The speaker ignored Professor Saberi.

"Our people's lives destroyed, by the thousands. Mine. Yours. From the beginning, all he ever wanted was to take our rights, our livelihoods, our due, our oil, our money."

"The Great Imam will get rid of him," shouted the religious man who had spoken first. He was now sitting with his friends at the head of the crowd. The room cheered.

"Your Great Imam believes in a God. That's no different than believing in a king," the man at the podium said.

The crowd at the front sprang to their feet, shouting. Someone threw prayer beads, which hit the speaker in the eye. "Blasphemy! Blasphemy!" the crowd shouted.

"Khomeini is saving us," called out the first speaker. "He is the only one who truly cares. The man is our saint."

Again there were cheers. "He is as pure as light," shouted someone else. "Look upon the moon, you'll see his face there," came a voice from the back.

Hearing this, Professor Saberi quietly put on his coat and left the room. Aria followed, but the room was so packed that she couldn't keep him in her sight. By the time she was outside, there was no trace of the white-haired professor.

The air was crisp and silent, and she breathed deeply. After a moment, she heard Hamlet call her name. He must have come to find her after she'd followed the old man.

"Want one?" He offered her a cigarette.

"No," she said. But he placed it between her lips and lit it for her, and she didn't resist. Behind him, Mitra was watching them both. Hamlet followed Aria's gaze and turned around, surprised. "Want one, too, Mouse?" he said.

Mitra took a cigarette and placed it between her lips. "You going to light this?"

Hamlet moved closer and lit it for her. Aria took a drag of her own cigarette and shoved her free hand into her coat pocket. "That first guy," she said. "I couldn't even understand him."

"That's because it was religious talk," said Mitra. "You never pray anyway, so you wouldn't understand those things."

"You're joking. It was all nonsense. And since when is an aya-tollah an imam? What do the mollahs know about politics?"

"You need to have some faith. They're close to God. Maybe they know better than those who aren't." Mitra took two deep drags of her cigarette and flicked what was left of it close to Aria's foot. "I'm going to hear more." She sauntered back to the house.

"She's a downright mule sometimes," Aria said, watching her go. "I thought this was a communist gathering. What are those turbans doing in there, Hamlet? What about that book you used to read?"

"Turns out we need their help. We need each other." Hamlet now flicked his cigarette away, too, and turned back toward the house. "Coming?" he asked.

Aria shoved her hands into her overcoat and walked in the opposite direction.

He ran after her. "Wait! Where are you going?"

"As far away from this shit as I can," she said.

"Can't you see what's going on here?"

"I see very well what's going on."

"Mitra's in there. She's not complaining. She's starting to see things clearly more and more," said Hamlet.

Aria whipped around. "She's only in there because of YOU. She's in love with YOU. That's all she sees. If you say jump, she says how high. Whatever you say, she says the same. She wouldn't give a shit about any of it if she didn't think she could impress YOU. For someone who claims to have such a clear vision of the future, Mr. Agassian, you can be so blind."

Hamlet stopped and watched the shine of Aria's leather boots disappear in the darkness. He felt the wind in the curls of his hair, and a heavy burden tied knots in his heart. So, the wrong girl was in love with him after all.

When he returned inside, the last speaker, the one who'd been heckled, approached him. There was a small bruise below his eye where the beads had hit him. He and Hamlet shook hands.

"Was that girl your friend?" the man asked. "The one who left?"

"Why do you ask?" Hamlet said.

"Is her name Aria, by any chance?" the speaker said. "I knew her father. A poor woman I met, down in South-City, told me she sometimes comes to these things."

TOCHAL WAS THE farthest mountain before the great Mount Damavand. Here the trails got steep, and there was nothing much to guide Aria. She'd forgotten to bring water, and for the life of her couldn't remember how she'd done this climb as a kid. She should have said yes when Maysi offered to pack food for her.

When she arrived at the café at the top, it was filled with men smoking hookahs. She searched the room for Hamlet, but he wasn't there. She stepped outside, hoping to find him, but there was no sign. All the way up, she had wracked her brains as to why he would ask to meet here. Perhaps it had to do with another of his fantasies about creating a great revolution.

She went back inside, and the server brought her tea and two sugar cubes. She drank her tea hot and played with the cubes, ignoring the men in the café and their looks of suspicion. Clearly, they thought she was too young, and too female, to be there on her own. Maybe they would assume she was the daughter of someone at the café. Or maybe they would wonder if she was a prostitute looking for work. And then she saw him, the speaker from the night before.

The man was sitting at the corner table, twirling a teaspoon in an empty glass. At just that moment he spotted her, too, and walked over to her table. "Rameen," he introduced himself. "And I know you are Aria. Mehri helped me find you."

"Mehri?" Aria asked, astonished.

"Yes. Mrs. Shirazi," said Rameen. "I think you know her. And you know me, too. How old are you now?"

She looked down at his hands and realized his thumbs were missing. "Twenty-four," she said. "Will you sit down?"

The server brought more tea, and Rameen pulled up a chair opposite her. "Do you work?" he asked.

"I study," she said. "Accounting."

"I always knew you were smart. Do you have a husband?"

"Why? Are you looking for one?" She laughed, but Rameen didn't laugh with her. "I'm sorry," she said.

"I thought maybe Hamlet . . . ," he said, then stopped himself. He took a deep breath. "I wanted to ask you about your father."

"He's dead," Aria said.

WHAT RAMEEN HEARD wasn't Aria's words, but the hollow echo of her voice and the rush of blood through his veins. The next thing he knew, Aria was bent over him, splashing lukewarm tea on his face. "I'm sorry," he said.

The owner of the café came out from the back and approached their table. "Everything all right?" he asked.

Rameen nodded. He wiped his face with a tissue, sat back in his chair, and picked up his own tea. The owner disappeared again.

"The last time I saw your father I was in prison," he began. "I was teaching him to read. For years, he would visit every Friday, after he saw you. But one day, years ago, he didn't come, and then the week after he didn't come again." His eye caught the light on the trees outside. "It's a beautiful place, this," he said with a smile at Aria. "But here is what I want to tell you. It was after your father had stopped coming, and a month after I left solitary, that I got the first letter. It simply said: *'What's coming is not for you. But please keep it safe. God be with you.'* That was all, a piece of plain paper with only those words on it. I did wonder if it was from your father. He had long ago asked me to help him write letters to you, about how much he loved you, how much he felt for you. He hoped you'd read them one day. But I lost those letters when I was sent to the prison in Shiraz. So now I wondered if he had finally learned to write on his own, and wanted me to read what he had written. But after this first letter, nothing arrived for another month. Like I said, I had hoped the letter was from your father. It would have been nice . . . I hadn't heard from him for so long, you see.

"Then a package arrived for me on a Monday. It was a box of baklava. The sweets were stacked in layers inside the box. The guards had eaten most of the upper layer, but there remained three full layers underneath. And beneath all that, taped to the very bottom of the box, was something wrapped in paper. I opened it in my cell, careful that no one would see. It was three hundred American dollars. A note came with the money. It said: *'More will come.'* And it did. Each month: another three hundred. Always hidden in boxes of sweets, with the guards having eaten the top layers. At first, I'd place the money between the pages of a book and hide the book in a sweet box. I'd become friends with one of the cooks and he'd stash the box for me behind a loose stone in the wall of the prison kitchen. Then the roll of bills got too big for the box and the spot in the kitchen. The cook leant me a suitcase with a lock. He gave me the key and I stashed the money there, in

tin boxes everyone thought had food in them. I was now convinced your father was sending these packages. The thing I
couldn't understand was how he was getting his hands on this
amount of money.

"Eight months later, a real letter arrived, not just a note. And
if anyone doubts that words can kill a heart and then ignite it with
life again, the words in this letter would have proven them
wrong. At last, I thought, your father had written to me. I considered that my mind was playing tricks, because like I said, when I
had last seen him, he couldn't write. But I convinced myself that
only a man like him could have written such beautiful words.

"The letters kept coming, once a month. For almost a year, I
was the envy of the other prisoners."

Rameen removed a letter from his pocket and read:

Dear Rameen,

*I wonder sometimes if it's possible for a generation to burn. I see
you as someone unreal, something from the myths of Ferdowsi. You
are to me like Rostam, the great warrior in the Book of Kings. I
have this image of you at birth, lifted high into space by a giant jinn,
as big as the universe, beyond clouds, beyond galaxies, and the
great Simorgh phoenix nestles you in her wing. You want to save
mankind like Rostam did. I know. You are the Rostam for those like
me, who have been struck down by the circumstance of birth.
When I was a child, I would sleep on rooftops under the night lit
up with stars. Our guardians would take us there and lay us down
on the concrete for fear that at night we would steal from the houses
we worked in. From the beginning, we had been marked as lesser.*

*I remember how you looked after Aria. I have regretted many
things in my life, but my greatest regret of all is that I allowed that
little girl to live. Why, in this world of deceit, where lies fall as*

freely as rain, must something precious be sullied? I feared for
her, that she would become like me, a monster. But perhaps,
my Rostam, you will right the wrongs I have done. Perhaps
there is a phoenix in all of us. And if you wonder why I write
well, I can only tell you that as a child I would put myself to
sleep with poetry.

"There are more," said Rameen. He removed a small box from
his backpack and opened it. Inside were letters upon letters, and
Aria's eyes grew large. He opened another, and read:

My Dear Rameen,
I have not seen Aria in some time. My childhood was no child-
hood. I barely remember the scent of my mother. The people
around me would never speak to me, only about me. "Should this
one do this job? Should they be separated? Should they sleep so
close to the china?" For every mistake I made I was beaten. And
for everything I did well, I was beaten again, this time by my own
kind, for fear I would become a favourite. And I, too, became a
victim of jealousy. One does not choose what one does. We are
moulded by the mud of our lives. If we are made of dirt, we shall
become dirt. I know I am dirt, Rameen. Aria and I have had such
similar lives, you know. I was left under a tree when my mother
died. But my father kept me. Whenever I looked at her, it was as
if I was looking back at myself. We are a nation of cannibals.

Rameen refolded the paper. "The total amount of money I was
sent over the past two years came to about forty thousand
American."

He held out an envelope for Aria. "It's all there. It's yours."
Then he handed her the box of letters.

With shaking fingers, Aria opened one carefully and read. Her face clouded. "My father didn't write these," she said. "I think he was already dead when this was written."

"But . . . who wrote them, then?"

"I recognize the handwriting," Aria said. "It was Zahra. And I don't want her money."

33

Aria spent a couple of sleepless hours in bed that night, thinking about Rameen and the day just past. She heard again the desperation in his voice as he implored her to take the cash, promising he would also send her the money Behrouz had sent to his parents for safekeeping. In the end, she had taken the cursed envelope. But where had Zahra found such riches? Why had she sent the money to Aria? And why had she written those letters to Rameen? There was no way of knowing, since Zahra had simply vanished after Behrouz's death. Aria stuffed the money and the letters in the bottom drawer of her dresser, under some old clothes, and vowed not to think about it.

When she could not will herself to sleep, Aria snuck downstairs, careful not to wake Maysi and Mana. She picked up the receiver on the phone and dialed. "Let's go to the club," she said.

Hamlet was on her doorstep within minutes. He had taken his father's Mercedes, and Reza was sitting in the passenger seat.

"Let's grab Mitra on the way. I don't like two against one," she said.

Mitra came reluctantly. "You couldn't have planned this, say, yesterday, could you?"

"You don't plan for the disco," Hamlet said. Reza and Aria laughed.

"Well, I'm not staying if there are drugs," said Mitra. She huddled under her coat beside Aria in the back seat.

"What drugs?" Aria said.

"They have cocaine. Everybody talks about the cocaine."

"That's the first thing I'm doing," said Reza.

"The police will get you," Mitra said.

"Bullshit," said Hamlet. "Everyone in this city drinks vodka and now everyone is about to snort coke. My ass, the police will get you."

"The police only get you if you're trying to save the poor," Reza said.

"Then long live cocaine and vodka!" said Aria. Only Mitra refused to laugh.

The club was smoky and smelled of sweat and alcohol. Aria lit a cigarette as soon as she walked in, and Reza headed straight to the bar. Music blasted from the speakers: "Jive Talkin'" by the Bee Gees.

Hamlet snatched Aria's cigarette, took a drag, and pulled her onto the dance floor.

After a moment, Aria pulled her arms away and walked back to Mitra, laughing. "He's crazy," she said. "Come, Mouse." She took Mitra's hand and found them a table, where she sat down and shrugged off her jacket. The sequined top she was wearing crisscrossed at her neck and revealed an open back. She took another drag of her cigarette and offered a new one to Mitra.

"You're not wearing a bra?" Mitra said.

Aria could no longer contain herself. "What's the matter with you?" she said. "Do you really think a plain shirt is enough for this place?" She bounced in time to the music. "How strange you are. Want a vodka-soda?"

"No," Mitra said.

"A beer, then?"

"All right. A beer. But put ice in it?"

"Ice? You're mad, Mitra Ahari. I'll be back. You watch Hamlet and make sure he doesn't break an arm, the way he's flinging himself around."

"He really doesn't know how to dance," Mitra said, but Aria didn't hear her.

Hamlet, oblivious, moved his body to the beat of the song. He struggled when the music changed, searching for new beats, stopping and starting. A few girls dancing close to him laughed, but Hamlet didn't care, and Mitra watched him not care. He closed his eyes when he found a rhythm, and the light reflecting off the broken glass of the disco ball became a cascade of colour across his face. Sometimes she could see him, sometimes not. He was moving light and colour, triggered by sound and rhythm.

He opened his eyes and saw her watching him. He smiled, lifted his hand, bent his four fingers toward his own body. "Come here," he said to Mitra. She shook her head no. He motioned with his hand again, and again she said no. He danced between the tables until he reached her.

"All alone?" he said.

She spoke loudly into his ear. "They're getting drinks!"

"Too bad for them," said Hamlet. He put his hand around Mitra's waist. "Come, you. We're wasting time." He pulled her to the dance floor and this time she didn't protest.

They danced in the light, and the other women in miniskirts around them tried to get Hamlet's attention. He had been that kind of boy, thought Mitra, and now he'd become that kind of man. But Hamlet held her and smiled.

"They're back," Hamlet yelled when the song ended. He pointed, and she saw that Reza and Aria were sitting at the table, nursing drinks.

"Anything new?" Reza was asking Aria.

"Nope," Aria said. She played with her drink, then picked it up and downed the whole thing. "Should have bought another."

"I'll get it," Reza said, standing up.

"No, I'll go myself," Aria said quickly, and left him there.

As the bartender made her drink, she looked out over the dance floor. She was glad to see Mitra dancing, glad she had brought them all out. Anything was better than staying in her bed, thinking about the day, not knowing whether to hate Zahra or hate life. How had she forgotten Rameen for so long? And why had he remembered her? He could have dropped the whole thing, taken the money himself, moved on with life. Yet the earth's magnetic field had played its mysterious trick, bringing them together, willing one toward the other, despite resistance. Now, as she watched Hamlet and Mitra dance, she envied her friends. Rameen's revelations rang loud and forceful in her memory. Here, where the youth of the country, privileged youth, indulged in a great act of forgetfulness through song and dance and whimsy, Aria could not forget. Were Zahra's letters a kind of apology? It was hard to believe, even hours later.

She watched Hamlet hug Mitra on the dance floor, take her hand, and walk her back to the table. Aria took her drink and joined them. "Not bad," she said.

Mitra laughed. "I guess I can dance a little after all. He helps." She pointed at Hamlet.

"Laughing suits you, Mouse," she said.

"Indeed," said Hamlet, and in an instant he had put his hand around Aria's waist and pulled her to the dance floor.

Aria glanced anxiously at Mitra, whose face had turned pale, a ghost among the flashing colours.

"You shouldn't have," Aria said loudly in Hamlet's ear.

But Hamlet didn't understand. "What? I'll teach you to dance, too."

Clueless and enraptured, he whisked her around the floor. Aria pushed him away, and turned back to Mitra. But the only one still sitting at the table was Reza.

"Where did she go?" Aria asked.

"Haven't a clue," Reza said. But he and Hamlet stood and did a circle of the club.

They found Mitra waiting outside. "It's time to go home," Aria told them, and put her arm around her friend.

IT WAS THREE months before Aria saw Reza again, this time in the cafeteria at school. His moustache was thicker. He was wearing a green jacket, a green turtleneck sweater, and green trousers with roomy pockets down the side of each leg. He looked like a soldier, she thought, without being one.

It was clear that many of the students knew him well. They said hello, and he smiled, shook their hands, and discreetly placed pieces of folded paper in their palms. Hamlet trailed him around the room. When he saw Aria, he smiled and waved, motioning for her to join them. She shook her head and returned to the book she'd been reading. Only when Reza was gone did she look up again.

Hamlet sat beside her. "What's your problem?" he asked, taking an uneaten piece of bread from her plate.

"I know what you're up to with Reza. There are agents all over the campus. Shame on you."

"Shame on me?"

"Yes, shame on you for wanting to talk to me when a million SAVAKis will see me with the two of you. *Let's have lunch, Aria. So sorry if it lands you in a cell.*"

Hamlet placed a dirty cassette tape in front of her.

"What's this?" she asked.

"Mozart! No, really it's our friend the ayatollah. Come with me and let's listen to it. Reza's not coming. I haven't listened yet. I figure if we've laughed enough at his book, we can laugh some more at his speeches." He grabbed her arm. "Come, just come," he said.

Aria gave in and followed him all the way to his home. In Hamlet's vast courtyard, she dipped her toes in the cold pool as he walked around it impatiently, trying to unjam the play button on his portable cassette player. "Damn thing," he said.

"Try wedging a knife in there," she suggested.

"No use. I have something else, though. It's a fancier player. My father just brought it back from New York."

"I'd rather die than use it," Aria said.

"Why?"

"Because your father probably bought it with blood money. The Shah's money."

Hamlet sat beside her and dipped his toes in the water, too. "Really, you'd rather die?"

"Who bought you that one?" Aria pointed at the broken player.

Hamlet lowered his head. "My dad did."

"Give it to me," Aria said. He passed her the player. She threw it in the pool.

Hamlet jumped up, horrified and speechless.

"We should dump this whole house in the pool," Aria said quickly. "And I want you to stop seeing that Reza guy. Last week they arrested twenty students."

"He's not a student anymore."

"They'll catch him, along with all the students he's recruited. Including you."

"Not possible," said Hamlet. "My father sells the Shah his diamonds, remember. They have breakfast together."

"You'd be surprised," Aria said.

Hamlet shook his head. "No. He's an asshole, but he's not crazy. We were about to listen to crazy. Unfortunately, you just threw that tape in the water."

"Shit," said Aria.

"But you're right." Hamlet looked from one side of the Olympic-size pool to the other. "Let's use this for what it's really meant," he said. He ran inside. Minutes later he was back with several small boxes. "Ready?" he said, and threw the boxes in the water.

"Have you lost your mind? What was in those?" Aria said.

"Look." Hamlet pointed at one of the boxes in the pool. Something glowed through a crack. Whatever it was, it sank with the box, and soon more shiny objects began to float away and sink.

Aria looked deep into the pool, and when the water finally settled she saw clearly. "Watches? You threw your father's watches in there?"

"These ones aren't watches," Hamlet said, and now he threw in more boxes. "These are the rings. Next, necklaces. And then, the world!"

After several minutes of this, Aria and Hamlet stood side by side at the edge of the pool. Empty boxes floated to the corners and back to the centre. From the bottom came the glitter of diamonds, gold, and silver.

"Do you think that if there was a plane flying above us, the pilot would think these were stars?" Aria said.

"That's something you'd have said when we were little," Hamlet replied. "And I would have laughed at you."

"Are you laughing at me now?" said Aria, her eyes on the water.

"Not at all," Hamlet said softly.

"So, shall we get more things to throw in?" she asked.

"I've already thrown in every piece of jewellery in the house," Hamlet said.

"Well, there are other things," she said, looking at him.

A few minutes later, they each stood again at the edge of the pool, carrying clothes made of silk and cashmere. "Mother will die," said Hamlet.

"Like everybody else who's died up there?" Aria glanced toward Evin.

It took a while for the clothes to soak up the water. "Isn't this just like washing them?" Hamlet asked.

"No, just wait. The chlorine will destroy them," said Aria.

After that, they turned their attention to rugs: long, heavy Persian rugs hand-woven by schoolgirls who ate once a day and were beaten if they didn't work fast enough. Then came the TVs, all three of them. Then the radios, and the cash Hamlet found in his father's coat pockets. They stopped only because there was no more room. When it was all over they stood at the edge again, watching the rugs and silks floating. Hamlet held Aria's hand. "Can I stay with you and your mother for a while?" he asked. "I don't think I'll be allowed back here ever again after my parents return."

Aria gazed into the distance, toward the Alborz mountain range. Mount Damavand looked back at her sharply, as if it were about to hand down a stiff punishment, a sentence she did not yet know about. "I'll ask Mana about you staying. But you know Mitra won't be happy about it." She examined the waves of Hamlet's hair, aware of his penetrating eyes and his silence. "But yes. All right, yes."

She placed a hand on his face, turned it to her own. "Stay away from Reza, that's all," she said, and kissed him, witnessed only by the mountains where the great Simorgh slept.

AT HOME THAT night, Aria was almost asleep when the phone rang. She quickly answered it before it could wake Mana and Maysi.

"I don't know what's going on with me. I do stupid things," Hamlet's voice said.

"What stupid things?" Aria asked.

"Men do stupid things."

Aria held her breath. Did he regret their kiss? After a moment, she said, "You should be kinder to Mitra."

"I'm not kind?"

"Be gentle, be careful. I'm going to tell her you kissed me."

"I kissed you? You kissed me."

"Men remember stupidly," she said.

"Do you think my father will be calm about what we did?" he asked.

"Yes. Armenians are calm. I think he will forgive you."

"Because we're Christian?" Hamlet said. Aria could hear the hint of a smile in his voice.

She laughed. "The serenity of Christ. Maybe," she said, and hung up.

The next day, Hamlet sent a message for Mitra and Aria to meet him along the road to Mount Damavand in the afternoon. The girls arrived first, and Aria told Mitra about the kiss. Mitra said nothing, but she turned her face away and kicked her bicycle tire. Aria stood nearby, letting the last of her cigarette turn to ash.

"It was stupid. So stupid. You're right, I do dumb things, Mouse," she said, hoping that some solidarity would linger between them. Snow fell, and for ten minutes they stood under it in silence as Aria tried to think of something more to say.

"Why did Hamlet ask us here?" she ventured.

Mitra shrugged, and Aria could see she was about to cry. She watched her friend look up from her angry study of the snow. "Because he's a bastard?"

They heard footsteps, and finally Hamlet appeared down the street.

"You're my best friend," Aria said quickly to Mitra.

Hamlet strolled toward them with his rolling gait and his thick boots, frowning slightly, oblivious to the tension. "Are you two getting lovelier and lovelier, or am I getting older and my vision blurrier? Have you been waiting long?"

"And you care?" Mitra said.

Hamlet turned to Aria. "I need to talk to you. Alone," he said softly.

"And leave Mouse?"

"Yes, now," he said. "Sorry, Mouse."

"I'm not leaving Mouse," said Aria.

"Fine. Mouse, follow us," he ordered.

The three of them strolled along the white-capped cobbled road that led to Damavand, Mitra walking slightly behind Aria and Hamlet, just within earshot, shuffling her feet. But what Hamlet wanted to talk about surprised both her and Aria.

"Reza's in trouble," he said. "They might shoot him. Execute him. I don't know. I don't know." He massaged his forehead and pulled at his hair.

Aria glanced at Hamlet. Was he joking? From the pallor of his face she saw he was not. "What did they catch him for?"

"Dancing. Or maybe it was doing a backflip. Who knows." Hamlet lit a cigarette.

"But I just saw him. The other day. He looked—"

"It was treason, Aria. For passing out flyers. Marxist ones," Hamlet said dully.

"For the Fadayan or the Tudeh?" Aria asked.

"What the fuck difference does it make? They're all the same. Could have been one of the smaller groups."

"But he wasn't fighting, he didn't kill anyone?"

"He did, inadvertently, I guess. Some military guy was shot by some kid who said he got the flyer from Reza. That's all I know."

"I told you to stay away from him," Aria said.

"I guess I'll have to now," Hamlet said. He ran his fingers through his hair again. Aria could hear the quaver in his voice, and she could see he was sweating.

"Okay, I can help you," she said.

"But you're not into helping, remember? You're into pouting and not laughing at jokes."

"Don't be angry with me. I didn't do this. And if they torture him enough he'll give them your name," said Aria. "There must be a way . . ."

"There is. A quarter of a million tomans. Do you have that?"

Aria hesitated. "His family . . ."

"His family lost most of their money. People like my shit of a father made sure of it."

"I have money," she said.

"Your mama has money, but I doubt she'd give it up for a thing like this."

"No. Me. I have money. My father left me a pension when he died. I get it monthly. I have since I was fifteen."

"That won't be enough. I know how much a military pension is worth."

"It's not just that. I have other money." She glanced back to see if Mitra could hear them, but she'd fallen back and was looking down at her footsteps in the snow.

Hamlet made a snowball and threw it down the road. "What other money? What are you talking about?"

"Before I tell you anything, I just want you to know that I'm okay. I won't be giving anything up. Let me give the money to you."

"Is it dirty money?" Hamlet asked.

"What does it matter what kind of money it is. If it saves a life? And saves you?"

"Because Reza won't want bourgeois money. That would go against everything he fights for."

"It's not. Far from it."

But Hamlet shook his head, unable to grasp the enormity of what Aria was saying.

"It's sweat money," Aria insisted. "Worked and sweated for. Clean as can be. It came to me through circumstances I can't tell you about. But it's good money. I just don't want it. What I want is for something good to come from it."

Hamlet stood still now, considering. Aria turned to see if Mitra had caught up, and saw that her friend was watching them. Aria was suddenly aware of how she and Hamlet had been walking in step, mirroring each other's movements. From Mitra's perspective, they must have looked like reflections of each other.

"I'm not sure we can pay you back very quickly," Hamlet said quietly.

Aria smiled. "I don't want it back," she said.

Hamlet reached the end of his cigarette and took a last drag. "I'm the one who should be the hero. Isn't that how it is in the fairy tales? The prince saves the princess, then marries her?"

Aria looked him in the eye. "Take it," she said. And she turned and walked back the way she had come, past a silent Mitra, her steps muffled by the falling snow.

34

Aria's taxi curved slowly through the alleyways, with barely room to move. The driver said it would be faster this way, but he had lied. They passed a boy and his two goats before a procession of vehicles blocked the way again. This time, it was two families, each with husband, wife, and two children, piled on their scooters, trying to squeeze past.

"You have to get off and walk!" the driver shouted at them, but the husbands waved him away. The wives wore long, black veils, and their children clung to them and each other.

"Enough! I'm getting out here. Here!" Aria said. She threw some bills on the seat beside the driver and opened the door. It scraped against a wall, but somehow she squeezed through, the driver's curses in her ears. In another minute she had made it to the main street. Little here had changed: the bearded men, the veiled women, the dirty-nailed children were all the same, only now there were more of them. And more of the people had cars, rundown and rusted but mobile. South-City was still South-City, but the Bazaar had fattened up the place. Things moved faster now, and everyone was busy. From one car's radio she heard the azan, the call to prayer. From another, she heard that famous pop singer, the Armenian one with the trembling voice whose song everyone was singing at the university these days. From another car she heard Led Zeppelin, and Jimmy Page's wailing guitar. Hamlet liked Zeppelin, too, but Mitra didn't. She turned red when Robert Plant bared his chest.

Aria made it across the road and launched herself into the crowds. Her steps were quick and timed to the passing seconds on her watch. She couldn't be late today, of all days, because today was Roohi's graduation. The girl from South-City had done the impossible, and Aria had to be there to celebrate over dinner with the family. She was about to make a run for it across the street on a red light when someone nearby said, "I wouldn't do that."

Aria turned in a full circle, searching for the source of the voice. Ten people around her returned blank stares—the women, from behind their veils, trying to decipher her, as if she were a secret code. The men had no interest in decoding her at all.

"The cars here are fast. You'll be flattened," the voice said again. This time she recognized it.

"Hamlet, where are you?"

The culprit pushed his way through the crowd. His sleeves were rolled up to his biceps, his shirt collar open, and he wore sunglasses and those bell-bottom trousers all the boys were now sporting. The waves of his wild hair were exaggerated by its length. If Mana saw him, thought Aria, she would hide him in the closet.

"Never cross the street around here. You'll die." He smiled at her.

"I know my way around, thanks," Aria said, unmoved.

The light turned and the crowd started to cross the street, so Aria and Hamlet followed them, on the lookout for rogue cars. When they reached a side street that branched into the alley that would lead to the Shirazi house, Aria stopped. "You can't come with me. What are you doing here, anyway?" she asked.

"I should ask you," Hamlet said. "Aren't you going to the Bazaar? It's just around the corner."

"Where were *you* going?" Aria asked.

"Well, you know there's not much to do at home, alone with your mother and Maysi," Hamlet said.

"You don't have to stay there all day. Your father forgave you. You can go home."

"I don't want to be around him," Hamlet said. "Anyhow, I wanted to update you on Reza. And your money. Things have turned out well. There'll be a trial later, but—"

"I don't want to talk about him. Not today. Anyhow, you have exams tomorrow." She knew his schedule well; like all the other law students, Hamlet was drowning in work. But nothing ever rattled him.

"I'll pass. It's all up here." Hamlet tapped his forehead.

"All that's ever been up there is dust," Aria said. "I really have to go." She started to walk down the alley.

He grabbed her arm. "Why haven't you kissed me again? We should talk about it, no?"

"Nothing to discuss. I have to go, and you can't come. Can you leave me alone now? We can have lunch at the cafeteria tomorrow."

"And we'll talk?"

"No, we'll eat."

"Accountants eat? I thought you were vampires. Plus Mouse will be there. I don't want to talk about this around her," Hamlet said.

Aria stopped walking. "My mother says to apologize to your father."

"Never. I know why I did what I did. And why won't you tell me where you're going? Is it to that family?"

Aria hesitated.

"What are they like?" Hamlet asked. "Do they pray ten times a day? You never say."

"It's five times. Muslims pray five times. Sunnis do, too. For Shias, like me, three times. And no, they don't."

"How many children are there?"

"Four," Aria said.

"Four what? Girls? Boys?"

"They're girls. You know this, Hamlet. But only two go to school."

"Ah. So they went in the end? No bazaar for them. Why only two?"

"The second one is graduating. This isn't your business."

"Why didn't the others go?"

"One was busy. The other one, sick. Like I said, this isn't your business."

They passed another group of South-City folk headed to the bazaar. "I hate this inferno," Hamlet said.

"Not as much as I do. Can I go now?"

Hamlet took her arm. "Can I meet them? Just to see. I want to know more about you."

Aria freed her arm, shook her head, and walked away. She kept on, not looking back, and headed down the winding stairs that led to another alley, then up a flight of stairs and a ladder that led to yet another. She could tell without looking that Hamlet had followed her. When they reached the green gates that opened to the Shirazis' dilapidated and rat-filled front yard, Aria turned to face him. "There's really nothing to see," she said again.

"There's everything to see," he said, standing beside her and studying the house.

A rattle sounded from the upstairs window. Behind it, Roohangeez was beaming. She gestured for them to come in, then disappeared. At the window, another face emerged: Gohar. And beside Gohar, still another figure stood, happily waving, her head barely reaching past the windowsill. This was the youngest girl, Tooba.

"Really, there is nothing to see," Aria said again. But this time her words sounded weak, and even she didn't believe the lie. Hamlet said nothing but put his arm around her shoulder. They both looked up at the window again, and this time it was Farangeez's face that filled the frame, a face stewed in discontent. Hamlet held his breath. There was everything to see.

GOHAR PLACED FOOD in front of Hamlet. He broke the bread and dipped it in the stew. "You're too kind," he said.

Aria fidgeted and cracked her knuckles. She was aware Mehri couldn't stop watching Hamlet, although, as always, it was Aria that she looked at the most, stealing secret glances as her husband asked questions.

"What do you do?" Mr. Shirazi queried Hamlet.

"Study," said Hamlet.

"Where?"

"Same school as Aria. Tehran University."

"What do you study?"

"Law. Aria studies accounting."

"Yes, I know. She's very smart. Why not accounting for you?"

"I can't really count," Hamlet said.

"What will you do with law?"

"It's criminal law I'm interested in . . . We'll see, but maybe human rights . . . no money in that, not like corporate law, but I think it'll work."

"What is corporate law?" Mr. Shirazi asked.

"Oh, business law," Hamlet explained. He felt the eyes of five girls upon him.

"Business. I have a business in the Bazaar. Can you help bazaari folk?"

"What sort of business?"

"Gold. I sell gold. And I can do some engraving."

"Well, corporate is really *big* business. There's oil and there's the metal factories."

"Yes, they make all the Shah's guns," Mr. Shirazi said.

"Husband!" Mehri said, but he waved his hand at her.

"So you're the one who just finished school," Hamlet said to Roohangeez.

Roohi blushed, and Aria jumped in. "She's twenty, but only because she started late. She's done so well."

"Aria taught our girl here. Got her reading. Then we sent Roohi off to school. Same with Tooba there." Mr. Shirazi pointed to his youngest. "She's at school now too."

Hamlet smiled and looked questioningly at the other two daughters, Farangeez and Gohar.

"Farangeez has helped her mother so much," Mr. Shirazi said. "And Gohar here." He grabbed his frail third daughter, sitting next to him, and pulled her into his chest. "We just love her so much we had to keep her at home with us."

"That's so nice," Hamlet said. He adjusted his posture on the cushion they had given him. "Do you always sit on the ground?" he asked.

"Hamlet!" Aria said.

Mehri turned red. She quickly left and returned with some tea, carefully placing the glasses in the centre of the room. Hamlet took a small sweet and washed it down with the hot tea.

"How did you meet Aria?" Mr. Shirazi asked.

"Oh, we've been friends since we were seven."

The Shirazis were quiet, and this time it was Aria who turned red.

"She's never told us about you. She likes to keep secrets," said Mehri.

Mr. Shirazi cleared his throat. "It's all right. Life gets too busy for us to stick our noses into each other's lives."

"I bet Aria has many other secrets," Farangeez said. "Another sweet?" She held forward the plate in her hand. "You can eat up and tell us all about her."

This time Hamlet refused her offer.

"You should come back and visit us again," said Mehri firmly.

And with those words, Aria and Hamlet knew it was time to leave.

"WHY HAVE YOU never talked about them?" Hamlet asked on the way home.

Aria lowered her head and said nothing.

"You've known them so long. All this time."

"I haven't really seen much of them lately. No time," said Aria.

He stopped her. "But you went today," he said.

Aria nodded silently.

"Anyway, I like what you do with that family. You shouldn't have kept it a secret so long."

"Mana sent me there at first, with Bobo. She said that if I helped them and taught the girls to read, there'd always be a place for me in heaven." She walked more quickly now, but Hamlet caught up to her and held her arm tight.

"Look at me," he said. "Why did you keep them a secret? Why?"

"No reason."

"Yes, there is. There must be." He squeezed her arm.

She pushed him away, tears in her eyes. "Fine. There is. Maybe it's because . . . I'm just like them, those girls. And when I was a baby I was left on the street to die. Are you happy? I'm a bastard. Maybe I come from rape. Is this what you wanted to hear? That I'm nothing to the world?"

There on the sidewalk, she told Hamlet everything. It poured out of her, like the waterfalls of the Alborz. She told him about the mulberry trees, the dogs, the winter night in the snow, about Behrouz, Zahra, Kamran, and the beatings.

When at last she was silent, he gently shook her. "I understand. I do understand. And even more now . . . I . . ." He took her other arm and kissed her there on the street, in front of anyone who passed. It didn't matter that they were sinning or that a mollah walking by would curse them, he thought. This wasn't a simple tryst beside a pool on a foolish afternoon. This time, the kiss meant he had seen all of her, all there was to see.

part four

ARIA

1977–81

ARIA DIDN'T KNOW how to tell Mitra that she and Hamlet were engaged to be married. But as things turned out, she didn't need to. Maysi ran into Mitra's mother at a neighbourhood shop and spilled her excitement. After that, Mitra became impossible for Aria to find. She skipped class and didn't answer the phone when Aria called.

Two weeks passed without a word or gesture, and Aria was desperate. One night, around midnight, she grabbed her wool blanket, a pillow, and sheets and quietly left her house. When she reached Mitra's doorstep, she laid out the sheets and pillow, and bundled up in the blanket. She tried to stay awake through the night, but fell asleep before dawn. In the morning Mitra stepped out and tripped over her friend.

"Are you crazy?" she said.

"At least this way you'll talk to me," Aria said.

Mitra said nothing and carried on down the walkway. Aria gave chase, dragging the sheets behind her.

"Stop bugging me. You have other friends to talk to," Mitra said.

"Mitty, did someone tell you? Did you hear?"

Mitra stopped but did not turn around. "Congratulations."

"Why are you so angry? We're all still friends." By this time, they had reached the street. Mitra ran ahead to a cluster of taxis gathered near the sidewalk. She hailed one and got inside before Aria could catch up.

After that, Aria tried other ways of reaching Mitra. She accosted her on campus, in the classrooms, and in the cafeteria, but Mitra had a facility for disappearing in a crowd. It was as though she had natural camouflage and could change her colours and textures at whim. "We should have called her Octopus, not Mouse," Aria said to Hamlet one day.

After a month, both Aria and Hamlet gave up. They had decided to marry quickly, and convinced their families it was for the best. Hamlet also promised to convert. He didn't need to be a Christian, he told Fereshteh. And anyway, Muslims believed in Christ.

"Yes, but he's not our God," Fereshteh said.

"He's a prophet, and that's that. Understood?" said Maysi.

"Yes," Hamlet said.

"You'll say the words?" Fereshteh asked.

"Yes."

"There is only one God, and only God, and Mohammad is His Messenger?"

"Yes."

"You'll say it in Arabic? At the mosque?"

"I don't understand Arabic."

"Neither do we," said Maysi. "You just say the words, boy."

"He can say it right here, Mana, and it will count," Aria said. "We don't need to make a scene."

"This is not a scene. You'll say it at mosque? In front of the clerics?"

"Yes, Madame Ferdowsi," Hamlet said.

"Won't your parents mind?"

"My mother may think all her crosses will catch fire, but such is life."

"They won't excommunicate you?" Fereshteh asked.

"I think they already have," said Maysi. "He spends half his days here."

"Quiet, Maysi," Fereshteh said. She turned to Hamlet and Aria. "I approve," she said.

—

HAMLET'S FATHER AGREED to the marriage on one condition: that he be allowed to pay for a lavish party. Hamlet's mother, on the other hand, did not accept her son's conversion, although she agreed to the marriage. "Once a Christian, always a Christian," she proclaimed, and clutched her cross. "Anyhow, he's been baptized," she said.

"Thank the great God, because he'd no doubt go to hell if he wasn't," Maysi said.

In the days leading up to the wedding, Hamlet tried to convince Aria to invite the Shirazis.

"And have your father hate me even more?" Aria said. "Imagine what he'd say when he saw their veils and dirty shoes." The one person she did consider asking was Zahra, although she had no idea where to find her anymore, or how to reach her. On a whim, two days before the wedding, she searched through the few belongings Behrouz had left her and found a number that she thought might be Zahra's. But when she dialed, a man answered. To her surprise, she recognized the voice. It was Rameen.

"I was just looking for a number," Aria said, flustered. "Zahra's. But I guess—"

"I have it," Rameen said. "She left it with a few of her letters. Do you want it?"

Aria paused for a long time. "No," she said.

THE FIRST NIGHT Aria and Hamlet made love, it was Hamlet who was scared, even though he had thought about this moment for years. Aria didn't desire him the same way he did her, but the desire did come. After their wedding night, she was the one who initiated their lovemaking every time. Sometimes she wished Hamlet had not been such a close friend. What if they'd met later in life, and had crossed paths like in the movies? She had to imagine him as someone different than her old friend when they were entwined, legs and arms wrapped around each other.

They had sex every night for the first two months, sometimes twice, sometimes more. He was more reserved than she thought he'd be, and always used the same position, said the same whispered words, gave the same kisses. In this way, sex, once forbidden, even wrong, became as commonplace in her life as brushing her teeth or driving. Still, it took some time for her to feel pleasure the way Hamlet had right away. It seemed so easy for him: Press the pedal and the car moved. She had to find her own way, and the more they made love, the more she learned how to make the pleasure happen. Would it have been this way with another man? She resigned herself to never knowing, and took comfort in the thought that Hamlet, too, would not know another. He had been just as virginal, fumbling that first night, as she had.

"I thought you'd have tried a few things, hanging around a guy like Reza," she said to him one night.

"What? With Reza?" Hamlet said.

"Not with him, God almighty. With other girls," she said.

"You think he's had a lot of girls?" Hamlet asked.

"I smell it on him."

Hamlet paused. "He never told me a thing."

"That guy likes his secrets," Aria said.

They conceived in late summer. She remembered the night well. It was the first night things became scary in the city. There were guns everywhere, and shootings, and the Shah set a curfew, ordering everyone home. People had to be at home by seven, with lights off by eight. There was nothing else to do but make love.

Later, they talked about Mitra.

"Do you think she's lonely?" Hamlet asked.

Aria wondered if he'd thought about Mitra during sex. She didn't mind, if so. She owed Mitra that much. Maybe, she thought later, the idea of Mitra had triggered the conception.

A MONTH LATER, on the same day Aria learned she was pregnant, Hamlet began his compulsory military service.

He'd been given dispensation to finish law school, but now he had to be a soldier like other men. He was officially the Shah's servant and there was nothing he could do about it.

During the last month of Aria's pregnancy, Hamlet was given leave. He and Aria both tried to reach Mitra again. They confronted her mother and swore on the life of their unborn baby that they would do anything if Mitra would speak to them, but Mitra sent back a note saying she was very sick and didn't want mother or baby to catch her illness.

In the last few weeks, as Aria's belly grew, she felt ravenous hunger and alarming pain. She especially longed for Mitra during this time, but her friend stayed away for all of it, a shadow blended with night.

Aria's labour lasted sixteen hours, and the baby came with difficulty. Hamlet wasn't allowed in the birthing room—it wasn't for men, except doctors. As Aria moaned, Hamlet dashed across the street from the hospital and bought a sapphire ring and ruby earrings.

The baby girl was born eight hours later, in the afternoon, with the noise of traffic outside drowning out Aria's screams and then the baby's. In one hand, Aria gripped the ring Hamlet had bought her. The nurse put the baby in her arms, wrapped tight to calm her. The infant trembled anyway.

"Let's give the baby those earrings," Aria said, and cried.

"We will," said Hamlet. He kissed Aria's head, touched his daughter's skin. "What should we name her?"

Aria thought of Fereshteh, Zahra, Mitra, Mehri. Not Massoomeh; that was for the lower classes. She sighed. None of those names would do. It was wrong for a Muslim to take the name of family, dead or alive.

"Shall we name her after Fereshteh?" Hamlet said.

"Muslims don't take the name of their mothers," she said.

"After my mother?" he asked.

"But you're a Muslim now," said Aria.

Two days later, they brought the still-nameless baby back to the Ferdowsi home.

It was on this same day that Mitra reappeared. She was standing by the lamppost in front of the house when Hamlet saw her. He waited, watching her for an hour from the window inside the door. She did not move from her place. When Aria and the baby had both fallen asleep, he walked outside, lit a cigarette, and looked in her direction.

She walked toward him. "Enjoying life?" she asked.

"So great to see you, Mouse," he said. "The baby—"

"Must be beautiful. I feel like I've missed all the fun," she said.

"Yes, but I haven't had much sleep in the past few days. How's your father?"

"They let him out again," she said. "The Shah's in a bad place. Figures if he lets all of the prisoners out, people will calm down, I guess."

"I know. The riots aren't helping. Aria wants to go to one of the demonstrations with the baby! Imagine that. Silly girl." He turned his face and exhaled smoke away from her. "Are you all right?" he asked.

"Why wouldn't I be? Seems like we'll all be okay, no? With Mr. Khomeini, you finally found your saviour," she said.

"Reza was the one looking for a saviour," said Hamlet. "I never was."

"I think I'm going to disappear for a while. You may never see me again."

"What do you mean?"

"Do you really love her?" Mitra asked, tilting her head at the house.

"Of course I love—"

"No, I mean more than me? I mean different from me? Do you love her in a different way than you loved me?"

"Of course I love you," he said. "Yes, of course I did. And do."

"Did you ever love me like you love her now? Did you ever love me like that?"

Hamlet took a few steps forward, and Mitra backed away. "Come inside," he said. "If you could see the baby. She has my eyes. Hair like a mop. Black as a crow's. Doesn't get it from either of us."

Mitra laughed. "Are you sure you're the father?"

"Silly Mouse." He motioned toward the door with his hand. "Please. Come inside. We miss you." He stood sideways, his body turned away from her. "Come," he said.

"So you can show me my unhappiness?"

"Mitra . . ."

"Have you named the baby yet?"

"Aria can't think of a name. Nothing fits, she says."

"There's still time," Mitra replied.

"You mean so much to me, Mouse," Hamlet said.

"I came to say goodbye." She took a few more steps back. "I think Spain's the best option for me now. I thought of going to the

Caspian, but it reminds me too much of you. Armenia's on the other side of it." She laughed and pointed at the roof of the Ferdowsi home. "We talked about our futures up there, me and Aria. She said she never wanted to marry." Mitra wiped away a tear. "And I told her about the kind of man I wanted: funny, strong, a little stupid. I told her I didn't want anybody like you, but I guess I was lying. I think life is meant to turn out the opposite of what we want. Otherwise we'd never learn anything. In Spain, people will talk to me and I won't know what they're saying. Maybe it was the same with you and me. I was talking and you didn't understand me, or I didn't understand you. Maybe one day there will be a universal language so we can avoid these misunderstandings. What do you think?"

Mitra smiled one more time, and for an instant Hamlet could see her wondering if he would follow. When he didn't, her face disappeared in the darkness, and then even her shadow was gone.

Mitra would never leave for Spain, or even for the Caspian; but in one sense, she was right. This was the last time she and Hamlet would ever see each other.

SIX YELLOW CANARIES were singing outside the window. From the living room, Mehri watched them. Silently, she gave each canary a name, one for herself, one for each of her daughters— even Gohar, the dying one, and even the one she'd once left for dead so many years ago in an alley lined with mulberry trees. Her other daughters sat near her, and her husband stood beside them. She had never told him about the fortune the baker had left her, and now she felt a terrible guilt. But at least what she'd done with it had soothed her other guilt. Her husband had made more money in recent years, and they had moved a few houses north, to this house with the view.

She had been sick for days, and her family was waiting for her to die.

From the window where the canaries sang, Mehri could also watch the boy in the house next door. He was a man, really, his face square, with a beard that had not been groomed and now covered his cleft lip. And he was dressed all in black. A week ago, she had watched him from her window as he had arrived home with a package tied to the back of his motorbike. He unwrapped it, and took out a beautiful white shirt and white trousers. From a pile of tools, he had picked up a can of spray paint. Then he'd laid his white shirt and trousers on the dirty ground, sprayed them black, and left them to dry under the sun. Mehri assumed these were the clothes he was wearing now, and she wondered if his shoes had once been white, too.

Now, across the room, her husband and the girls had gathered around the radio. A loud voice repeated a warning: Everyone was to stay inside or deal with the consequences. The Shah would make certain of it.

"My fault. All my fault," she mumbled, feverish. The canaries sang to the sounds of her pain, and the boy next door rode off. She turned her head to look at Mr. Shirazi. He couldn't go to work because the bazaaris had shut down the Bazaar as a sign of defiance against the Shah. Lights were out in every home, but echoing from distant rooftops, cries of "God is great" could be heard. They tumbled through the clouds and onto the empty city streets.

AS THE CANARIES sang to Mehri across town, Aria paced her apartment, her baby in her arms and her pinky in her mouth to keep her quiet when the inevitable gunshots rang out. Streets away, Fereshteh and Maysi sat knitting in their usual spots in the Ferdowsi living room, cocooned in their silence. The lights were dimmed and the radio hummed in the background. Aria had called earlier to say that Hamlet was not yet home, and the women were worried he might have been detained. When the phone rang again, they jumped. Fereshteh waved at Maysi to sit still, and answered it herself.

"Don't worry," Fereshteh said into the receiver. "They'll know he's on the people's side. Him wearing some uniform won't mean a thing."

Then the lines were cut, as they had been continuously since the revolution first started, months ago.

Aria gently bounced her still unnamed baby. She had not been able to name her since Mitra disappeared.

Fereshteh placed the receiver down and resumed her knitting, only to realize that, despite trying to follow the pattern, she had gotten the colours wrong. Now she had to unravel and start all over again.

"Why is she in that house all alone? Why doesn't she bring the baby here?" Maysi said.

Fereshteh ignored her maid. She glanced toward the other end of the hall, where her father's old gramophone sat, dusty from years of neglect. A record had been left on it, collecting dust, its black sheen turned ashy. She walked over and placed a finger on the record's surface. The name of the song had worn off. She swiped her finger across the plastic, brought her finger to her mouth, and blew the dust into the air. If Jafar could see this, the shock would kill him. She found a tissue in her pocket, wiped the rest of the dust away, and placed the needle on the edge of the record. The wooden pivot that held the needle creaked as it moved. Bits of the wood had begun to chip off.

"Is this really the time for music?" Maysi said.

"What better time?" replied Fereshteh.

The faint wail of a cello sounded through the gramophone's horn. "Remember, Maysi? No, of course you don't. You were much too young then, you and that Zahra."

"I'm going to cook up something in case that child decides to come over with my baby. I hardly ever get to see my baby," Maysi said.

But Fereshteh was listening to the music: a Vivaldi opera, *Il Farnace*. As it gently played, she quietly recited to herself the words of the grieving father: *"I feel my blood like ice coursing through every vein. The shade of my lifeless son afflicts me with terror, and to make my agony worse, I see that I was cruel to an innocent soul; to my heart's beloved."*

KAMRAN'S MOTORBIKE SKIDDED along the edge of a curb. He lost control for a moment, then steadied himself. In the short time he'd been outside, crowds had begun to gather. Small groups moved onto the main streets through adjacent avenues and alleyways, joining the larger throng.

Kamran turned his bike onto the sidewalk, then back on the street again. He'd been riding in zigzags like this since leaving home. It was a good way to make a statement, he thought, to show people who was really in charge.

"Not on the main road!" a passerby yelled. "Stay on the side-walks with that thing!"

Kamran ignored the man. If he was going to be shot, so be it. Nothing would stop him on his mission to get to the meeting place before all the weapons were handed out. All he cared about was Khomeini and the great gift the old man was about to bestow on his people.

"They've set up barricades at that end. Go another way!" someone else yelled. This time there was nothing Kamran could do. He pulled into an alley, leaving Pahlavi Street behind. He stopped his bike and got off for a better look. Soldiers had placed sandbags and trucks across the street; beyond that, he was unable to see. An old man wearing a suit and tie and smelling like cologne approached him.

"They're everywhere," said the man. "You got a helicopter? Because that's your only chance to fly past those Shah-loving bastards."

Kamran glanced at the man's tie. Khomeini had said ties were Western, signs of wealth, and that men who wore them couldn't be trusted.

"The only option now is fire," the old man said. He pointed down the alley. "In the garbage bins, people are making Molotov cocktails. Fire." The old man's hands shook, as did his head. "The men have been giving lessons to the women, too."

A string of bullets flew through the air. Kamran jumped on his bike and drove away.

ARIA PUT THE baby's lips to her nipple but she had no milk. She didn't even have the fake kind, the black market kind. Everything had been disappearing: food, money, people. She wished she'd told Hamlet to pick up something on his way home, but then again, it was unlikely anyone would sell him anything if he was wearing his uniform. Perhaps he'd thought to change.

She could hear distant cries coming from somewhere near the South-City. With the baby in her arms, she walked to the bedroom window, where she could see onto Youssef-Abad Street. Clouds of smoke were rising in the distance.

She turned away and looked down. "What shall I name you?" she said softly to the baby.

THE NOISE HAD drowned out the canaries and deafened Mehri. Crowds were forming outside the house, along the street. Despite all the government warnings and curfews, it seemed like more people than ever were gathering.

"What if they come in to get us, Baba?" asked Roohi.

"No one's going to do that," Mr. Shirazi said. "The bad ones won't be coming here." He turned to his wife. "I'm going out. If anyone knocks, if they're bleeding to death or even not bleeding to death, open the door. I don't care who it is."

"What if it's a bad man bleeding to death?" asked Roohi.

"I don't care who it is," said Mr. Shirazi. "You must open the door."

The sounds around them grew louder, like waves about to crash and break.

RAMEEN PEDALLED DOWN the narrow roads of Darakeh. It was only at the last minute that he had decided to forget his fears. He would join this protest, and no threats or anxiety about returning to Evin would stop him. He wasn't afraid of being tortured again.

He made it to Pahlavi Street and passed the city barracks near Laleh Park, thinking of Behrouz. As he pedalled, Fereshteh and Maysi looked out their front window, watching the firelight; Aria settled with her unnamed infant inside her car; Kamran rode his old motorbike, leaving a toxic trail; Hamlet slowly wove his way through the ruins of a city that was shedding its skin; and Mehri felt suffused with light, weightless for the first time in twenty-five years. The lightness guided her outside, to a stairwell at the end of her balcony, then up each stair. And to her own astonishment, there she was, a veil wrapped around her small, bird-like body, standing on a rooftop along with thousands of others, or maybe millions, crying out in unison, "God is great."

Helicopters whirled above them all, carrying snipers ready to shoot.

IT WAS NOT yet night, but clouds of smoke from fires in the garbage bins had turned the sky black. Kamran tore off a piece of his sleeve and held the rag to his mouth to keep from breathing the toxic air. He slowly rode to a street corner, and from there he saw eight men tumble out of a small Volkswagen whose engine had caught fire after getting shot by a sniper.

Kamran was desperate for a rifle. He'd heard the mosques were giving them to the people, and that the main headquarters, where Khomeini was to be taken upon his return, was a girl's elementary school. Several clerics had already gathered there, planning their next move. He watched the men from the Volkswagen fire bullets at the snipers and longed to be among those clerics.

Suddenly, his eyes began to water and he could no longer breathe. It was as if his heart had collapsed into his lungs. Something had exploded, and the searing heat was blurring his vision. He knew there were thousands of people around him, but he could no longer see or hear them; all he felt was this burning. He fell to his knees and quickly looked up at a rooftop nearby. He saw what looked to be a rifle, but whoever was holding it pulled back. It was then he realized there was a body beside him. He dropped to the ground and covered his head. As he lay there, he felt something warm on his left cheek, something liquid. The liquid had leaked into his mouth. With his head down, he turned over the body beside him. It was a girl, probably no more than fourteen. Her eyes were partly open and stared back at him. She was smiling in her death.

Many years afterwards, when his hair had turned grey and people addressed him as "sir," when he was rich and feared, Kamran would tell people that he had once seen a dead girl smiling. It was a beautiful smile, he would say, on the most perfect lips he'd ever seen. And he would smile himself as he said this, but his lips were nothing like the girl's.

BULLETS FLEW PAST Rameen as he pushed his bike along the street, at the end of which he saw a crowd screaming and pushing against barricades. He turned his bicycle around and went in a different direction, toward the sound of weeping. It was coming from a man who was hunched over a dead girl, a pool of blood around her. Rameen couldn't see the man's face, in part because there was another man on top of the weeping man. This second man had a beard and was all in black. He was trying to pull the other man away from the dead girl.

"Brother, look out!" Rameen yelled. He had spotted snipers on the rooftops. A string of bullets flew by. They landed somewhere near the three interlocked bodies, but no one was hit.

"Get down!" Rameen yelled again. This time, he tossed the bicycle onto the sidewalk and lunged at the group. He got a good grip on the weeping man, who was now trying to lift the girl's body. Rameen pulled the fellow away and flattened him to the ground. He looked at the other man, the younger one with the beard, who was sitting to the side with his arms wrapped around his own body. More bullets whistled past and the crowd dispersed as people ran into the alley or closer to the building, where they'd be out of view. But when the firing stopped, they returned to the centre of the square again.

"Is this her father?" Rameen asked the younger man.

"I don't know. I just saw the bullet; I mean, I heard it. Hit her straight in the chest, and she fell . . . then this man ran at her. I don't know."

"There's blood on him. But I think it's the girl's," said Rameen. He unzipped the older man's jacket but couldn't find a wound. "You okay?" he shouted.

The older man wept and said nothing.

"Come," Rameen said to the younger man. "Help me help this guy."

The younger man stood up. "Ambulance!" he shouted.

"Not so loud," said Rameen. "They'll shoot you."

"It's coming. Over here! Over here!"

Beside Rameen, the old man was hunched over the girl again, but he wasn't trying to lift her anymore.

The ambulance, riddled with bullets, pulled up in reverse. "Hurry," the driver shouted, and a second man hopped out of the passenger seat and kicked the rear doors open. "Throw her in," he said.

Rameen and the younger man with the beard slid the girl's body into the back of the ambulance and helped the old man in beside her.

"The rest of you okay?" the driver asked.

"Fine," said Rameen. "But the old fellow—look after him."

"Get off the streets," the driver said. "You have no idea what's going on." He shut the door and was gone.

Rameen wiped away the sweat on his forehead with his shirt-sleeve. "What's your name, brother?" he asked.

"I saw a bullet hit that girl. Passed right by my own head."

"My name's Rameen." Rameen held out his bloody hand, and the younger man shook it firmly.

"I'm Kamran. And I tell you, God knows everything, brother. If only I had a gun myself. I saw the sniper who killed that girl, up there somewhere. I saw it with my own eyes. If only I had a gun."

ARIA STEERED HER car out of the driveway and onto 41st Street in the Youssef-Abad neighbourhood. One end of the street was barricaded, and the other was filled with the thumping feet of thousands of marchers. From their cheers she could tell they were civilians, not soldiers. She was surprised the procession had made it this far north and wondered just how long it would take for people to reach Niavaran Palace. She thought fleetingly about the silverwork Mana's father had made there. Would they destroy everything?

The baby was crying harder now. Blocked from entering the main streets from one end of the avenue, she had no choice but to make her way through the narrow alleyways and pull onto Pahlavi Street, which was filled with the revolutionaries pounding on and kicking cars. If no one was inside, they would flip the car over.

Someone kicked one of her headlights and she heard it break. She pressed her foot harder on the gas and managed to get past the congestion to where an empty strip of road briefly lay open between North-City and South-City. Patches of black smoke choked the air and bonfires flared in garbage bins. Aria drove slowly, afraid someone might jump in front of her. She heard distant bullets and wondered where Hamlet was now.

ALONE ON A rooftop, a figure in black held her arms to the sky. "God is great! God is great!," Mehri shouted, and the echo returned to her, fuelling another spontaneous cry. Never before had she felt the power of her own voice as she did now. It shook, and the building shook with it. It gelled and danced with a thousand other voices. So she cried out again and again, "God is great! God is great!" until she could cry no longer.

Farangeez and Roohangeez had sped up the stairwell after her, followed by Gohar.

"What is she doing?" Roohi asked.

"I don't know," Farangeez said.

"She'll get shot."

"No, she won't."

Roohi shoved her defiant sister. "Yes, she will. And what if she dies?"

"And if she does? Still nothing will happen. Do you understand?" Farangeez grabbed her. "Who says we need a mother anyway? Maybe if our stupid mother had died we wouldn't be the way we are. Maybe I'd have gone to school and Gohar wouldn't be sick all the time. Maybe you wouldn't be so scared of the world, you stupid girl. What do you know of anything? You've hardly been to school. You can hardly put two sentences together. All you know about the world is what other people have put in your head, and all because you had *that* mother. You know where our father likely is? He went to the Bazaar, to protect the shop. He cares more about his pocket than he does his daughters. You think he'd do that if he had sons? Don't you see anything, Roohi? You stupid girl."

Farangeez pushed her sister away and sped back down the stairwell. The others stared at their veiled mother as she stood facing the city, her back to them.

Mehri stepped farther onto the rooftop ledge and began to call out, "God is great!" again as the city on fire burned into dusk.

—

KAMRAN AND RAMEEN ran toward a row of houses. They were not alone; some fifty others ran behind them, toward open doors. Rameen slammed the first door shut, and he and Kamran fell to the floor.

"What is happening, Mr. Rameen?" Kamran asked as gunshots ricocheted outside.

"The elders have left their doors open for the young," said Rameen. Suddenly the door opened again and five more people rushed in. Together, the group of them squeezed along a corridor. "There isn't space here for everyone. If more people come in, we'll crush each other."

The corridor was dark. Kamran felt along the wall for a light switch but found none.

"Come in, come in," a voice in the darkness said. A man opened a door along the corridor and motioned them into a living room. "Sit, children, sit," he said. "Water? Somebody, water?"

The man was elderly and tall, with a long face and long fingers, and, from what Rameen could see in the gloom, skin as translucent as a jellyfish. Another man, younger and sturdier, although he walked with a cane, came forward.

"Tell them to come in, Jafar, quickly. Have a seat, sons. We'll get you water. Have a seat."

In the living room, Kamran and Rameen sat on the edge of a couch that was already packed with several others. A woman, elderly but younger than the two men, came in through a back door with glasses of water on a tray.

"What happened, children?" she asked as she passed out the glasses. A burst of answers came at her from a dozen different mouths.

"They opened fire."

"Tried to kill all of us."

"Psychopaths."

"God will deal with them. Great Imam Hossein, he will deal with them."

"It was the ruthless Shah and his ruthless scum."

Then the younger men began to argue.

"Why bring a fake god and imams into it? Man stands alone."

"We'll destroy the Shah one day."

"Imam Khomeini will deal with him, that's who."

"He's an imam now? Wasn't he just an ayatollah yesterday? When will you fanatics learn?"

"The communists will get the Shah, that's who."

"The English did this."

"Who made him an imam?"

"No, the Americans did this."

"Democracy will save us."

"Khomeini will save us. Islam will save us."

The elderly woman held up her arms. "Quiet, children. It's no use talking over each other. I can't make sense of any of this. Who wants more water? And soup. Husband, is the soup ready? Mr. Mammad, is the soup ready? Hurry, Mister, hurry!"

Mammad emerged from the kitchen, pushing a cart. "Coming, wife," he said.

On top of the cart, a pot steamed. "I'm sorry we haven't got any bread left," Mammad said. "The last round ate it all."

"There are still more kids outside, Mammad," said Jafar.

"Jafar, we haven't got any more room. They'll have to find someplace else. Madame Nasreen, please pass the bowls to these children while I go around the room."

On the couch, Rameen noticed that Kamran was whispering to himself. He leaned in to hear. "The devil's water, the devil's water," Kamran said repeatedly. Now the others were watching him, too.

"What's wrong with him?" said a man on Kamran's other side.

"I don't know," said Rameen.

"His lips are blue," said someone else.

The old man with the cane came close and shook Kamran. "Wake up, boy!"

"Please don't shake him like that. I'll help him," Rameen said. He grabbed Kamran's shoulders. "You all right? Hey, you all right?"

For a moment, Kamran came back. He stared into Rameen's eyes. "I know that woman," he whispered. "The old one with the water. We've got to get out of here. Guns. We need guns."

"Do we have a lunatic here?" said a girl at the back of the room. "You just got here, buddy. Let it calm down a bit. Didn't you see all the snipers on the rooftops?"

"Shut up!" Kamran shouted. "We'll destroy them, you stupid woman!"

Rameen held him tight. "Kamran, don't talk like that. Show respect."

"I'll talk however the fuck I want to whomever the fuck I want. We'll build our army and cut them to pieces. Wait till those snipers taste God's army."

"Brother, calm down," said Rameen. "Not today. Not today."

Kamran turned around. "Swear on Imam Hossein's life? Do you swear on the Imam's life? Imam Hossein and Imam Khomeini and . . ."

"He's an imam now, brother?" said Rameen.

"And on Saint Zahra's life and Saint Maryam's life, and the Great Prophet, that we will crush the devil-king who took our food and took our homes and took our lives and took our fathers and took our women. SWEAR IT!"

"I swear, brother, I swear," said Rameen. He tried to put his arms around Kamran to calm him. The other men were standing now, ready to grab him, too.

"We'll destroy the names of all the devil-kings before him, do you hear me, woman?" He moved toward the girl who had angered him.

The girl laughed. "Going to change history, are you? What next, Moses never parted the waters? Will you rewrite the Quran?"

"He's in shock," said Rameen.

"Children, the soup is ready," Mammad said, nervously watching this exchange. His heart ached.

Rameen led Kamran into the darkness of the corridor. He could hear Nasreen saying soothingly to the others, "Yes, the soup will get cold if you all don't eat up. We haven't got much power left to heat it up again."

From the darkness of the corridor Kamran called out to her. "I remember you. From that day."

"Why are you talking like that, son?" Nasreen said. "Are you hurt?"

Rameen wrapped his arms around Kamran's chest. He could feel the younger man's body tremble. "You ruined my life, didn't you?" Kamran called out again to Nasreen. "Why? What was wrong with me? You wouldn't let me see her."

"Enough, brother," Rameen said. "Let's go." He led Kamran to the door. "What have I done?" he could hear Nasreen say, bewildered. "Husband, what was that boy saying?"

"Come, wife. The kids are hungry. That boy is lost."

As they left the house, Kamran nearly fainted in Rameen's arms. The blood rushed from his head, leaving one memory, of the day long ago when he had brought Aria chocolate, and the woman who had opened the door told him his kind did not belong with hers.

THE FIRES MADE the city hot. Revolutionaries ran toward Aria's car, and she veered to the side, thinking they wanted room on the road. But one of them knocked on the window. "Get out of the car," he said. Sweat and grime covered his face. His eyes were red with exhaustion and fear.

"I'm driving to my mother's," Aria said.

"Out of the car!"

"I have a baby. I'm going to my mother's."

"Get out of the car now," the man said again. He held up his Kalashnikov so she could see it.

"Please. The house is right there," she said.

"When Khomeini arrives he'll deal with the likes of you," the revolutionary said.

Within seconds, a dozen men had surrounded the car. Two of them beat the ends of their rifles into the fender and doors. Then came a round of gunfire, and deafening sounds like tiny explosions. Suddenly, the front of the car began tilting; the tires had been shot. The car crashed against the pavement. The baby's cries had turned to whimpers, as though the growing chaos was giving her inner calm. The louder the sounds of the outside world, the quieter the baby became. Now the revolutionaries began rocking the car back and forth. Aria pulled her baby out of the carrier, and when she sat back up the men were gone. They had run into the shrubbery on the meridians and sidewalks.

A bullet hit the car door, another hit the bumper, another the hood, then a series drilled a straight line along the passenger side. Aria leapt into the back seat and threw her body over the baby.

Bits of felt floated around her. There was broken glass every-where as the windows shattered. She could smell gasoline. Then the car exploded.

Within seconds, Aria was on the pavement, crawling on her knees and one arm while clutching her baby with the other. Her hands were covered in blood from where broken glass had cut into her arms. The hem of her skirt had caught fire and she kicked at it till it died. Then she stood and started to run, looking down as she did so. Her boots, her good velvet ones, were still on. Her hair had come loose and she realized her shirt matched the colour of the blood that covered her. She had just enough time to wonder why such a thought would occur to her at a time like this when, suddenly, there they were, the French mahogany doors of Mana's home. There wasn't much light to follow, only the opaque glim-mer of the tall lamppost outside. She could still hear the gunfire but it was farther away now. The battle had moved into the ave-nues nearby.

Aria looked down. The baby wasn't crying, and her own arm was still bleeding. Suddenly the doors opened, and there it was, the face of an angel. "Why did you go outside? Why did you come?" Mana screamed. Aria fell into her arms.

"Massoomeh," Fereshteh yelled. "Massoomeh, help us!"

Maysi pried the baby from Aria and walked quickly into the house with the baby's head tucked under her chin. Then she turned and noticed Aria's arm.

"It's nothing," Aria said quickly.

"Thank God it didn't puncture a vein," said Fereshteh.

"Miss Aria," Maysi said urgently.

"Stop worrying, Maysi, it's nothing."

Fereshteh searched her daughter's face and then her arms for more cuts and bruises. "Why did you go out into the streets? Didn't I tell you to stay home?"

"Miss Aria," Maysi said again, in a low voice.

"I wasn't going to sit at home worrying about you and Maysi all day. I'm already going crazy not knowing where Hamlet is."

"Miss Aria, Miss Aria. No."

"What is it, Massoomeh?" Fereshteh asked.

"The baby's bleeding."

"No, that's my blood," Aria said. "Give her to me."

"No, miss, no. The baby's not moving." Maysi's face had turned pale. "I'm going to be sick, Miss Aria. Please. Help me, Miss Aria." She held the baby up. A stream of blood trickled down the blanket wrapped around her body and dripped onto the carpet below, onto the woven wreaths and vines and various blooming flowers of its design.

"Unwrap her," said Fereshteh. Her voice was trembling.

They placed the baby on the couch. Layer by layer, they peeled off the cloth until she was naked. Around the waist and down her round legs, the baby was drenched in blood.

"What has happened?" Aria said. She wanted to scream but found she couldn't. The room started to spin.

Fereshteh pushed Aria to the floor and made her lie flat.

"Madame, I'm going to die," Maysi said.

"What has happened?" Aria said, still on the floor.

"Call an ambulance, Massoomeh," Fereshteh said.

Maysi lifted the receiver, then put it down. "Madame. The lines aren't working," she said.

Outside, Maysi made Aria lean on her to keep steady. Fereshteh held the baby as they ran down the sidewalks, through the dust and smoke. When they came to an intersection, they stopped and checked for mobs and gunfire. Then they kept running, trying to find help. "Our baby's bleeding," Massoomeh screamed. Aria fainted a second time, and Maysi slapped her face and held her up again. They covered three blocks in this way. Smoke filled the air, and they could hear the calls of "God is great" from roof-tops. Then, from out of the haze, a figure emerged. He was young, bearded, and wore a leather jacket with the collar up, a black turtle-neck underneath. His rifle was pressed to his shoulder and his finger was on the trigger. He marched toward them.

"What is it, mother?" he asked Fereshteh. But after one look at the baby, his face changed. Suddenly, his friends appeared too, from the road behind him. They were dressed alike, with unkempt beards and cropped hair. One turned and yelled to the others behind him.

"They kill babies! Brothers, they kill babies!"

Without asking, the first man scooped the baby out of Fereshteh's arms. "Look at what they're doing to us, mother," he said. He turned and showed the baby to the others. "Go tell everyone that the Shah kills babies. Brothers, go tell them the Shah kills babies!"

THE HOSPITAL HALLS echoed with the screams of the dying, and, louder still, the wails of those watching them die. There were no beds left for the men with the Kalashnikovs, the old women, the teenage boys, the doctors and nurses who hadn't slept in days.

Still, the men with the Kalashnikovs shouted, "Make way! A baby's dying."

No one listened, because there were a hundred others dying too.

"They're trying to kill *us*," said a doctor. He was crying.

Aria's baby had turned blue. The doctor took one look, grabbed her, and ran into an operating room. The men with the Kalashnikovs followed, but the nurses caught them at the door and pushed them away. While each man took out a rosary and began to pray, repeating Khomeini's name, Aria and Fereshteh and Maysi held each other.

"They're killing babies," one of the men shouted, holding his rosary to his forehead.

Fereshteh called out to him, "Whoever did this wasn't aiming for the baby. It wasn't a soldier. It was one of you!"

The men stared at her with blank eyes. "You are mad, mother," another of them said. "This was on purpose. On purpose! The soldiers aimed for that child."

"We'll destroy every last one of them," said his friend.

Aria could no longer contain her rage. Inside the next room, her unnamed baby lay dying. "You've got it all wrong," she said fiercely. "Everybody's got it all wrong. From the very beginning, everybody's had it all wrong."

KAMRAN WRAPPED HIS arms tightly around Rameen's waist. The motorbike was dirty and burnt, but it moved. They'd left Rameen's bicycle, bent and misshapen, back where snipers had fired and the girl had died. And they had left behind the house with the old people, and the young ones who had mocked him.

Rameen drove fast. It was Kamran, looking to the side, who saw the soldier first. He was lying face up, his shirt drenched in blood.

"Brother, do you see him?" Kamran shouted.

They slowed and made a circle, then Rameen killed the engine. They ran to the soldier, fell to their knees, and lifted his head.

"He's one of them," Kamran said.

"He's breathing," said Rameen. "But his wound is on the head."

"From a bullet?"

"Don't think so. Something else. The skull is dented. Look here. Someone beat him."

"Because he's a soldier."

"Most likely."

"You think he deserted?"

"I don't know," said Rameen.

"He better have, or I'll kill him myself," Kamran said. He took off his leather jacket and placed it around the soldier.

"Come on, let's get him up," Rameen said.

As they lifted the soldier, they could hear sirens coming closer.

"Get him to the bike," said Rameen.

"Wait!" Kamran unrolled one of his sleeves and tore it off. He wrapped it around the soldier's head, and slapped the man's face gently. The soldier made a faint sound. "What happened to you, brother?" said Kamran. "Who got you, the communists or the Muslim brothers?"

"What does it matter?" said Rameen impatiently. His arms were growing tired.

It was clear the soldier couldn't answer, and Kamran soon gave up and grabbed the rifle lying beside him. They seated him on the bike between their own bodies, and Rameen rested the man against Kamran's back. "Ride," he said.

Kamran steadied the bike as he rode through the smoke. Night had begun to settle, bringing a pause, and for a moment all he could hear was the wounded soldier breathing hard. Suddenly the sound of crying erupted. At first Kamran thought it was from the sewers, and he stopped to investigate.

"Do you hear that, Mr. Rameen? Or is it just me?"

"I hear it," Rameen said. "It's music."

"It sounds like someone, some thing, dying," said Kamran.

"It's an instrument, sir, I promise you," Rameen replied. "That's a reed, an old Persian reed. Someone up there is playing it." He pointed to the rooftops. "It's old music, about the reed separated from its reed bed. In old lore they called this the sound of separation."

Kamran started the bike again, and they sped through the crowds. Barricades had been installed, and they saw more fires, and more soldiers in groups lining the streets. As they turned a corner, a soldier spotted them. He shouted, "Hey, stop! I said stop!" But Kamran opened the throttle, and the bike moved faster. Rameen looked back to see more soldiers following, a few on motorcycles, some running, several in a jeep.

"I'll shoot them," Kamran said. "I don't care."

A soldier on a bike caught up and rode alongside them. "Slow down!" he shouted, and tried to wave them down.

"Think he recognizes this guy?" Rameen said.

"I don't care," said Kamran. "I'll still kill them." But before he could steady his rifle with one hand, the jeep cut in front. He jolted the bike to a stop.

"We're trying to help this fellow," Rameen said. He steeled himself, expecting to be shot.

Kamran pointed his rifle at the soldiers. "The Shah will go, and we'll die if we have to," he yelled, his voice shaking.

"We know," one of the soldiers said. He held up both his hands. "Relax, relax. We'll help you. Here." He pulled something from a pocket and Rameen held his breath, expecting a gun or a grenade. But what the soldier offered him was neither.

"Here. Take it," the soldier said, and he handed Rameen a flower. The other soldiers followed, each taking a flower from his pocket, rifles on the ground.

Miles away, not far from the city centre, Hamlet was undoing the top button of his shirt and taking off his beret. The order had travelled through the chain of command—not from the generals, for they no longer mattered, but from the captains on down: the soldiers were not to kill one more citizen. Hamlet held the flower he'd been given and walked into an angry crowd. Some of the people screamed they would kill him, but before they could do a thing, he held out his flower.

MAYSI WATCHED THE chaos of the hospital swirl around her. Outside, the rattle of rifles and homemade bombs continued. She looked at the blood on Fereshteh's hands and chest. It had run down her dress and stained it. If she hadn't known better, she'd have thought it was Fereshteh with a bullet in her heart. Aria had fainted again, and the nurses gave her some medicine to make her fall asleep. Now she lay on a bed in the corridor as police and doctors ran past, carrying corpses. One of the bodies was that of a child, a girl no more than fourteen. Blood poured out of her mouth, and the attendants just dropped her onto the floor and rushed to the next emergency. For a moment, she lay there, exposed, before a nurse ran over and threw a white sheet over her body. Maysi noticed that the sheet did not turn red, which meant the blood on her face had already dried. She'd been dead for a while.

At least that girl had lived for a little while, Massoomeh thought. She directed a brief prayer toward the baby in the operating room. "Better to live with a hole in your heart than not live at all," she whispered aloud. She looked over at Aria, watching as the girl's chest moved up and down with such ease that Massoomeh thought she must be having a beautiful dream.

Fereshteh, seated next to her, hardly moved. "You should wash your hands," Massoomeh said.

"No," Fereshteh said. "I lost one baby. I won't lose another."

Maysi pictured Fereshteh's baby boy. "Maybe it was for the best," she said. Fereshteh did not reply.

A little later, the three women were sent home with good news. There was no hole in the baby's heart; the bullet had just grazed it and the child would be fine. A police car took them home, weaving through the smoke and rubble left after the day's protests and shootings. Along one avenue a woman was washing blood off the pavement, while on another, four men were holding a lamb. They cut its throat right there and its blood poured onto the street. This act reminded Maysi of her childhood; there had been a sacrifice for every birth and every death. Maybe with that poor lamb's blood, peace would come.

When she fell asleep that night, listening to Aria's sobs, Massoomeh dreamed of another sacrifice. She hadn't dreamed of it in years, but now the faces and sounds appeared to her again. The dream was about a real night, a night years ago, when she had gone to the kitchen after hearing strange sounds. Fereshteh was eight months pregnant at the time, and Massoomeh had let her sleep. There was nothing in the kitchen when she got there but a draft. The back door that led to the garden had been left slightly open, and she shivered in the cold air. Across the garden was the home's other half, where the Ferdowsi men lived and Jafar polished his coins. She saw a faint light coming from the attic. In her dream the light flickered, but she knew that on the real night it had stayed bright and unmoving. Above the attic was the rooftop where she and Zahra used to lie, staring at the stars. That night, Maysi had slowly climbed the winding stairs that led to the top. It was as she neared the second floor that she heard the sounds. Even in the dream, she couldn't tell what they were.

She reached the landing of the second floor and saw a long shadow on the wall coming toward her. When she turned round, the young boy Jafar was standing there. "What have you been doing?" she asked. "What is that sound? Is someone screaming?"

Jafar was playing with a coin. "It's been happening for years," he finally said. "You hear them, too? I thought I was the only one."

"Why haven't you said anything? Where's it coming from?" Massoomeh asked him.

"From my head. The sounds come from my head."

His madness was clear to her then. "Where's your brother?" she asked.

"His room is at the other end. He never hears the sounds. They're from my head."

Massoomeh kept climbing, and Jafar followed her. As they neared the attic, the sounds, the cries, grew louder. The door was locked, but she opened it as she always had, by sticking a hairpin in the keyhole, then tilting it upward and to the right. In the dream she did it much faster than she had that night. But Jafar was still amazed.

The gardener boy, Mahmoud, was on top of Zahra when they walked in. One hand was over her mouth and the other around her throat. Her face was red, her screams muffled as he thrust himself into her. 'You'll give me a thousand babies if I tell you to," he was saying.

A few moments after the door opened, Mahmoud turned his head and saw Massoomeh. He jumped off Zahra, who turned to Maysi with a face full of terror. "No, no," she said.

Mahmoud pulled up his pants and patted back his dishevelled hair. "What the fuck are you doing here, maid?" he asked.

"You reptile," was all Massoomeh said.

Jafar was looking at the floor, turning his head from one side to the other. "I have to go now. I have to go. I hear them. They're in my head."

"It's okay," Zahra said through her tears. "Just leave."

"We'll leave. We'll leave," Jafar repeated.

"Please. Just leave," Zahra begged Maysi.

Now Mahmoud turned toward her. "You breathe one word of this, maid, and you'll be on the streets before daylight. I'll make sure you're known as the greatest liar there ever was."

"What about him? Will you make him a liar, too?" She looked at Jafar.

"He's mad. You think they'll believe him?"

When Mahmoud realized Massoomeh wasn't afraid of him, he threw a fist in her face, stopping just before the punch. "I'll destroy you," he said. His eyes bulged in the room's dim light. He looked like one of those monsters she'd seen in drawings and old movies.

"Do you want to come?" she said to Zahra. But Zahra just lowered her head.

As Massoomeh walked away, down the stairs and into the garden, Mahmoud's words echoed in her ears. *You'll give me a thousand babies if I tell you to.* And then Massoomeh understood why Zahra had stolen Fereshteh's necklace. If she was about to bear a child, at least it would have some inheritance, a start to life. Even if that start was stolen. "We must take fortune where we can find it," Maysi whispered.

Sitting in the hospital that day, she had wanted to tell Fereshteh that if her baby boy had lived, he might have become a devil like Zahra's son, and maybe Fereshteh would have become another Zahra, poisoned by the gardener boy who'd run off to Qom.

Zahra had left the Ferdowsi home soon after that night. She had lied and said she was getting married, but Maysi knew the truth—even if Zahra did get married for real, years later, to that younger man, Behrouz. After losing her own son, Fereshteh had often said to Maysi that she wanted to meet Zahra's boy. But Zahra never came back to visit—not until the day a blind girl arrived, riding on her back.

FIVE MONTHS LATER, Kamran and Rameen watched as Khomeini's plane landed on a vast tarmac surrounded by crowds of excited people. The plane's door opened and Khomeini, adorned in typical cleric garb, with his white beard and black eyebrows arched like the horns of a ram, stepped out. He waved at the crowd in a manner that suggested he was counting every one of them, and that each was of importance to him, an importance that he guarded in the secret world of his inner life. The pilot stepped out to stand beside him, and when the people who'd gathered to watch—at least two million, Rameen would later hear—saw this man take the hand of their beloved leader and lead him down the stairs, they screamed even louder than they had on the burning streets during the days that brought them here. The world stopped in that moment, and witnessed their ancient nation at last defeat the tyrant. The last of the Shahs was gone.

Rameen realized he was crying. His vision blurred as he looked out upon the vast field of people, wondering how many of them had lost someone, how many had suffered, how many understood what this new freedom would mean. Of course, there'd been a time when these thoughts would not have pleased him; when he would have been bitter that it was a religious man who brought them to this moment, when he himself had spent so many years in prison because he refused to accept leaders ordained by God. But his fears had settled when, in the days before his return, Khomeini had promised that he would not mix religion and government. He did not want power, the great man said. All he wanted was to return to his simple cottage in Qom, the city where he had learned his faith, and spend his days kneeling before God's mercy. This was what men of faith were meant for, he said. Let the politicians deal with politics.

Rameen glanced at Kamran. They hadn't seen each other since that day on the motorbike five months ago. He remembered taking Kamran home that night to his terrified mother and his determined sister, neither of whom seemed surprised by the mania that had befallen their loved one. It had happened before, his mother said. Rameen left quickly, hoping the kid would be all right. But this morning, when he awoke to the news that Khomeini was on the plane, his first thought had been to find the young man again, to see if things really were okay. He wanted to spend this special day with Kamran—they'd been brothers in war, and now were brothers in victory.

Still, it had been a surprise when a very sane-looking Kamran stepped out of his door, grinning widely, dressed in an army uniform with a rifle slung across his shoulder, and embraced him. Rameen hadn't recognized the uniform; its tailoring was different from the old ones he himself had worn. A crest with a symbol Rameen had never seen before was pinned to Kamran's lapel, and again on the side of his upper arm.

"What is that, friend?" Rameen had asked, pointing to it.

"Brother, you're not up on the news. It's the sign of our victory. Come closer. What does it look like to you?"

"Four curves, two concave, two convex. What does it mean?"

"Read it, brother. It says 'Allah.' Look closer." Kamran brought his arm toward Rameen's face, then lightly slapped his cheek. "It's all about God now, brother. This is what truth tastes like."

Rameen had grabbed the back of Kamran's neck. "Happy to see you, Kamran. You're looking well, even if you worry me a little with that uniform. Should I salute or something?"

Kamran pulled at his sleeve. "Nice, isn't it? Our own new army. And I've changed my name. It's Ehsan now."

"That so? What was wrong with your old one?"

"Kamran's too Persian, no? Anyway, Ehsan sounds better."

"It's Arabic," said Rameen.

"The Prophet's language," Kamran nodded.

"Do you speak it?" Rameen asked.

"Not yet. But I will," said Kamran.

Rameen touched Kamran's uniform and eyed his rifle again. "Are we going to war with someone?" he asked.

"Nah. We're supposed to take care of anybody who starts trouble. Know what I mean? It's defence. In case people start getting ideas, especially Westerners wanting to throw their filth on us. You'll hear more about it soon enough. They need men, brother. You should join up. My mother and my sister are in this army and have guns, too. Take a look." He gestured toward the open door behind him.

Rameen poked his head inside the house and saw a woman, veiled in black, holding a rifle. "You're not kidding," he said, stepping back out.

"It's all about security," Kamran replied. "You win something, brother, you fight like mad to keep it."

The two men walked to the landing strip together, and to his surprise, Rameen found it was true: He felt secure with Kamran beside him. It was as if no one could touch them.

◇

HAMLET TINKERED WITH the antenna on the TV set. It was brand new, made in 1979. He adjusted both poles until the image finally turned from grainy black and white to colour—although this made little difference, because what the screen showed was thousands of people dressed in variations of black and grey. Those were the men. The women, at the back of the crowd, were covered in their black veils. This was one thing about Islam that confused him. His mother, grandmother, aunt, and great-aunt all wore headscarves, but their Christian way of doing so was different from what he was seeing now. Why hide the face, the teller of tales and secrets? But maybe that was it, he thought: Women's stories and secrets were dangerous.

Hamlet peered more closely at the image on the TV. At the head of the crowd, Khomeini stood tall, doing what had become, since his return months ago, a trademark. He raised his hand as though to wave to the crowd, yet it looked as if he was counting them, slightly moving his fingers back and forth in a manner too subtle for those far away to notice. Only on television could you really see it.

In the time since his return, Khomeini had become a master orator. Every day he appeared in public to talk about his vision, and about how the people could help create his utopia. "The evil vermin that called himself your Shah has gone," he said. "Your lives now will change, and flowers will bloom all around you." Already he had made several promises, which he enumerated precisely:

1. The price of oil would be raised. No longer would the West steal our most precious commodity.
2. There would be more meat. The farming industry would thrive, as more land would be taken from the

aristocratic and privileged, and distributed to the real men of the land. (Like Robin Hood, Hamlet thought, and laughed a little.)

3. Women would never be mistreated again, for the purity of Islam and the veil would save them.
4. There would never again, in this country, be a poor person. Starvation would be a distant memory.
5. The people's pockets would be filled with money. Why not? Was this nation not overflowing with oil, bestowed upon them by God?
6. There would be peace. Forever. Prison walls, army barracks, tanks, would be empty. Forever.

"The evil vermin that called himself your king has gone," Khomeini said again.

Hamlet sighed. Khomeini had spoken these proclamations for months now. Was there even a point to turning on the TV anymore? The images were always the same: crowds praying or marching. He strained to listen for his infant daughter's breathing in the next room, but he couldn't hear her. He thought of the scar from the bullet that had grazed her chest, and got up to check on her. Yes, her tiny chest was moving as she slept. He watched her breathe and wondered what her life would be like.

After a few minutes, Hamlet returned to his TV and fiddled with the antenna again, managing at last to summon a different image. This one showed women protesting. One of them held a sign that read: "Freedom for Our Daughters." A reporter asked the woman a question, and she replied in a heavy peasant accent. "I have worn hijab my entire life. It's what we were raised with. But it's been my prison and my hiding place. I know what my prison is, but I was never able to leave it. I have eight daughters. I don't want my daughters to hide. I don't want them to fall into this prison, too."

"But what if your daughters want to be veiled?" the reporter asked. Hamlet noticed a symbol on the microphone and peered more closely at the screen. He'd seen it before, he realized, on the lapels of some of the new soldiers, the Revolutionary Guards.

ARIA SAT NEAR Mehri's bed, and Roohi and Gohar sat beside her. They watched Mehri's frozen face, her eyes rolled to the back of her head, her breathing shallow and quick. She had been this way for a week. And today she was dying.

Aria kept watch for a few hours before getting up to leave. Her baby would be missing her, and she had promised Hamlet she would be home before too long. "Do you need anything? Hamlet can get it for you," she said quietly. Farangeez was at the doorway, and she looked away. She was refusing to talk to Aria.

As she got close to the door, Aria felt a hand on her shoulder. It was Gohar.

"What is it?" Aria asked.

"I'm sorry . . . about Fara," Gohar said.

"It's fine," Aria said. "If she doesn't want to talk to me, she doesn't have to." She turned to leave.

"Wait." Gohar grabbed her hand. "This is for you." She placed something inside it, an envelope. "It's a letter," Gohar said. "From mother. I wrote it out for her, years ago."

"You can write?" Aria asked.

"Yes, I did learn a little, watching you with Roohi. The others don't know about the letter. We wrote it together. I'm not sure she ever wanted you to read it. It was just something she had to say. But now, with how things are . . . I don't know."

"Why don't you just tell me what's in it?" Aria said softly.

"I can't."

As she walked to the car, Aria heard a swell of commotion coming from the other end of the street. Sudden panic had filled the neighbourhood. She was startled to see more than a hundred men running toward her from every direction, as if the days of the revolution had returned. She instinctively covered her face with her arms, but soon realized the men were running past her. She stopped a boy who was trailing behind.

"Where is everyone going?" she shouted above the din.

"American embassy, lady. Didn't you hear the news? They've caught Americans. A hundred of them."

As it turned out, the boy was both right and wrong. A hundred Americans had not been captured; sixty-six had. A group of university students, the religious kind, whom everybody now called the Hezbollahi, had taken them. Aria stopped at a bread shop where people were clustered around a black-and-white TV. "It's a disaster," the baker told her. On the television, a woman was speaking perfect English. She wore a tight headscarf, so that not a single hair showed, and spoke about the captured embassy workers and condemned America.

When Aria made it home at last, she faced her own disaster. Hamlet wasn't anywhere to be seen, but the neighbour Mrs. Taheri ran toward her, the baby in her arms. "They killed him! They killed him!" she screamed, and fell to her knees.

Aria dropped Gohar's envelope, which by now was crumpled into an unrecognizable ball, into a bag on the hall table. "Who? Who did they kill? Where's Hamlet?"

"They didn't kill him, missus," said Mrs. Taheri, trying to calm herself. "But they will kill him. They took him away. They wouldn't let him go, even with the baby. I heard his shouts from the court-yard. They were going to take the baby, too, but I pulled her away. They'd have had to kill me first."

"What do you mean they took him? Who took him?"

"They looked like the Hezbollahi type, Mrs. Aria, dear. The Revolutionary Guards, the ones who wear those military uniforms."

Aria grabbed her baby. "Did they say why they took him? What did he do?"

"I don't know. My heart was beating so fast . . . I don't know. They just came through with one of those military trucks, and there was a tank outside too. I heard them say he committed some crime, something against the Islamic Republic."

"Where did they take him?" asked Aria, but as soon as she spoke the words, she knew. Before Mrs. Taheri could answer her, she had run into the streets, heading toward Evin.

MILES AWAY, HAMLET sat in a cell. He'd been arrested, he'd been told, "for aiding and abetting the escape from punishment of an enemy, Reza Navidi, who had been prepared to overthrow the glory of the Islamic Republic, and who was responsible for the recent deaths of three Revolutionary Guards, upon whom he and two accomplices had opened fire."

Aria begged to see him in Evin but was turned away. A female guard, speaking through a grille, told her that if she came back the next day, perhaps her luck would change. As she walked away from the prison and back to the city centre, Aria realized the Revolutionary Guards were everywhere, even among the women in black veils who were filling the sidewalks, some hopping down from tanks, many, almost all, with AK-47s and Kalashnikovs strapped over their shoulders. Their veils weren't worn in the usual Islamic way, to render them demure and discreet. Instead, it seemed to Aria that these women wore their veils brutally; the black garment, blowing with the strange wind that day, was a heavier weapon than any rifle, dispersing violence in the streets through the women's eyes, challenging whoever dared to look back. As the wind beat against the veils, the flaps made rippling sounds not unlike bullets fired from a barrel. Tap, tap, tap, the veils went. And the women's words were like bullets, too.

"Stop!" one of them said, stepping in front of Aria. "Where is your hijab?" she yelled. Two others joined her. "Stop!" they shouted.

Aria did as she was told. "What do you want of me?" she asked.

"Is this not an Islamic republic?" the first woman said. "Where is your veil?" She took her Kalashnikov off her shoulder and pointed it at Aria.

"I'm sorry." Aria remembered hearing that Khomeini had designed the new style of veil himself. They had been shown on television, along with other preferred styles for women: long pants, flat shoes, jackets that covered the neck and came to the knees, and hair slicked back tight under an even tighter headscarf. Now one of the women grabbed Aria and took a heavy scarf out of her bag. She whipped it around Aria's head, pushing her hair underneath the fabric. It hurt, but Aria didn't allow herself to wince.

"In the name of Imam Reza and Hossein and Imam Khomeini, watch yourself," the woman said. The other two pulled out rifles from under their veils. Aria stepped back.

"You're lucky your clothes are not vulgar, sister," said one of the other women. "But God almighty will decide what to do with you in the end. And get this off." She pulled a tissue from a bag, grabbed Aria's face, and wiped off the light colour from Aria's lips.

"You're nothing more than a whore," she said. "Are you not? Are you not a whore?"

Aria's face hurt, but she said mildly, "Of course, ma'am. So wrong of me. I was in a hurry and forgot. I promise it won't happen again."

"Next time it does, you'll see the inside of a prison, sister," said the first woman, her tongue as bitter as a lemon. At last, they let Aria go and moved on to the next woman walking by, as if they were mousetraps and the women mice.

WEEKS PASSED, AND each day Aria made the trip to Evin, only to be turned away. Then early one morning the phone rang. When Aria answered it there was nothing but silence, and she hung up. A few minutes later the phone rang again, and again there was silence. This pattern continued through the morning, until at last a man's voice said, "Be at the front gates of Evin. Noon." When Aria began to speak, he hung up the phone.

She was at the gate at noon. Twenty minutes later, it opened, and under the tall lampposts she could make out Hamlet's smiling face, half covered by the shadows of the prison walls. As he walked toward her, he limped.

They embraced, then got in the car. Aria drove, her arms shaking. Frost had set on the windshield and snow had turned the city white.

"How did you get me out?" Hamlet asked.

Aria was silent.

"How did you get me out?" he asked again.

"I didn't," Aria said.

◇

MITRA PULLED THE thin covers up to her chin to keep warm. For the third time that day she had refused to eat. Her lawyer had come by a little earlier and made yet another attempt to convince her to tell the truth. He didn't believe her story, he said, just as he didn't believe there was justice in this world. But of her innocence, he was certain.

The next morning the guards brought her soup. Mitra touched the bowl; it was hot, and she could see small bits of chicken mixed into her broth. Even in Evin there is humanity, she thought.

In the afternoon she was interrogated again. There were four others in the room: the judge, the witness, her lawyer, and a guard. Mitra eyed the judge warily: He had a turban on his head and seemed to be a mollah. Mitra had never seen a mollah act as a judge before. How could someone whose entire life was spent grazing through the Quran have enough time to navigate the pages of law books?

"Let's go over this again," the judge said. "The money that was used to bail out Reza Navidi from Evin prison, after he was charged and convicted of passing out communist propaganda and encouraging uprisings against non-communist regimes, came directly from you. The bail money was yours, yes?"

"Yes," Mitra said. Her lawyer shifted in his seat.

"And by your testimony, and despite the testimony of Reza Navidi himself, Mr. Hamlet Agassian played no part in procuring this money?"

"Yes."

"Yes he did, or yes he didn't?"

"Yes, he played no part," Mitra said.

The judge fumbled through the papers on his desk, then cleared his throat.

"And why, miss, would you confess to such a thing? When a

man was already in prison in your place, sparing you guilt and possible consequences?"

Mitra did not answer.

The judge continued. "You see, there is no logic here, miss. I'd believe you if you had something to gain. But I cannot see what that would be." He looked at the guard. "Would you agree?" The guard nodded. "See, Miss Ahari, even an idiot like this fellow isn't fooled."

"Everything I have told you is true," Mitra said. "And I have nothing more to say."

The judge laughed. It was the same laugh she'd heard for the past three days, ever since she replaced Hamlet in Evin.

For six more days Mitra remained silent and alone in her cell, until, unable to get anything different out of her, the guards put her in a room with eight other women. The room was covered with kilim rugs, and thin mattresses had been placed along the wall. The rugs smelled nice, as if they had just been brought from the provinces by the village girls who made them. Sometimes at night, as Mitra lay on her mattress, she wondered what stories existed in the fabric of these rugs, in their weaves and patterns, in the dye that coloured them, and in the geometric shapes and the symbols for rivers and plateaus, and in the birds that lined the borders, especially the brave hoopoe bird, the dove, and the sparrow.

Two of the women in her group had children with them. One had two toddlers, the other an older child, a boy. Mitra slept apart from the others. She didn't know what they were in here for, or why the children were with them. Were they communists? Mojahedin? Shah-lovers? None of them seemed the type. A couple had asked her about her crime, but she walked away, not caring to engage.

On her fifth day with the group she was told she had visitors: a young woman named Bakhtiar and an Armenian man. She refused to see them. The next day she was told the Bakhtiar girl had come again, but Mitra informed the guards she didn't want to see anyone, ever, not even her own mother. Any letters she received remained unopened, and after a few weeks the guards didn't bother delivering them anymore. The pile she already had stayed hidden under her mattress.

She was a model prisoner, and her lawyer said he was trying to get her ten years, but with three uniformed men dead, he wasn't sure he could manage it. The men, after all, had been Revolutionary Guards, the light of a new Iran.

On the nights when Mitra lay awake, she thought about Reza. She knew he'd been killed immediately when hundreds of Guards had stormed his hideout and shot the rebels, along with anyone else nearby, just in case. She heard that amongst the innocent had been two children, a mother, and two men with moustaches—shot because Stalin had a moustache, too, and who knew, perhaps these men were communists like him.

One night the noise of the children crying was joined by the sound of a television, bringing her out of her thoughts. The TV projected grainy images of the captured Americans. Blindfolded, they walked down the steps of the embassy as people cheered and burned American flags.

"There's talk of letting them go, of making a deal with Reagan instead of Carter. It could have been Carter. But he's not their president anymore," said a young woman whose hair had turned grey. She shook her head. "I don't know where this rage comes from," she said.

Another woman, the one with the older boy, had an answer. "From that time when they destroyed Prime Minister Mossadegh," she said. "Remember, in '53, what they did to him? How those

Americans interfered? Now these madmen want revenge. What do you think this revolution is about?"

"It's about a great cause," the grey-haired woman said.

"Madmen hide behind their causes," said the woman with the boy. "Only the sane are without cause. And now the whole world will pay. You just pray they shoot you before you see real hell. This wasn't about Mossadegh, not for them." She motioned to the TV, where Khomeini, surrounded by other mollahs and a handful of ayatollahs like himself, sat supine and serious, angry yet content. Proud of his progeny for having finally served America, the great Satan, with the blow it deserved.

In the mornings the women marched in the grassless court-yard after the men had had their turn. They walked in circles, one way for ten minutes, the other direction for another ten, repeating these steps for an hour. After several weeks the man who ordered them to march, the new head of the Revolutionary Guards, got bored. First, he ordered the other guards to blindfold the women before they marched. When he got bored of that, he told the women he was going to kill them.

Mitra, blindfolded, was led outside with her cellmates. Her hands were tied behind her back. She and the others stood in a line. A male guard, his beard fully grown, a turtleneck under his uni-form's open collar, placed a megaphone to his lips and commanded: "You are not to move. If you move, a bullet will enter your head."

When the first bullet was fired, those who thought they had been hit screamed. When more bullets were fired, those who thought their friends were dead sobbed, and the mothers, scared their children had seen everything, froze in silent agony.

The blindfolds were untied, and the guard bellowed into the megaphone: "What wimps you godless scum are." The women looked at each other and saw that not a single one of them was dead. The guards had fired blanks into the sky.

HAMLET AND ARIA sat in silence at the Ferdowsi dinner table as Maysi picked up their plates and Fereshteh held the baby in her arms. They hadn't spoken of Mitra for days, and even then, had only commented fleetingly.

For a time Hamlet considered finding witnesses to prove he'd been the one who gave Reza the money. But he'd hesitated, torn; doing so would have brought it all back to Aria, because the money had been hers. Aria thought about making her own confession, but one look at her baby changed her mind.

Tonight they ate dinner slowly. Aria was separating each grain of rice from the next, and cutting her meat into smaller and smaller bits. When she swallowed them, her throat ached as if there were a lump inside.

Hamlet took a drink of his black-market whiskey, and Fereshteh shifted the baby from one arm to the other.

Aria removed a pamphlet from her pocket, unfolded it, and showed it to the table. "I've been trying to follow what it says to do when I'm outside," she said. It was a step-by-step guide, like the kind for assembling dining-room tables and baby cribs. Hamlet grabbed it and flipped through the pages. It showed the different garments that went into the making of, as Hamlet read aloud, *"Proper Islamic attire for the Islamic women of Iran: For those who do not wish to comport themselves in the traditional black veil, a more modern option is possible, with blessings from our great leader, Imam Khomeini."*

"So they've turned him into an imam already," remarked Hamlet.

"Keep reading," Aria said.

Hamlet scanned the instructions on the first page. They began with the headscarf: Only three colours were allowed, black, dark blue, and brown. The scarf was to be fastened tight under the chin, with even lengths hanging off the knot. The top of the scarf, covering the head, was to be pulled forward, so that one could only see the triangular shape of the woman's forehead, with all hair covered. Ears, especially, were not to be shown. The next page gave instructions on the upper body: All women were to wear long sleeves and turtleneck shirts. If they did not have a turtleneck, the scarf was to be long enough so that the skin of the neck was entirely covered, in case the male gaze found and violated its purity. For the lower body, no skirts were allowed. All women were to be dressed in pantsuits, and again, only three colours were allowed, black, dark blue, brown. All pantsuits were to be non-form-fitting, longer than the ankles, and never tapered, to avoid showing the shape of the legs. All shoes must cover the entire foot and only three colours were to be worn; black, dark blue, brown. The body must be covered with an overcoat.

Hamlet tore the pamphlet's pages and threw them across the room. "Are they inventing their own Islam? You don't have to do this. And what about the women I work with? They're expected to walk into a courtroom dressed like this?" He shot up from his chair, swung open the long glass doors of the balcony, and disappeared into the darkness outside. Fereshteh and Aria could smell the burning of his Camel cigarettes, which Aria knew he had bought at the black market that morning. In the kitchen Maysi was washing the dishes, the water running hard so she couldn't hear a thing.

"I'm worried you won't be able to survive on Hamlet's income anymore," Fereshteh said. "And he's Armenian, he—"

"So? Those people had no respect for him before, and they'll have no respect for him now. I think his people are used to it. Just like the Jews. As long as we don't admit we don't believe in God, we'll be fine."

Fereshteh shifted the baby again.

"Here, give her to me," Aria said. "Maybe I'll cut hair for extra money. Or I could always sew dresses," she added.

Fereshteh looked at the baby. "You still haven't named her," she said. "And soon she'll be old enough to know. A name's not as important as you think."

"A name means everything," Aria said, brushing a few strands of hair from the baby's forehead.

Hamlet came back inside. He paced around the dining table trying to find something useful to do, a dish to take to Maysi or napkins to throw away. But Maysi had cleared it all, and Hamlet was left with a sickness in his belly. "Remember when that son of a bitch promised us he was going back to his shit of a house in Qom?"

Aria shushed him. "Lower your voice. You don't know who might be listening outside. It carries all the way into the courtyard."

"Fuck the courtyards in this shit of a city. All our problems are because of those courtyards." Hamlet circled the table a third time. "And did you read the papers today? Now Saddam wants to attack us. Some revolution we had."

"Quiet," Aria said. "Shouting won't help."

"Staying silent will then, I suppose? Is that what you'd tell Mitra now if you saw her? That we're letting her rot away while we pretend we haven't ruined ourselves?"

"Shut up," Aria said. "Just shut up. And don't talk about her. You don't have the right to talk about her."

But Hamlet raised his voice. "So we'll just sit here and forget she's in that hell because of us!"

"Because of YOU!" Aria yelled. "You, Mr. Agassian. Because you messed with her head all those years."

"So you'd rather have me locked up in there?"

Aria looked up in anger, but her voice was quiet. "Sometimes, yes. Sometimes I think it would be better than this guilt."

Aria and Hamlet didn't speak to each other for the rest of the night.

The next morning Khomeini announced that they were at war.

And that afternoon, in the courtyard of Evin prison, a woman who had flinched when bullets were fired into the air finally did have a bullet put into her head, and bled to her death in the arms of her two young children.

HAMLET SAT AT his desk at the law firm and wondered why he had not yet gone crazy. He was witness to a deep cesspool of humanity, from the pile of papers, dossiers, and documents stacked in front of him to the new cases that kept pouring in every day: spousal abuse, women wanting divorces (hard to get with the new sharia law), wives killing their husbands for beating their children, husbands killing their wives for beating their children.

In the top drawer of his desk were the letters he had written to Mitra. She had sent them all back, unopened. He picked up his pen, thinking he would write her again today. Maybe this time she would read and listen to what he had to say. But just as he began, a knock sounded on the door.

"What is it?" he asked.

"Phone for you," his secretary replied. "And you will probably want to go home after."

Hamlet picked up the phone. On the other end of the line was a warden from Evin. "You should sit down," the voice said.

THE GUARDS TOOK Mitra and the women out into the yard again. "March clockwise," they said. Then: "March counter-clockwise." There were a few women guards now, with rifles underneath their black veils. The male guards acted the same way as they always had, especially the one who liked to press the megaphone to his lips and shout so loudly that no one could understand what he said.

When the prisoners were rounded up after the march, Mitra was kept outside.

"You're going somewhere else," the guard with the megaphone said.

Mitra guessed that he was the one who had shot her friend in the head as her two children watched. But she was wrong. The guard who shot the woman had professed it was an accident and pleaded to retain his dignity and his job, but he had lost both anyway. He'd been sent home with a month's pay and a reference from his head officer. Later, he enrolled in the Basij, the plain-clothes militia who carried machetes and knives in their coats and stabbed those who said the wrong thing. He was told he'd be a better fit there.

Mitra could feel the guard with the megaphone walking behind her. He was breathing heavily into her neck, and she wondered why he had such laboured breath when he was still so young. As they walked through Evin's halls, she heard the echo of her own footsteps. They went deep into the prison, past the common quarters and the cafeteria, and even past Ward 209, from which most of the screams were heard. The guard guided her, a hand on her back. He was strangely gentle. At last, they stepped into a room where there were four chairs around a table and a single light hanging from a wire above it.

"Sit down," the guard said. "The judge is coming."

The man who stepped through the door a minute later was a cleric, with the full beard, turban, and long robes. As he entered, the guard who had guided her suddenly kicked her chair. "Stand when a judge walks in the room," he said.

Mitra stood up. "Mollahs are now judges?" she said lightly. "How quickly they get their degrees."

But this mollah wasn't like the one she'd met before. This one hated her.

The guard kicked her chair again. "Shut up."

"Where is my lawyer?" Mitra said.

The judge sat in one of the empty chairs. He scratched his head and shuffled the papers in front of him. "Already one minute wasted," he said, without looking up at her. "You have two more."

"Where is my lawyer?" Mitra asked again.

"What makes you people think you deserve lawyers?" the judge said.

"Then why am I here?" Mitra said.

For the third time, the guard, half hidden in the shadow behind her, kicked her chair, and this time he removed the rifle that had been hanging over his shoulder. "Shut up, woman. No more shit out of your mouth. You can sit down now and wait for your sentence."

Mitra tried to see the guard in the shadow. "What sentence?" she asked.

It was the judge who replied. "This is your trial. Do as the officer asked you. Two minutes wasted. One minute left." He licked his lips then wiped them with his thumb.

Mitra sat down.

"Now," the judge said, "Miss Mitra Ahari, do you admit to the aiding and abetting of a former Marxist, a threat against the Islamic Republic of Iran, and all the world of Islam and its prophet, Mohammad, peace be upon him?"

"I helped a man who was mistreated by the previous regime," Mitra said.

"And this man was Reza Navidi?"

"Yes."

"And he was a member of the Tudeh?"

"No."

"Still, was this man trying to spread anti-Islamic beliefs?"

"I don't know the details of his activities," Mitra replied.

The judge raised his voice. "Was this man plotting to destroy the purity of Islam and our revolution?"

Mitra said nothing.

"Was this man not a traitor to everything we have died for?"

"This was before the revolution. And he was fighting against the Shah," Mitra said quietly.

"Was he not a traitor to our great Imam Khomeini and everything he has done?"

"It was before the revolution," Mitra said again.

"I don't care when it was, Miss Ahari." The judge wrote something down. When he was done, he finally spoke: *"Bismillahir Rahmanir Raheem*: In the name of God, the Compassionate, the Merciful; *as salaam alaykom ramatullah wa barakto*: May the peace of God be upon you, and His mercy and blessings. By the power invested in me by the Islamic Republic of Iran, and the Absolute Guardianship of Islamic Jurists, who through the guidance of our great leader, Imam Khomeini, carry out the justice of our nation, I hereby sentence you to death by hanging, for the crime of treason, conspiracy against the leadership of this nation, and against the purity and sanctity of Islam."

He paused. "Take her away," he said to the guard hiding in the shadows.

KAMRAN SHOWED HIS identification when he and the prisoner reached Ward 209. His new name was written clearly next to the symbol of his new country: Ehsan Jahanpour.

The guards allowed him and the prisoner to pass, and soon they came to a door at the end of the hall. Kamran unlocked it. The room was empty. He adjusted his cap and his rifle, stepped to the side to let the prisoner through, then shut and locked the door behind them. He and the prisoner stood in darkness, and waited.

After five minutes, two other guards with prisoners of their own knocked on the door. Kamran unlocked it, let the prisoners in, and stepped into the hallway. The other guards walked away.

Kamran waited outside. He stroked his beard and felt the gap on his upper lip. After a couple of minutes, the two guards returned, one carrying a chair in front of him, the other carrying one under each arm. The first took a piece of paper out of his pocket and read aloud. "Hossein Talebjam, Vahid Alborzi, and . . . who's yours?" He looked up at Kamran.

"Mitra, something . . . Aha," Kamran said. He unlocked the door to the cell once more, and all three guards, each now carrying a chair, went inside.

With the blindfold still around her eyes, Mitra was gently guided to stand on one of the chairs by Kamran's unsure hands. He then stood on the chair and grabbed hold of the noose that hung from the ceiling. The other two guards did the same with their prisoners. Kamran placed the noose around Mitra's neck and stepped down, losing his balance a little while holding on to her to steady himself. One of the other guards, still fiddling with the knot of his prisoner's noose, laughed at him.

At last the three guards stood in front of their captives.

"Hey, do you know what to do?" one of the other guards said to Kamran.

Kamran nodded.

"Well, just in case you don't, it's like this." The guard kicked the chair from under his prisoner and the man dropped until his feet were inches from the ground. His body didn't move.

Mitra was between the other prisoners. She listened for the sound of dying beside her, but heard nothing. Her hands were cold and she couldn't swallow. On her other side she could hear the heavy breathing of the other prisoner. The more the silence of the first man's death lingered in the room, the more the second man began to lose control. He started to cry, and then the chair beneath him went flying across the room as his guard decided to have mercy.

It was Mitra's turn next.

This is easy enough, Kamran thought. One kick and he would never have to think about it again. And it would right a wrong. He looked up at the figure of the woman in front of him. She was so high up on the chair but looked so small. Her hair fell over her blindfold. He studied her movements. She wasn't breathing hard, but there was something strange about how she was holding her head. It was tilted down, as though she were looking at him. And for the first time, he wondered if he had seen her before, outside of prison. With her eyes covered like this, and her hair down over her face, she somehow looked familiar.

He kept looking at her and kicked the chair. It moved only a little, and Kamran realized that he was trembling. One of Mitra's legs fell off the chair and she balanced on the other one. The other guards looked at Kamran and he stared back at them, as if in apology for his sudden weakness.

Now he kicked the chair harder, so hard that it broke as it hit the wall. Mitra dropped and her neck stretched sideways as it broke. Kamran watched it elongate as she began to sway from side to side, hitting the bodies of the two men beside her. For a second she was still, then Kamran noticed she was pulling up one of her knees, trying to bend it. When she couldn't do so, she wiggled her feet back and forth.

"She's lighter than the men," said one of the other guards. "Takes her longer." Her neck stretched more, making her body grotesque. Her feet were still wiggling. It must be automatic, Kamran thought. She couldn't be fighting. More seconds passed and Mitra's body finally stopped swaying.

The room was still, the three bodies dangling motionless. The guards stood there for a while, making sure the prisoners were dead, so they wouldn't have to do it all over again. Kamran took out a cigarette. He tried to light it but his hands shook too hard.

"Let me," said one of the other guards.

He had only taken one drag when he realized the second guard was eyeing him.

"It's a sin to smoke," the man said.

"Right," Kamran replied. He threw his cigarette on the floor and ground it under his boot. He wiped the sweat from his face with his sleeve. His throat and neck ached.

"God is great," the second guard said. "Let's take them down. It's done."

epilogue

1981

Aria sat in Ferdowsi Square and opened the letter Fereshteh had left on the counter at home. "It's from Evin Prison," Fereshteh told her. "From a man you know. His mother came by with it. She said he's been incarcerated again—something about him getting into more trouble for being a communist—and has been writing for a while, but you're not responding. So he asked her to deliver it by hand."

Dear Aria,

I will try again. Because I must make this clear. I explained things in more detail in the previous letters. But one gets tired of the details, and you realize how irrelevant they are. They say life is in the details, but the details only make up the whole, and in the end it's the whole that matters. There was a mistake in my story, the one I told you long ago in the café. But it was an error that was easy to make. Remember the letters? The ones from Zahra? And the money? The letters were from Zahra, but not the money. The money was someone else's. It was an easy mistake to make because the letters from Zahra and the packets of money started coming at the same time, after your father stopped visiting. I made the mistake of thinking they were connected. Until a little while ago. I was sent another letter, one that exposed my error.

*I don't have much energy to explain, but here is the letter
I was sent. I was told you had a copy. One of your sisters gave it
to you, but you never responded.*

*I have known of that Shirazi family all these years. Your
father told me about them. Maybe you have read the letter from
your sister, and you know the truth now and don't care. But your
sister had two copies and only gave you the one. So once again, I
am charged with the task of sending something to you. Here it is.
I leave you with the letter.*

*Yours in heart and mind,
Rameen*

With a start, Aria remembered the letter from Mrs. Shirazi,
the one Gohar had given her on the day Hamlet was arrested. She
had forgotten it entirely; in such a short time, so much had happened. She searched through her purse, and there it was, hidden
underneath the makeup she wasn't allowed to use anymore. Her
fingers trembled as she opened the envelope. She read it slowly
and fearfully.

Dear girl,
*I am not good with letters so please forgive me. I cannot write. I
have asked Gohar to write this letter for me as I tell it to her. She
has studied a bit. From Roohi's old books. I apologize that
she will know our secret. I must confess to you. At some point in
my life, I made a mistake. Would another mother have done
what I did? Maybe all your life you have believed that you were
left to die. It is easy to believe this. But in my heart, when I
search it enough, I know this is not true. How does a mother
ask for forgiveness? I will not ask here. I will only hope. And I*

hoped for many years in my life. I prayed to the good God to forgive me. One day he finally did. I think he did.

The day you were born, a man and his wife, an old friend, helped bring you into this world. Were it not for this man you would have died. But sometimes people find goodness in themselves they didn't know was there. I never heard from this man after you were born, because while he brought you here, he also turned you away. You were different, and he was raised to fear our kind, to hate us. Because of his fear I had to give you up. No doubt this act poisoned him with guilt and he lived with it for the rest of his days. When this man died, Aria, he chose to right his wrongdoings. He gave me everything he had, all of his money. He left his bakery to his wife, but nothing else. Everything else was for me. I put this money aside but the girls found it one day, and so did Mr. Shirazi. None of them said a thing to me. For you see, they too knew this money was not mine to keep. It was sent to me for you, from a man who wanted forgiveness for his mistakes.

When you were younger, Mr. Behrouz searched for me for years because he wanted you to have a better mother, a good mother, not the kind his wife, Zahra, was to you. This was before the madame found you. So when the money came to me from the baker, around the time you were 15, I knew I could trust Mr. Behrouz. I told him I would send small amounts to him monthly so that it would not raise suspicion with his wife and he could find a place to put it, and he should keep the money for you, and give it to you when you needed it. But then when he died not long after, I had nowhere else to send it. Four years I waited, not knowing what to do. I hid it away from the girls, especially Farangeez. I was afraid she would take it from me. She's that kind of girl. Then, after all those years, I remembered a young man Mr. Behrouz would talk about. I don't know what made me think of him. I remembered how Mr. Behrouz told me stories of how Mr. Rameen would look after you, and he also told me that Mr. Rameen was in some prison. I found out that he had been put in that big new one, Evin. So I began sending him the money there, to save for you. I thought if Mr. Behrouz trusted him, so should I. And he would find a way to get it to you. I thought this money might help you someday.

I know the madame has been good to you, but she hated our kind as well. She was raised with the same fear as so many others. Is it not possible a grieving mother might want to right a wrong—even in the place of my other daughters? I always said to myself, At least they had a mother; but I left the first one motherless. Let me give her something in life. With help from the good God I hope that Mr. Rameen did get the money to you, my child. I have never met him, but from the stories I heard he is a good man. Of course, sometimes in stories those who seem good are bad, or those who seem bad are good. We can never know. But I always hope. And if the money did ever reach you, I hope it was of some help. That you used it for good. And maybe erased the curse of my actions. Please know that your mother, this helpless woman that I am now and was then, never meant you harm.

Your mother, Mehri

The streets around the square were unusually quiet that day. There was the odd honk of a car horn, the sudden calls of mothers to their children, hungry birds in search of a meal, the cries of the meat and nut vendors—and yet, the day felt subdued. After reading the letter, Aria walked through the square with her baby in her arms. Her daughter, now two, felt heavy. And she still didn't have a name.

Her daughter tugged on the headscarf Aria now wore (it had happened after all, in spite of Hamlet's anger) and the garment fell off her hair for the third time. Aria scolded her: "Honey, if you do that Mummy will get in trouble for showing her hair. Don't make the bad people come after us." She looked at her child to see if she understood. But the little girl only laughed in a fit of giggles like other children her age.

Aria thought of her own childhood and all the times she had laughed. The memories came flooding back: Ferdowsi Square, even quieter back then than it was today; nights and days on Zahra's balcony; Zahra, whom she had for a few years now believed to be good. But now Aria understood that her letters to Rameen had been self-serving. Maybe they had been an attempt at apology or a way to explain what she had done so that her name wouldn't be marred forever. There were those in life who were lost, Aria thought, lost within their own echoes, like Narcissus at the pond.

She thought now of the cinemas and Kamran bringing her chocolate bars; how the two of them used to run hand-in-hand from streets to alleyways. She remembered the doll in Zahra's garden, Mana and her garden, Behrouz and his mountain.

Her daughter giggled again as a row of cars drove past. Aria noticed how the faces of the drivers looked destroyed, as if sullied by life's heaviness. The American prisoners had been let go, but the country was at war now. Children were being sent to the battlefields. Tehran used to look beautiful under the white tapestry of snow, but now it was always dark. Even the people wore dark clothes.

She crossed the road to a bench on a patch of grass near the square's centre. Her daughter in her lap, she adjusted her scarf again for fear of exposed hair and the inevitable punishment. She could see the Revolutionary Guards—they were called SEPAH now—on the corners of the square. They were everywhere these days, just like the SAVAK agents from before. Still, the soft sounds in Ferdowsi Square were beautiful, and the air here smelled like the Tehran she had always known.

Aria closed her eyes and breathed in the last drops of sunlight. She thought for a long time about the letter, and about the money, how it had changed hands and hiding places so many times, how it had disguised itself.

She allowed herself to think of Mitra.

"Night is coming," said a voice behind her. Aria opened her eyes. The woman sat down beside her on the bench. "Night, night," the woman repeated.

Aria knew this woman, dressed from head to toe in red. It wasn't the old dress she used to wear, the way Aria remembered her.

"You're still here?" Aria said.

"Where else should Yaghoot be?" said the woman in red. "Night, night. Baby?"

Aria nodded.

"Some babies come from love, some come from fear. Not hate, fear. There is no such thing as hate."

"What?" Aria said.

"Hate. No such thing. How old?"

"She's two," Aria said.

"Nice age. Nice age."

"Are you still waiting for him?" Aria asked.

"What else to do but wait? Name?" Yaghoot nodded at Aria's daughter.

"Name?" Aria looked at her daughter. "I don't know. Two years and I still can't think of the right name. They say I'm crazy."

"They say I'm crazy, too," Yaghoot laughed. "Names mean

everything," she said. "Think the world would be like this if there were no names?"

"Aren't you afraid?"

"Of what?"

"We're not allowed to wear bright colours anymore. They'll arrest you."

Yaghoot laughed again. "How can they arrest *you* when *they're* the ones in prison? Hmm?" She laughed harder, cackling like a witch.

"If you don't wear red, he might not see you, right?"

"I wear red, I wear red, I always wear red," said Yaghoot. "Red, red." She moved closer to Aria. "What if he doesn't see me? I cannot disappear. He told me to wear red. So I wear red. I must be seen, you see. *Ghermez*." Yaghoot pointed to Aria's daughter.

"Red?" Aria waited for an explanation.

"Her name. *Ghermez*. Red," Yaghoot said again.

Aria looked into her daughter's face. With her black eyes and hair, she and Aria were so different. The child had taken after Hamlet's family. Yet under the light of the sun, she could see the underlying red in her daughter's hair, like canvas beneath paint.

"Name my baby after the colour red?" Aria asked. "Are you crazy?"

"Always. Red," Yaghoot said again. "Love. Rage. Heart. Blood. Have blood, have heart, never disappear. He will find you. Red."

Yaghoot patted Aria's head, then her daughter's. "Red, Red, Red," she sang. "After me. Yaghoot. The ruby."

Aria opened her purse. She looked at the small sack she'd been carrying inside it for years, then pulled it out. "I have something for you. Do you like gifts?"

"I like many things, darling," said Yaghoot. "Many things, many things, many things."

"Bracelets? With beads? I have some red ones." She opened the sack and pulled out a few.

Yaghoot came closer, mesmerized by the beadwork. She touched the tips of her fingers to the bracelet. "Ah. They're from a lover."

"I don't know," Aria said quickly. "But you can have them. You could sell some if you need the money."

Yaghoot looked into Aria's eyes and smiled. "You don't sell love, darling. But nice, nice." She cupped her hands together and waited.

Aria placed a few bracelets into Yaghoot's hands, then the entire sack. "Wait!" she said. "I'll keep just one." She searched through the jewellery, the beads clicking against each other and making a sound she liked, as if they were shells tumbling beneath the sea before being carried away by waves. "I'll keep this one."

"White you like?" Yaghoot said. "Okay, that's okay." She bowed to Aria, tucked her white hair beneath her red headscarf and walked away.

Aria gazed after her for as long as she could before the old woman faded into the traffic, holding the small sack of bracelets tight against her hip. The final glimmer of sun began to disappear. Tehran was becoming darker, the silhouette of the Alborz Mountains hovering over it like some creature from the fables, as though the mythic Simorgh would rise with a body of fire from behind the peaks and protect the city with its wings. For a moment, as Aria watched, the last gold and yellow of the sun melted into the coming black of night, and all was red.

acknowledgments

I would like to thank the following friends for their support throughout the years: Hossein Mousavi, Taylor Orton, Amy Hill, Hal Wake, Viren Thaker, Chris Baron, Rachel Rose, Janet Hong, Julia Von Lucadou, Shirin Mehrgan, Sarvenaz Ghassemi and Maryam Najafi.

A special thank you to my Canadian editor, Lynn Henry, for her talent and for having faith in this book. Thanks to everyone at Knopf Canada.

Thank you to my UK editor, Mary Mount, at Viking UK, for her trust and vital input.

A heartfelt thank you to my wonderful agent, Karolina Sutton. Thank you to Caitlin Leydon. I owe a debt of gratitude to Margaret Atwood for her incredible support.

Thank you to Maureen Medved for her guidance. Thank you to Dr. David Heilbrunn for all his help.

And to Myriam Khalfallah, thank you for everything and more.

Most of all, an eternal thank you to Homayountaj Mansouri and Ezatollah Bakhtiari.

AUTHOR'S NOTE: On page 280 a segment of Sohrab Sepehri's poem, "The Footsteps of Water" is an original translation from the Persian to English by Karim Emami. I have loosely translated another segment of the poem in the epigraph.

Some elements of this story were inspired by real people and events, but the novel itself is a work of fiction.